Shiz Gate

Southstairs

The Emerald City

Westgate

The Palace

Gillikin

The Madeleines

Munchkin Mousehole

Mockbeggar Hall

Restwater

Yellow Brick Road

The Pine Barrens

The Free State of Munchkinland

Quadling Kells

Qhoyre

Bengda

Country

Waterslip

Ovvels

Son of a Witch

SON

OF A

WITCH

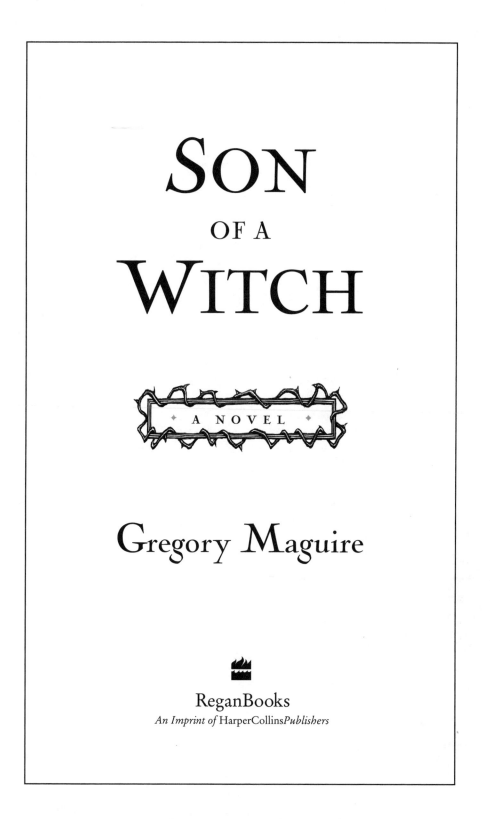

* A NOVEL *

Gregory Maguire

ReganBooks

An Imprint of HarperCollins*Publishers*

Mag

HarperCollins books may be purchased for educational, business, or sales promotional use. For information please write: Special Markets Department, HarperCollins Publishers Inc., 10 East 53rd
Street, New York, NY 10022.

FIRST EDITION

Designed by Judy Abbate
Illustrations by Douglas Smith

Printed on acid-free paper

Library of Congress Cataloging-in-Publication Data

Maguire, Gregory.
     Son of a witch : a novel / Gregory Maguire.
        p. cm.
     ISBN 0-06-054893-2 (cloth)
     1. Witches—Fiction. 2. Oz (Imaginary place)—Fiction. I. Title.

PS3563.A3535S66 2005
813'.54—dc22
ISBN-13: 978-0-06-054893-3

                                                                            2005046232

05 06 07 08 09 WB/RRD 10 9 8 7 6 5 4 3 2 1

L. FRANK BAUM's second Oz novel, *The Marvelous Land of Oz* (1904), was dedicated to the actors David C. Montgomery and Fred A. Stone, who performed the roles of the Tin Woodman and the Scarecrow in the first theatrical version of *The Wizard of Oz*.

In that spirit, *Son of a Witch* is dedicated to the cast and creative team of the musical *Wicked,* which opened on Broadway in October 2003—the night before Halloween.

To Winnie Holzman and Stephen Schwartz, foremost and first, for their vision; to Wayne Cilento, Susan Hilferty, Eugene Lee, Joe Mantello, Stephen Oremus, Kenneth Posner, and Marc Platt and his associates, for bringing visions to life; and, among all the capable cast, most especially to Kristin Chenoweth (*Galinda/Glinda*), Joel Grey (*The Wizard*), and Idina Menzel (*Elphaba*), for bringing life to visions.

I HAVE NO FEAR that the poetry of democratic peoples will be found timid or that it will stick too close to the earth. I am much more afraid that it . . . may finish up by describing an entirely fictitious country.

—Alexis de Tocqueville,
Democracy in America, 1835, 1840

ALL COWS were like all other cows, all tigers like all other tigers—what on earth has happened to human beings?

—Harry Mulisch,
Siegfried, 2001

Contents

Son of a Witch

Under the Jackal Moon

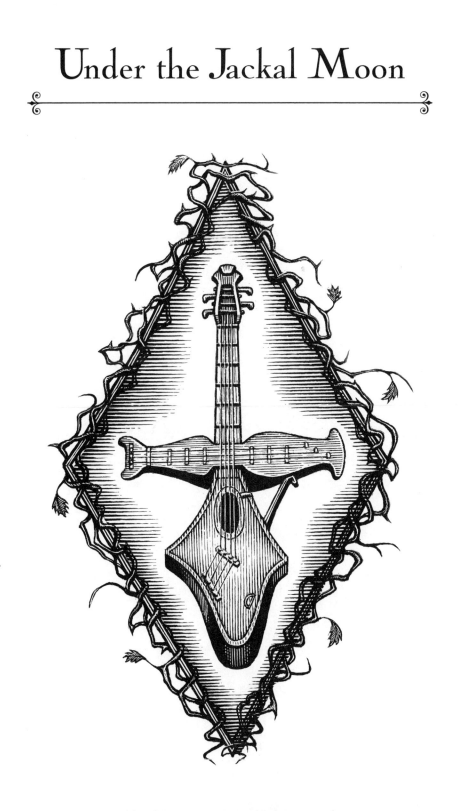

The House
of Saint Glinda

SO THE TALK OF RANDOM BRUTALITY wasn't just talk. At noontime they discovered the bodies of three young women, out on some mission of conversion that appeared to have gone awry. The novice maunts had been strangled by their ropes of holy beads, and their faces removed.

Her nerve being shaken at last, Oatsie Manglehand now caved in to the demands of her paying customers. She told the team drivers they'd pause only long enough to dig some shallow graves while the horses slaked their thirst. Then the caravan would press on across the scrubby flats known, for the failed farmsteads abandoned here and there, as the Disappointments.

Moving by night, at least they wouldn't make a sitting target, though they might as easily wander into trouble as sidestep it. Still, Oatsie's party was antsy. Hunker down all night and wait for horse hoofs, spears? Too hard on everyone. Oatsie consoled herself: If the caravan kept moving, she could sit forward with her eyes peeled, out of range of the carping, the second-guessing, the worrying.

With the benefit of height, therefore, Oatsie spotted the gully before anyone else did. The cloudburst at sunset had fed a small trackside rivulet that flowed around a flank of skin, water-lacquered in the new moon-light. An island, she feared, of human flesh.

I ought to turn aside before the others notice, she thought; how much more can they take? There is nothing I can do for that human soul. The digging of another trench would require an hour, minimum. An additional few moments for prayers. The project would only further agitate these clients as they obsess about their own precious mortality.

Upon the knee of the horizon balanced the head of a jackal moon, so-called because, once every generation or so, a smear of celestial flot-sam converged behind the crescent moon of early autumn. The impact was creepy, a look of a brow and a snout. As the moon rounded out over a period of weeks, the starveling would turn into a successful hunter, its cheeks bulging.

Always a fearsome sight, the jackal moon tonight spooked Oatsie Manglehand further. *Don't stop for this next casualty. Get through the Dis-appointments, deliver these paying customers to the gates of the Emerald City.* But she resisted giving in to superstition. Be scared of the real jackals, she reminded herself, not frets and nocturnal portents.

In any case, the light of the constellation alleviated some of the color blindness that sets in at night. The body was pale, almost luminous. Oat-sie might divert the Grasstrail Train and give the corpse a wide berth be-fore anyone else noticed it, but the slope of the person's shoulders, the unnatural twist of legs—the jackal moon made her read the figure too well, as too clearly human, for her to be able to turn aside.

"Nubb," she barked to her second, "rein in. We'll pull into flank for-mation up that rise. There's another fatality, there in the runoff."

Cries of alarm as the news passed back, and another mutter of mutiny: Why should they stop?—were they to bear witness to every fresh atrocity? Oatsie didn't listen. She yanked the reins of her team of horses, to halt them, and she lowered herself gingerly. She stumped, her hand on her sore hip, until she stood a few feet over the body.

Face down and genitals hidden, he appeared to have been a young man. A few scraps of fabric were still knotted about his waist, and a boot some yards distant, but he was otherwise naked, and no sign of his clothes.

Curious: no evidence of the assassins. Neither had there been about the bodies of the maunts, but that was on rockier ground, in a drier hour. Oatsie couldn't see any sign of scuffle here, and in the mud of the gulch one might have expected . . . something. The body wasn't bloody, nor decayed yet; the murder was recent. Perhaps this evening, perhaps only an hour ago.

"Nubb, let's heave him up and see if they've taken his face," she said.

"No blood," said Nubb.

"Blood may have run off in that cloudburst. Steel yourself, now."

They got on either side of the body and bit their lips. She looked at Nubb, meaning: It's only the next thing, it's not the last thing. Let's get through this, fellow.

She jerked her head in the direction of the hoist. One, two, heave.

They got him up. His head had fallen into a natural scoop in the stone, a few inches higher than where the rain had pooled. His face was intact, more or less; that is to say, it was still there, though shattered.

"How did he get here?" said Nubb. "And why didn't they scrape him?"

Oatsie just shook her head. She settled on her haunches. Her travelers had come forward and were congregating on the rise behind her; she could hear them rustling. She suspected that they had gathered stones, and were ready to kill her if she insisted on a burial.

The jackal moon rose a few notches higher, as if trying to see into the gulley. The prurience of the heavens!

"We're not going to dig another grave." That from her noisiest client, a wealthy trader from the northern Vinkus. "Not his, Oatsie Manglehand, and not yours, either. We're not doing it. We leave him unburied and alone, or we leave him unburied with your corpse for company."

"We don't need to do either," said Oatsie. She sighed. "Poor, poor soul, whoever he is. He needs no grave. He isn't dead yet."

✦ 2 ✦

IN TIME, when the travelers had rejoined their cronies and relatives in the Emerald City—in salons, in public houses, in taverns of exchange—they heard more chatter about the hostilities they had managed to side-step. Rumor flourished. Forty, sixty, a hundred deaths resulting from the skirmishes between the Scrow and the Yunamata. Barbarians, the lot of them: They deserved to kill off each other. But not us.

Rumor could be wrong, of course, but it couldn't be uninteresting. Two hundred dead. Twice that. Mass graves, and they would be found *any day*.

But the luxury of safety came later. First, the Grasstrail Train still had to resume its snail's progress through the Disappointments. Geographical variety—the hills, mountains, dales and forests that made the rest of Oz so memorable, such a heartland—was in short supply here. Just flats, shales, more flats, grey as pulped newspapers.

The prospect was dispiriting, and the notion of having to carry an invalid with them didn't improve matters. Oatsie Manglehand's clients had paid good hard cash for her service. Some originating from as far away as Ugabu, and others having joined the group along the eastern foothills of the Great Kells, they considered their own safe travel should be Oatsie's sole concern.

Oatsie reminded them that they didn't have a vote. She'd never represented that her clients would travel unencumbered by waifs and strays. Indeed, by terms of their contracts, she was free of liability should any of the travelers be murdered on the trail by a fellow passenger, a stowaway, a hitchhiker, a native. Oatsie had promised to lead the caravan as safely as she could, relying on her knowledge of the terrain and its populations. That was it. Period. To that end, she'd chosen a new route intended to avoid the current hot spots of intertribal conflict, and so far so good. Right?

The invalid was loaded aboard.

Despite her bravado, Oatsie was indeed sensitive to her clients' fears, and in a way she was glad to have the unconscious young man with them. It distracted the travelers, while he remained oblivious of their re-sentment.

She bedded him in the third carriage back, requisitioning from her clients the warmest of winter robes. She mounded him into a cocoon. There he languished, day and night, not so much fevered as feverless—an equally worrying condition. After a day of trying, Nubb was able to spoon a few tips of brandy between the lad's lips, and Oatsie fancied she saw his muscles relax in a new way.

She couldn't be certain of this. She was no doctor.

Of one thing she was sure, though. With his arrival, the mood of the Grasstrail Train changed. Why? Perhaps this: If the poor creature had been beaten to within an inch of his life, and lived, there might be hope for all of them. Think about it: *His face hadn't been scraped.* People re-laxed. The nasal buzz of prayers around the supper campfire gave way to a quieter mood. Song returned, in time.

We'll make it. We deserve to. The privilege of life has been accorded us, see? We've been saved. Must be for a reason. Spines straightened, eyes grew bright and moist in a rapture of gratitude at the plan of the Un-named God.

Another week and they had rounded the landmark rocks that marked their U-turn north, and they left behind them in the Disap-pointments the greatest threat of ambush.

In this month of Summersend, the wind flicked the strands of oakhair in the forest that grew between the lakes. Squirrels spilled nuts on the skarkskin roofs of the wagons. The air was more watery, too, though both lakes were out of sight beyond the miles of woods on either side.

As the oakhair forest thinned and they reached the Shale Shallows, the shady surround and homely walls of an old settlement solidified in the middle of walnut-colored fields. The first stone building they'd seen in six weeks. Despite its steep, aggrieved gables and pinched outbuild-ings, despite its battlement defenses, nothing—not even the Emerald City—could seem more welcome a sight just then.

"The Cloister of Saint Glinda," they buzzed. "How holy it appears."

The maunts who lived within were divided into ranks. Some took vows of silence and lived cloistered. Others took vows of indulgence.

They indulged in teaching, tending the sick, and operating a hostelry for those traveling between the southern Kells and the Emerald City. So the broad carved doors were swung open when the Grasstrail Train pulled up. The welcoming committee, a band of three middle-aged maunts with well-starched collars and bad teeth, stood at attention.

They greeted Oatsie with frosty politeness. They were suspicious of any unmarried woman who had found a way to live single, apart from female community. Still, they offered her the traditional wipe of the face with sweet rosefern. A fourth maunt, sequestered behind a screen, played a welcoming anthem, poorly. Harp strings snapped, and the sound of a most unmauntish oath issued forth.

The travelers didn't care. They were almost in heaven. To anticipate beds!—and a warm meal!—and wine!—and a captive audience, ready to thrill at the story of their journey!

In this last item, though, the maunts gave bad value for money. At once their attention was riveted by the invalid. They carried him into the loggia and hurried to collect a stretcher so he could be hauled upstairs to the infirmary.

The maunts were beginning to shift the fellow to private quarters when the Superior Maunt wafted by, fresh from her morning devotions. She greeted Oatsie Manglehand with the least of nods, and glanced upon the broken lad for a moment. Then she waved her hands: Remove him.

She said to Oatsie, "We know him. We know this one."

"You do?" said Oatsie.

"If my memory hasn't begun to fail me," the Superior Maunt continued, "you should know him, as well. You took him from us some years ago. Fifteen was it, twenty? At my age I don't apprehend the passage of time as I ought."

"He'd have been a child twenty years ago, an infant," said Oatsie. "I never took an infant from a mauntery."

"Perhaps not an infant. But you took him just the same. He traveled with a disagreeable novice who served for several years in the hospice. You were conveying them to the castle stronghold of the Arjikis. Kiamo Ko."

"He was with Elphaba?"

"Now you remember, I see you do."

"The Wicked Witch of the West . . ."

"As some called her." The Superior Maunt sniffed. "Not I. Her name here was Sister Saint Aelphaba, but I seldom called her anything. She was more or less under a vow of silence—her own. She needed no addressing."

"You recognize him from youth to now?" said Oatsie. "You've seen him since?"

"No. But I do not forget a face."

Oatsie raised her eyebrows.

"I have seen so few faces," explained the Superior Maunt. "We will not talk now. I must have Sister Doctor here to look the boy over."

"What *was* his name?"

The Superior Maunt vanished without answering.

By nightfall, as Oatsie's clients finished their nightcaps, the next generation of rumors was launched. The man-child was the Emperor's confessor. He was a brigand trafficking in the sex trade. He spoke in the voice of a Loon. Except for a single rib, the man-child had broken every bone in his body.

Many of the rumors were contradictory, which in the aggregate made them all more amusing.

• 3 •

IT WAS A HARD TIME. It had been a hard time, in Oz, for some time (for all time, said world-weary students). The Superior Maunt, too tired for colloquy, removed herself to her chambers and settled in a rocker. Amid trappings more severe than what her younger colleagues could tolerate, she rocked a little and thought, as coherently as she could. (It was a habit of hers, to forestall the onset of vagueness, that she review a strand of history from time to time.)

The Witch—so-called—had lived at the cloistered mauntery a decade and a half ago. One couldn't forget *that*—to the Superior Maunt's knowledge, no one else in Oz had ever been born with skin as green as new lilac leaves. But Elphaba had kept herself to herself, accepting without complaint such assignments as were meted out. She'd lived there for, what, five, six, seven years? And then, the Superior Maunt had hired Oatsie Manglehand to escort the close-lipped novice back into the civilian world. The small boy had tagged along, neither warmly included nor shooed away.

What had his name been, and where had he come from? An urchin left behind by one of the gypsy bands that scavenged for petty mushrooms among the roots of oakhair trees? The Superior Maunt couldn't remember the lad's provenance. Someone younger would know.

Elphaba had gone. Off to Kiamo Ko, there to stew in her own private penance. The Superior Maunt occasionally listened to testimonies of sin confessed by her sisters, but during her tenure as a maunt, Elphaba had never petitioned for an audience. Of this the Superior Maunt was quite sure. Though the nature of Elphaba's sins had been of great interest to the under-entertained sorority, Elphaba had never obliged.

Bit by bit—the news filtered through even to an outpost like this— the maunts learned of the slow evolution of Elphaba into a Witch, by dint of her rash behavior, her unexpected family ties. (She'd been sister to Nessarose, the Wicked Witch of the East, as some said. For the love of the Unnamed God, who could have expected *that*?)

The Superior Maunt sighed, chiding herself for the pleasure she took in remembering her contempt for those days. How she had leapt up from her prayers and clapped her hands, to hear that the long reign of the Wizard of Oz had drawn to a close at last, and the merciless old bastard disappeared into the clouds in a hot-air balloon advertising some obscure commercial tonic. Then the surprise ascendancy to the Palace throne of Lady Chuffrey, née Glinda Arduenna, of the Uplands. A sort of prime minister pro tem, until things could be sorted out. (She'd come out of nowhere, politically speaking: money to burn, and a certain sort of style, but who might have guessed the vacuum left by the Wizard's departure would suck in a society wife with a penchant for glitter gowns?)

"Not a terrible choice." The Superior Maunt began talking aloud, to keep her thoughts straight. "And I say this without need to reflect nicely on our own Saint Glinda, for whom Lady Chuffrey was probably named. Or renamed herself, *Galinda* a rural name, *Glinda* the more sophisticated: the saint's name. Clever move." No, *Glinda,* as she became known popularly—a single name, like a house pet, like a lapdog!—Glinda managed to run an open court for a while, and much that had gone wrong, at least in that prior atmosphere of Wizardic secrecy, was corrected. There was an inoculation initiative, very thoughtful. Some schools for millworker girls, of all things. Good programs—expensive to run, though. It had seemed generous and intelligent from the perspective of a cloistered spinster—but what kind of perspective was that?

Then Glinda had stepped aside. Ever the dilettante, she'd grown bored with governing, people assumed, and had taken up collecting miniature furniture with a vengeance. Well, to be fair, maybe she'd been pushed out. For a while a puppet government replaced her. A right dolt, calling himself a Scarecrow. Rumors had flown that he was no real Scarecrow, that he wasn't even the Scarecrow associated with the Visitor: Dorothy. He was just some out-of-work bum dressed up to fool the masses. Being paid every weekend at the back door, probably—but by whom? Glinda's people? Her thwarters? The banker barons of industrial Gillikin? Who knew? In due course he was booted out by the latest nuisance, the next hollow man, reeking with glory: the sacred Emperor.

The long years since Elphaba had driven her wild broom across the sky had been quiet—on the surface. Certain atrocities had ceased, and that was good. Other atrocities replaced them. Certain diseases subsided, others had taken grip. Now something was agitating the Scrow and the Yunamata in the West, something so fierce that agents from one or both of the tribes were striking out at neutral parties.

Like the junior maunts sent out on a mission by the toadies helming the motherchapel in the Emerald City. Those sycophantic biddies! They'd cluck themselves to death if their Emperor asked it. Their emissaries, those innocent young things, had stopped here at the Cloister of Saint Glinda for nourishment and cheer. Where were their faces now, wondered the Superior Maunt. She hoped she'd never see them again, neither in her dreams nor in a parcel in the delivery of post.

She was drifting off to sleep in her rocker. She arose, groaning at the pain in her joints, and tried to pull her shutters tight. One of them stuck and had to stay as it was. She'd meant to have it seen to this afternoon, but with the arrival of the caravan, she'd forgotten.

She visited the toilet reserved for her private use, and dressed in her rough gown for the night. When she settled herself on her horsehair mattress, she hoped she would drift off quickly. It had been a taxing day.

The jackal moon looked in her window at her. The Superior Maunt turned her head so as not to meet its eye, a folk custom with which she'd been raised seven, eight decades earlier, and never shaken.

Her mind went briefly to those days in the Pertha Hills of Gillikin, days sharper and more wonderful in memory than what she could apprehend of current life. The taste of pearlfruit leaves! The water on her father's wagon roof when the rains came. The rains came so much more often in her youth. The snow smelled of things. Everything smelled. Wonderfully or not, it was wonderful that they smelled. Now her nose hardly worked at all.

She said a prayer or two.

Liir. That was his name. Liir.

She prayed to remember it when the time came for her to wake up.

✦ 4 ✦

THE NEXT MORNING, before Oatsie Manglehand gathered her band together for the final push to the Emerald City, she took Nubb to a small plain parlor. There they met with the Superior Maunt, Sister Doctor, and Sister Apothecaire.

When the Superior Maunt sat down, the others sat. Since she abstained from morning tea, the others abstained.

"If we are to help this boy, we must share what we know," began the Superior Maunt. "I've picked up all sorts of hearsay. A report from Sister Doctor, if you please."

Sister Doctor, a beefy woman with questionable credentials but proven expertise in diagnosis, wasn't sanguine about the prospects for the invalid. "He appears to have suffered little from exposure, so he will have been left for dead only shortly before you found him."

Oatsie didn't speak to this. She didn't want to begin by contradicting a professional woman, even if she thought Sister Doctor had to be wrong.

Sister Doctor pressed on. "He is a shattered man, quite literally. It isn't mine to guess how he came to be so wounded, but his state is like nothing I've ever seen. One of his legs is broken in multiple places; both his wrists are sprained. One of his shoulder blades is cracked. Many of his ribs. Four of his fingers. Three of the bones in his left foot. Not a single bone punctured the skin, however. And, apparently, no blood loss."

Not unless the blood ran off in the rain squall, thought Oatsie, but kept still.

Sister Doctor rubbed the back of her neck and grimaced. "I spent so much time setting bones that I could do only a cursory exam of his organs. He is breathing shallowly and with difficulty. The phlegm that runs from his nose is both yellow and bloody. This suggests respiratory troubles. Sister Apothecaire has her own notions about this—"

"To start with the question of the discharge," began Sister Apothecaire, somewhat overenthusiastically, but Sister Doctor spoke over her.

"Sister Apothecaire can speak presently. I utter no opinion about her . . . conjectures."

"The heart?" asked the Superior Maunt, overriding the old tired conflict.

"Working." Sister Doctor grunted as if in disbelief at her own answer.

"The guts?"

"The word might be *wobbly*. I suspect an imploded spleen or the like, and septic poisoning. There's a funny color in the extremities and on certain contusions that I don't care for at all."

"What color is that?" asked the Superior Maunt.

Sister Doctor pursed her lips. "Well, I'm a bit overtired. We worked all night, you know, without resting. But I should have said there's a green tinge to the bruises, ringed with a plum-yellowy margin."

"Suggestive of internal bleeding, you think . . . or a disease? Or maybe something else?"

"He may be comatose or he may be brain-dead. I have no way of knowing. Though his heart is good, his color, as I say, is not, so circulation may be failing. The lungs have been compromised severely—whether by a preexisting condition or by some aspect of his adventures I cannot venture an opinion at this time."

"To conclude—" The Superior Maunt rolled her hand in the air.

"Death by nightfall, maybe tomorrow morning," said Sister Doctor.

"We could pray for a miracle," said Nubb. Oatsie snorted.

"Sister Apothecaire will handle treatment," said Sister Doctor, making it sound as if she thought prayer would be a wiser course.

"*You* could pray for a miracle," said Sister Apothecaire to Nubb. "I have other work to do."

"Sister Apothecaire," said the Superior Maunt. "You have something to add?"

Sister Apothecaire pushed her spectacles down her nose, then removed them, huffed upon them, and wiped them clean on the hem of her apron. She was a Munchkin and exhibited the Munchkin farmwife's passion for hygiene—not a bad attribute for a person in her profession. "It's all puzzling," she agreed. "We have made him as comfortable as we could, and as the mercy of our mission requires. With tape we have bound his limbs to splints and shims. Should he live, he may regain some degree of motor function."

"What does that mean?" asked Oatsie. "Speak clearly to the ignorant. Me."

"He may be able to sit up, to use his hands, if his nerves are not shot to hell. He may be able to walk, in a fashion; that is unlikely, but as I say we aim for the stars. What is more troubling is the discharge from his membranes. The nose, most obviously, but the other orifices as well. Ears, eyes, anus, penis."

"You've had a chance to do some initial work in the laboratory," prompted the Superior Maunt.

"Indeed. Just a start. I've found nothing definitive, nothing I haven't seen before, either in my station here at the mauntery or in my prior position as Matron's Assistant at the Respite of Incurables in the Emerald City."

Sister Doctor rolled her eyes. Sister Apothecaire never lost an opportunity to publish her credentials.

"Can *you* supply us with a hypothesis?" asked the Superior Maunt.

"It would be rash to do so." Even sitting, Sister Apothecaire was shorter than her peers, so her sideways glance at her disapproving colleague required her to poke her chin up, which perhaps gave her a more combative expression than she intended. "Whoever he is, I do wonder if this lad was from high altitudes. The mucous seepage may be due to the systemic collapse of arterial function due to a sudden change in air pressure. I haven't seen such a symptom before, but the Fallows are very low ground indeed compared to the highest peaks of the Great Kells."

The way Sister Doctor murmured "mmmmm" made it plain to all what she thought of her colleague's hypothesis. She straightened her spine as if to say, hurry up; her longer spine gave her height over her colleague, which she liked to use to advantage.

The Superior Maunt intervened. "Do you agree with Sister Doctor that death is imminent?"

Sister Apothecaire sniffed. The two didn't like to agree on anything, but she couldn't help it. She nodded her head. "There may be more to learn," she added. "The longer he hangs on, the more chance I'll have to study his nature."

"You will study nothing in his nature that isn't directly related to the easing of his afflictions," said the Superior Maunt mildly.

"But Mother Maunt! It is in my charge as an apothecaire. The syndrome he dies from may afflict others in time, and this is an opportunity to learn. To turn our noses up at it is to discount revelation."

"I have delivered my opinion on the matter, and I expect it to be observed. Now, to you both: Is there anything we can do for him that we are not doing?"

"Notify the next of kin," said Sister Doctor.

The Superior Maunt nodded and rubbed her eyes. She lifted a saucer of tea to her lips now, and without hesitation the others did the same.

"I propose we get one of the sisters to play music for him, then," she concluded. "If our only contribution is to ease his death, let us do what we can."

"Preferably not the sister who was torturing the harp when we arrived yesterday," muttered Oatsie Manglehand.

"Have you anything to add, Oatsie?" said the Superior Maunt. "I mean aside from your critique of musical performance?"

"Only this," said the caravan guide. I won't bother to apologize for contradicting them, she decided. "Sister Doctor proposes that the boy would have been set upon by brigands and left to die only shortly before we found him. But the terrain out there, my friends, is flat as a rolled-out tart crust."

"I don't follow," said the Superior Maunt.

"The body had to have been lying there for longer than Sister Doctor suggests. I would have seen the marauders in retreat. There was no place for them to hide. There is no tree cover. You know how bright a night it was; I could see for miles."

"Puzzling indeed."

"Do you use magic in your ministrations?"

"Oatsie Manglehand," said the Superior Maunt tiredly, "we are a sorority of unionist maunts. Such a question." She closed her eyes and rubbed her forehead with old, bowed fingers. Over her venerable figure, Sister Doctor and Sister Apothecaire both nodded silently to Oatsie: *Yes. We do. What little we're capable of. When we need to.*

The Superior Maunt continued. "Before resting for the night, I recalled his name. The boy was named Liir. He left the mauntery with Sister Saint Aelphaba—well, Elphaba, I suppose; she never professed her vows. Do you remember the boy at all, Sister Doctor?"

"I had just arrived about the time Elphaba was setting out," said Sister Doctor. "I remember Elphaba Thropp a little. I didn't care for her. Her moods and silences seemed hostile rather than holy. Of the many urchins who are abandoned around here, however, I remember even less. Children don't interest me unless they are gravely ill. Was he gravely ill?"

"He is now," said the Superior Maunt. "And somewhere, if his mind is still able to dream, he is still a child in there, I presume."

"Very sentimental indeed, Mother Maunt," said Sister Doctor.

"I do remember him, now you give his name," said Oatsie Manglehand. "Not well, of course. In the better years I make three or four separate runs, and we're talking twelve, fifteen, eighteen years ago? I have packed more than a few children onto heaps of worldly goods, and buried some by the side of the track as well. But he was a quiet lad, unsure of himself. He shadowed Elphaba as if she were his mother. Was she his mother?"

"Oh, dubious, very dubious," said Sister Doctor.

"There is the green tone to his bruises," Sister Apothecaire reminded them.

"I blush when I'm embarrassed, Sister Apothecaire; this does not relate me to the radish," said the Superior Maunt. "Well, we'll have to ask around. Most of the older sisters who might have remembered Elphaba are dead now, and the others are in their second childhood. But Sister Cook, if she hasn't been guzzling the cooking sherry—or perhaps if she has—she will know something. She always slips food to the children loitering in the kitchen yard, and she may remember where the boy came from.

"Meanwhile"— and the good woman rose, to signal that the meeting was done—"we will do our best with Liir, whether he be witch's spawn or the reject of a gypsy mother. It hardly matters on one's deathbed from whom one has been born, does it? The world is the womb now, and the Afterlife waits for one to be born into it."

She turned rheumy eyes on Oatsie Manglehand. The wagoneer could see that the Superior Maunt was waiting, hopefully, for her own deliverance from this world and delivery unto the next. Oatsie accepted the old woman's cool hands on her forehead, knowing the gesture was intended as a blessing, a forgiveness . . . perhaps a farewell.

"The wind is high," said Oatsie Manglehand. "If we leave now and find the water level low enough at the near ford, we'll make the far bank of the Gillikin by nightfall."

"The Unnamed God speed your progress," murmured the Superior Maunt, though her eyes had shunted inward, as if already on to the next problem. Indeed, she was. Before Oatsie had finished tying the strings of her boots, she heard the Superior Maunt say to her colleagues, "Now you must help me on the stairs, ladies, for I will go to visit our invalid."

"She's a tough old bird," muttered Oatsie to Nubb.

"Let's get out of here," said Nubb. "Don't want to stay under any roofs that house a son of a witch, even if it's holy roofs."

• 5 •

THE MAUNTERY, the oldest bits of which dated back several hundred years, was conventionally arranged around a courtyard. The vernacular of austere Merthic style—flattened stone columns, bricked quoins devoid of plaster or wash—was indicative of the speed with which defensible households had needed to be raised.

Up far too many stairs, the surgery included an office crammed into a closet, where Sister Doctor kept her notes and manuals. In a storage space under some eaves, Sister Apothecaire filled oaken cabinets with her unguents and restoratives, purgatives and negatives. (Small, as many Munchkins still were, she could work upright in a space too cramped for her colleague to stand upright in, so she got the private office. Endless grousing over this.)

The surgery also gave onto two largish dormitories. The right-hand chamber served the poor and ill of the domain. The left chamber was reserved for ailing maunts. Through here, behind a stout door, loomed an odd-shaped space, the finial of a corner tower. Inside, therefore, it was a round room, with narrow slitted windows looking in three directions. The room had no true walls or ceiling, just sloping rafters that met at the top of the conical space. A bedbound patient could stare up and see how the roof planking traversed the ribs. There were bats, but they were cleaner than most of the patients, so they were let be.

It's like nothing so much as being inside a witch's hat, thought the Superior Maunt as she paused to catch her breath. Then she pushed aside the curtain and entered.

Liir—if it was he, and she was rather certain it was—was laid upon the high bed more like a corpse than an invalid. "He's been given no pillow?" asked the Superior Maunt in something of a whisper.

"The neck."

"I see." Well, there wasn't much to see, really. His braced limbs were swathed in wide strips of gauze, his chest bound, his head undressed, and that dark hair cleaned with oil and herbs. His eyes, behind slits in the bandage, were closed. The lashes were long and feathery. "He has not been torrefied, has he? You have tucked him up like a victim of burns."

"The skin needs tending for the sores, so we cannot fully immobilize him."

I suspect not, thought the Superior Maunt.

Her eyes weren't what they had been. She leaned forward and looked closely at the seams where Liir's upper and lower eyelids met.

Then she lifted his left hand and studied his nails. His skin was clammy, like the rind of a valley-skark cheese. The fingernails were crazed.

"Pull back his loincloth."

Sister Doctor and Sister Apothecaire exchanged glances and did as they were bade.

The Superior Maunt had had little reason to become an expert in the male anatomy, but she showed no sign of pleasure or revulsion. She gently shifted the member this way and that, and lifted the testicles. "I ought to have brought my reading spectacles," she murmured.

She needed help straightening up. "Very well, do him up again," she said. Her maunts obliged.

"Sister Doctor," said the Superior Maunt. "Sister Apothecaire. I will not have you loosen his bindings to show me the bruises you report. I rely on your perspicacity. However I make note here, and will do so formally in the Log of the House, that I observe no sign of greenness in his skin. I will tolerate no murmur belowstairs that we are harboring any sort of—aberration. If you have been indiscreet enough to propose such to your sisters, correct the damage at once. Is this understood?"

She didn't wait for an answer, and turned back to the body.

It was hard to take the measure of a man who displayed the flaccid composure of a corpse. No brow is noble when it is dead: It has no need to be. This lad seemed about as close to death as one could be and still harbor hope of recovery, yet the sense she had about him was neither tranquil nor restive.

He was a young man, with youth's agreeable form: That much was apparent despite the bandages. The young suffer and die, too, and sometimes it is merciful, she thought. Then she was filled with an unseemly glee and selfishness that she had lived a long odd life of her own, and it wasn't over yet. She was in better shape than this poor benighted kid.

"Mother Maunt, are you yourself?" asked Sister Doctor.

"A tremor of digestive grief, nothing more."

She couldn't put her finger on it. She turned to go. There was Sister Cook to interview next, and other pressing matters of the day. As Sister Apothecaire fussed with the bedclothes and Sister Doctor dived to confirm the pulse, the Superior Maunt sighed. "We will do our duty, and no more than our duty," she reminded them.

They stood to attention. "Yes, Mother Maunt."

Neither tranquil nor restive, she thought again: It is as if his spirit is not here. His body is not dead, but his spirit is not here. How can this be?

Blasphemy, and bad science besides, she lectured herself, and scooted away as fast as her arthritic limbs could manage.

♦ 6 ♦

THE SUPERIOR MAUNT had long since given up supervising Sister Cook. For one thing, the ancient maunt had little interest in cuisine, her stomach having been soured by too many decades of regrettable food served under bad kitchen government. Those appetites remaining to her, after all these decades, concerned feeding the spirit alone.

So, pausing at the thresholds of the mauntery's kitchens, the Superior Maunt felt a faint queasiness.

Given where the mauntery was situated—on the back route from Quadling Country—the establishment took in its share of Quadling girls deemed too plain or unruly for marriage, or too dull for the mild professions—teacher, governess, nurse. Sometimes their families reclaimed them. More often, the girls ran away, but at least they were older and better fed when they struck out on their own.

Still, while in residence, they were as a population docile enough, and they made good kitchen assistants. Looking for Sister Cook, it occurred to the Superior Maunt that a Quadling girl might sit with the convalescent upstairs.

"Sister Cook?" called the Superior Maunt, but her voice was rusty. "Sister Cook?"

There was no reply. Into the kitchens ventured the Superior Maunt. A few quiet girls worked in a sunny corner, kneading vast tough pillows of bread dough with their bare knees. The peasant practice was generally frowned upon, but the Superior Maunt passed by the novices, pretending not to notice, as she didn't feel up to delivering a chastisement.

Sister Liquor was high on a ladder, giving each purple glass bottle of savorsuckle brandy a quarter turn. She was singing to herself and swaying on her rung.

"Mercy," murmured the Superior Maunt, and kept going.

The pantry offended with the promise of lunch: bread, moldiflower root, rounds of aged skark cheese, and soft blue olives, the kind even donkeys refused to eat. It's not *that* hard to keep your mind on higher things when this is the daily fare, observed the Superior Maunt.

The outside door was open. Beyond the pantry, in the walled orchard, wands of pearlfruit trees twitched and shuddered in the wind. The Superior Maunt went through, as much to catch a breath of fresh air as to see the severe autumn colors of pearlfruit leaves, which shaded from granite pink to a hesitant periwinkle.

In the emerald grass near the well several novices sat on their aprons. They'd taken for a little outing one of the palsied biddies in a wheeled chair and kindly thrown a tartan over her lap. The ancient maunt—older even than the Superior Maunt, by the look of it, or more infirm, anyway—had pulled her shawl over her forehead, to keep the morning sun out of her eyes. Two of the novices were husking pearlfruit pods. A third was fingering some sort of instrument, a kind of zither or dulcimer with lengths of catgut strung along two axes, one set perpendicularly above the other. The effect of her plucking and slithering was more tympanic than melodic. Perhaps the thing was out of tune. Or the player untalented. Or even that it was a foreign way of making music. Still, the other novices seemed not to mind, indeed, even to take pleasure from the droning sounds.

They leaped to their feet at her approach, scattering their work in the grass. They were Quadlings, the younger three of them. "Girls, please," said the Superior Maunt. "To your tasks." Then, deferentially, "Your health, Mother."

The older maunt nodded but didn't look up. Her eyes were on the fingers of the girl playing.

"I was hoping to find Sister Cook," said the Superior Maunt.

"She's in the mushroom cellar, harvesting for a fungal soup. Shall I fetch her?" asked one of them.

"No," said the Superior Maunt, looking one to the other. "Are you all first-years?"

"Shhhh," said the crone.

The Superior Maunt did not like being shhh'd. "Are you professed, the lot of you?"

"Shhhh, he's coming."

"Mother, I have work—" said the Superior Maunt. The sister in the chair raised her wrinkled hand. She had no fingerprints, no lifelines on her right hand—no identity, no history, nothing to read, as if her hand had been burned clean of individuality through some chastening flame.

Only one old biddy had this hand. "What are you on about, Mother Yackle?" asked the Superior Maunt.

The old creature didn't answer, didn't look up, but she did crook one hobbled finger skyward. The Superior Maunt turned. All kinds of romance and lore about visitors from the sky, from sacred scripture to rabble-rousing prophecies. The sky was hard to ignore.

It wasn't the sky, though, that Mother Yackle was indicating, but one of the trees. Out of it fell a ruffling cascade, like a stack of ladies' fans sliding silkily off a credenza. A scatter of brazen feathers, red winking. A gold eye set in a pear-shaped skull.

A crimson pfenix! Male, to judge by the plumage. The species was rumored to have been nearly hunted to extinction. The last known colonies of pfenix lived in the very south of Oz, where the watery acres of marsh began at last to dry out, and a strip of jungle thought to be seven miles wide still defeated travelers to this day. This fellow—blown off course, perhaps, or deranged by disease?

The pfenix landed on the center of the musical instrument that the third girl was playing. She looked up in some alarm; she hadn't been attending anything but her music. The pfenix craned his head and fixed first one, then another golden eye on the Superior Maunt.

"If you're looking for the talented one," said the pfenix—well, the Pfenix, if he spoke—"this is the one for you. I've been watching for an hour, and she takes little notice of anything but her music."

The women said nothing. Talking Birds were not uncommon, but they rarely bothered to speak to human beings. What a specimen this Pfenix was! His rack of tail feathers fanned out laterally, like a turkey's, but a Pfenix just as easily could unfurl his close-coiled camouflage feathers, which spiked globally all about him, affording a sort of private chamber of airy, concealing, fernlike fronds. A mature male Pfenix aloft in full display could look like a shimmering globe in the air.

"Do you know the boy who has been brought here?" asked the Superior Maunt, beginning to govern her own awe.

"I don't know any boys. I don't consort with your kind at all. I am a Red Pfenix," he added, as if they might not have taken it in.

The Superior Maunt disapproved of vainglory in all its forms. She turned to the musician. "What's your name?"

The girl looked up but didn't answer. Her face was not as ruddy as some Quadlings—less red, more umber. Its shape was pleasing, proportioned along the lines of an oakhair nut: broad brow, high cheekbones, sweet swollen cheeks like a toddler's, a small but firm chin. The Superior Maunt, who did not pay much attention to the looks of her novices, was surprised.

She was too beautiful to be a natural maunt, so she must be a moron.

"She doesn't speak much," said one of the novices.

"She's been here three weeks," added the other. "Her whispered prayers are in a dialect we can't decipher. We think she cannot raise her voice."

"The Unnamed God hears anyway. Where do you come from, child?"

"Sister Cook will know," said the first novice.

"Up, girl, up," said the Superior Maunt. "You have been chosen by a Red Pfenix. You don't talk much, but you understand our tongue? Just the one I need." She offered her hand to the musician, who rose, reluctantly. The Red Pfenix nestled in the grass and set to ridding himself of lice.

"Can I send for a bowl of scented water, something? Is there a way we can offer charity to you?" said the Superior Maunt. "We don't have visits from the likes of you often. In fact, I think never."

"I'm only passing through," said the Red Pfenix. "There's a Conference farther west. But the music drew me down."

"You love music?"

"If I loved music I wouldn't have stopped. She doesn't play very well, does she? No, I don't love music; it interferes with my homing devices. I was merely curious to see an instrument like this again. The sound of her playing reminded me of a time I had seen one long ago; I'd quite forgotten. But thank you for your charity. I require nothing but a little rest."

The Red Pfenix looked at the musician, who stood shyly in her pale grey novice's skirts. "She's a puzzle, that one is," said the Red Pfenix.

"Got him!" shouted Sister Cook, coming up from behind with a snare, and indeed she had. The Red Pfenix squawked and thrashed; all the eyes in his plumage contorted. The scream was horrible. "Pfenix steaks!" said Sister Cook. "I have just the recipe!"

"Let him go," said Mother Yackle.

It was not her place to speak next, and the Superior Maunt was irritated. She knew Sister Cook was thinking: Pfenix steaks! With knobs of butter, and tarragon mustard, and small new potatoes roasted in the same pan . . .

"Let him go," said the Superior Maunt, more sternly than Mother Yackle.

"Shoot," said Sister Cook. "I spend fifteen minutes creeping up on this bird, and with my lumbago I actually manage to catch it, and you say 'Let him go'?"

"Do not question my authority."

"I merely question your sense," said Sister Cook heavily. She turned the snare over, and the Red Pfenix exploded away from the orchard, cursing.

"He was on his way to a Conference," said Mother Yackle.

"Enough," said the Superior Maunt. "Enough of this. Sister Cook, who is this novice? Where did she come from?"

Sister Cook was grinding her teeth in annoyance at the missed opportunity. "Candle," she muttered. "Left here by a gypsy cousin for safekeeping, said he'd be back in a year. Either she'd be mauntified by then or he'd reclaim her, but I said I'd take her on. She causes no trouble because she can't gossip with the other girls, and she knows how to make a mean marrow gravy. I've had her working with Sister Sauce on the feast day roast."

"Can you spare her?"

"Can I spare a Red Pfenix is a better question, and the answer to that one is *no*."

"We don't eat Animals," said the Superior Maunt. "I know times have changed, but it's in our charter. We don't eat anything that can talk back to us, Sister Cook, and if I find you have been butchering behind my back . . ."

"I can hardly spare her," said Sister Cook, looking at the musician. "But if you make her take that unnerving domingon with her, I'll call it even."

"Domingon, is that what it is. I'd read of them, but never seen one. Come, my daughter, domingon and all." The Superior Maunt gestured, with as tender a smile as her crabbed old mouth could assume. The girl rose. She took the Superior Maunt's hand in an easy, unaffected way— the other girls snickered. Yes, she must be simple.

"I had come looking to ask you what you remembered of a novice we once housed—the strange green girl, Elphaba."

"Before my time," snapped Sister Cook, and left.

Mother Yackle scratched her nose and yawned.

The Red Pfenix was still screaming in the sky. He circled the towers of the mauntery, safe now, and recovering the ability to be affronted. He was like a clot of blood swimming above the infirmary.

"Did you say there's a boy in the house?" asked Mother Yackle. She let her shawl slip back, and raised her bleary, milk-clotted eyes toward the Superior Maunt. "Did he bring back the broom?"

• 7 •

THE SUPERIOR MAUNT was going to need a long rest after lunch, she knew: all these stairs. A certain penance regarding the joints. But she exerted herself, and Candle lent a willing arm without being asked, which was a good sign that the girl wasn't hopelessly slow.

The sun was high enough overhead by now that the room had grown warmer and begun to sink into noon shadow. The young man lay as he had lain, twitchless, blanketed with an unnatural calm. Sister Apothecaire and Sister Doctor had brought their small chores close, so they could be nearby while they worked—Sister Apothecaire, the grinding of herbs in a mortar, and Sister Doctor the annotating of symptoms in a ledger. Sister Doctor sat on one side of the bed, Sister Apothecaire on the other.

"You know this novice?" said the Superior Maunt.

Her colleagues neither admitted familiarity, nor dissented.

"She's a garden girl with an instrument called a domingon. I have heard of these but never see one. Apparently Candle has a small talent at music. Perhaps in the long hours on watch over Liir, she will develop it. Candle, meet Sister Doctor and Sister Apothecaire. You will have seen them at table or in chapel if not elsewhere."

It was not the professional maunts' obligation to bow, but when Candle did not bow either, Sister Apothecaire, out of social anxiety, gave a lurching sort of bob that might have meant any number of things.

To the older women the Superior Maunt said, "There are matters more pressing for you to attend to than the continual observation of our new guest. I have a different assignment for you."

"Mother Maunt!" replied Sister Doctor. "Far be it from me to question your discernment. But I must remind you, in loyal obeisance of course, that while you govern the spirit of this House, I supervise the health of the individual souls within it."

"As to such treatments that may be required," began Sister Apothecaire, but the Superior Maunt held up her hand.

"I will hear no objection. Candle seems a simple soul, but she can sit here and watch the boy. She understands my instructions. If he so much as speaks, she will let someone know. She can practice her scales and perhaps grow in skill. If he is to die, let him be comforted by the peculiar drone of her instrument. This is my wish, and I have made my point."

She cupped her hands before her in an archaic, formal gesture that meant "be it thus" or, depending on the expression of the speaker, "enough out of you, you."

Nevertheless, Sister Apothecaire protested. "I'm well aware of this girl, she doesn't know enough to come in out of the rain. You are making a terrible mistake—"

"In this rare instance Sister Apothecaire is correct," said Sister Doctor. "Should any wound suppurate, or a complication develop—"

"I have other jobs for you two," said the Superior Maunt. "Your insistence at brooking my will convinces me. You two are the ones for the next job at hand."

They paused in their flailing, affronted and curious.

"I haven't yet told you what I recently learned about the three missionary novices from the Emerald City who stopped here some days ago," said the Superior Maunt. "Their small party was ambushed and they were all killed. Scraped, I'm afraid. Someone will need to find out who did the deed, and why."

She turned. "Finish your nostrums and reinforce your binding spells at once, enough to last till dinner anyway, and come with me. I shall nap briefly instead of taking a meal, and we will convene in my sectorium when the lunch prayers are concluded."

She was untrained in their profession. How did she know they'd used several illicit binding spells? This was why she was the Superior Maunt, they guessed. She didn't know medicine but she knew women.

There was nothing for them to do but obey. Walking slightly in advance of them, the Superior Maunt couldn't help but smile faintly to herself. The medical women *were* good, solid folk. They were merely curious, curious as hell, like the rest of the House. And whatever was troubling Liir, inside or out, he would recover or decline more comfortably without being smothered by the attentions of middle-aged maunts.

The Superior Maunt paused to catch her breath. Stairs were the devil. Her two colleagues respectfully froze in place while she wheezed. The willpower of women, she thought. These two, and me besides. I make the awful choice to put them in danger. If anyone can manage the task at hand, they will. Keep them safe, she prayed.

But why do I even have to put my dear sisters in jeopardy? Because my colleagues in the motherchapel dare to send young innocent missionaries into the wild—without so much as a guide. No Oatsie Manglehand for them—just faith, innocence, and courage born of stupidity. Damn the Emerald City for leaning down upon us all. Damn those—those *bath mats* in the motherhouse, for yielding to the influence of the government!

She didn't utter a private apology for the oath. She felt she'd earned the right to swear internally, now and then. When it was warranted.

◆ 8 ◆

CANDLE HARDLY GLANCED at Liir. She sat on a rush-seated chair and rubbed the calloused pads of her right fingers over the upper strings. A faint harmonic vibration buzzed in the lower strings, almost inaudible— a sensation in the air more than a sound.

The light heaved in its uncertain tides, as clouds too thin to see washed across the sky. The room chilled slightly.

Candle let her fingers wander up the frets. She was a skilled musician, more skilled even than the kitchen sisters knew—skilled, and talented besides. This domingon was missing a vital part, and couldn't peal

or chide or keen as she would like to require of it. Still, to keep her fingers alert, from the domingon's double necks Candle drew dull incom-
plete sentences. They had no power to comfort; this she knew. But she
would tease the lengthy imponderable sounds out into the air anyway.
She had seen the Red Pfenix in the sky. So it was her playing that had
called him down, was it? She could do it again, and more besides.

Abroad

✦ I ✦

THE DOMINGON PLAYED ON. Unheard by Liir in his state, it had its effect nonetheless.

✦   ✦   ✦

HE WAS LIVING IN THE CASTLE called Kiamo Ko at the time, but he wasn't present at the death of the Witch.

The Witch had locked him in the kitchen with Nanny and that jittery Lion. Showing surprising resourcefulness for one so dotty, Nanny had driven the handle of a one-egg iron skillet into the rotten wood of the doorjamb. Getting the idea, Liir and the Lion gouged at the hinges until the door fell heavily inward.

Chistery, the Witch's Snow Monkey, had skittered ahead of them up the stairs to the Witch's tower-top chambers. But Dorothy was already coming down, her face glutinous with tears, the badly burned broom stinking in her hands. "She's gone," sobbed the girl, and Liir's heart had gone out to her—whose wouldn't? He'd sat on the step and snaked his arm around her shoulders. He was fourteen. First attraction is awkward under any circumstances, he supposed, but this was extreme. It wasn't as if he'd ever seen people being tender. And she was a saint from the Other Land, for pity's sake.

The girl couldn't control her shock, so it took Liir a while to understand what she was blubbering about. The Witch was *gone*. His earliest memory, his bête noire, his Auntie, his jail-keeper, his sage friend—his mother, the others had said, but there'd been no proof of that, and she'd never answered the question when he'd asked her.

Dead, dead and gone, and after her own inspection, Nanny wouldn't let him up to the parapet to see. "The sight would turn the holy blind," she murmured, "so it's a good thing I'm an old sinner. And you, you're just a young fool. Forget it, Liir." She pocketed the key and began to warble in an unfamiliar mode, some dirge from her backwater childhood. "Sweet Lurlina, mother of mercy, shroud of the murdered, shawl of the missing . . ."

Nanny's pagan pieties were somehow unconvincing. But on what basis could he say that? He'd left the unionist mabuntery too young to absorb any of the tenets of faith that supported the cloistered way of life. From the distance of a skeptical adolescent, unionism seemed like a thicket of contradictions. Charity to all, but intolerance toward the heathen. Poverty ennobles, but the Bishops had to be richer than everyone else. The Unnamed God made the good world, imprisoning the rebellious human being within it, and taunting humankind with tinderbox sexuality that must be guarded against at all costs.

Lurlinism was no more sensible, to judge by how Nanny spoke of it. Random episodes of mildly erotic dalliance, as Lurlina effectively wooed Oz into being. Privately he thought it was downright stupid, though, being prettier, it was also easier to remember.

Perhaps he just didn't have the feeling for faith. It seemed to be a kind of language, one whose gnarled syntax needed to be heard from birth, or it remained forever unintelligible. But he wished he had a faith now, some scrap of something: for Elphaba was dead, and to act as if the world were no more changed than if some branch of a tree had snapped off—well, it didn't seem right.

She whipped up in his mind, the first brutal memory as sudden and insistent as a bee sting. She was yelling at him. "The Wizard's soldiers kidnapped the whole family and left you behind? Because you were useless? And you followed after them anyway, and they *still* managed to elude you? *Are* you useless?" Even then he had known she was less angry at him than frightened at what had befallen the other residents of the castle while she was away. Even then he had known she was relieved he'd been spared by virtue of being insignificant. Even then he'd smarted at the rebuke of the term. Useless.

"I'll take the broom," said Liir at last. "She can be buried with it."

"I need it, to prove she's dead," said Dorothy. "What else would do?"

"I'll carry it for you then," he said.

"You're coming with me?"

He looked around. The courtyard of the castle was more silent than he'd ever seen it. The Witch's crows were dead, her wolves, her bees. The winged monkeys were huddled on top of the woodshed, paralyzed with grief. With the Arjiki villagers in the settlement of Red Windmill down the slope, or scattered in cottages on the leeward side of the mountain, Liir had had little contact.

So there was nothing to keep him in Kiamo Ko but Nanny. And old as she was, she would soon lapse into her usual fog of deafness and abstraction. In a week she would forget that the Witch had died. Besides, even in her best days she'd never known where Liir had come from. Neither had she seemed to care. So it was no hardship to leave her.

"I'm coming with you," he said. "Yes. And I'll carry the broom."

It was too late to leave now, so they busied themselves instead. Liir fed the monkeys. Dorothy tried to make a meal for Nanny, who wept and said she wasn't hungry and then ate all her portion and the Lion's besides.

After washing up, Dorothy settled cozily in the crook of the Lion's neck, as much to calm him as to take comfort herself. Liir climbed to the Witch's room and looked about. Already it was as if she had never lived there.

He thought of the Grimmerie, that perplexing book of magic. He had never been able to read it. Wherever the Witch had put it last, he let it be. No matter. No Flying Monkey would be able to gibber a spell out of it, and Nanny's eyesight was too poor to decipher its odd scrambling text. It would be too heavy to carry, anyway.

Books have their own life, he thought. Let it take care of itself.

Turning to leave, he caught sight of Elphaba's black cape. A bit worse for wear, its hems threadbare, its collar much sampled by moths. Still, it was thick, and the days would only get colder. He put it over his narrow shoulders. It was far too large for him, so he looped the ends around his forearms. He looked, he supposed, like a small silly bat with an oversize wingspan. He didn't care.

The horizon was frosted with a greenish smear, as if ranks of camp-fires from distant tribes had divined the news already and were burning an homage to Elphaba before the sun could set on the day of her death.

He could smell her in the collar of the cape, and he wept for the first time.

LIIR DIDN'T BOTHER to say good-bye to Chistery. Let the Witch's most beloved Flying Monkey take care of himself now. Why else had she taught him language, but so that he could keen when she was gone?

On the road, the Lion and that little yapper, Toto, lagged behind with the other two who had been waiting for Dorothy—the Scarecrow, the man of tin—both of whom gave Liir a serious case of the creeps. The wind was brutal and the streaky clouds massed to the east, and if Liir wasn't mistaken, before long rain would fall.

Dorothy asked perfunctory questions, but she was more interested in making sure they didn't lose their way. How would *he* know if they went off course, he asked her—it had been seven or eight years since he'd come from the maunery with Elphaba, and he'd never left the neigh-borhood of Kiamo Ko in all the time since. Dorothy had much more re-cent experience of the greater landscape.

"Yes, well, those Flying Monkeys carried me the last bit," she said nervously, "and I can't claim to have had my wits about me enough to have taken note of landmarks. Still, we're going downslope, and that's got to be right."

"Everything is downslope of Kiamo Ko," Liir told her.

"I like your confidence," she said. "Tell me about yourself, then."

He suspected his memories of young childhood were like anyone else's: imprecise, suggestible, and largely devoid of emotion. He didn't recall defining moments—maybe there weren't any—but he did remember the sensation of things. The shafts of light slanting through the mullioned windows high up in the gallery, pinning silent maunts to their silent shadows on the stone floor. The smell of asparagus cream soup, a little maple syrup drizzled on top. The smell of snow in the air. Liir had been attached to Elphaba, somehow, he remembered that: he'd been allowed to play with his broken wooden ducky in the same room where she sat and spun wool.

"Was she your mother?" asked Dorothy. "I'm terribly sorry to have killed her if she was. I mean I'm sorry anyway, but more so if you were related."

The girl's directness was puzzling, and Liir wasn't used to it. The Witch had never hidden her emotions, but nor had she explained them, and in many ways living with her had been like sharing an apartment with an ill-tempered house pet.

He tried to be honest, but there was so much he didn't know. "I started out with her," he said. "How, as a toddler, I came to be among the maunts, I can't say. No one has ever told me, and the Witch wouldn't talk about it. I remember other women from those times, Sister Cupboard and Sister Orchard, and some of the more playful ones, the novices, who kept their own names, Sister Saint Grayce, and Sister Linnet. But when it came time for Elphaba to leave, they wrapped up my small packet of clothes, too, and I was lifted up to a seat on a wagon, and we joined a party that went through the Kells, stopping here and there until we got to Kiamo Ko."

"It's awfully out of the way," said Dorothy, looking around at the unpeopled slopes of pine and potterpine, and the slides of scree, and the scraggles of mountain lavender going to seed.

"She wanted to be out of the way. And besides, it's where Fiyero had lived."

"Your father?"

Liir was as doubtful of his paternity as he was of his maternity. "He had meant something to her, to the Witch," he pointed out. "But what, I don't know. I never met him. Can you imagine the Witch would sit down and pour out her heart to me?"

"I can't imagine anything about her. Who could?"

He didn't want to talk anymore. The death was too recent, the shock of it was beginning to wear off, and what began to show through was anger. "In a general sense, we're going southwest, and then we'll cut east through Kumbricia's Pass," he said. "I've learned that much by listening to Oatsie Manglehand when she comes through guiding a party. There are tribes around and about."

"We saw no one," said Dorothy, "not for miles."

"They saw you," said Liir. "They had to. That's what they do."

"Not nice, to be spying on us. We're very chummy," she said, putting on an aggressively friendly face. Any party of scouts witnessing it would do well to keep themselves hidden.

Before long the rain came, and he was glad, for it stopped their conversation, which had turned into prattle. A heavy rain, the drops like pebbles. He could see no shepherd's hut out here, not even a clump of mountain arbor to shelter beneath. So rather than sit in the mud and let the rain wick through their undergarments, they trudged on.

Their confidence about their course ebbed, though, what with the shrouding of hilltops—all landmarks wiped out of view.

"Liir, I have no confidence in your sense of direction," said the Tin Woodman, politely.

"Nick Chopper! You're heartless!" said Dorothy.

"Ha bloody ha. And you're an orphan," he replied. "I'll rust in this downpour. Does anyone think of that? No."

"Don't carp. I don't deal well with conflict," said the Lion. "Let's sing a song."

"*No,*" they all chorused.

"What'll you do when you find yourself courageous—assuming the Wizard grants you what you wish?" asked the Scarecrow, to change the subject.

"Invest in the market? Join a troupe of music hall buskers? How the hell do I know?" said the Lion. "Strike out on my own, anyway, and find a better class of associates. More simpatico."

"You?" asked the Scarecrow of the Tin Woodman.

"What will I do if I find myself with a heart?" scoffed the Tin Woodman. "Lose it constantly, I imagine."

They slopped on. Liir didn't think it was his place to continue the conversation, since he hadn't been present at their initial audience with the Wizard. When no one else spoke, though, he said, "Well, Scarecrow, your turn. What'll you do with your brains?"

"I'm thinking about it," he answered, and would not discuss it further.

"Oh, Toto!" shrieked Dorothy suddenly. "Where's Toto?"

"He's wandered off to do his business," said the Lion. "Just between you and me, it's about time he learned to be private about it. I know you dote on him, but there is a limit."

"He'll be lost," she cried. "He couldn't find his way out of a cracker barrel. He's not very bright, you know."

After a respectful pause, the Tin Woodman observed, "I *think* we've all noticed that."

"I hate to be obvious," added the Scarecrow, "but you'd have saved yourself a heap of trouble if you weren't too cheap to invest in a leash, Dorothy."

"There he is," she cried, pitching up a small slope.

The clueless creature was finishing his evacuation at the base of what looked like an ancient traveler's shrine to Lurline. A weathered statue of the pagan goddess gazed blindly out into the storm. The statue was life-size, if you accepted that goddesses have the same stature as humans. Little more than a lean-to for protecting the statue from the elements, the structure could afford no room for the travelers to crawl in out of the downpour. After a while, though, Liir thought of standing on the shoulders of the Lion and slinging the big black cape out over the shrine's roof. Using the scorched remains of the Witch's broom as a pole, he rigged up a black tent under which they could huddle. The Lion's mane reeked, but at least the travelers were protected from the worst of the rain.

"This cape is larger than it looks," said Dorothy. "And the water isn't soaking through."

"Maybe she hexed it waterproof. She didn't like water," said Liir.

"So I've learned," said Dorothy.

"Who does?" added the Tin Woodman, squeaking his joints.

"Tell me more about her," continued Dorothy.

Liir didn't oblige. He found Dorothy congenial enough—but it had been so long since he'd had anything like friends his own age! At Kiamo Ko, when he'd first arrived with Elphaba, Fiyero's three children had allowed him into their small society, but slackly, without much interest. The girl, Nor, had been the only one ever really to play with him. Though he had been little more to Nor than that dog was to Dorothy, a presence to boss around, Nor *had* been kind. That first Lurlinemas, she'd given him the tail of her gingerbread mouse, because no one had thought to make him a gingerbread mouse of his own.

And besides her? No one else to play with, once she and Irji and the rest of the ruling family—Fiyero's survivors—had been kidnapped by the Wizard's forces garrisoned at Red Windmill. Yes, he'd bravely followed, but fecklessly. They'd given him the slip. He had had to return to Kiamo Ko and face the screeching. Then the Witch had prohibited Liir from fraternizing any longer with Commander Cherrystone of the Gale Forcers or from making new friends among the lice-ridden urchins of Red Windmill.

So Liir had lived a lonely life. It could have been worse; he was fed and he was clothed more or less warmly. He had his chores, and the winged monkeys, largely inarticulate, at least didn't go out of their way to move if he sat down nearby. Was there supposed to be more to a childhood? Rehearsing it to tell Dorothy, it seemed a spare, botched thing, and he suppressed most of it.

Of late, the Witch had become more irritable than usual, complaining of sleeping problems. Nanny—her nanny, at one point, and her mother's nanny before that—was well into her eighties and good for little by way of coherent discussion. Liir had been left to talk to himself, and he'd found himself less than stimulating as a conversationalist.

Dorothy's curiosity seemed flat to him, though, perhaps artificial. He wasn't able to tell if she was really curious about his life, about the Witch, or if she was just marking time. Maybe steeling her own nerve by hearing the sound of her voice. He felt leery. Perhaps, the son of the Witch or no, he had inherited from exposure to Elphaba a mild sense of paranoia, as if everyone were after some scrap of vital information that they were unwilling to ask for directly.

He fussed and rolled his eyes and tried to imagine how to change the subject. He didn't want to talk about his toddler days in the mauntery or his boyhood in Kiamo Ko. He was bereft of family, now, something of a hanger-on to Dorothy's party, something of a guide without a clue out here in the cruel terrain. He just wanted to concentrate on the job.

He was glad, therefore, when the Lion started and said, "What's that?"

"It's night coming on," said the Tin Woodman.

"Night coming on makes a sound like the Crack of Doom?" complained the Lion. "Never did before. Shhh, everyone. It wasn't thunder. What was it? Shhh, I tell you."

The Tin Woodman observed, "You're the only one who's talking—"

"*Shhh,* I said!"

They shhhushed.

The downpour made a symphony. An undertone of susurrus—rain at mid-distance—accompanied the solo vocalists rounding vowels of rainwater—*plopp*—*plopp*—or, as Liir thought, of Auntie Witch, Elphaba Thropp—*Thropp*—*Thropp.*

"Did you ever notice how rain sounds like a domingon?" asked the Scarecrow.

The Lion put his paw to his mouth: Shhhh. His grimace was anything but fearsome; he looked like an overgrown child in lion pajamas.

Then they heard what he was hearing, and before they could do anything about it, a stone at the base of the statue of Lurlina was shifted to one side. Up from the earth poked the paw of a creature. A badger, a beaver? Something brown, whiskered, and sensible. A slope grite of some sort, larger than its valley cousin.

"You've some nerve, besmirching the memory of Lurlina with your prattle," said the Mountain Grite. His jowls made a saddlebag flapping noise as he spoke.

"Nerve," said the Lion. "I wish."

"We're merely sheltering from the storm," said Dorothy. "May we have your blessing to stay here?"

The Grite bared an impressive collection of incisors and canines.

"What business is it of yours?" said Liir. "We're not bothering you."

The Grite looked around, as if assessing whether he might take them on all at once and get the better of them. Apparently not. "My digs, if you want to call it that," he said at last, "are directly below. You're a big heavy lot, and you're going to collapse the walls of my lodging."

"A bad place to build," said the Tin Man, for whom the teeth of a Mountain Grite weren't much of a threat. "An insult to Lurlina, actually."

"Maybe, but I dig deep, and if the whole thing gives and you tumble in, you'll starve to death down there. And the stink of your rotting corpses won't appeal to the spirit of Lurlina, however beloved of the natural world she is said to be."

"The storm can't last forever," said Dorothy.

The Grite came forward a little. "Quite possibly I have rabies, you know. Fair warning. I bite first and I don't ask questions."

The Lion sighed and removed himself from the makeshift tent. Out there, the deluge sloped on him like a fountain coursing over a sculptured lion.

"We're not going to let some overgrown rodent chase us into the storm," said Liir. "If you bite me, I'll bite you back, and return your own rabies to you. Go away."

"That's a capable awning you have." The Grite wrinkled his face. "My eyes aren't what they used to be. What is it?"

"It's a cape," said Liir. "What business is it of yours?"

"That's the Witch's cape," said the Grite. "I don't believe it. Where did you get it?"

"I took it," said Liir.

"More fool you. She'll have your head before nightfall."

"She's dead," said Dorothy. Smugly.

The Grite's eyes bulged, and he pushed his face nearer to Dorothy, who flinched and drew back from him: He wasn't an especially handsome specimen of his family. "The Witch is dead? Can it be true?"

They nodded, each one of them.

"Oh, the shock of it." The Grite clutched his paws and worried them back and forth. "The shock of it! The Witch is dead?"

The wind itself answered in a kind of obbligato descant: *The Witch is dead!*

"Get out of here," said the Grite in a colder voice. "Go on."

"I thought you'd be glad," said Dorothy.

The retort was crisp and censorious. "We held her in considerable regard. There have always been some Animals who would have marched at her side, right to the gates of the Emerald City, had she believed in armies, had she ever given the word. You'll find no comfort among us."

"She was my friend," said Liir. "Don't confuse us with assassins."

"You're a fledgling. You could barely manage to befriend her cape, let alone the Witch herself." To Dorothy he added, "Move along, little Miss Thug and accomplices, before I call on reinforcements to deal with you." The Grite sniffed the raw air as if expecting to find proof of their assertions in the smell of the revised world. "The Witch is dead. It can't be. Wait till Princess Nastoya hears. Wait until the Wizard hears."

He was lost to his own ruminations, and turned to look up at the statue of Lurline. "Give us guidance!" he said. "Speak, for once."

The storm thundered very nearby. Everyone shuddered but the Grite. "I mean, speak in a language we can understand," he clarified. But the storm, or Lurline within its might, didn't oblige, and indeed, moments later the worst of the downpour was done, and the thunder shunted elsewhere.

The Grite continued. "I have no reason to give comfort to mine enemy, but there you are. You may be villainous, but you are young, some of you, and perhaps might learn to repent. I'm told that Wizardic battalions are encamped on the banks of the Vinkus River. Find the Wizard's forces and they will protect you. That's my advice to you."

"The Wizard's armies will *protect* us?" snapped Liir. "The Wizard of Oz is a menace!"

"Of course he is. A despot, a suzerain, call it what you will. The boss. And you've abetted him in his campaign to wipe out the western resistance. This news will travel fast, my friends." Every time he said the word *friends,* it sounded less friendly. "But take protection where you can. When the word of the death of Elphaba Thropp spreads through these hills, you'll have a very difficult time of it. I won't answer for what happens next. You've heard my advice. Heed it."

"I'm not giving myself up to any corps of the Wizard's army," said Liir. "If there are forces down the eastern side, we'll keep to our plan to veer west, and take our chances through Kumbricia's Pass. It'll be a longer route but a safer one."

"Perhaps we'd better get going," said Dorothy, nervously.

"You had better go on," agreed the Mountain Grite. "I won't join a posse against you, but nor will I lie to my friends about what I've learned here today. The clouds are passing over. If you've intended to take the hairpin track down the western slope of Knobblehead Pike, you've overshot. You'll have to back up. You won't reach the river valley before dark. Shelter under a black willow; you'll find a stand of them where the track levels out and circles a bit of highland swamp. You'll be safe there."

"Thank you," said Dorothy earnestly.

"Don't be a fool," said Liir. "Thank him for what?"

"You," said the Grite to the Lion, "are a turncoat. You ought to be ashamed of yourself. I'd be especially wary if I were you. Animals don't take lightly to traitors. If you were more of a Lion, you'd know that."

"I did nothing!" said the Lion. "I was locked in the kitchen!" His tail twitched eight or ten times.

THE GRITE KEPT HIS WORD and ratted on them. Before the travelers had finished washing the next morning, a scouting party of Scrow appeared at the edge of the black willow grove. Riding bareback and nearly naked on their purple-white steeds, they looked like wild centaurs in the mist. Without a word but with considerable glower the Scrow contingent circled the grove. There, the travelers were kept loosely penned. Attempts to negotiate were fruitless; they had no language in common.

The languages of Oz. Liir had never thought about them. The father tongue had always seemed universal; even Dorothy spoke without peculiar inflections or special difficulty. True, the dialect of the mountain clans, the Arjikis, was characterized by the growling of syllables halfway down the throat—but the difference had made little impression on Liir. He could still understand the Arjikis.

So why would the isolated Mountain Grite speak the common tongue with clarity and effect, while the Scrow clung to a language only they understood?

Right up to the end, the Witch had kept trying to teach the winged monkeys to speak, as if to be able to testify might save their lives some-day. So much bound up in language . . . The language of spells themselves—*spells,* of all things! A way to order sounds to make things shift, reveal what is hidden, conceal what isn't . . .

He wished he had a skill for language. He wished he could spell magic as, with effort and increasing control, Elphaba had learned to do. He would bind the Scrow frozen, and he and his companions would walk away safely. But this was beyond him—like everything else.

The Scrow scouts tossed the travelers hanks of repugnant dried meat and smoked corn. It was clear Dorothy and company were to wait here. A day and a half later, the leader of the Scrow arrived, traveling in a slow-moving caravansary that with considerable care negotiated the path to this low-lying western ridge of Knobblehead Pike.

The party included a translator, so Liir found himself requesting an audience with the Highness behind the shabby drapes of the palanquin. He wasn't skilled at bargaining. "The only thing I request is that we, uh, hurry," he said. "My friend Dorothy wants to get safely to the Emerald City; she has an appointment with the Wizard. Then she intends to travel abroad somewhere."

And I with her, he thought to add, but didn't. Would she have me? And if not—what else am I going to do?

The translator was an old, gnarled Scrow gentleman who, despite his tribal appurtenances, had been trained in the university environs of Shiz. "Very well," he said. "I don't see why we should dally. It is in all of our interests, after all. Give her Highness a chance to compose herself, and we shall let you know when she's ready."

Dorothy said, "We don't think much of crowned heads where I come from. Who is this Highness?" The interpreter left without answering.

"How rude," said Dorothy. "Well, who *is* she, this Highness? Might it be the Ozma everybody goes on about?"

Liir explained. "The last Ozma disappeared many years ago, kidnapped as a young girl when the Wizard came to power. Nanny believed the child had been bewitched in a trance, never to grow older by a day until the moment she was released from the charm, like a fairy-tale princess. Then she would rise up and smash the mighty in their comfort, and return the monarchy to its rightful place. But Auntie Witch always pooh-poohed that. She said the child had probably been murdered long ago. The remains of the Ozma Tippetarius would be found deep in the bone bins of the Palace, along with her ancestors, if anyone were allowed to look there."

"I believe in Ozma," said the Scarecrow staunchly.

Mindless fool, thought Liir, but said nothing more.

The court of the Scrow didn't keep them waiting for long. When the sun had reached its zenith, attendants unrolled a green carpet with a puckered selvage. Shapeless pillows, sour with mildew, were placed about. "Stand until her Highness is seated," the translator said, arranging in a kind of lattice pattern the remaining hairs on his pale domed head. "Then you may be seated, too."

She was helped out of her compartment by six retainers. Her muscles were of little use in holding up her bulk, and her large, sagging face twisted into seams of overlapping skin. She grimaced at the pain of every step. An old woman, a monolith of an ancient Scrow matron, easily the size of all her retainers standing together. Like a queen bee among drones.

Her face was scored with green and purple smudges, some sort of ceremonial marking. The waft of vetiver and lily water, pleasant enough, couldn't entirely disguise an animal odor.

"Princess Nastoya," said the translator in comprehensible Ozish, "may I present Dorothy Gale, of parts unknown, and her companions, a Lion, a Scarecrow, a gentleman clad in Tin, and the boy about whom you've been told." He then repeated the lines in Scrow, to indicate how he would go on.

"How do you do?" said Dorothy, curtseying.

Princess Nastoya was lowered to the ground so she could regard them while reclining on her side. Her spine was preternaturally long, as if she possessed extra vertebrae. The servants propped her knees on a yellow cushion, and her elbow on another, and they arranged a small mountain of cushions behind her so she wouldn't roll backward.

The interpreter began a flowery biography, but the Princess cut him off. Her voice was low, tympanic, as if her nasal passages were large enough for the storage of melons.

"I am sore with disbelief," she said, the interpreter translating. "I had only known that the Witch sent out Crows to call for help. Before they could reach me, they were attacked and their flesh devoured by a posse of nocturnal rocs."

"How do you know about the Crows?" asked Liir. "If they were eaten by rocs?"

"Nocturnal rocs are mute beasts," said the Princess, "but the attack was witnessed by a Grey Eagle who keeps an eye on a certain district for me. He drove the rocs away from one Crow, who managed to pass on the message of the Witch's embattlement before dying. The Eagle delivered the message to me as I was closing a convocation with some of the southern Arjiki clans."

"The Witch ought to have been told about that," said Liir. "She considered herself an honorary Arjiki, sort of."

"I won't be lectured on strategy or protocol," replied the Princess. "In any case, I did invite her. But I never knew if my invitation got through. I was told that she was distracted with grief over the death of her sister."

"She was . . . unsteady . . . at the end," admitted Liir. "I'm not sure how much she could have done for you, or if she would have bothered. In truth, she was kind of a hermit. She kept to herself." Even when it came to me, he remembered.

"I'd have put the case forcefully to her, had I gotten her attention," asserted the Princess. "She was no fool. She saw that when the breadbasket of Munchkinland was ruinously taxed by the Emerald City's chancellors, it had to break away and form a Free State. If pressed, we here in the west will do no less than that ourselves. My attempts to build an al-

legiance with the Yunamata have come to naught, and the Arjikis can enjoy their own insularity, obstinate slope dwellers!—but we Scrow will
not stand by and let our Grasslands be plundered. The Wizard is amass-
ing an army on the eastern slope of the Kells. I know how he works, you
whippet."

The Princess groaned. "She might have been a help! But it is too
late. I hear through the report of a Mountain Grite that the peculiar
woman is dead. Elphaba."

The interpreter pronounced it wrong. "EL-phaba," said Liir.

"Is the murderer here among us?" asked the Princess.

"It was an accident," said Dorothy. "I didn't mean it." She put the
end of one of her pigtails into her mouth and chewed it.

"The deceased was a curious creature," said the Princess. "I only
met her once, but she impressed me with her stamina. She did not seem
the type to die."

"Who does?" said Dorothy.

"Speak for yourself," muttered the Lion. "I die a little bit every day,
especially if there are unfriendly faces in the room."

Through her factotum, the Princess continued her message. "You
are in grave danger. Not least from me. Murder and theft of the Witch's
belongings, the way I see it, but even worse: doing so in collusion with
the Wizard."

Liir protested, sputtering. "Not in collusion with the Wizard!"

"Well, the Wizard of Oz *did* ask me to kill her," admitted Dorothy.
"No use crying over *that* spilt milk. He did, and I won't lie about it. But
I didn't intend to do it. I just wanted her forgiveness for the accidental
death of her sister. And then there was the bucket of water. And how
was I to know? I mean, we don't have witches back home in Kansas. We
wouldn't hear of it."

"You've got it all wrong," interrupted Liir. "Listen, Princess Nastoya, please. I lived with the Witch all my life. There's no question of
theft. I am the next of kin."

"How so?"

He couldn't answer. The Princess pressed her point.

"Can you prove it?"

He shrugged. His skin was neither green, like Elphaba's, nor musky ocher, like Fiyero's children and widow. Liir was rather pasty, in fact; not a convincing specimen of anything, when you got right down to it.

"It is no matter," said the Princess. "I would not kill you. Oh no, I would not. But others might, and I wonder if I could prevent them. We have no sway with the Arjikis, as the collapse of my recent campaign shows."

"Why would the Wizard's armies bother to raise a hand against us?" asked Liir. "The Witch is dead, and the ruling family of the Arjikis—the house and line of Fiyero—has been obliterated."

"Even the daughter?" asked the Princess.

Liir's mouth dropped. "Do you mean Nor? Have you heard otherwise about her? What can you tell me of her?"

"I have capable ears," she answered, but continued. "Can you prove the Witch is dead?"

"You want us to bring her back to life?" Liir scoffed. "You might as well kill us now, if that's your demand."

The Princess indicated that she wanted to stand. "It's the neck, it creaks under the weight of too much heavy thinking," she said. It took nine men to cantilever her to her feet, and then they brought her a pair of jeweled canes as thick as newel posts. She leaned forward and fixed Liir in the eye.

"You would be of no help at treaties, you boy-calf," she said. "But you wonder what *do* I want of you."

She let her mirrored shawl slip off her shoulders, and three black ivory combs clattered to the ground from her knotted hedge of thick white hair. The air grew very still, and clammy; there was a sense of Presence. The Princess closed her eyes and droned, and her hair seemed to pick at itself, and then to gather into a sleek sliding thing, and it ran off her back into a white coil on the ground. The shapeless gown of cotton geppling shifted on her hips, appeared to draw itself up into a peplum or a bustle, and then it snaked off.

Liir had never seen an unclothed woman before, old or young—only little Nor on washday, lithe in the copper tub, when she'd been a girl of four or five. The effect of a naked Princess was startling, the print of silvery hair at the groin, the pockets of flesh folding one over the other, the bosom flattened by age and gravity. Dorothy murmured "Goodness!" as if she thought she must be witnessing exactly the opposite.

If this was magic, it was still spelling time. The Princess's nose was lengthening, uncoiling, and the skin on her cement-colored cheeks stretched and thickened epibolically. Her eyes, which had been little more than slits in the folds of her face, lost their ovoid shape, rounded into marbles. A net of fine hairs sprouted on her brow and pate, her cheeks and chin and dramatically hostile nose. And ears:—yes, they were capable and then some.

More or less like an Elephant head, though not planted on an Elephant body.

"Perhaps I ought to have given you more warning," she said. "It seems I've upset the girl." Dorothy was retching into her apron, and her dog appeared to have had a nervous fit and passed out. "I have little use for niceties at this stage in my life, though."

Liir didn't trust himself to speak.

"I am an Elephant," said the Princess Nastoya. "From the Wizard's pogroms against the Animals, I have been in hiding as a human all these long years. I'm admired by the Scrow for my longevity and what passes for my wisdom. In exchange for their protection, for a home in the Thousand Year Grasslands, I have performed my duty as a leader. But of late, young boy-thing, I am unable to shuck off my disguise with the ease I once had. Though Elephants pretend to immortality, I believe I am dying. I must not be allowed to die in this half-form. I will die as an Elephant. But I need help."

"How can I be of service?" asked Liir. As if I could do anything, he added to himself.

"I don't know," said the Princess Nastoya. "I once told Elphaba Thropp that if she needed help, she was only to send word, and I would put all my resources under her command. I never thought that the reverse would happen. That the time would come for me to apply to her for her knowledge of Animals, her native skill at spells and charms. But I have started too late, I see, for your companion has murdered my only hope."

"Dorothy was not to know," said Liir.

"Any murder at all, of any sort, is a murder of hope, too."

"It's disgusting, actually," whispered the Lion to the Tin Woodman. "Do you know, my stomach is turning as we speak."

"I don't have a talent at spells," said Liir. "If that's what you're asking."

"How do you know?" asked the Princess. "Have you tried? Have you studied?"

"I'm not a good student, and furthermore I'm not much interested."

The huge proboscis whipped up from nowhere. Her nose-digits grabbed his chin. She would crush his skull, chin-first. "Get interested," she said. "Get interested, or get help. If you're not to be murdered for your crimes against Elphaba—and that might yet happen—get yourself enough knowledge from someone, somewhere, to help. Was there a book, a Grimmerie? Did Elphaba have associates? I don't care how long it takes, but come back to me. I can't die like this. I won't. In the end, all disguises must drop."

"You confuse me with someone else," he said. "Someone with competence. Someone I never met."

"This isn't a request," she said. "It's an order. I am a colleague of Elphaba's." She lifted her nasal limb from Liir's chin and blew her own horn in his face. His eyes stewed in his skull, and some of the hair at the front of his scalp was raked bloodily away by the force of the blast. "If you claim to be a relation of the Witch's, you will figure out what to do. She always could."

"Well, not always," Dorothy corrected her helpfully, "as is woefully apparent at this moment in time."

"I will pay you," concluded the Princess, apparently addressing Liir alone. "I will keep my ears to the ground for word of your abducted friend—Fiyero's cub, Nor. Nor, was it? Come back to me with a solution and I will tell you all I've been able to learn in the meantime."

Liir couldn't speak, but he held out his hands, palms up, in a gesture even he couldn't read. Accepting the task? Protesting his inadequacy? Whatever—it didn't matter. The Princess was done with them. She turned her massive Elephant head, wobbling on its all-too-human spine, and a dozen Scrow rushed to hold her up. They cloaked the acreage of her buttocks, as if to protect her from a sort of ignominy that, anyway, could never have attached itself to her. Even a half-thing, trapped in a decaying spell, she was too much herself for shame to apply.

"SHE DIDN'T KEEP ONE OF US as a hostage," said the Lion, almost delirious. "I was sure it was going to be me. But I could never have dealt with it."

"She trusted us," said Liir.

They settled into a pattern of traipsing day after day, under skies of broken cloud and brittle light. To avoid the Wizardic armies, they kept to the western base of the Great Kells. In places the upright thrusts of the mountains rose from the grassland floor as cleanly as the front of a corncrib meets a level floor: one could almost mark with a pencil where the plain stopped and the slope began.

They rested where they could. At least it wasn't a bad time of year to be making their way cross-country. They skirted the edge of the Thousand Year Grasslands, ants in single file on the fringe of a carpet of prairie. After several weeks, they reached the verdant apron that rose into the gorge known as Kumbricia's Pass, a high and fertile valley affording the quickest way through the central Kells.

Liir remembered it vaguely from years past. The air was dense and damp, and the ground quilted with decaying vegetation. If Princess Nastoya had not been able to engage the local Yunamata tribes in a treaty against the Wizard, it was likely she hadn't been able to extend her offer of protection through their territory, either. But the Yunamata kept themselves hidden, as was their way.

Beyond, heading downslope toward the Vinkus River and eventually the Emerald City, the world seemed cold and sore. The year was moving on. The occasional foothill farmhouses were crude, almost derelict, roofing thatch thick with mildew, gardens thin on the ground. If bread was offered, it was offered sullenly. No locals would take them in and provide anything like a mattress. The corner of a barn and a blanket crusty with pigeon droppings were the best the travelers could hope for. Still, exhausted with plodding, they slept hard and dreamlessly.

To Liir, it wasn't a question of how many days or weeks it took to reach the Emerald City, but how many hours a day he had to trudge before he could sink back into a safe sleep again. Not sleep, something richer: blissful annihilation. So he could forget the sideways throb of his flattened heart kicking: *You. You. You.* He kept the thought of Elphaba there, unwillingly; it pressed painfully against membranes so interior he had never known their existence before. *I hated you. You left me. So I hate you more than I used to.*

The Kells dwindled, the scrubby flatland spread its wastes in fields of shattered stone. Oakhair forests began first to fringe the horizon, and then to loom with oakhair breath and the sound of wind in their leaves . . . Little of this registered on Liir without his wanting to say, "Look, look—the world you hated so much that you left it behind. It's so weird. I can see why."

He couldn't say this. He could hardly think it, with Dorothy rabbiting on about Auntie Em and Uncle Henry and various forgettable farmhands. *Elphaba,* thought Liir. *Elphaba,* he felt. *Elphaba.* The world without you.

How am I to manage?

THE KELLS HAD LOOKED CLEAN, conceived by a keen architectural eye, and thrown up with confidence. By contrast, the Emerald City, on first sight, seemed organic, a metastasis of competing life-forms. Liir had never seen a settlement larger than a hamlet before, so he was flummoxed at the way the City punched itself against the horizon. Flummoxed, and daunted.

"Don't be scared," said Dorothy, catching his hand. "Think of it as a thousand farmsteads piled on top of one another."

"And *that* isn't a scary notion?"

"I am going to find myself here," declared the Tin Woodman.

"I'm going to lose myself," said the Lion.

"Just try to blend in," said Dorothy. "Act natural."

"Now that *would* be acting," said the Tin Woodman, and barked one calf percussively against the other to underscore his point.

"Come on," said the Scarecrow, "we're in luck." He indicated a motley crew of traveling players advertising a silly new show done mostly with puppets. They were amusing the guards, and in the commotion the Yellow Brick Road Irregulars and Liir managed to sidle undetected through the City's west portal. They debouched into a broad square. Judging from the stink of skark manure, the space served as a holding pen for beasts of transport while cargos were being unloaded and bills of lading composed. Plain granite storehouses faced the yard, and bears—or possibly even Bears, talking beasts, though they weren't talking now—were hauling sacks of grain and crates of produce. "Ho," yelled the overseers. Some were Munchkins, a third the height of their laborers. Their landing whips loosed splatters as of red rain.

"We're meat here, meat," groaned the Lion. "Not that it's all about me, but I feel so *exposed*."

"The Lion's right. Come, let's duck down this alley," said Liir.

"I'd expected a bit more fuss," said Dorothy. "I mean, like it or not, the Witch is dead, and you'd think the word would have gotten out." She held her own nose with one hand and Toto's nose with the other. "Kansas boasts henhouses sweeter than this."

They wandered through commercial districts, crossing wide boulevards lined with dying cypress trees. Some were splintered in half, pulled down for such tinder as they might provide. Many open spaces, around fountains memorializing successful military campaigns, were filled in with makeshift homes, some cardboard, or oilcloth stretched over chicken wire. Cooking pots stank of dinner. The broken spout from a fountain still trickled a little: a common toilet. "Ugh," said Dorothy. "My earlier visit didn't take me through this neighborhood."

"You had civic guides," guessed Liir. She nodded.

The people of the boulevards ducked behind the shawls tacked up as curtain-doors, or hid their faces in sheets of old newsprint when the travelers passed. "You'd think we were leprous," said Liir.

"Perhaps we're too clean," said Dorothy. "We shame them."

Liir didn't think Dorothy was as clean as all that, but her eyes were bright and her step sure, and perhaps that counted more than cleanliness. "Maybe they're used to police action against them, and they just don't know which side we represent," said Liir.

"Oh, really," said the Tin Woodman. "Look at us: a man of straw, a man of tin, a Lion with a bow in his hair like a lapdog! A girl, a boy, a surly little dog. How could we possibly be authorities? We're too—"

"Unique?" asked Dorothy.

"Lacking in camouflage?" asked the Lion.

"Fabulous?" proposed the Tin Woodman.

"Ridiculous?" asked Liir.

"All of the above," decided the Scarecrow. But the indigent seemed not to be convinced and avoided the peculiar travelers.

WHEN THEY REACHED the great piazza before the Palace of the Wizard, Liir wanted to hang back. The Witch had despised the ruler of Oz; how could Liir show his face? "Don't be a sissy," said the Lion, "I've got that covered for us all."

"It's not fear," said Liir, though it was, in part. It was also anger, he realized. How capable, how flexible anger was: he could feel it for the Witch, who had gone and died on him, and for the Wizard, the orchestrator of her murder, both at once. Then why, for Dorothy, did Liir feel nothing but an increasing exhaustion? Perhaps he harbored a zesty secret anger toward her, too, but if so it kept itself in disguise. If Liir lashed out at Dorothy—well, what would he have left in the world? Who? Pretty nearly nothing. Just about nothing at all.

"Well, we can't wait while you dither," said Dorothy. "You'd be a fool to pass up this chance. The Wizard can give you your heart's desire, after all. He's good at that."

He remembered a conversation with Elphaba, suddenly.

What do you want, Liir, if the Wizard could give you anything?
A father.

"He's like Santa Claus." Dorothy's eyes were button bright with apostolic zeal.

"Don't know what you mean."

"*Santa Claus?* Jolly old elf! Magic as anything. At Christmas every year he comes to your home and leaves you treats, if you're good. Or if you're not, coal in your stocking. We don't always have extra coal in Kansas so once he filled my stocking full of manure. I cried like the dickens but Uncle Henry said it was punishment for me singing too brightly in the hog pen. I was scaring the pigs shitless, he said, and here was the proof."

"The Wizard of Oz puts manure in your socks?"

"No! Listen and stop being an idiot. I just mean the Wizard is *like* Santa Claus: he's a charitable sort. Come and get what you need. What's to stop you? What do you have better to do?"

He wobbled. If the Wizard was handing out rewards, why shouldn't Liir deserve one? He was an orphan now. He didn't need to say who he was, did he?—or where he came from?

"He owes you lots." Dorothy was solemn with assurance. "Without your help, we wouldn't have gotten back alive. The creepy Yunamuffins hiding on the trail, that repulsive Elephant monster, queen of the Scrow-folk. I had jeebies crawling all over my heebies."

"Maybe I will," said Liir.

What do you want, Liir, if the Wizard could give you anything?
A father.

The Wizard couldn't give him a father or a mother, but maybe he could give him some news of Nor. Now that the Princess Nastoya had awakened a hope that Nor might still be alive. Or maybe the Wizard had gotten hold of the missing Grimmerie, somehow. With it, Liir might figure out how to help the Princess shuck off her disguise. In any event, even to approach someone as mighty as the wonderful Wizard of Oz would be, for Liir, both a novelty and an accomplishment: he was hardly more than spinster spawn, and had seen little of the world of men.

"Well, come if you're coming; we're off," said Dorothy, so Liir hid the Witch's cape beneath an ornamental flowerpot in a corner of the deserted café where they had been sitting, and went with them.

Dorothy's strategy for getting the attention of the proper officials at the Palace doors was simple. "I'm Dorothy," she said, "you know. *The* Dorothy."

The guards gawked. Ministers were summoned, and arrangements made for an interview almost at once. "You're not allowed," said the Secretary of Audiences to Liir. "You aren't part of the original contract."

"But I'm here to ask the Wizard for help," said Liir.

"Piss off."

Dorothy shrugged, grinned too broadly, and straightened her apron. "Don't fret, Liir. We shouldn't be more than an hour. All we have to do is show up, and I'm sure the Wizard will grant our requests. We'll meet back at that café tonight and decide what to do to celebrate before I leave."

"Are you sure you want to leave?" asked Liir.

"Of course I'm leaving," she snapped. "This is my exit interview. Why do you think I put myself through this indignity? I didn't ask to kill the Witch, but having done it, I'm going to collect my reward if I can possibly manage it."

He bit his lip. "Then may I come with you?"

"You wouldn't feel at home in Kansas. Few do. Besides, you're supposed to be un-bewitching that old freak elephant noggin. Are my pigtails even?"

She kissed him in a bruisingly incidental manner. Full of stupid trust, she turned and hurried after her friends. The ceremonial doors banged behind them.

Liir went back to the café. Using up almost all the coin he had, he waited with mounting horror and then failing hopes. She never returned. He never saw her again.

She hadn't been much, that Dorothy. Priggish, in a way, proud of her wide-eyed charity. Her kindness, at first magnificent, had come to seem a bit—well, cheap. After all, she'd also oiled the Tin Woodman, and soothed the timorous Lion, and discussed differences between the gold and silver standards of foreign currency with the Scarecrow, who seemed for all his brainlessness to be following the whole discussion. She'd cuddled that rank little dog of hers. In light of all that, her solicitousness to Liir seemed nothing more than the Next Good Deed.

Nonetheless, she had been brave, one foot in front of the other, all the way to the Vinkus, all the way back. When the bells began to toll throughout the City, and Liir finally worked up the nerve to ask someone why, Dorothy wasn't mentioned at all. "The Wizard is deposed," they said. "The Wicked Witch is dead, but the Wizard is deposed anyway. Some other good witch has been hired to oversee Oz in the interim."

"Dorothy?" he asked. "What about Dorothy?"

"Dorothy who?" they replied. The cult of Dorothy had yet to take hold.

ONCE, YEARS BACK, in one of the barns at Kiamo Ko, Liir had been horsing about with Nor and her brothers. The children of Fiyero and his wife, Sarima, were high-tempered, and they had persuaded Liir to sit on one end of a timber that they intended to pivot out over a pile of hay below. He could jump to his safety! It would be fun, they said. And so it would have been, had not one of them—Manek, probably—leaped off the balanced end before Liir was fully positioned. Afraid of smashing himself on the stone floor of the barn, Liir had lurched to safety across the edge of a cart. The falling beam failed to kill him.

However, he knocked the wind out of his chest, and for a minute or two he was unable to breathe. He could feel his lungs kicking, and his heart kicking back, but he thought he was dying. The faces of Irji and Nor peered down over the edge of the loft at him. Lying on his back, stretching in vain to open his windpipe, he looked up at their faces contorting with laughter and mild concern.

What Liir remembered, in as near to extremis as he had experienced in his short life, was how embroidered these last few impressions of the world seemed. How the light breaking over the crowns of Irji's and Nor's heads seemed shaped like segments of overlapping fins, tying the bright expressions of his friends to the rafters, the cobwebs, the knotholes, the looped ropes, the stray feathers. All of a piece, all of a piece, he thought: why did I never see it before, and now I will die and never see it again.

Then he didn't die, but lived. His breath punched itself back into place, and he wailed and his torso hurt and everything splintered into disjointed elements. As angry as he felt at Manek for making him the butt of a well-planned prank, he was distressed at the loss of his fine moment of apprehension: The world belonged together like this. The pieces related to each other. There was no contradiction, deepest down. Complexity, yes, but not contradiction. Only connection.

Now, hunched beneath the doorway of a shuttered butchery in the Emerald City, with Dorothy so newly met, and just as quickly vanished, he remembered the incident in the barn at Kiamo Ko. There is no resolving a good mess, he thought. Every breath one takes is a waking up into disjointedness, over and over.

He rocked hard enough to build plum-colored bruises on his shoulders. They hurt when he prodded them, and he prodded them to make them hurt.

He had nowhere to go, nothing to do. By day and night he meandered like the other bits of human trash that drifted up and down the boulevards. Filching from merchants, begging for pennies, relieving themselves in public without concern for decency or hygiene.

Nightly he returned to the café, in case his sense of dread had been for naught, and Dorothy might still make good on her promise and come back for him, at least to say good-bye. A lucky thing, too, for on the fifth day Liir was turning over newspapers looking for scrag-ends of butter pastry when he was tapped on the shoulder. He turned, half expecting that the café owner had summoned the police as he'd been threatening. Instead, Liir found the Scarecrow.

"You're still here," said the Scarecrow. "Somehow, I thought you would be."

"Where is she?"

"She's gone, you know that." The Scarecrow sighed. "You knew she would go. She was a Visitor, not of our kind; that kind can't stay, you know."

"How do you know? Maybe you just need to invite them."

The Scarecrow affected a superior attitude, and that was his only answer. "A lot is going to change in a very short time," he said. "I hope it's for the best, but it could get ugly in the interim. I thought it smartest to let you know. If I were you I would get out of town."

"No one wants me," said Liir, scoffing. "No one cares to come looking for *me*! No one knows who I am, not even myself. Do you mean that because someone tittered that the Witch was my mother, I'm in danger?"

"I don't mean that," said the Scarecrow. "I don't know if anyone here knows or cares whether the Witch had children, or who they might be. I just mean there's talk of a cleanup of this neighborhood." He straightened up—he'd been limping, an odd thing for a Scarecrow—and cast his clumsy gloved hand down Dirt Boulevard, where the denizens of the evening were in their cups. A small crowd had gathered around a couple of half-naked teens making dirty right there on the ground. The tatterdemalions were pelting them with bits of food and egging them on. Elsewhere, bottles emptied of their beer smashed on paving stones. A baby cried piteously.

"What is happening?" said Liir.

"The Wizard has left, and Dorothy is gone, and Lady Glinda Chuffrey, née Arduenna of the Uplands, has been importuned to supervise a government until something more permanent can be arranged."

"Glinda! I heard of her. The Witch used to talk about her sometimes. Well, she'll do some good, won't she?"

"Doing good, cleaning house, takes a mighty strong broom," said the Scarecrow. "Speaking of which . . ."

The Scarecrow looked this way and that. The kids on the ground, wheezing and humping in their throes of lust, had secured the crowd's full attention. The Scarecrow reached into his waistband and, hand over hand, drew out a stake. No, a pole—the handle of the broom. The Witch's broom. Aha. Hence the limp.

He gave it to Liir. "No one wanted it," he said. "No one needed it for anything. It served its purpose and was going to be thrown out."

Liir accepted it with resignation; one more thing to carry back to the home he no longer had. "What do you mean, things are going to get ugly? Seems to me they're pretty ugly around here already."

"Well, I mean, for the ceremony of Glinda's elevation, they'll have to relocate the urban poor. For one thing. Glinda's quite tidy and likes things just so."

"You seem to know a lot all of a sudden. The brains are working?"

"There's talk that Lady Glinda will eventually yield, and put a wise Scarecrow on the throne," the Scarecrow said, pride—or derision—making his voice sound odd. "After she cleans up the Wizard's affairs. And there are those who think that the charmed child Ozma will be located in some cave almost at once, now that the Wizard's gone. Sounds cynical and desperate to me, but what do I know of government? I've had more access to information the last few days than the rest of my life put together."

"A wise Scarecrow on the throne? *You?*" said Liir, incredulous. "Sorry, I don't mean to imply—"

"I," said the Scarecrow, "or someone like me. Frankly, to human beings, all Scarecrows look the same, which is odd, since we seem to be much more individual than humans. But we're made in their image and likeness, so all they see in us is themselves, and one mirror is as good as another, I guess."

"Do you want to be king? Now that you're so smart?"

"Now that I'm so smart, I know enough not to let on what I want," said the Scarecrow. "We should move away from here, you know."

Liir roped the heavy cape around his arms and took the scorched broom. "Any ideas?"

"Just—away. This is all so unseemly." The Scarecrow indicated the throng. "You're very young for all this."

"You're younger than I," said Liir.

"I was born old," said the Scarecrow. "That's how I was made."

"I don't know how I was made," said the boy. "That's part of my problem."

They crossed a small canal into a quieter street and came to rest on a fundament to which ranks of small private barges and blunt-boats were tied up for the night. The smoke of cooking fires, the smell of boiled beans and potato stew hung in the air.

"I miss Dorothy," he said.

The Scarecrow replied, "It's the Witch you miss, isn't it?"

"I hated her too much to miss her."

"That's what you think."

"You think your own thoughts, and leave me mine." He was outraged at the presumption. "What did you know of the Witch? Auntie Witch? Elphaba Thropp? She was my . . . she was my witch!"

The Scarecrow paid no attention. "It's starting, listen," he said. He held up his hand. The sounds from Dirt Boulevard had altered; a percussion of horses' hoofs, hundreds of them, came thrumming forward, a scatter of shouts turning into screams. "I waited too long," the Scarecrow said. He bundled Liir onto the nearest canal boat. A bearded old coot with a sawed-off hand turned and raised a hot skillet at the Scarecrow, but the Scarecrow deflected it with his gloved fist, and the man tumbled into the filthy water. "Loosen the mooring, push away," said the Scarecrow, "the neighborhood will be in flames by dessert time."

• 2 •

CANDLE PUT DOWN the domingon to rest. Her fingers were swollen with long red welts. She'd been working hard. The young man—they called him Liir, was it?—breathed shallowly, but regularly. And he hadn't twitched a muscle in the hours since Candle had started playing to him.

At the sound in the doorway, she turned. She expected the Superior Maunt, but it was her grouchy kitchen boss, Sister Cook.

"*Someone* landed a cushy job where she can sit all day," said Sister Cook, without real resentment, but she had eyes only for the victim. Hardly nightfall the first day, and the maunts in the cloister of Saint Glinda couldn't curb their curiosity. "He's not much to look at, is he?"

Candle made a soft sound in her throat, a kind of purr. A demur?

Sister Cook wasn't sure. She knew Candle to be capable of following in-structions, so whatever the girl's limitations were, they didn't include deafness or lack of language understanding. She just didn't speak up; with her it was mostly glottal molasses.

Sister Cook wrinkled her nose, as if considering the merits of a joint selected for the holiday roast. A gauze sheet, nearly transparent, casting lavender shadows on the lad's near naked form. The coverlet was woven tightly, affording warmth, and was light enough to be whisked away when medical attention was required. As the evening came in, the blood blisters under the skin on this face looked like medallions of honor—or maybe the sites of subcutaneous leech colonies.

"I came to make sure you were all right," said Sister Cook at last, having taken her fill. She turned back to Candle. "Here. We all must do our part."

She pulled from her apron pocket a long red frond, fringed with airy, asparagus-fern stamens. Candle started, and the sound in her throat was clearly revulsion.

"Not to worry, it was a willing sacrifice," said Sister Cook. "I was alone in the yard mincing the cord onions when that Red Pfenix ap-peared again. He was distraught. He'd been attacked and wounded by something; he was bleeding from the throat and couldn't speak."

Candle shrugged and hit her chest with her hand, turning it outward.

"Sister Doctor and Sister Apothecaire hate to administer to Animals, you know that," said Sister Cook. "But it doesn't matter. They couldn't even if directed to. The Superior Maunt sent them away after lunch. Off on some investigative mission about those Emerald City novices who had their faces scraped. So what was I to do?"

Candle reached out and touched the Pfenix feather.

Sister Cook said, "Nearly shorn of life, he came back here. He pulled out his axial feather himself and walked up to me with it in his beak. Swans sing when they die; Pfenix do, too, but he couldn't. So you make music for him, please. Out of respect; we're having Pfenix breast tonight."

Sister Cook shoved both her hands in her apron pockets. "Pfenix

breast, though I've diced them small and disguised them as chicken fin-
gerlings so our dear old Mother Rush-to-Judgment doesn't have a con-
niption stroke. Don't forget to come down when you hear the dinner
bell; we don't get Pfenix around here very often, Animal or otherwise."

She lingered a moment longer and watched Candle hold the red
feather. It was almost two feet long and still retained some of its vital
elasticity. "Well?" said Sister Cook. "I can't stand here forever. Play a
dirge for the Pfenix, who never made it to his Convention or his class
reunion or wherever he was going. He was interested in your playing, I
saw. Honor him by accepting his gift."

Candle tried to remember what she had seen of the domingon
when it was played by its maker. She had swooned, for music or love or
both, and in her exhilaration, maybe she'd overlooked an aspect of the
instrument's construction. Maybe it had had a pfenix feather, and the
master had removed it—pfenix feathers weren't easy to come by. And a
Pfenix feather, freely given besides! What she might learn to play now.

She leaned down and laid the quill end of the feather against the
empty notch at one end of the domingon's lower soundboard. It settled
in perfectly, as if the domingon had been built to accommodate this exact feather. Then Candle gently coaxed the feather flat. There was a
hasp at the soundboard's far edge, a leather tooth on a sprung hinge
that clamped down hard to hold the pinion end of the tailfeather in
place.

Candle turned the pegs, listening to calibrations of tuning too precise for Sister Cook to appreciate. Then Candle flung out both her hands
at Sister Cook: Go! Go!

"Ungrateful, the both of you," said Sister Cook. As she descended
the stairs, she heard the first few notes of an exquisite instrument being
played by an expert. So suddenly it took her back to school days—when
she was a nervous slip of a thing at Madame Teastane's Female Academy,
not the cow she'd become—that she had to steady herself against the
wall. She was thirteen, and suffering her first menses. Coming back from
a dawn visit to the cold lavatories on the third floor, she'd spotted a red
pfenix on the roof of the Master's lodge. The trees had been airy, just

budding, struck with first light, and the bird had looked like red cloisonné set in warm stone. A stab of loveliness unmerited, unexpected. It had cheered her then. She continued down the stairs back to the mauntery's kitchens, cheered again at the long-forgotten thought, though perhaps she was also happy to anticipate a fine, fine meal that night.

Southstairs

THE SUPERIOR MAUNT made it her business to get to the infirmary on a daily basis. She didn't like what she saw. The young fellow made no discernible progress; indeed, a yellowish sweat rolled off him, hinting of turps. His skin was cold to the touch. He was still breathing, however.

"You may wipe him down when he becomes too clammy," she said to Candle, and showed her how. The girl seemed reluctant to touch her charge, but did as she was bade.

Holy intuition, the Superior Maunt felt, did not figure among her own administrative talents. She was a common-sensist. She thought the Unnamed God had given her a brain to use, not to ignore as a snare of the devil. She had tried to lift herself up by clear thinking, and others, too, when she could.

Nonetheless, it was intuition as much as charity that had inspired her to call for a musician. This Candle seemed perfect: demure, even of temper, and increasingly proficient at her instrument.

The Superior Maunt wasn't overly worried that whatever had befallen Liir—whatever it was, those bruises, those broken bones!—would afflict her pair of investigators. The young missionaries from the moth-erchapel in the Emerald City, whose faces had been scraped—the boy himself—were possessed of the loveliness of youth, youth's fine igno-rance of its own fleeting grace. The same couldn't be said of Sister Doc-tor and Sister Apothecaire. Through long years of dedication and hard work, they had grown wizened and doughy, respectively. They would be safe from the attention of those who wanted to despoil the innocently beautiful. And their training in medicine had fostered keen observational skills; they could protect themselves, if anyone could.

The Maunt Superior noted that though her hearing wasn't good anymore, the music of the repaired domingon had a way of traveling. The entire mauntery was filled with its soft phrases. Sister Linenflaxen said it was elegiac, damn it, Candle was wooing the lad to his final sleep. She should play something peppier. Everyone else said *shhhh*. The whole place had fallen under a sort of spell. They were waiting to see what would happen, but the music made them patient.

Sister Graveside ironed a fresh winding cloth and refilled the corked jug with anointing oil, to be ready.

CANDLE WAS MORE OBSERVANT than the Superior Maunt credited, though. She could see that Liir's respiration responded to her choice of music. He went through periods of rhythmic breathing, like someone sleeping peacefully enough, followed by patterns of shallow flutterbreath.

Restored to glory by the feather of the Pfenix, the domingon had become responsive: the harmonic overtones hung in the air and comple-mented one another. When the invalid seemed too agitated, she would bring him back with long furling phrases. But too many of those and she was afraid he would deliver his last, deep outgo and breathe in no more: and then he would be dead. So she would agitate him with pizzicato comments and thumb-struck flat-tone responses, to alert his lungs and stimulate his heart.

She was guiding him. She knew it. She just didn't know where he was.

✦   ✦   ✦

LIIR WAS IN THE STOLEN BLUNT-BOAT with the Scarecrow, heading along one of the waterways of the Emerald City. It was a week or two after the Witch had died. There was trouble behind, and darkness ahead, but the windows of the town mansions that lined the canal—one flight above street level, above the barricaded stables and stout front gates—threw trapezoids of gold light onto the stinking canal water. Liir and the Scarecrow passed in and out of one another's view.

"What *will* you do?" asked the Scarecrow. "Where will you go?"

"I have no place to go," said Liir. "I'm not going back to Kiamo Ko. Why should I? Only old Nanny there."

"Have you no obligation to her?"

"*Now* you ask me? In a word, no. Chistery will mind her well enough."

"The Snow Monkey? Yes, I suppose he will. Well, the story of Dorothy is done. We won't see her like again."

"And a good thing, too," said Liir. "Off and away with the fairies, just like that, and not so much as a decent good-bye!"

"Her departure was precipitous," agreed the Scarecrow. "Glinda made the arrangements in something of a hurry."

The light from a party, candles laid out on a balustrade. The music wafting out open doors: agitated phrases, comments and responses, from some instrument with multiple voices, or many instruments playing very close together. Haunting!

The Scarecrow said, "Don't fasten on Dorothy. Only unanswerable longing lies down that road. Gone is gone."

"How wise you are, now that you're packed with brains. Everyone got some party favor from the Wizard except me. Everyone's got somewhere to go."

"Don't look to me for a map, Liir. Figure it out for yourself. What about your friend, Nor? That Princess Nastoya seemed to think she might still be alive. Maybe you could find her."

"First I better learn a trade and find a way to support myself. Or watch how the pickpockets practice their trade. Sure, I would like to find Nor, but I'd like to fly, too. Not bloody likely without some help."

"I can't be much help."

"Too highly connected now, I'm sure. Too chummy with the chief cheeses."

"I have my own plans. Appointments to keep. I'm out of here as soon as I can."

"I thought that Glinda person had singled you out for a lead position in the government. That's what they're saying on the streets, where I pick up my news and other garbage."

"Lady Glinda doesn't confide in me. I've heard she intends to rule for six months or so, and then abdicate in favor of a straw man. Who?— well, as I've admitted, one scarecrow is as good as another. Do you think anyone would notice the difference? When a scarecrow blows apart in a gale wind, the farmer just props up another one. It's the job to be done that's important, not who does it."

"That's what they used to say at the mauntery," said Liir. "If a maunt dies and goes to the Afterlife, another maunt comes to take her place. Like replacing a pane of glass. It's the work that's important, not the individual who does it."

"Well, I'm keeping my own counsel about my plans," said the Scarecrow, "and I'm not long for the Emerald City, I'll tell you that much. One day you're a celebrity, the next day you're hauled off to jail."

They contemplated this as they came upon a weir. From here, a system of locks stepped the water level down steeply until it disappeared into a fortified grate. Above, armed members of the Emerald City Guard were having a smoke around a brazier. "Better not get their attention," said the Scarecrow.

"What's over there, that the canal is guarded?" whispered Liir as they regarded their situation.

"Not sure. Couldn't say. But it might be Southstairs."

"Southstairs? What's that?"

The Scarecrow made a face in the gloom. "The high-security prison for the heartland. Don't you know anything? I've only been here a week and I know that."

"Why would they be guarding the canal grate?"

"Who knows? Maybe they're afraid there'll be a move to liberate Southstairs. I'm told a lot of professional Animals ended up there over the decades, cheek by jowl with murderers, pedophiles. Rapists. Political pamphleteers."

"The Wizard's gone. Why aren't they just throwing the gates open?"

"You want the murderers and rapists back in the neighborhood?"

"Well—no. No, but for the dissenters."

The Scarecrow frowned. "Dream on. Who's going to take it upon themselves to decide which is which at this point? The job of personal fiscal betterment is far more urgent."

"Hard to argue with that. And I bet the suppressed Animals agree with you. Are they on the move, do you know? Or hanging low until they see what develops?"

"Look, I got you safely away from Dirt Boulevard before you were swept up in a purge. I'm not going to deliver you to Southstairs so you can check on the Animals there. Let's turn about."

The Scarecrow piloted the blunt-boat backward until there was room enough to swing it around. Their route took them back under the balustrades where the fancy-dress ball was in progress. The laughter was more unguarded, even strident, the music brassier. "Lots to celebrate these days, for those of the right station," said the Scarecrow. "Good news indeed. Could be another Victory Gala."

"Celebrating the Wizard's departure?"

"Celebrating the Witch's death," said the Scarecrow. His face was impassive. "Oh, sweet Oz, it's Glinda's house!" He tucked his head down. "Liir!"

"She doesn't know me," said Liir. He scrambled backward along the boat to its squared-off stern, a small elevated platform for the loading of goods. Craning, he could see a woman leaning her hips against the carved stone balustrades of the balcony. The light from the ballroom fell on her golden hair, which was swept up on her head in a bubbly mass of curls hooped by a diamond tiara. He couldn't see how old she was, nor her expression, for her face was turned away. She was trim and fit, though her shoulders were slumped—grief, or despair? Or boredom? She dabbed a handkerchief at her nose.

Liir didn't speak, he didn't call out—what did he care for Lady Glinda Chuffrey? Auntie Witch had mentioned her only in passing. Sometimes with grudging respect, more often with disapproval. As he watched her, something echoed along the waters of the canal, a sound— as if a private, smoky slide of music accompanied their blunt-boat, counterpoint to the party pandemonium.

Lady Glinda turned, and gripped the rail with both hands, and leaned over as their vessel was slipping beneath a pedestrian bridge. "Shit!" hissed the Scarecrow, and stayed the boat in the shadows by throwing his weight against the pole. "She's seen us!"

"Who is it?" called Glinda. "Who's there?—I almost thought—"

Liir wanted to speak up. The Scarecrow clapped a gloved hand against his mouth tightly. Liir struggled, elbowed the Scarecrow, but he wasn't strong enough to break free before Glinda shook her head as if in disbelief, straightened the epaulets on her ball gown, and returned to her affair.

"What's the matter with you?" railed Liir, when the Scarecrow had let him go.

"What's the matter with *you*?" said the Scarecrow. "I'm trying to keep a low profile in order to help you, and you have to go and signal the heads of state and alert them about it?"

"I didn't signal her!"

"Well, she must have a sixth sense then, for she turned, and she saw you."

"She doesn't know who I am. She doesn't know I exist!"

"And let's keep it that way."

✦ 2 ✦

THE ANIMOSITY THAT OBTAINED between Sisters Doctor and Apothecaire subsided once dusk fell on their first evening away from the Mauntery of Saint Glinda. The women erected the frame of thin skark ribs and fixed the waterproof awning to it. Then they huddled together under a blanket. When the wolves of the oakhair forest howled their midnight requiem, the Sisters mangled their devotions into such a gabble of syllables and sobs that, had the Unnamed God been condescending to listen, it could only have concluded that its two emissaries were afflicted with sudden-onset glossolalia.

"The Superior Maunt thought it safe to send us out on an exploratory mission even though the faces of those three young missionaries had so recently been scraped," said Sister Apothecaire the following morning, which dawned damp and windless. "I trust her in every particular," she added fiercely, unconvincingly.

"Our charge is clear," said Sister Doctor, "safety or no. We are to make an effort to address the tribal Scrow, if we can locate them, and certainly the Yunamata. We must enquire about the disaster that struck those missionaries. With the conviction of our faith in the Unnamed God, no harm will befall us."

"Do you propose the missionaries were in greater danger because their faith was weak?" asked Sister Apothecaire.

Sister Doctor's lips became thinner as she folded the awning away. "Cowardice, said the Superior Maunt, will not serve us in this task."

Sister Apothecaire relented. "Cowardice is a dubious attribute. Yet I possess it in spades, so I hope on this venture to learn how to use it to my advantage if I must. All gifts come from the Unnamed God, including cowardice, and self-repugnance."

The mules dropped their heavy hoofs on the path, picking a way between ranks of thin trees with branches nearly empty of leaves. Little cover.

"Perhaps," said Sister Doctor, "the Superior Maunt sent *us* out because we would be better able to tend to each other, medically, were we attacked."

"If we survived. Well, I've no doubt that our skills here in the wilderness will prove useful. After all, I do speak a dialect of West Yumish."

"When you've had a bit too much seasonal sherry."

They laughed at that and proceeded in companionable silence until Sister Apothecaire couldn't stand it. "Now Liir is Candle's responsibility. Funny little thing. What can she bring to Liir that we can't?"

"Don't be stupid. She can bring youth and charm, if she can get his attention. She can give him a reason to survive. This is something neither you nor I could do. If he opened up his eyes after a long coma and saw either of us right off, he'd probably kick the bucket in a nonce."

Sister Apothecaire did not murmur assent. She was rather proud of her looks. Well, her face, anyway; her figure was regrettably lumpy. "Perhaps," she said distractingly, "Candle has a natural talent that the Superior Maunt can sense."

"What sort of talent?" Sister Doctor shifted in her saddle and turned to peer at her colleague. "You don't mean a talent for magic? That's distinctly forbidden in the order."

"Come come. You know perfectly well we resort to it when we must. Not that we're very good at it. I need hardly remind you that these are dangerous times. Perhaps the Superior Maunt thinks that in the rehabilitation of the boy, such a talent is called for."

By the straightening of her spine Sister Doctor signaled that she did not intend to second-guess the Superior Maunt's motives. Sister Apothecaire regretted having brought it up. "Well," she continued, falsely jolly, "I don't have much of a sense of Candle one way or the other. If she's got common magic or common sense, it's news to me either way."

"She certainly has no talent for music." Sister Doctor sniffed. "I do remember the day she arrived, though. I happened to be suturing one of the novices in the kitchen. I turned to ask kindly for water, and there was that Candle, her rickety domingon slung over one shoulder like a crossbow. Mad old Mother Yackle had her by the hand, as if she'd just created her out of calves' foot jelly. 'The gypsy Quadling, her uncle leaves her to us,' said Mother Yackle."

"Mother Yackle doesn't speak and hasn't in years."

"That's why I remember the event so distinctly."

"Did you see the Quadling uncle?"

"I went to the window, and he was making his way rather hurriedly through the kitchen garden. I called out to him, for there are procedures for the introduction of a novice, and this wasn't one of them. But he wouldn't be stopped, merely called over his shoulder that he would be back in a year if he was still alive. It's rare to see Quadlings this far north these days. I imagine the poor girl is quite lonely."

"Well, yes. No one speaks Quaddle."

"I believe the term is Qua'ati. So is Candle mute or is it that she just hasn't anyone to speak her native tongue with?"

"I don't know."

Perhaps it was Candle's silence and self-control that had inspired the Superior Maunt to choose her for keeping vigil over Liir. The maunts began to regret their tendencies to bark and spark at each other. Thinking on their noisy failings, they fell into a silence now.

IN THE FOLLOWING FEW DAYS, they came across their share of blue squirrels, bald egrets, and disagreeable emmets. The egrets kept to the ground cover, rarely taking wing; the emmets preferred the bedding. It wasn't until near dusk on the fourth day that the maunts came across an Animal, a lone and pagan Water Buffalo in the shallows of a cove of Restwater, Oz's biggest lake.

"Oh, oh," moaned the Water Buffalo at their approach, "not the missionary voice traveling in twos! Not again! I bury my own waste, I only speak when spoken to, I lick my knees fifty times a night before I sleep—what more am I to do to appease the fates? I don't want to be converted! Don't you understand? Oh, all right, get it over with. I'll lapse before nightfall, I promise you. I can't help myself. Perhaps I'm too far gone for you to bother with me?" He peered, both gloomily and hopefully, at them.

"We're not converters," said Sister Apothecaire. "We haven't the time."

"And who cares about you? You can go to hell," said Sister Doctor, meaning to be cheerful. This was the right note, as it happened; the Water Buffalo began to smile.

"Scarcely see a soul coming from your direction who doesn't have designs on my immortal soul," said the Water Buffalo. "It used to be I was worried about my hide. I always thought a soul was private, but it appears it can be colonized against your will if you don't watch out."

"Well, we *are* maunts," admitted Sister Apothecaire.

The Water Buffalo winced. "*No.* Say it ain't so. You're plates of glamour and glasses of fashion, as anyone who rests a sore eye upon you would have to agree."

"Don't be mincing," snapped Sister Doctor. "These are perfectly respectable clothes for traveling in."

"Depends on where you want to get to," intoned the Water Buffalo.

"Look, we can evangelize like the best of them, if that's what it's going to take—"

"Sorry, sorry!" said the Water Buffalo. "I'll be good. What's your game?"

They told him. He knew nothing of the attacks on the young maunts and their scrapings, nor had he ever heard of Liir or his misadventure. But he had seen airborne battalions of trained creatures flying so high that he couldn't make them out. "Something's amiss," he said. "I know there's been an attempt to call a Congress of Birds out in the west, but lately I've seen few Birds brave enough to fly at anything like a decent height."

"We can't patrol the skies right now," said Sister Doctor. "It's the Scrow or the Yunamata we need to find."

"The Scrow rarely venture this far east. However, you may come across a small band of Yunamata, if they haven't moved off yet. They're down from Kumbricia's Pass. I came across them bathing this morning. We all minded our own business. They don't have anything to do with the Unnamed God, so they don't bother me, and I don't bother them. They rinsed their totems and washed their hair, and one of them gave birth to a baby underwater. They're rather froggy folk when it comes to birthing. They circulated a birth pipe around, passed out in the sun for an hour or so, and then gathered their things and left. They seemed to be heading southwest. Several dozen of them, no more."

"If you see them, tell them we're coming," said Sister Doctor.

"Jubilation, they'll be over the moon," drawled the Water Buffalo. "If you want to meet up with them, better *not* tell them you're coming, honeys."

The sisters moved on, but before they had lost sight of the Water Buffalo, Sister Apothecaire thought to turn and call, "We forgot to ask your name!"

"Only the chattering classes of Animal have names!" the Water Buffalo replied cheerily. "And there hasn't been a professional Animal the length and breadth of Oz for thirty years. If I don't have a name, I can't be targeted as a potential convert, can I?"

A moment later, when he was out of sight, his voice rang toward them thinly: "Though if you had to locate me, I suppose I'd answer to Buff . . ."

"Weird creature," said Sister Apothecaire a while later.

"He'd survived, a talking Animal in the wild," Sister Doctor reminded her. "It can't have been easy. After the Wizard's banishment, the Animals didn't rush for reassimilation. Who could blame them, with all they'd been through."

"Sounds as if the creature's been dogged by zealots, though."

"Indeed. Well, the Emperor is a devout man, and wants all his subjects to enjoy the benefits of faith, I suppose."

ANOTHER NIGHT, and the wolves howled more fiercely than ever. The dawn seemed full of its own arcane purpose, a pale light leaching through grey cloud-hemp. The maunts ventured out across the Disappointments. Then, easy as playing at knackers, they came upon a group of Yunamata doing winter rush-work.

"Hail," said Sister Apothecaire in Yumish, "or have I said *hell* by mistake? Hello? Yoo hoo Yunamata? We come in peace."

"What are you saying?" said Sister Doctor. "They look mystified."

"I'm addressing their tribal gods," said Sister Apothecaire, and in Yu-mish, "I. Good. Good one. Good human person woman being. I. Good thing. Where is the library?" In her anxiety it was all she could remember.

"They look amused," said Sister Doctor.

"That's respect," said Sister Apothecaire. But amusement was better than hostility, so she began to relax, and more of the plain tongue began to return to her.

The Yunamata were known for keeping to themselves. Nomadic, but not a horse culture like the Scrow, this Vinkus tribe was fleet of foot and economical of domestic impedimenta, needing only a few pack animals to carry their belongings. Generally they sheltered in Kumbricia's Pass or the forested slopes of the Kells south of there. What were they doing out in open country?

Sister Doctor, who never liked to go slumming as a veterinarian, felt she could sniff out an Animal tendency: the Yunamata looked as if they might all have one giant, docile Frog among their ancestors. Way, way back. Nothing like webbing between their digits, no long flickering tongues, no, no; they were human through and through. But an amphibian sort of human, with leathery skin, narrow ridiculous limbs, and thin lips that seemed partly withdrawn into their mouths.

One could laugh at the silliness of them. Laugh—and then be carved to shreds, for when aroused they could be a formidable enemy. The Yunamata had skill with knives. Mostly they used their serrated tools—lethal curved blades set in handles of the hardest mahogany—for aid in the construction of their tree nests, where they harbored at night. Those same knives could carve a pig or eviscerate a minor canon with equal efficiency.

Sister Apothecaire set out to convince the Yunamata that the maunts were abroad neither to betray the clan nor to convert them. Just in case, like the Water Buffalo, they'd previously been targeted as a population ripe for conversion. As a group, they listened, promoting no spokesperson among them. By turns they mouthed small neat phrases. Sister Apothecaire took pains to translate these remarks to her colleague carefully, and to question her own understanding if she had any doubt. She didn't want to assent to human martyrdom merely because she'd forgotten some nicety of Yumish grammar. *Was* there a retractional pluperfect subjunctive in Yumish?

"You are going on quite a while," said Sister Doctor after an hour or so.

"I am doing my job and trying to see if we're going to be invited to stay for supper," said Sister Apothecaire. "Leave me be."

"I hope they aren't teetotalers. I think I'm getting a sniffle."

When the conversation had concluded at last, and the Yunamata retreated to prepare a meal, Sister Doctor said, "Well? Well? I deduce from your smug expression that they're not about to sharpen their blades to scrape our faces from us. Though I'd like to hear it put directly, to ease my mind."

"They speak by indirection. They know about the scrapings. They have seen evidence of it. They say it must be the Scrow. The Scrow have a tradition of royalty, and their queen is an old woman named Nastoya who has been in declining health for a decade. Were we to fulfill the mission assigned us, we would next have to hunt for this Princess Nastoya and reprove her about these infractions. The Yunamata insist that the Scrow must be in allegiance with the Emperor."

"Ridiculous. If the Scrow were in allegiance with the Emperor, would they be scraping his emissaries? Or are the Yunamata lying?"

"Look at them. Could they lie?"

"Don't be soft. Of course they could. The most purring of cats can still kill a bird within half a purr."

"I suppose I believe them," said Sister Apothecaire, "because they *admit* to their capacity for vengeance. But they also have told me that this is the season of the jackal, and out of wariness of the moon's opinion, they take a vow of gentility. Babies born under the jackal moon are considered lucky. Babies born in Restwater are luckier still."

"Are you sure you've understood correctly? Throughout Oz the season of the jackal is considered dangerous."

"Perhaps it's a kind of propitiation," said Sister Apothecaire. "They mentioned the Old Dowager, a kind of deity who harvests souls. She sounded a bit like Kumbricia. Do you remember Kumbricia, from your schoolgirl lessons in antique lore? Kumbricia, the oldest witch from the time of creation? Source of all venom and malice?"

"I turned my back on such things when I entered a unionist mauntery," said Sister Doctor. "I'm surprised you remember such poppydegook."

"I don't know if we're getting a meal," said Sister Apothecaire, gesturing, "but look, it appears we're getting a pipe of some sort." A delegation of Yunamata was approaching with a communal smoke.

"A vile habit," snarled Sister Doctor, but she determined to do her best at being sociable, and stomach such barbaric customs as courtesy required.

• 3 •

No ONE AT THE MAUNTERY, Candle included, knew enough about musical instruments to appreciate the domingon she arrived with. It was made of seasoned wrenwood by a master from the Quadling Kells, and Candle had first heard it played at a summer festival. The master himself performed, using his fingers as well as a fiddle bow and a glass emulant that he kept tucked under his bearded chin when not required. Now Candle recalled that the domingon *had* been fitted out with a feather, though at the time Candle had thought it merely ornamentation—and a sexy fillip at that.

She had thought she was in love with him, and had slept with him before dusk, but a few days later she realized it was the music she had loved. What she heard in its music: a coaxing, an invitation to remember, to disclose. Perhaps because her voice was small and high, she couldn't project, and she imagined it would be more gratifying to play music than to speak. Mercilessly she pestered her uncle to circle back and buy her the domingon; she'd been surprised when he obliged.

Candle was not simple, not in the least, but her debility had made her a still person. She listened to church bells, when they pealed, trying to translate; she watched the way the paper husks of an onion fell on a table, and examined the rings of dirt that onion mites had left in parallel rows on the glossy wet inside. Everything said something, and it wasn't her job to consider the merit or even the meaning of the message: just to witness the fact of the message.

She was therefore a calmer person than most, for there seemed no dearth of messages from the world to itself. She merely listened in.

For a week now she'd been playing the domingon until her fingers ached, watching and listening for the language of Liir's recovery. It wasn't unusual that she had had experience with men; Quadlings were a casual sort in matters of sexual prudence. The carnal experience had neither scarred her nor much interested her. Through it, at best, she had learned something of the human body, its hesitations and reservations as well as the surge of its desires.

In the infirmary, as her eyes moved from the instrument to the invalid, she felt she was picking up some news. Was it some minor language of olfactory signals, an arcane pattern of eye twitches, a hieroglyph etched in the beads of his sweat? She didn't know. She was sure of this, though: Liir's body seemed the same in temperature, comportment, and color. But he was going through a phase of crisis, and would either awaken for sure or die at once: no middle ground.

She didn't know if she should go get the Superior Maunt or if she should stay at her post. She was afraid if she left, if she dropped the domingon on the floor even for the twenty minutes it might take to find the Superior Maunt and get counsel, she would lose Liir for good. Wherever he was, he was lost, and the music of her instrument was his only hope back.

So Candle stayed seated and played till her own fingers bled, in ripples of waltz, as if nothing were wrong. The blue of the sky thinned till it was pierced with star prickers, and then the jackal moon rose and slowly lumbered over till it could look in the window and watch for itself. Watch, and listen, as Candle played Liir through his memories.

"She'll be there," said Liir.

"Who? Where? Are you talking about Elphaba?" said the Scarecrow.

"Of course not. I'm talking about Nor. The girl I knew. Maybe my half-sister, if the Witch really was my mother and Fiyero my father, as some have guessed."

"In Southstairs? A girl?"

"Can you tell me why not?"

The Scarecrow didn't answer. Liir thought: Maybe he imagines that someone as insignificant to the mighty Wizard of Oz—a mere girl, no less—hardly merited imprisonment. Maybe he thinks she might as easily have been murdered, or tossed onto the streets to drift and starve. How long had it been anyway since she had been taken from Kiamo Ko? Two years? Three? But then Princess Nastoya had implied that Nor might have survived . . .

They had circled the canals a bit longer and found a place to berth underneath some rotting trees by the side of a pub. "I can't stay with you for much longer, you know," said the Scarecrow. "I only came to give you the Witch's broom, and to wish you well, and to protect you from the clearing of Dirt Boulevard. I have my own path to follow. I would see you safely to the other side of the gates of this troubled city if I could. If you would let me."

"I'm not going," said Liir. "Not without Nor. Or not without finding out what has happened to her."

At a crossroads, unwilling to move, they sat disconsolate.

"Look," said Liir, at graffiti dashed sharply and sloppily on the pub's side wall. It said HAPPY ENDINGS ARE STILL ENDINGS. "You've done your work, you've kept your word to Dorothy. I have the broom. But I won't be ushered out of harm's way. What's the point? I have no happy ending—cripes, I've had no happy beginning, either. The Witch is dead, and Dorothy is gone, and that old Princess Nastoya has asked us for help. As if I could! Just because Elphaba would have!"

"You needn't fulfill some promise Elphaba made. If you're not her son, you have no obligation there."

"Well, there's Nor, too. Call it a promise to myself."

The Scarecrow held his head in his hands. "The Tin Woodman has left to cultivate the art of caring. He has his work cut out for him, poor sod. The Lion is suffering severe depression; his cowardice was his sole identifying trait, and now he's pitiably normal. Neither of them can help you much, I'm afraid. You should get yourself out of here while you can. Start over."

"Start over? I never started the first time. Besides, it's not getting out that I need to do. It's getting in."

The Scarecrow pushed a hand against his heart and shook his head.

"Into Southstairs," said Liir.

"I know what you meant," said the Scarecrow. "I'm not stupid. Now."

"You're the one I need to keep on my side—"

The Scarecrow interrupted with a brusqueness that might have been meant kindly. "Don't bother to look for me. You won't find me. Save yourself for someone you might recognize. I'm not in your story, Liir. Not after this."

So they took their leave, with little fanfare or fuss. The friendship between them was no larger or more hopeful than the shape of a scorched broom, which Liir waved halfheartedly as the Scarecrow loped out of sight, once and for all.

The boy sat in the bobbing blunt-boat and listened to the sound of laughter spilling out the open windows of the pub. The smell was of beer and vomit, and old urine splashed against the wall. The moon was invisible behind the clouds. The sound of a tentative waltz, beguiling and minor, hung over the stinking waters of the canal and the desolate boy there.

THE NEXT MORNING, Liir presented himself at the servants' entrance of the town house he'd passed the night before.

"We don't give handouts and we don't need another coal shoveler, so get yourself out of here before I assist you with a boot in your behind," said the houseboy.

"If you please, I'm not looking for food or work. Sir."

The houseboy smirked. "Toadying bastard. Call me *sir* again, and I'll beat the crap out of you."

Liir couldn't follow. "I meant no disrespect. I just want to know how I can get an audience with Lady Glinda."

The houseboy's sneer needed rearranging with a good swift kick, Liir decided, but when the houseboy guffawed, his voice was less hostile. "Oh, a simpleton. Pardon me, I didn't realize. Listen, the very Margreave of Tenmeadows, Lord Avaric himself, hasn't been able to get her lady-ship's attention. She's got her hands full, what with the goings-on in the Wizard's Palace. The people's Palace now. Or should be. Or will be. What, you want to fling yourself in her lap and call her *mother*? More urchins have tried that already than you could fit on a barge and drown in Kellswater. Now get off with you."

"Whatever mother I don't have, it certainly isn't *her*." He held up the broom and shook it in the houseboy's face.

"What's that then?"

Liir said, "You tell Lady Glinda that a boy at the back gate has the Witch's broom. Tell her Dorothy gave it me. I don't care how long you take, I'll wait."

"That thing? That's a corpse of a broom. Not fit for kindling."

"It's been through a lot. That's how you know it's the real thing."

"You're a stubborn bugger. I can't be standing here chewing the fat all day. Tell you what. Do me some magic with that broom and I'll see what I can do for you."

"I can't do magic. And the broom isn't a magic wand. It's a broom. It sweeps."

"Sweep a floor with that thing, you'll leave char marks, and I'll be the one cleaning up after you. Get out of here, now. Go on."

Liir raised the broom again and tilted it forward. The houseboy shrank back, as if afraid flecks of scorch would fall on his livery. Notic-ing this, Liir decided it would be worth his while to wait around and see what happened.

His instincts proved sound. The houseboy wasn't able to resist gos-siping about his conversation with Liir. Just before noon, a housekeeper came out, tucking her apron strings in and wiping crumbs from her lips. "Love a grouse, you're still here, and that's a good thing!" she gabbled. "The houseboy's been docked a month's pay for being silly-headed! Get over here, Her Haughtiness wants to see you at once! You reek, haven't you washed? The pump, there, boy, scrub your grubby armpits and wipe that smirk off your face. This is Lady Glinda that lives here, not some cow-mistress. And hop smart, you. She's waiting."

HE WAS BROUGHT TO a lady's parlor and told to behave and touch nothing.

He could look, though, and he did. He had never seen an upholstered chair before. He'd never seen one chair face another chair that looked identical. Cushions everywhere, fresh flowers, and gleaming crystal bubbles set on little stands. A collection of commemorative baubles, he guessed. To what end?

A fire of aromatic woods burned in the dainty hearth. Why a daytime fire in such a well-built mansion, when the citizens outside couldn't get close enough to a brazier to warm their hands, let alone soften their supper bricks of congealed molasses?

He wandered to the window to open it, let in some air. It looked out over the canal where he and the Scarecrow had drifted the night before. From this height, he could see the rooflines of the fancy houses. Palaces, almost, or palaces-in-training. Beyond the chimney pots, beyond the roof gardens, the cupolas and spires and domes, two more massive buildings rose: the domed Palace of the Wizard, in the dead center of the City, and off to the right, the steep bluestone ramparts of the prison known as Southstairs.

It was like looking at a picture in a book—not that he'd seen all that many books. Only the Grimmerie, and that only from a distance. Here, the etched rooflines seemed like a hundred man-made hills. Set here and there to delight the eye with infinite variety in depth and perspective.

Under every roof, a story, just as behind every brow, a history.

He hardly believed he had summoned the nerve to come here. But it was all he could think of to do. The Princess Nastoya had promised, in exchange for his helping her, to listen for news of Nor. But why work backward? The Princess would have to be scrubbing the news of the Emerald City to learn about Nor. Whereas now—he was here already—

so let Princess Nastoya work out her troubles for herself. Liir had all the City before him. He would be forthright and claim what he wanted for himself. On his own terms.

"The Lady Glinda," announced a man's voice. When Liir turned, the door was already being drawn closed behind her, and Lady Glinda came near.

It was like being approached by a decorated holiday tree tiptoeing in jeweled slippers. Lady Glinda was the most exceedingly dressed person Liir had ever seen. He almost flinched, but knowing that Lady Glinda had been a friend of Elphaba's stiffened his nerve. "How do you do," she was saying, in a voice like a piccolo blowing soapsuds. She tilted her head. Was it an upperclass gesture, like a genuflection? Ought he pivot his head in reply? He remained upright. "Liir, is it?"

"Yes, ma'am."

He had never called anyone "ma'am" in his life. Where had *that* come from?

"They said it was Liir. I thought I might have misheard. Please, won't you sit—" She took a better look at the state of his clothes and changed her mind. "Would you permit me to take a seat? I'm not resting well these days, and it's a strain."

"Of course." He realized he was to remain standing, though he drew a little nearer. Settling gingerly on a chaise longue upholstered in peppermint stripes, she arranged a bolster at the small of her back, and then reclined, lifting one ankle up from time to time. Maybe she had a twitch.

"I'm told you have something to show me, a talisman of some sort. You've got it wrapped in that shroud. A broom, a witch's broom. *The* broom? The broom of the Wicked Witch of the West?"

"I didn't call her that," he said.

"How did you come by it? Last I heard of it, that Dorothy Gale was humping it around the Palace like some sort of a trophy, brandishing it for all to see."

"I'm told she's gone," said Liir.

"She is." The tone of authority was convincing. Tired, regretful, convincing.

"Gone the way old Ozma is gone? Disappeared? Done in?"

"Gone is gone," said Glinda. "Who knows, maybe Ozma herself will be back someday. I wouldn't hold my breath."

"And maybe Dorothy, too? Or is she gone too far to come back?"

"You ask bold questions of a lady you've just met," said Glinda, and she looked at him sharply. "And you haven't answered mine. How did you come by Elpha—I mean the Witch's broom?"

"You can say Elphaba to me." Liir unwrapped the broom and held it up for Glinda to see.

Glinda didn't look at the broom. She was staring at the Witch's cape. She hoisted herself to her feet and reached to touch its hem. "I'd know this anywhere. This is Elphaba's cape. How did you come by it? Answer me, thug—thief—or I'll have you thrown in Southstairs."

"Fair enough, I'm headed there anyway. Yes, it's her cape. Why wouldn't it be? I took it when I left her castle. I'm her—"

He couldn't say *son*. He didn't know. "I'm her helper. I came from the castle with Dorothy. When the Witch melted, all that was left was the broom. The Scarecrow brought it back to me after Dorothy vanished. No one else wanted it."

"It's a burned stick. Throw it on the fire."

"No."

Glinda reached out a hand, and Liir took it. She wanted help getting up. "Let me look you in the eye, young man. Who are you? How did you come to be at Kiamo Ko?"

"I don't know, and that's the truth. But I served the Witch and saw Dorothy safely to the Emerald City, and I need your help."

"You need *my* help? What for? Bread, cash, a false identity to help you slip sideways through the cracks? Tell me what you need, tell me why I should help, and I'll see what I can do. In memory of Elphaba. You knew her." Her head tilted again, but up, this time, and it was to keep the sudden wetness from spilling into her carefully colored false eyelashes. "You knew my Elphie!"

He would not indulge in cheap grief. "I want to find out what happened to a girl kidnapped by the Wizard's men a few years back. She lived at Kiamo Ko when we got there."

"We?"

"The Witch and I . . ."

"The Witch and you." Her hands reached out hungrily for the cape and rubbed its hem, as if it were leaves of thyme or hyssop. "What girl might that be?"

"Her name is Nor. She is the daughter of Fiyero, one-time prince of the Arjikis, and his wife, Sarima, also kidnapped that very day. You knew Fiyero."

"I knew Fiyero." It was clear Glinda did not want to speak about him. "Why should I bother with you?"

"Nor was his daughter. She was my—" Again, he couldn't say *half-sister*. He didn't know. "My friend."

Glinda reached out and took the charred broomstick and cradled it. "I know about friends."

"Friends have children," Liir said carefully. "If you can't help your friends, you can help their children. Do you have children?"

"I do not. Lord Chuffrey was not so inclined." She reconsidered. "I mean to say, he is so very old. Old and wealthy. His interests lie else-where."

She drifted among the occasional tables. "I don't know why this girl you mention was taken away, or, if she proved that much of a worry, why she should still be alive."

"Everyone knows the Wizard is gone. Surely his enemies don't need to stay imprisoned? If she's alive, why shouldn't she be released?"

A rustling of stiffened tulle sounded in her underskirts. "How do I know you are telling the truth?" she said at last. "These are such treacherous days. I've spent my adult life up till now in salons and theater boxes, not in closed assembly with grasping, pinching . . . *ministers*." She spat out the word. "Insects. And I thought girls at school were devious. Here, every impassive expression hides a bloated ambition for—for dominance, I suppose. And any one of my so-called loyal cabinet could be sending you in here with a tale designed to catch at my throat. I must have more proof you are who you profess to be. This may not be Elphie's cape you're sporting. Maybe my sorrow tempts me into seeing what I would love to see. This may not be her broom. Tell me more, you Liir. How did her broom come to be so burnt?"

"I'm not sure. In truth, I didn't see her die, I only heard what Nanny and Dorothy and the others said. I was locked downstairs. But the broom burnt, that's all I know."

"Anyone could tell a lie!" cried Glinda. "Anyone could burn a broom and make up a story about it!" She beat herself on the breastplate with a clenched fist, and suddenly rushed across the room, overturning a small table and shattering some china dolls. She flung the broom in the fire. "Look, I could do it, too. There's nothing to it."

"Take the broom, burn it," he replied. "Take the cape and burn it, too, or sew it into a hairshirt and wear it under your fancy ball gowns. It doesn't matter. Give me a way to get to Nor, and to get her out; you can have whatever you want. I will come back and serve you as I served the Witch. I have no other plan for my days alive once I answer the question about Nor."

Glinda collapsed on the nearest stool and wept. She needed a man to come and take her in his arms, to give her a shoulder. Liir wasn't a man, nor was his shoulder made for a highborn lady to weep upon. He stood foolishly by, twisting his hands, averting his eyes here, there.

"Look. Glinda, look." In his excitement he forgot to use her title.

She raised her eyes and turned to where he was pointing.

The fire still danced and hissed. Some trick of physics caused the flue to hum faintly like an old folk melody, as if someone were on the rooftop playing an instrument. The music was not merely consoling— and it was that—but commanding: look, it said, look. The broom lay on the back of a log that seethed with flames of pumpkin and pale white. The broom was untouched.

"Sweet Oz . . . ," said Glinda. "Liir, take it. Take it back."

"I'll burn my hands!"

"You won't." Glinda chortled a few syllables in a language Liir couldn't understand. "This is one of the few spells I could ever really master; it came in handy when my husband required me to hand him the burnt toast on the mornings I thought it my wifely duty to prepare his breakfast. Go on. Grasp it and bring it back."

He did, and Glinda was right: the broom had not only neglected to ignite further—but it also wasn't even warm to the touch.

"A burnt broom that has had enough, and refuses to burn further . . . Keep that with you," said Glinda. "I was wrong to doubt you. Whoever you are, however you came by it, this is the Witch's broom. And so I must trust you to be telling me the truth."

She shrugged and tried to smile, and almost began to blubber. "Elphie would know what to do!"

"Tell me what *you* know," he said, as softly as he could.

"I don't have access to the register of prisoners in Southstairs Academy, which is the place your—Nor—is most likely to be if she wasn't murdered long ago. I'm not even sure a register is kept. But I know someone could get you in, at least. Whether you could find Nor or get her out, or yourself either, I can't guess. But I can make introductions for you; in memory of Elphaba, I will do that much."

"Who would help me? A friend of yours?"

"No friend of mine, but a bereaved member of her family. Next of kin to the dearly departed Elphaba Thropp, the Wicked Witch of the West . . ."

"But I thought Elphaba's sister was dead!" said Liir. "Wasn't Nessarose—killed by Dorothy's clumsy house?"

"Yes, she was. But didn't you know? Didn't Elphaba tell you? She had a brother, too. A younger brother named Shell."

◆ 4 ◆

IN COMING TO THEIR SENSES, Sister Doctor and Sister Apothecaire were gratified to find they still possessed their faces. The pack mules were nowhere to be seen though, nor their food supplies, nor their hosts.

"What is that engine in my brain?" said Sister Doctor, after she'd vomited into some ferns.

"I feel as if the jackal moon had been down here snouting around in an unseemly manner." Sister Apothecaire adjusted her garments. "It must be the effects of the ceremonial pipe."

"And that's why the Yunamata never built a city nor invented algebrarish nor bowed to the Wizard."

"With a smoke that kicks like that, who needs a city or an Emperor?"

They ambled in oppressive daylight. "I suppose we should think about what we're doing," said Sister Doctor.

"Yes. If the Yunamata are right, then the Scrow must be responsible for the scrapings. So we're liable to wander into hotter water if we are able to find them."

"I think that's our calling, isn't it?"

"Hmmm." They had a choice: to venture farther into the foothills of the Kells, and make their presence known to the Scrow—or to go back and claim they'd failed. Without discussing it further, they pressed on. Duty weighed more heavily than dread.

THE MAUNTS KNEW that their professional skills—to be loving, to be devout, to be local in their attentions and spiritual in their desires—had not prepared them to be government envoys. Still, since their mauntery served as a way station for those who acted upon the stage of the world, the good sisters considered themselves at least as broad-minded as any other cloistered soul.

Sister Doctor and Sister Apothecaire, nonetheless, were unprepared for the breadth of the Scrow camp when they came upon it. More than a thousand clanfolk, they estimated, maybe fifteen hundred, and a virtual zoography of physical types. The nomads tented in patterns that followed their occupations.

Some castes managed the animals, primarily a huge herd of sheep collected from fell-swards to be penned for a late winter lambing. Other castes specialized in creating sumptuous hangings and carpets from the wool of those same sheep. A contingent of fierce-browed young men with slender, tapering dark beards seemed to be a kind of clerks' collective, running here and there with instructions, corrections, assessments, revisions. Older men and women—some much older—managed the care of children with surprising mildness and efficacy.

At the center of the hubbub rose a tented pagoda. Around it, a good many brass urns issued an aroma of raspberry and heart-of-musk. It didn't take the maunts long to realize that the incense wasn't devotional, but hospitable: the smell from the Princess's pagoda was, well, a stench.

First fed on a peppery broth that seemed to clear both their sinuses and their brains, the maunts were then allowed a chance to pray and compose themselves. It was almost dusk when they were brought into a tent to meet an ambassador of some sort.

"Please, sit," he told them, and sat as well. He was a portly man on the threshold of old age. One eye wandered as if bedeviled by an interior vision it didn't appreciate. His skin was the color of fine whisky. "We hope you have been made comfortable. Or comfortable enough."

The maunts nodded. Their approach had been greeted without apparent alarm, and they'd been welcomed respectfully.

"Very good, very good," he said. "Even in these uncongenial times, with the Emperor cudgeling us heathen into conversion through the force of his holy mace, we pride ourselves on clinging to our customs. Charity to visitors ranks high among our traditions. My name is Shem Ottokos."

"Lord Ottokos, you speak very well," ventured Sister Doctor.

"For a Scrow, you mean," he said, taking no offense. "I had a university degree at Shiz, back in the days when there was more collegiality at college. I studied the languages, ancient and modern."

"You had a notion to be a translator?"

"My notions are insignificant. I am the chief interpreter for her Highness now. I assume you have ventured into our tribal lands to gain an audience with the Princess?"

Though the maunts believed the native land of the Scrow to be significantly farther west, on the other side of the Great Kells, theirs wasn't to quibble. "Yes," said Sister Doctor. "We have work to complete. We are investigating the cause and agency of the recent spate of scrapings. If it would suit the Princess to grant us an audience, we should be able to clear up our concerns and be on our way almost at once. Is the Princess up to seeing us?"

Without answering, he stood and flicked both his hands, which the maunts took to mean: *Come*. They followed him from his tent and toward the royal pavilion in the center of the camp.

"She has not been well for more years than anyone can remember," said Lord Ottokos as they walked. "She has little energy for idle chat and I will not bother to translate anything that would upset her. I would suggest you contain your remarks to ten minutes, no more. When I get up to leave, so shall you."

"We might have brought tribute . . . ," murmured Sister Apothecaire.

"*Sister!*" said Sister Doctor sharply. "We are maunts of the House of Saint Glinda! We do not bring tribute to a foreign princess!"

"I meant a cake, or a witty novel," she explained unhappily.

"She has no need of cakes or novels," said Lord Ottokos. "Meaning no disrespect to our Princess, I would recommend that you breathe through your mouths. It is not considered impertinent to hold your sleeve in front of your nose. Try not to gag, though; it upsets her Highness."

The maunts exchanged glances.

The interior of the pavilion was dark and dank. Even chilly, come to that. Eight or ten heavy stone caskets with perforated lids slowly exhaled sheets of moisture that hung, nearly visible, in the air. Ice, thought Sister Doctor. They've carried ice down from the higher Kells, where it lasts all year long. And the cold serves to tamp down the smell of rot. Now that's a labor, for ice is heavy, and the higher Kells are not convenient . . . Perhaps that's why they're so far from their normal territory at this time of year, for easier access to the ice pack up the eastern, more gradual slope of the Kells . . .

Sister Apothecaire, whose eyes had adjusted more quickly to the gloom, pinched Sister Doctor's elbow and indicated a massive mound of reeking laundry on a low table. It was rolling on its side and opening its eyes.

"Your Highness, may I present Sisters Lowly and Lower-even-than-that," said Lord Ottokos, before he remembered to speak in his own tongue. "Ladies, the Princess Nastoya acknowledges your presence."

She had done nothing of the sort. She had not spoken nor even so much as blinked.

Lord Ottokos continued. "The Princess enquires after your health, assumes it is sufficiently robust or you wouldn't be here, and compliments you on your courage. Have you news of Liir?"

The maunts turned to each other, but in the darkness of the pavilion they could scarcely read each other's expressions. "Liir?" said Sister Apothecaire faintly. She was beginning to need her sleeve, as had been proposed.

"The boy who denied he was Elphaba's son. Is that not why you came to us? To tell us of him? Where is Liir?"

Sister Apothecaire began, "Why, that's uncanny, I never—"

But Sister Doctor cut her off, saying "We came to discover why the Scrow are scraping the faces of unarmed travelers."

Lord Ottokos made his mouth into a pucker—amused, distressed, it was hard to tell. "I repeat, have you news of Liir?" he said.

"If you're not interpreting our comments to your senior, need we have this conversation here?" said Sister Doctor.

"My good Sister," said Lord Ottokos, closing his eyes briefly, as if experiencing a spasm, "the Princess Nastoya entertains visitors only once every several weeks. Do not waste her time. She is waiting to learn what you have to say."

"We *have* seen Liir, we have!" said Sister Apothecaire, unable to govern herself any longer. "He was found not all that far from here some days ago, and brought to our mauntery for recovery, if he can be recovered."

"Sister!" barked Sister Doctor.

Sister Apothecaire shot her colleague a look that seemed, vaguely, to imply: *Give it a rest.*

Lord Ottokos turned and spoke to Princess Nastoya. For the first time, she stirred; that is, her face stirred. Beneath its greasy robes her body had kept up a constant slow stretching, twitching, creaking. Her eyes widened, and globes of ink-colored tears collected in the folds beside her nose. She was a woman in mighty distress. When she spoke, the voice was deep and plain, a laundry mistress's voice, no sonority to it. She said only a few syllables, but the language of the Scrow must have allowed for much meaning in enunciation and pronunciation.

"Forgive my not getting up," began Lord Ottokos's translation. "I am stricken, a creature severed unnaturally in two by decisions made long ago, when the Wizard of Oz set public policy against thinking Animals. Now, one part of my nature is nearly dead and the other clings to life waiting help."

"I have training in surgery, and my colleague in applications—"

Lord Ottokos spoke over Sister Doctor. "I have entrusted the boy Liir with a task, and I have been waiting his return these ten years. Ten years is a decade to a woman, marking the difference between maiden and matron, matron and crone, crone and harpy—but to an Elephant it is only a breath. A long, foul breath, but only a breath. I know the loyalty of Animals, I know the fickle allegiances of men. Because Liir was possibly a flitch of Elphaba, I had placed my trust in him all these years. I have hoped he might discover or invent a solution for my dilemma. And I have been patient—an Elephant is patient. And you come to tell me you have found him. Bless you, my daughters. Is he coming back to me at last?"

"He is not well," said Sister Doctor.

"He *was* not well," corrected Sister Apothecaire. "Perhaps he's improving. We've been traveling, so we can't report developments in his state."

"Why does he not arrive?"

"Something happened to him," said Sister Doctor. "We don't know what. Perhaps what attacked our sister maunts attacked him, too. He is sunk in a strange sleep from which he may not awake. If we knew what had attacked him, we might better invent how to treat him. Lord Ottokos, *ask her my question!*" she said suddenly. "It is pertinent!"

Lord Ottokos obliged this time, and muttered something to Princess Nastoya.

The reply. "We do not scrape the faces of maunts, nor of mice, nor sheep. We do not treat others as we have been treated. You must hunt the barbaric Yunamata and find out from them why they have taken against travelers."

"It isn't the Yunamata," said Sister Doctor, and in making the remark out loud she suddenly felt certain about this for the first time; she had been dubious up until now. "They wouldn't do such a thing. Can you be sure your people are not forgetting their traditions under the burden of sorrow they feel at your condition?"

"My people, as you call them, are not even my people," said Princess Nastoya. "They honored me years ago and made me their princess, and even in my decay they will not allow me to abdicate. They are a nation that has elevated charity beyond what is possible even in the precincts of your religious order. If out of fealty to me they would rather be governed by a Princess who is partly a corpse, how could they raise a hand against defenseless travelers?"

"The young maunts who ventured this way were intent on conversion," admitted Sister Doctor. "They were sent by the Emperor himself, we hear."

"None of us admires the Emperor's zealotry. But intention to convert is hardly a reason to kill people and defile their bodies. The murderers you seek aren't among the Scrow. Don't waste your time considering the matter. It is the Yunamata or it is someone else. Or something else. Perhaps they had a disease."

"No disease makes one's face fall off," said Sister Apothecaire firmly.

"If you know so much, what is my disease?" said Princess Nastoya.

"We should have to examine Your Highness," said Sister Doctor.

"Enough," interrupted Lord Ottokos. "I won't translate such a barbaric notion. The Princess has dismissed you. You may leave."

But the Princess spoke over her interpreter, and he was bound to listen. He bowed his head and continued, "She says again—and she has too few words left to spend in life to say it a third time—where is the boy Liir?"

"But he is not a boy any longer. We have told you what we know." Sister Doctor put her sleeve to her nose; in her line of work she knew the smell of putrescence all too well. "He is in a comatose state not six or eight days' journey from here, though perhaps nearer to the Emerald City than you would like to venture."

Lord Ottokos snapped, "We are not imbeciles. We know where his body is. You have told us. That is not the question."

The maunts blinked at him.

"Where is he?" Lord Ottokos repeated. "Where is *he*?"

"We don't know where he is," said Sister Apothecaire. "Our talents are not that fine."

Princess Nastoya shivered. Handmaidens came forward to withdraw shawls drenched with sweat and other seepage. "Let me help," said Sister Apothecaire suddenly.

"Don't you dare," said Lord Ottokos.

"I do dare. What are you going to do, have me scraped? Sister Doctor, a vessel of water and some essence of citron—lemons, limoncelli, parsleyfruit, anything. And some vinegar reduced to the usual."

Princess Nastoya began to weep then, full tears of a nasty vintage. They fell on Sister Apothecaire's bare hands and burned them; she was not halted in her work. "What has she said just then, in that low murmur?" she asked Lord Ottokos, who stood sputtering and clutching his beard in rage and disbelief.

Finally he submitted to this dotty, disobedient woman. "She said she wishes she could be scraped," he finally allowed.

"We can't do that," said Sister Apothecaire. "Vows of gentility and all that. But she can be made more comfortable. Sister Doctor, that pillow. The head. Watch the neck. What a weight upon this spine! Where *is* the dratted vinegar reduction?"

✦ 5 ✦

FOR A MOMENT, TO REST HER HANDS, Candle set the domingon down. The sound box thunked with a hollow expression. Its cavity was a kind of womb, she thought; how ineffable the secrets born there.

She wasn't given to reflection herself, but she was tired. For a moment she allowed herself to remember her arrival here a month or so before. The one called Mother Yackle had been dozing on a bench in the sunlight; she'd looked up with a start at Candle's approach. She had stretched out a wilted hand, peering with an expression canny, severe, and resigned. Resigned: that was much the way Candle had felt at that moment. Her uncle had tricked her here; he hadn't wanted to keep her any longer. "The way you're going, you'll be pregnant soon enough, if you're not already—and I can't take a child and a child's newborn with me on the road." It seemed he'd bought the domingon from its maker as a way to bargain with her. Go into the mauntery for a year, and the instrument is yours. Do with it what you will, and I'll be back to get you in good time. There's not much left for us in our home marshes, but you'd be ruined in the north. They'd spit at you, your easy ways; they'd laugh, your little voice. Stay here, and remember me wherever I am.

That kind of remembering was another skill, but now she was attending someone else, and her uncle meant little to her.

Candle took Liir's hand in her own. A clamminess. Was his color fading? Or was it just that the sun was setting, and the jackal moon was rising later than it had? The shadows lengthened and browned. By comparison his skin was bleached like an old, sun-whitened bone.

She took up her instrument again and leaned the edge of the minor bridge right on the edge of his bed. Her fingers running into the treble range, they danced in contrapuntal jiggery at the top register, not six inches from his right ear.

Where *was* he?

✦   ✦   ✦

LADY GLINDA SAID TO LIIR, "I can tell you have no intention of leaving that charred broomstick behind, but if you try to walk into a public space carrying it over your shoulder like a blunderbuss you'll be taken for a fool, or at any rate noticed. I think what you are after is something a little more like camouflage."

She paused to regard herself in a convenient looking glass in the stairwell. Adjusting her everyday tiara, she conceded, "It must be said that camouflage is not an effect I have ever strived to master. Still, we'll do what we can."

Liir followed her down the marble steps of the central staircase. The place had gone quiet. "Goodness, everyone takes off for a smoke the minute my back is turned," she said. "Where are the kitchens, anyway? Through here?"

She stumbled into a cloakroom, and then opened the door to a closet where two of the belowstairs staff were involved in recreational exercises. "I beg your pardon," she said, and shut the door, and then locked it.

"Eventually they'll have to thump to be released, and one of them is bound to be cheating. Heaps of fun. But where's the kitchen?"

"Have you just moved here?" asked Liir.

"Don't be silly. Lord Chuffrey had this place long before we married. But I don't cook for myself, if that's what you mean. Nothing other than the toast that I mentioned earlier, and that's done in the breakfast hall. Ah, here we are."

A half-flight of stone steps descended into a cavernous whitewashed kitchen. A dozen members of the staff were sitting about the table so deep in conversation that they didn't hear her coming. "Lady Glinda," said a bootblack, and they all leaped up with guilty looks.

"Glad to be recognized in my own home," said Glinda. "I hate to interrupt what are probably well-intentioned plans to kill us all in our beds, but if you don't mind? A minor request for whichever of you has just a moment to spare?"

They melted away, all but the housekeeper and the houseboy.

"He's about the same size as the bootblack," said Glinda, pointing to Liir. "Suit him up in House of Chuffrey colors and find some decent shoes, and get him a leather satchel on a sling. You know, that long cylindrical thingy that Lord Chuffrey's guests use to carry their arrows when they go hunting in the country. That ought to accommodate the filthy old broom, I think."

"Asking your pardon, Lady Glinda," said the houseboy. "We've no such satchels on the town premises. They're all down to Mockbeggar Hall."

"Do I have to think of everything? Haven't we friends? Haven't we neighbors to borrow from? Aren't there shops still serving the public? Need I go tramping to the marketplace myself with a sack of coins between my teeth?"

The houseboy fled. The housekeeper pursed her lips editorially.

"Don't speak. Don't. It's only a temporary appointment," said Lady Glinda. "Just for the day, in fact. Now feed up this boy; he hasn't had a square meal for weeks, I can tell. And when he's equipped as I require, return him to the Yellow Parlor."

Lady Glinda climbed the stairs, muttering "Kitchens!" in disbelief, leaving Liir behind.

"Well, peel off those beggar's weeds and wash in the cauldron room, just there; I won't have you staining her fancyfart's good livery with your dirty limbs," said the housekeeper. "I'll put out some food, and you be grateful for it, for it's out of our own downstairs supply, and we don't take kindly to ravenous upstarts here in Lord Chuffrey's establishment."

"WHERE ARE WE GOING?" He peered out the window of the carriage.

"Put your head back. Servants don't gawp out of carriage windows."

How odd to be five feet higher than the street. It was not an experience to which he was accustomed. The carriage lurched under arched spans of stone, stopped for a squadron of uniformed cavalry on display, sidelined along a merchants' parade, and picked up speed along Dirt Boulevard. Cleared of its village of indigents, the roadway showed signs of its original elegance, though its parallel rows of trees were in bad shape. It looked as if the grounds were being used for military drills.

Where had all the itinerants gone? "Where *are* we going?"

"To the Palace," Glinda said. "Where you'll keep your head down and your mouth closed. Are you scared?"

It seemed too personal a question for a woman to ask a boy. Perhaps she realized this. She continued, "I was, the first time I came here. It was with Elphaba. We were older than you are now, but only by a few years. And in many ways we were more naive. Well, I was, anyway. And I was terrified. The wonderful Wizard of Oz! My stomach just about dissolved in its own acids."

"What happened?"

"What happened?" She turned the question to herself, examining it. "History happened, I suppose. We saw the Wizard, and we parted ways—Elphaba went underground, as it were, and . . . in time, I hugged the limelight." She sighed. "With the best of intentions, and with limited success."

"And now?" he said, not because he was interested, but because he didn't want any more attention on himself.

"Now, I hold the key," she said. "Now, for the time being, I am intended to stand in for the mighty on their thrones. It's all I'm good for."

"Are the mighty deserving of thrones?"

"That's an Elphaba question, and out of your youthful pouting mouth it sounds preposterous. Like most of her superior cavils, it has no easy answer. How could I know?"

She sighed. "Sit *back,* I said. Yes, I'm nervous. You'll find in time most people are. They simply learn better how to disguise it, and sometimes, if they're wise, how to use their anxiety to serve the public good. Perhaps being jittery helps me pay closer attention. You know, I didn't want the hard work of government. They all say I need to clean house. Clean house! That presumes I've cleaned a house before. I say, hey, what are the servants for? Decoration?"

She was speaking to herself, in a way, but she was also trying to cheer him up. He turned his head, confused by her kindness, and busied himself from watching, at an acceptable angle, as the buildings nearer the Palace hove into view. One mammoth ministry was strapped with bas-relief marble panels depicting various historic Ozmas in characteristic poses. They looked at once venerable and ludicrous, and the pigeons of the Emerald City paid them no high compliment.

"But why are we going to the Wizard's Palace?"

"The people's Palace, now," said Glinda derisively. "Though what the people are going to do with their own palace I have no earthly idea." She chewed on a nail. "There's a clandestine entrance to South-stairs from the Palace. Of course there had to be, a means of instantly spiriting away any treasonous Palace upstart sniffed out in the court. Though the common criminal condemned to serve time is more publicly lowered in a cage into the pit that drops down inside those bulwarky ramparts. You see, it's mostly underground, Southstairs. It's the most impregnable prison in Oz. Nobody who goes in via the cage comes out that way."

"How do they come out?"

"In pine coffins."

SHE DABBED A SACHET doused with oil of clove and root-of-persimmon behind her ears. By the time the door to her carriage was opened by a staff member of the Palace, Lady Glinda had become more regal. Her chin went up, a jeweled scepter was provided for her right hand. Her eye flashed with a steeliness Liir had not noted earlier.

"Lady Glinda," they murmured. She deigned to supply the briefest of nods, as an indication that she was not deaf, and walked by.

Liir followed in something closer to terror than he had ever experienced before. He expected to be rushed away and beaten before he could even begin to protest. But Lady Glinda's penumbra of influence extended eight feet behind her, it seemed, for his progress was unquestioned, and he gained the threshold of the Palace without anyone's objecting.

The place was a maze, and he lost his bearings almost at once. Accompanied by a Palace flunky, Glinda and Liir swept up grand staircases, along arched corridors, past ceremonial chambers and receiving parlors. Another staircase or two, another corridor or three, and at length they traversed a long dingy room, where dozens of staff members were perched on high stools above ledgers. They splashed ink in their nervous abjection, though not on Glinda in her celestial blue gown.

Behind a wall with an interior window, the better for supervising workers, stood an office with a desk and some chairs. An elegant man absorbed in a newssheet was tipped back on the hind legs of his chair, his ceremonial boots propped on the desk and his saber stuck in the soil of a potted fern. "Commander," said Lady Glinda, "we're here. Show some respect, or pretend to anyway."

He leaped to his feet with ostentatious speed. Liir blinked and gaped. "Commander Cherrystone!" he said.

"You've met?" said Glinda. "How droll."

"I'm drawing a blank," said the Commander, wrinkling a brow.

"At Kiamo Ko," said Liir. "You were head of the Gale Forcers at Red Windmill. It was your men that kidnapped Fiyero's widow, Sarima, and her sisters and her children."

Commander Cherrystone smiled deferentially and offered Liir a hand. "Kidnapped? We took them into protective custody for their own good. How were they to know the depravity of the Witch they were harboring?"

"And how well did you protect them?" said Liir.

"Ooh, the boy has spit, has he," said Commander Cherrystone, wiping his sleeve. "I like that, son, but please. This is my best dress uniform." He was equable and seemed to take no offense.

Liir glared at Glinda. "You've taken me here, to him—betrayed me to the very man responsible for Nor's abduction?"

"Recriminations, they get us nowhere," said Lady Glinda. "And how was I to know? Consider it poetic justice: Now he must help you. Because I say so." She turned to Cherrystone. "Look, Commander, I've laid it all out. You got my note? The boy wants to see Fiyero's daughter, if she's still alive. As an officer and a governor of the prison, you can make the arrangements, can't you?"

"It's an institution with its own appetite, is a prison," said Commander Cherrystone. Rather approvingly, thought Liir. "I can't say I remember you, lad, but my work involves many postings. And in none of them have I ever before met a soul who wanted to enter Southstairs voluntarily. You understand: No promises that you will leave it. Either dead or alive. It might be your tomb."

"My name is Liir," he said. He tried to lift his chin as he had seen Glinda do. "We *have* met. I liked you. You seemed decent."

"I tried to be decent, within reason," he replied. "Anyway, I had little choice if I wanted to gain the trust of that knotty little clan in Kiamo Ko."

"What happened to Sarima?" asked Liir. "Fiyero's widow."

"Everyone dies. It's a question of where and how, that's all."

"Oh, bandying, bandying, please, my head," said Glinda. "I feel I'm back at Shiz. The Debating Tourneys: what a migraine. I need a tonic. Are you going to do this for me, Commander?"

"I wouldn't be here if you didn't require it," he answered. "Ready, lad?"

"I'm ready," Liir answered. He turned to Glinda. "Ought I take off these silly clothes?"

"What, and go naked into Southstairs? I wouldn't recommend it," said Commander Cherrystone. Glinda waved dismissively. Then she tucked her hand against her mouth and bit her knuckles. It was hard to know if her pretty ways were studied or innate.

"Oh, oh," she managed, "I don't know that I'll see you again . . . and you remind me so of her."

"I haven't Elphaba's talent," said Liir simply. "I'm not worth mourning, believe me."

"Her power was only part of it," said Glinda. "She was brave, and so are you."

"Bravery can be learned," he said, trying to be consoling.

"Bravery can be stupid," said Commander Cherrystone. "Believe me."

The boy didn't move forward to touch her or kiss her. In Kiamo Ko, only Nanny had been the kissing type, and Liir hadn't figured much in her affections. So he merely said, "Well, good-bye, then. And don't worry. I'll take care."

They looked at one another. In a moment Liir would lose heart; he would do the shaming thing that the houseboy had predicted. He would let Nor's life reach its destiny without intervening—in exchange for having someone stand in as a mother. Lord knows Elphaba hardly had!—and here was Glinda, blinking back tears or something.

She looked at him almost as if thinking the same thing. The moment passed, though. "You do your work," Lady Glinda told him. "Ozspeed. And don't forget your broom."

"Her broom," said Liir.

"Your broom," she corrected him.

◆ 6 ◆

THE ROOM GREW SUDDENLY COLDER. Night was drawing in, and the rump flank of the wind hinted at the winter to come. Candle rose to draw the shutters closed. The jackal moon was at its most self-satisfied; soon the constellation would wane and its elements return to their ordinary, lonelier orbits.

She shuttered most of the windows for the first time, but she couldn't fix one shutter securely; a rope of ivy with a stem stout as a forearm had grown across a corner. Candle took an extra sheet and hung it as best she could against the chill.

When she came back to Liir, she became alarmed. She felt his brow. His skin was colder still, and his blood pressure seemed to be dropping.

She wasn't suited for work of this seriousness. She laid down her instrument on the floor, determined to run and get Sister Cook or the Superior Maunt. She found her way blocked.

The figure stood in the doorway, veil drawn to cloak the features. Candle reared back, startled.

The veil dropped. It was only the addled elderly maunt, the senior biddy in the place, the one known as Mother Yackle. What was she doing here?

"You can't leave," said Mother Yackle. "There's no one else here to do what needs to be done."

Candle picked up her domingon and raised it threateningly. Quicker than could have been imagined, Mother Yackle slid back into the shadows, and closed the door behind her, and locked it.

Candle thumped against the door, and threw her shoulder against it, but the heavy thing was quarter-sawn oakhair wood, and cross-built. She couldn't waste her time clawing at it with her fingernails. Liir was failing.

She turned her attentions to the rest of the room. Not raised in the arts of medicine, she didn't recognize much of what she found in the cupboard. A large mortar and pestle for the grinding of herbs. Several fresh-nibbed pens, with sheets of paper and a stoppered jug of ink, for the making of notes. Unguents of disagreeable viscosities. The body of a mouse on the bottom shelf. A few old keys—none of which fit the room's only keyhole.

She sat down and played a few rapid runnels, in mischief mode, to concentrate her apprehensions. She felt for his pulse again, and brushed his hair away from his forehead. Even his scalp was cold.

She took off her tunic and tried to wave it from the window. Though she couldn't attract attention by yelling, maybe someone in the kitchen garden would see her signal. But a wind came up and took the tunic away, and that was that.

At length she relied on what fate had provided her. She took the cleanest of the pen nibs and sharpened it further by training it along the stone windowsill. Releasing Liir's left arm from its splint, she propped it up against a transept of the domingon, so his hand was raised in the air, a salute. To the extent that she prayed—which wasn't much, even in these environs, even at this drastic juncture—she begged for her hands to be steady. Then she tried to play Liir's bicep as she might her domingon, running her hands in light, feathery scales along the skin. She settled on a place near the inside of the elbow, and using the nib as a lancet, made a neat incision.

She caught his blood in the mortar, and when she'd filled it she rushed to the window and dumped it out. There, jackal moon, you want your blood offering, there it is. She collected a second portion, then a third, and she took off her habit to bind Liir's arm and stop the flow.

In only her broadcloth shift she shivered, and her fingers trembled. Nonetheless she returned to her instrument. Her musical figures went wobbly, but she kept on.

◆　◆　◆

AFTER GLINDA HAD GONE, Commander Cherrystone took no more notice of Liir than he might a napping dog. He disappeared behind his newspapers, humming to himself. Liir sat on a stool, waiting; something had to happen sooner or later. He watched the Commander's well-trimmed nails hold the page, listened to various admonitory hums and clicks and editorial *humphs* breathed nasally. The career soldier was a fit man, a calm one, and his lack of attention to Liir seemed suitable. What was hard to fathom was the Commander's composure. It was under his command that Nor and her family had been abducted, yet he seemed so oblivious to Liir's contempt that Liir began to doubt himself. Maybe there was more to the ruling family of Kiamo Ko than he had known.

Not until the business day in the Palace came to an end, and the dozens of civil servants left their desks for home, did the Commander sit up. "Your guide will be along presently—ah, there he is."

A handsome younger man with a keen, guarded expression blustered into the room. "Can't have kept you waiting more than a tockety-tick, have I? Witches' britches, the Palace staff gives you the once-over!

Thought things would loosen up once the Wizard abdicated." He shucked a jacket from his shoulders and slung it across the desk. "You notice. Nice, eh? A clothier in Brickle Lane. Yes, it's black-market Munchkinsheep wool, I'd have nothing else. Feel that weight."

"You've a prettier penny to spend than a military man does," observed the Commander dryly.

"She is not that young and I am not that choosy: conditions for a bargain. Bartered it mostly. Fuck, I'm hungry. This is the boy, then. Got a crumpet or a butter roll anywhere, Cherryvery?"

"This is Liir. You're to take him below and help him as best you can. I know you've your mind on other matters, so I don't pretend to expect you will be thorough in your assistance. But do try. He seems a good sort."

The young man shot Liir a glance. "He looks too wet to be after what I'm after down there."

"I suspect he is," said Commander Cherrystone, "but all good things come to those who wait, and he may grow into a sexual nature before he emerges, if he ever does. Liir, this is Shell."

"The Witch's brother?" Liir felt he had to check.

"The same," said Shell, flexing his fingers. Liir wasn't sure that he could see a resemblance, but Shell looked capable and cunning both. "Are you ready?"

Does he know who I am, wondered Liir. Has Shell ever heard of a Liir? A boy who might be his nephew?

"I'm ready."

Commander Cherrystone flicked a speck of dust off his dress weskit. "The usual arrangements about your return, Shell. Liir—I wish you luck."

He left, locking them into the office. Shell looked at Liir more closely, and his nose twitched as if on the scent of something. Then he shrugged and said, "I'm ready for an ale. You ready for Southstairs?" Liir nodded.

Shell went to an installation of cubbies for the sorting of interoffice mail. Liir couldn't see how his fingers fussed, nor at what, but in a moment the whole wooden unit slid aside on a secret track. Behind, a plain door, and Shell had the key for it.

"Is this where Southstairs got its name?" asked Liir, pointing to the flight of timber steps that descended treacherously, without benefit of railings, into the gloom.

"Dunno. Never thought about it. Let's go. I hope your thighs are good. Watch your step."

"Was your sister a martyr?" asked Liir, innocently as he could.

"Which sister?" he answered, but before Liir could reply, he continued. "Martyrdom implies a religious faith, and Nessarose had so much faith that no one else in the family could breathe. Elphaba affected a salty agnosticism; I never knew whether it was genuine or not. For me to consider them martyrs, I'd have to have faith, and I don't—not in unionism, the faith of my father; nor in the other varieties that clot the calendar with their hobbledehoy feast days. It took all the fancy dancing I could do not to be tarred as a traitor-by-family-association. Luckily, I have little interest in government, and I'm rather good at dancing, as it happens. Look . . . Liir, is it . . . I prefer to save my breath. Shall we not chatter like choirgirls on an outing? That okay with you?"

Liir didn't answer. The wind siphoning through the slitted windows above made a sound almost like a spiral of music. He wanted to ask Shell if he could hear the strange effect, but he kept his own counsel.

They grew colder and colder as they descended. Soon Liir had to put out a hand, not just to feel his way in the gloom, but also because his legs threatened to buckle beneath him. The wall was damp, here and there soft with wet clinging growth.

Eventually the sound of their steps began to echo, and then it was clear a light was burning below. At last they reached a stone floor from which several dark corridors led.

"Here I usually stretch," said Shell, and showed Liir how. Liir rubbed his muscles as directed. When they were ready, Shell took a club from a pile on the floor and lit it from the torch affixed to the wall. "Do the same; we won't spend the rest of eternity together, you know," he said. "Light is helpful. These are limbs of irongrowth stock, so they burn a good long time."

"If we're not going to stick together, how will I find my way out?"

"I don't know. I assume you're clever, though." Shell's nonchalance was cruel. "Very few emerge from here. Only the guards."

Liir tried to memorize all of everything, just in case—but he intended to stick with his guide no matter what Shell might think about it.

The way was dank and sour, sometimes cut with a sulfurous gust. The torchlight made a tidal rush against flattened arches of milk grey stone. Parts of the walls were bricked, though the work was ancient and the brick face crumbling.

As they walked along the crushed cement and scattered rubble, and Liir got his breath back, he tried to think of how to speak to Shell. The man was in his late twenties, maybe early thirties, and a certain class of fop; even Liir, knowing himself a rube and a naïf, could see that. But Shell's eye was keen and his manner, variously courtly or casual, always suave. He was taller than Elphaba had been, sleek where she had been spiky.

As it happened, Liir had no time to ask questions. The path ended in a flight of shallow steps leading farther down. They were reaching the outskirts of Southstairs—not so much a prison as an underground city. The sounds of carts, and a murmur of voices. Somewhere, someone was playing a stringed instrument, far away; somewhere, someone must be cooking, for there was a grievous smell of rendered bacon fat on a hot griddle.

"The cowhand of mercy prepares his rounds." Shell swept off his hat and left it on a ledge; a curl of yellow plume bobbed in the gloom.

"Will you lead me to Nor?"

"I've promised to take you to the central registrar, but I've a few stops to make first." Shell patted the satchel on his shoulder. "Some folks need my attention, and it would be unthinkable to postpone their medications to rush you by first. You don't mind?"

Liir did. "No, of course not."

Around another corner, down a few more steps, and they came to a greasy waterway, not unlike the canals above in the Emerald City. "Come on then, if you're coming," said Shell, leaping aboard an abandoned canal dory. He seemed to be growing cheerier by the moment.

At length, the narrow waterway ran into a wider channel that curved beneath a high ceiling of rock face supported here and there with beams and buttresses. On either side of the channel, padlocked doors were set flush into the stone walls. Sometimes the doors gave out onto ledges or a path between cells; more often, just onto the water.

The stench and the noise grew. Before long Liir and Shell passed grey-clothed laborers hauling buckets of supper one way, buckets of feces back.

"Didn't think a country kid would wrinkle his nose at a rural perfume," observed Shell, berthing the canal dory. "You'll stay and guard this; more than once I've had my vessel nabbed while I was at my errand of mercy." He opened the flap of his satchel and removed a small glass syringe filled with a urine-colored solution. He wiped the needle with a clean cloth and then tapped the plunger once to make sure it worked. "Ripe and ready, she is," he murmured. He looked sideways at Liir. "It's humbling to be able to help those who suffer."

With a practiced hand, he quickly undid the lock on a door and slid through, closing it behind him.

Despite his intentions to cling to Shell like a burr, Liir didn't have the nerve to follow, nor was he tall enough to peer through the small window high in the door. But there was a gap at the bottom between the door and its sill. By sinking to the floor of the dory, Liir could make out the movement of figures inside. Apparently Shell had set his torch in a wall stanchion. His voice sounded soothing, even hypnotic, but the prisoner crouching against a back wall scooched her bare feet underneath her skirts. Shell's boots drew near until he was standing flush against her. She moaned or whimpered, and her feet curled the farther under her skirts. Mercy was hard to accept, Liir guessed. Shell's feet rocked from toe to heel, with a comforting rhythm, and his heels began to lift from the floor.

At the sound of someone approaching, Liir turned.

"You, what're you lying there for?" A portly Ape with a ring of keys, dragging his knuckles on the ground. He was wreathed in his own weather of cheap cologne, protection against the smells, and he wore a collar made of mangy ocelot fur.

"I'm visiting," said Liir. "With permission of Lady Glinda. I'm accompanying a man named Shell, who is inside tending to the needs of the sick."

"I'll say he is, and he's sicker than most," said the Ape. "But what Lady Glinda dictates means nothing down here; we're our own society. Have you a writ of passage from the Under-mayor?"

"We're on our way to get one. But Shell needed to stop first."

"He sees to his needs. I'll see to yours. Come with me."

"I don't think I'd better."

The Ape insisted, and Liir called out repeatedly for Shell, who emerged, cross and agitated. "What're you bothering my boy for?"

"Oh, he's your *boy*?" asked the Ape. "Ever the surprise, Shell."

"He's under my care for the moment. Leave him be, Tunkle."

"You give our Miss Serenity her weekly jab?" asked Tunkle, jingling the keys.

Shell replaced the syringe. "You interrupted me. I'll go on to the next."

"He's a one-man festival of fun," said Tunkle. "I wouldn't get too close if I were you. He gets fairly hot and bothered over all these errands of mercy."

Shell showed no sign of taking offense. "Clear off, Tunkle. We know the ropes. We're on our way to the Under-mayor. We'll just take our time, that's all. You want a lift?"

"Not on your life. I go upside once a month and I can find my own fun, Master Shell; I don't need your fancy imported sort." The Ape spit in the waterway and let them go by. "Watch your back, lad."

Making no effort to lower his tone, Shell remarked to Liir, "Tunkle. A collaborationist. Saved his own hide, during the Wizard's campaigns, by signing on to bully his own." Still, his tone was neutral, as if this seemed a reasonable enough strategy.

Liir asked softly, "How far are we from the Under-mayor's office?"

"A stop or two, or three," said Shell. "There's more than one would like my attentions, but I pick and choose, trying to be fair. I can't be all things to all people, now, can I?" He brushed his lapel and made ready to continue his missionary work.

LIIR DIDN'T KNOW how much time had passed before they finally reached the Under-mayor's quarters, but Southstairs grew progressively warmer, stinkier, noisier, brighter the farther in they floated. Shell made two or three more stops, always, it seemed, to tend to young women— Liir could hear their voices, supplicating, sometimes weeping, once cursing Shell. But Liir couldn't see them, nor did he want to.

Shell became more distracted as the hour passed, his bespoke clothes more disheveled. At length, however, they reached their destination. A foreman's cabin stood freely beneath the lofty ceiling from which, in the stronger light, Liir could make out rock structures, strange candelabras of dripped stone frozen in place.

The prison Under-mayor was a sallow man, skin soft and pale as bleached linen. He looked as if he hadn't seen the sun in many years. Multiple rings on every finger, even his thumbs: like a fence for stolen jewels. His name was Chyde. "You're raising someone up in the paths of righteousness, I see," he said, cheerily enough, to Shell. "I'm not used to thinking of you as concerned about the morals of the young."

"One does what one can," said Shell.

"I thought your motto was one does whom one can. But never mind that. You bring news of the starlight goddess?"

"Glinda's all right. She's coping. The City's a mess up there, but you'll have heard all about it."

"You always have a special slant, though." Chyde located some beer and a few stale rings of fried castipod. Liir declined, but Shell tucked in.

"Well, after all these years, it's a right rich stew up there, that's for sure," Shell conceded through a mouthful of flaky breading. "The Wizard's departure was weirdly unexpected, given he's been in power for so long. Still, with so many having schemed behind the scenes to oust him, you'd think they'd have gotten their signals straight about what ought to happen next. Lady Glinda is looking in, a glamorous figurehead, and no one knows if she's got a scrap of brain in her noggin. The trade unions should be rising any day, but the municipal militia wasn't quite prepared to recognize a socialite for a queen. Hence, in loyal support of *course,* the guard has been on the offensive, clearing out the neighborhoods where the rabble is more likely to rouse. Glinda thinks it's urban revitalization. So it's an interesting time, a sweep of forces with everyone assessing the power of the other. Heads will roll, of course. It's merely a question of in what sequence: who gets to laugh first, and who next, and whose laugh is cut off by the guillotine blade."

"And you'll be stealing in and out of the bedchambers of the wenches and the wives and the widows . . ."

"The wives laugh neither first nor last, but they do laugh best!"

"I live a quiet life down here," said Under-mayor Chyde to Liir. "It's part of your dad's program of good works to fill me in on the local gossip. I could go northstairs if I could trust a soul, but I don't trust a soul. And the minute the selfish bastards up there remember their relatives down here, if they ever do, I'll be hamstrung before morning and bled by noontime. I've never felt I could leave my post, but especially not now. Not if I want to survive through these interesting times."

"He's not my father," said Liir coldly.

"Oh? I thought I caught a resemblance," said Under-mayor Chyde. "Well, more's the pity. You're training an apprentice, are you, Shell?"

Shell yawned and drained his beer. "No. I promised Lady Glinda I'd deliver this spawnling to you. He's searching for a prisoner."

"We're all searching for someone," said Under-mayor Chyde in a drawl. "People pay me well to begin searches I can't somehow ever manage to complete." He flashed his jeweled hands. "Care to make a contribution to the exhibit, lad?"

"He's not buying your silence or your service," snapped Shell. "Get on with it, Chyde-ey, or I'll report your side business to the authorities. Lady Glinda has an interest in jewels herself, as it happens. A more seemly interest. She might not like to hear—"

"Name?" interrupted Chyde.

"Her name was Nor," said Liir. "Is Nor. About, oh, sixteen? She was abducted by the Gale Forcers at the castle of Kiamo Ko, out west. In the Vinkus."

"I can't say the name sounds familiar, but we house an exclusive clientele, some of whom like to keep a low profile. We respect their wishes, of course."

"Her father was the prince of the Arjikis."

"A crowned head? Well, if she's here, she must have one of the private suites. You haven't been to offer her your particular brand of solace, Shell?" Under-mayor Chyde snapped his fingers with a clink and said, "Jibbidee, bring me the two green ledgers. No, sorry, the ocher ones, if she's a Winkie."

"She'd be young still," said Shell. "Or young-ish. I do have some standards, Chyde."

An elf with ears in an advanced state of decomposition appeared from a cupboard and scrambled about a rickety bookshelf. "Thank you, Jibbidee," said Chyde, without inflection, and the elf returned to his cupboard and shut the door behind him when his job was done.

"You might remember the circumstances of her registering," said Shell. "It was the same castle where my sister lived until recently."

"Oh, *that* Kiamo Ko. How could I be so slow?" Chyde slid a pair of spectacles off his pate and down to his nose, and squinted. "My former wife, save her blessed hide, always said that I'm such a big-hearted guy, you know, everyone's story gets to me, and so I can't keep them straight. My heart bleeds for all. One and all." *Harumph.* "Part of our marital problems, but so be it."

He glanced up over the top of his lenses and fastened on Shell for the first time. "I am sorry about your sisters, though, Shell. Both of them meeting their ends within such a short time. It can't be easy."

"We weren't close," said Shell, studying his nails.

"Munchkinland's in revolt, now that Nessarose is dead. It has to be said she ruled with an iron fist, for all her piety."

"Spare us the civics class. I'm in a hurry, Chyde," said Shell. "Can I leave the boy here for you to finish with?"

"Some poor widowling just aching for your attention, I know, I know . . ."

Liir put it together at last. What a dolt am I! "Are you sleeping with your patients?" he blurted out. "I mean—you know—"

"Patients," mused Chyde. "Nice touch."

"I am seeing to their needs," said Shell, without apology or shame. He patted the satchel. "The comfort I supply is greatly appreciated. And of course they want to show their gratitude. What else does a lady in chains have to offer? She couldn't accept charity. It isn't done in polite circles. So she pays as she can. I'm not so cold as to deny them the chance to show their appreciation. It seems a fair exchange to me."

I'm not sticking with him even if he is my maybe-uncle. Forget it. New plan needed. I'll improvise. "You're disgusting," said Liir. "I mean, really. That's disgusting. You're disgusting. I can't believe it. It's—it's monstrous."

"Oh, I'd need to be a good sight more ambitious to make it to monstrous." Shell laughed. "Chyde? Sometime this week would be nice."

"Might as well leave him." Chyde turned to another volume. "Nothing is coming to light. Are you sure she's here?"

"I'm not sure of anything, but this is the natural first place to start, I suppose," said Shell. He stood and smoothed down his clothes, and offered his hand to Liir. "So we take our parting now, comrade. I hope the rest of your day is as amusing."

Liir thought about biting the hand, but Shell would only make another joke. So the boy tucked his own hands high up in his armpits. "We'll meet again," said Shell. "Likely it'll be down here, since it isn't easy to obtain an exit visa. Sweet dreams, Liir-boy."

He spun on his heel and disappeared almost at a run.

"Oh, the energy of the young," said Chyde, sighing and continuing to flip pages. "You know, I'm not coming up with anything so far. What did you say her name was again?"

◆ 7 ◆

IN THE WESTERN DISAPPOINTMENTS, on the last evening of this jackal moon, the Scrow herders sent their dogs out to round up the sheep earlier than usual. Other workers erected a double row of pliant, bindweed fencing around the far edge of the fold's perimeter. Unless cloud cover prevented it, the celestial beast would brighten the night more brilliantly than at any other time in a generation. It would make a good night for scavengers.

Sister Doctor and Sister Apothecaire had done what they could. They had provided comfort to the old Princess that her own staff could not. She was happier, though the mood in her tent, when she was asleep, was ugly. The Scrow were a proud people—well, what people weren't?—and they were suspicious of foreign clinical practices.

The interpreter put it to the women as gently as he could.

"You should move on," said Lord Shem Ottokos. "We have told you what you came to learn—that we know nothing of the scrapings of those colleagues of yours. If your profession is the extension of charity, you have performed your mission. You've benefited Princess Nastoya mightily. There is no reason to linger, and danger to you if you do."

"We're told you are hospitable to strangers," Sister Doctor reminded him.

"Strangers, yes; that is the way of the Scrow," said Ottokos. "After several days, you are less strange than you once were. You become familiar, and therefore, like family, less agreeable. I'll be happy to provide you with a supply of food, but I recommend that you start home this very evening and take advantage of this unusually bright night."

Sister Doctor said, "In the question of scrapings, we haven't convinced you that the Yunamata are blameless. So why would you send us into danger?"

"You've been so good; we'll provide what we can manage by way of an escort," said Lord Ottokos, and left.

"The nerve!" said Sister Apothecaire. "We're being disinvited. I believe I'm offended."

"Are you going native?" Sister Doctor asked her Munchkin colleague. The tone verged on the cruel.

"They're adorable heathen," said Sister Apothecaire, somewhat wildly.

"Yes. Well, they'll seem less adorable if they conquer their aversion to scraping the faces of their visitors. After all, when you were a child you were an adorable heathen, too, but you got over it."

"I don't appreciate your wit, Sister Doctor."

It began to seem for a short while as if the maunts might disobey the instructions of their superior and split up. However, the Princess Nastoya requested a final interview with them, and she felt well enough to sit up on her pallet.

"Have you taken the full measure of my ailment?" she said, through Shem Ottokos. "To avoid the pogroms of the Wizard against the Animals, I went deeply underground many years ago, accepting a witch's charm as a way to hide myself. I am an Elephant, and want to go to my death as an Elephant, but I am cursed to remain in this human body. I used to be able to change for a brief time, but infirmity and age have eroded those talents, and now I am trapped. I fear the Elephant within me has been dying for some time, and may be in part dead already; but I would join it, if I could only have help. Ten years ago I asked the Witch's boy for help, but he disappeared. Now through your exotic skills you have helped me rally, and so I must press this request. Please return to your hive and collect the boy, the man, Liir. Bring him here or send him here; get him here safely. He may not be able to help me, but even the most blessed of witchcraft has gone underground in these trying times, and he is the only one I know who might be able to help."

"Do you really think he is Elphaba's son?" asked Sister Doctor.

"He had her cape, he had her broom," said Princess Nastoya. "Maybe he wasn't her son, but he cared about her life, and he may have learned something anyway. What other course can I take?"

"We've never even seen him awake," admitted Sister Apothecaire. "It would be hard to promise we could persuade him when we don't know what he's really like. Yet."

"In return for his help, I'd promised him something in exchange." She began to wheeze a bit, and Ottokos collected her phrases haltingly. "I want—to tell him what I've heard—about—the word on the street in the Emerald City."

"I'm sure he'll be fascinated," said Sister Doctor. "If he ever wakes up."

"The threat to Animals during the Wizard's reign crowded me—humanward—and I have been safer than many. Now, as our violently holy Emperor demands all our souls, I want to go to my death as an Animal: proud, isolate, unconsecrated. Find him for me. Hurry. I will give you—two rare male skarks to ride—and a panther to travel by your side as far as the forest. You will travel faster on the backs of those beasts than you did on foot or on mules. If you aren't ambushed by soldiers or wolves or any other enemy, you may make it by sunrise. At the edge of the forest the panther will turn back, but the skark will keep on, and by then the worst of the jackal moonlight will be spent."

The maunts nodded their heads and rose to take their leave. They didn't expect to see Princess Nastoya again, dead or alive, an Elephant or a human. They didn't want to tire her with further discussion. But it was she who raised the last point, when they were almost beyond addressing.

"My friends," she said. They turned. "You have been kind to me, and good to each other. I am not so far dead that I haven't seen this. How can you perform such works in the name of the Unnamed God, whose agents belittle us so?"

"The Unnamed God does not descend from the Emperor," explained Sister Doctor. She was afraid that an obscure point of contemporary unionist theology might be lost on a pagan, but she was reluctant to treat the Princess like a fool. "The Unnamed God, whatever they may say in the Emerald City these days, is still in its essence unnamed. We have as much a right to work in its name as anyone else."

"Hardly seems worth the bother to believe," murmured Princess Nastoya. "Still, life itself seems more than patently fantastic, and we believe in life, so I'll let the matter drop."

THE RIDE WOULD BE SWIFT but rollicking. These skarks were large of pelvis, supported by longer back legs than other skark varieties. Around their legs circled the panther like an eddy of black oil, constantly swishing by.

Lord Shem Ottokos escorted them safely out of the camp. Sister Apothecaire was disappointed that there were so few Scrow to wave good-bye to them. "You'll have noticed the creatures circling," said Ottokos. The maunts looked uneasily at each other. "In the sky, I mean."

"Vultures?" said Sister Apothecaire. "Sensing the carrion of Princess Nastoya? She would supply a healthy portion of carrion to a bevy of vultures."

"They are higher up than vultures, I think," said Ottokos. "So, according to the laws of perception, they must be larger than vultures. Besides, vultures wait for the body to die before approaching. I fear they are a squadron of attack creatures who don't wait until the meat is dead. Perhaps—well, I hardly dare say it. Dragons."

"Dragons are rare in the first place, and in any case docile," snapped Sister Doctor. "Menacing dragons are only mythology."

"Myth has a way of coming true," said Ottokos. "I'm merely saying *Be careful*."

"How kind to set our minds at ease, just as we depart from your protection." Sister Doctor looked livid.

"You have the panther. Nothing will get by her."

"Good-bye, then," said Sister Doctor. "I hope you have learned something from us."

Sister Apothecaire sniffled into a souvenir shawl that she'd bought at an inflated price from a Scrow weaver.

Shem Ottokos watched them leave. He did wish them well, at least as far as the mauntery, and the completion of their task for his Princess. Beyond that, he wished them nothing at all: Let their Unnamed God go on unnaming their lives for them.

THE SNOUT OF THE JACKAL moon poked over the line of the trees.

Liir was nearly grey. The bleeding was staunched, but his heart was lurching. Candle worked at her throat, trying to scream for help, but she could not make that strong a sound.

No, she thought, the poor cold boy, no. Not this.

She put her domingon down and rubbed his shoulders. Then she removed his splints and braces and massaged his arms and legs. The air was turning from chilly to icy, and the extra blankets were in the hallway, beyond the locked door. She felt something lurch in him—he, who had been absent for so long—something kicked and resisted the death that seemed to be settling upon him. His breath was halting. A long moment without a breath; another.

She leaned over his brow from above, and held his newly bearding cheeks in both hands, and laid her nose next to his, and breathed into him, and kissed him besides.

✦ ✦ ✦

"WELL, *THERE'S* SOMETHING FOR YOU, NOW," said Chyde. "It never hurts to read the small print, my lad. Jibbidee, my walking stick? And it's not even that far, though in a quarter I rarely get to visit myself. Let's go."

The elf came forward with a walking stick, and Chyde stood erect, or as erect as he could. Long years of desk work had crushed his hips cruelly, and his posture was poor. Still, at a new angle, he was able to look Liir over a bit more thoroughly than he'd yet managed.

"You hadn't ought to have arrived with a firearm," he said with sudden harshness. "You'll leave that with Jibbidee at once, my lad-ee-oh."

"It's no firearm. It's a broom."

"Show it me."

Liir opened the satchel and displayed the top end of the charred broom-pole.

"Let me see the length of it, to be sure it's not a blunder-bulleter in disguise."

The broom was withdrawn and Liir handed it over. "A right wreck of a thing, but for the new growth," said Chyde, handing it back.

"What?"

Liir didn't ask again, but felt it. The broom handle was notched with young nubs, and two of them had split, revealing modest embellishments of pale green leaf, like tiny rare broaches pinned to an old bit of scrap wood.

"It can't grow!" said Liir in amazement. "It can't do that."

"Put it away," said Chyde. "Some folks haven't seen a green leaf

✦ 116 ✦

growing in twenty years. You don't want to get them all weepy now, do you? Mercy is the name of the game in this trade." He kissed a vulgar emerald on the knuckle of his own middle finger, paying obeisance.

They set off, not in the direction of the waterway, but along a broad passage that served as a commercial parade for the underground settlement. More humans in evidence now, part of the vast employment network that kept Southstairs running, though the shops and stalls were largely staffed by elves who seemed to have raised obsequiousness to an art form. Here and there, the nice contrast of a grumpy dwarf. The noise was ordinary chatter and gossip, and it was some time before Liir realized what made it seem strange. For once, there was no little strain of music playing off to one side. Well, who would play music in a prison, after all?

The roofs of the cavern rose higher overhead, passing out of view into darkness. More of the structures were freestanding, supplied with their own tiled roofs, like buildings on any aboveground street. It felt like a city of the dead. Eventually Liir could see why: this must be the oldest district in Southstairs. It certainly seemed the most decrepit, so far. Above it, all at once, the claustrophobic blackness of cave-dark gave way to the blackness of a different sort: a moonless night, with scratchy scarves of cloud being drawn by the wind across ancient, disaffected stars. It was the middle of Southstairs, the original geologic bucket that must have suggested itself as a natural prison to the first settlers of the Emerald City.

"Stars, they give me the creeps," said Chyde. "I hate to come this way."

They found a set of steps leading farther down. Chyde asked for directions once or twice, and sent Jibbidee scampering to check the marks on buildings. "This'll be it, I guess," he said. "It's an Animal district, so you'll forgive the stench. Hygiene isn't their strong suit, as you know."

The air was so cold, though, with a wind whipping in from above, that the smell seemed negligible. At any rate, Liir was too excited to care. He found himself bobbing up and down, and once he nearly grabbed Chyde's hand to squeeze it. So what that Shell was a bounder, that Lady Glinda was a glamorous airhead! They'd done something good; he'd gotten here. He'd find her, his only peer and friendmate, his half-sister if that version of history was true—the girl who befriended mice, and shared her gingerbread, and who had giggled at bedtime, even when threatened by a spanking. He would liberate Nor, and then—and then—

He couldn't think beyond that. Just to see her, someone he had known once, back when the world had been something other than tragic, back when Elphaba had been stalking about the castle out west in her robes and rages! Back when home was still home!

Jibbidee skittered forward, back, anxious and irritable. "What, what's the matter, thingy?" asked Chyde. "Cat got your tongue? Ha-ha." He turned to Liir. "It did, you know. That's why he can't talk. It'll grow back in time, but at the moment it's a bloody little stump."

They pressed into a building, more a pen than a set of salons. A Sow was lying in straw trying to warm some Piglets, most of whom looked to be dead. Improbably, the runt had survived, but it was not long for this world.

Chyde voiced what Liir was himself wondering. "An odd place to put a girl child. What was I thinking of? You. Sow. We're looking for a girl, a human girl child. Name of Nor. The register puts her in this unlikely spot."

"She had some developmental problems," explained the Sow without opening her eyes. "Some lodgings coordinator decided that, among the likes of me and mine, she wouldn't seem as offensive."

"Where is she?"

"I would construct a good story if I had the strength," said the Sow, "but I'm conserving what energy I have left for my litter. In fact, the girl's own story is good enough. Do you remember when the butchers came through a week or ten days ago to cull the crop because a roast of loin was required? Some celebration Upside. It was the Wizard's deposal, wasn't it?"

Chyde looked slantwise at Liir. "We don't sacrifice Animals for ceremonial meals, don't be silly," he said hastily. "You're talking through your postdelivery deliriums, Sow." He twisted rings on his fingers, turning some jewels palmward, other jewels out.

"Whatever," she said. "My deliriums remind me about a couple of

Horned Hogs, long in the tooth if they'd still had teeth, who were going to make better rump roasts this year than next, I'll tell you. They knew their days were numbered. One of them had broken off a horn trying to escape, and the bone spur was sharp and useful. Didn't you read the report on this?"

"I've fallen behind. Terrible workload, and no one to pick up the slack. Jibbidee's next to useless. Where is the girl, that's what I want to know."

"I'm telling you. The Hogs entered a kind of suicide pact, and the bull killed the bitch and then himself. They arranged it to be done on the same slab of old door on which they'd have been carried out for slaughtering anyway. A kind of final comment on the quality of life at Southstairs."

"Only the best is good enough," said Chyde.

"So they let themselves putrefy, and we neighbors left them to it for as long as we could stand it. It bought us all some time. But you know as well as I that the entrails of Horned Hogs breed a kind of maggot that likes to burrow into human orifices, especially the airless ones—"

"Stop . . ."

"And there's little less airless than Southstairs—"

"I don't want to hear about it—"

"So your colleagues had to cart the carcasses Upside. They had no choice."

Chyde said softly, "You'll get a huge extra bucket of slops for this. Keep on."

"I had no way of suspecting that the poor suckling Nor had a functioning brain left in her skull," said the Sow. "But apparently she did. She climbed onto the door-slab and pulled the Hog carcasses over her. I certainly hope for her sake she plugged all her valves. I saw her chewing candlewax once, so maybe she was softening it for just such a purpose. Anyway, hidden by corpses, she was carried away a few days ago, though what happened to her once she left our happy home I can't say."

"The very least of my concerns," said Chyde. He glanced at Liir, who was tremblingly pale and gulping for air. "You take it so hard, lad? Why is that? Sounds like she got out—something you'd never have persuaded me into allowing. Don't weep, silly boy." Then he said, "Jibbidee. The runt."

"Oh no you don't," said the Sow, struggling to her feet. The elf was defter, though, and he had scrabbled over the boards and across the straw, and snatched the Piglet before the Sow could position herself in full defense. "You bastard!" she cried.

"I've been remiss; I haven't noticed. Poor Sow: You've far too much on your mind. This should relieve you of distractions." Chyde grabbed the squealing Piglet from the elf and hurled it against a beam. His aim was true; the blood spattered and the body fell with a thud into the slop trough.

In shock Liir fell against the fence, and the maddened Sow went for him, but Chyde, laughing, pulled the boy away in time. "You should've let someone know these shenanigans were going on," he said to the Sow. "Being a squealer isn't such a bad thing in a Pig. And we all have to do our duty—you, me, and the least little daisy in the field. Eh? Eh?"

◆ 8 ◆

THE PANTHER HAD GONE as far as she would go, and turned back. Now the canopy of oakhair limbs formed over their heads. In the short time that they'd been away from the mauntery, however, the wind had scoured the trees of their last leaves. The jackal moon, though sinking toward the horizon, still watched Sister Doctor and Sister Apothecaire as their high-rumped skarks fleet-footed it through the forest. The unnamed creatures still circled overhead, following their progress.

"I could use a moment to pee," called Sister Apothecaire at one point. "A Munchkin woman doesn't have as large a bladder as some others."

"Winter wolves come out at dawn," Sister Doctor replied, "so shut up and hold your bladder if you can, or pee in your saddle."

+ 9 +

CANDLE HAD SEEN ENOUGH OF DEATH to know that Liir was about to die. She was breathing him and kissing him as best she could, rubbing his limbs to encourage what warmth remained. His scalp was like ice. She took off her underskirts and tried to wrap them like a turban around his head, to keep his brain alive. From time to time she went and kicked against the door, hoping to arouse some maunt doing midnight devotions, but she couldn't keep up the effort. She couldn't stay away from him. As he grew more distant and colder, she grew warmer in her panic, and climbed atop him and tried to rescue him with her own warmth. She kissed him and licked his eyelids as a cat might, trying to open them. She didn't know what his eyes looked like, even, and she was stretched naked upon him like a wife.

+   +   +

LIIR BROKE AWAY FROM CHYDE, stumbling, his eyes shut against the tears and the memory of the blameless Piglet. Just like that, without cause! What then, thinking they had some cause, might they have done to Nor?

"Be it on your own head if you get lost down here," called Chyde, not much alarmed. "You won't get far, and there's none to help. Come back to headquarters when you've had enough wheeling about and I'll get you a hot meal. There's no reason for me to be inhospitable, you being a guest of Lady Glinda and all. I'm not unreasonable. I live to serve, as my dear former wife always knew me to say."

Liir lurched, first running, then sinking almost to his knees and catching himself, then running again. He didn't know how to find the waterway on which he and Shell had arrived. He threw down his torch, hoping it would catch something on fire and turn the place into the hell it seemed, but the torch only rolled once or twice and then dropped into a canal. There it sizzled out, and the stick bobbed like a hard new turd.

The dark was less intense, though, than he'd reckoned on, and in a moment he thought to look around. He was in a small square of faceless buildings, just a few bolted doors, possibly a warehouse district. It was empty of pedestrians and fairly quiet, too, as this place went, and above him was a scatter of starry deep.

His only thought was that there was nothing left, nothing to live for, nothing to wait for, nothing to remember. The stars were cold and he couldn't leap to grasp them, to pass fist over fist along their lofty network of knobs, arrive someplace new, and, if not safe, at least less heinous. They merely mocked, as stars were created to do.

He hugged himself, for here the wind swept in without interference. He pulled the cape like a blanket about him, and clutched the broom as if it were the Piglet, and he could will it back to life. His tears came hot and desperate, the only warmth in the universe.

The broom twitched once or twice, and he took it out of the satchel. It shook itself slightly, and seemed firmer in his grasp. The old dusty straws at the back end, bound in a bristly fagot for sweeping so long ago, were freshened with green—even in this starry half-light he could see the color. Cattails, or grass tips in seed, something like that. He didn't know the plant.

He threw his leg over the broom without thinking and he held on tight, and he rode it up the draft from hell, and into the night.

+ 10 +

WHEN SHE HEARD THE KEY IN THE DOOR OPEN, she came to her senses, and collected her hair from where it had spilled across his face, and climbed down.

Mother Yackle was smiling almost as if she had a sensible thought in her head, though according to the other novices Mother Yackle had been senile for as long as anyone could remember. The old crippled creature pulled the door aside and dropped her head, as if affording Candle some privacy as she composed herself.

Liir stirred, and sighed. Though his eyes remained closed, the lids both twitched, just faintly. One hand clenched, then released.

By the time the jackal moon was gone for another generation, and the Superior Maunt and her returning agents, Sisters Doctor and Apothecaire, had made it up the steps to the infirmary, Liir and Candle were gone, too.

The Service

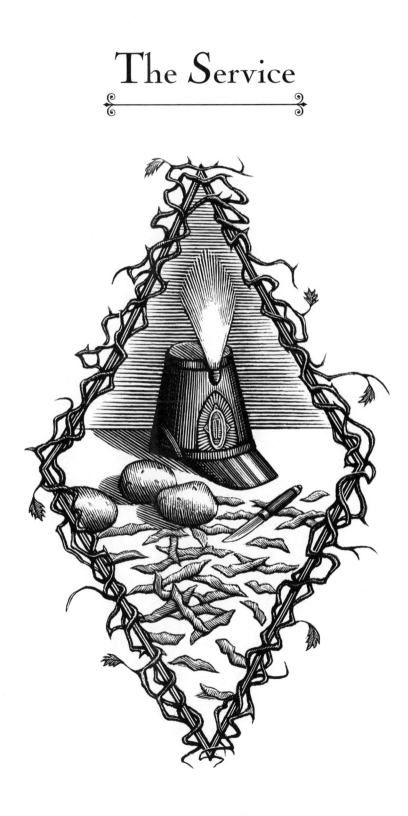

A NOTION OF CHARACTER, not so much discredited as simply forgotten, once held that people only came into themselves partway through their lives. They woke up, were they lucky enough to have consciousness, in the act of doing something they already knew how to do: feeding themselves with currants. Walking the dog. Knotting up a broken bootlace. Singing antiphonally in the choir. Suddenly: This is I, I am the girl singing this alto line off-key, I am the boy loping after the dog, and I can see myself doing it as, presumably, the dog cannot see itself. How peculiar! I lift on my toes at the end of the dock, to dive into the lake because I am hot, and while isolated like a specimen in the glassy slide of summer, the notions of *hot* and *lake* and *I* converge into a consciousness of consciousness—in an instant, in between launch and landing, even before I cannonball into the lake, shattering both my reflection and my old notion of myself.

That was what was once believed. Now, it seems hardly to matter when and how we become ourselves—or even what we become. Theory chases theory about how we are composed. The only constant: the abjuration of personal responsibility.

We are the next thing the Time Dragon is dreaming, and nothing to be done about it.

We are the fanciful sketch of wry Lurline, we are droll and ornamental, and no more culpable than a sprig of lavender or a sprig of light-ning, and nothing to be done about it.

We are an experiment in situation ethics set by the Unnamed God, which in keeping its identity secret also cloaks the scope of the experi-ment and our chances of success or failure at it—and nothing to be done about it.

We are loping sequences of chemical conversions, acting ourselves converted. We are twists of genes acting ourselves twisted; we are wicks of burning neuroses acting ourselves wicked. And nothing to be done about it. And nothing to be done about it.

IN SOME MORE HUMBLE QUARTERS of Oz, gossip had long held that El-phaba Thropp, the Wicked Witch of the West, had been born a wise soul, already formed, somehow conscious. Why else the mouthful of sharp choppers, not so much baby pearls as python's teeth, which some folk insisted she'd sported at birth? She came into the world with ad-vance knowledge of its corruption, and in the womb she had prepared for it as best she could, by growing those teeth.

That was what was said, anyway.

Not everyone is born a witch or a saint. Not everyone is born tal-ented, or crooked, or blessed; some are born definite in no particular at all. We are a fountain of shimmering contradictions, most of us. Beauti-ful in the concept, if we're lucky, but frequently tedious or regrettable as we flesh ourselves out.

The governesses of the monied classes often held that a child ought to be kept from witnessing cruelty and ugliness, the better to preserve some ounce of innocence. Rural grannies and spinster aunts—like the Nanny who had helped raise Elphaba—neither mollied nor coddled. They be-lieved it was better for a child to know what befalls a chicken when the feast of Lurlinemas rolls around. Better to learn—from a distance—the tricks perpetrated on the weak, the distractible, the unlucky.

Both pedagogical stances, however, relied on a common assumption. Growth and change were viewed as a reaction to conditions met. One might as easily argue, however, that it is the world's obligation to respond to children. By force of personality, by dint of their vicious beauty and untamed ways, children tromp into the world ready to disfigure it. Children surrender nothing when faced with the world: it is the world that gives up, over and over again. By so giving up, of course, it renews itself—that is the secret. Dying in order to live, that sort of thing.

You could catalog the thousand ways people shrink from life, as if chance and change are by their nature toxic, disfiguring. Elphaba, with her sympathies far more substantial than her luck, had at least wrestled with the questions. She'd shoved, and barked, and made herself a right nuisance.

By contrast, the Quadling girl, Candle, was an interpreter savant, translating the text of a world whose fundamental nature she hadn't yet grasped, and maybe never would. Did the difference between an Elphaba and a Candle come down merely to a question of focal depth: the big picture versus the little picture?

For his part, Liir had not been a bright child. Even on the edge of puberty he had given little thought to the paradoxes of his existence. He had imagined himself to be more like Chistery, the chief Snow Monkey, than like Nor and her brothers, Irji and Manek. Chistery had a slipsy-doodle sense of language, but he tended toward steadiness. He did his chores without complaining or forgetting, and asked for nothing beyond his basic needs. Even at fourteen, Liir hadn't been much more demanding than Chistery.

But Liir remembered that Nor had addressed the stars, had sung harmony with mountain streams, had loved all creatures whether their initial letters were written Great or small—Animal or animal. She was nuts as a nut tree in a nut forest, of course: that was what he had thought without realizing he was thinking anything at all. That silly Nor was a creature apart. Not just as a girl—though that, too, of course—but as a fragment of human possibility. She had had a sympathetic imagination, and Liir?—he could barely count.

Children often define themselves in relation to their parents: emulating them or working hard as possible to avoid resembling them in any way. Since the identity of both his parents was in doubt, Liir couldn't see himself as taking after anyone for sure. Certainly not Elphaba. In her final months, stooped, crabbed, scrabbling from desk to podium to window ledge, she was more like a quivering scorpion than a woman. At rest her fingers tended to curl up like a claw, or like the petals of a flower gone a bit blowsy: her hand was always out, always open, ready to take what found its way there and seize it. Not at all like Liir, who cowered.

Among the human kind, thought even the most jaded and bitter of Animals, there are many ways to be wrong, but there are only a relatively few ways to be young. In their generous apprehension of the world, for their insatiable appetite for the world, the young are to be forgiven.

SOMEWHERE IN THE SULFUROUS UPDRAFT above the great maw of Southstairs, Liir was born out of a dark vile womb and thrown into the night. He came into himself perched on a broomstick dozens of yards above the highest watchtower. Here was a cushion of wind, billowing him almost onto his side, causing his shins to tighten automatically against each other, his arms instinctively to wrap the broomstick harder. It was Liir and wind and height and stars, it was alone and alone and alone; the understandings were distinct and differentiated, and then suddenly annealed by a process he couldn't name. Maybe fear of heights! His *Liirness* applied, suddenly, applied to himself and no one else.

He didn't know what *Liirness* might mean, and he was sorry Elphaba wasn't around to raise a mocking eyebrow and sling a caustic remark. He might have been hurt by her sly digs, but he could have relished that hurt, too—he saw now. Survived it? Transformed it?

A hurting Liir was a real Liir.

However he'd come to be here—settling on an unstable bolster of thermal, learning to slide up the banister of the night—there was no else doing it but Liir.

The Emerald City gaped at him, but it didn't understand what it saw. He was just a touch of ash from a hearty fire, a scrap of tinder tossed in the winds. Winds that were damned strong; they snatched at the hem of his cape and unrolled it off his shoulders until it trailed behind him, a stain.

For his part, he saw the City the way few others had. Well, Elphaba must have! And anyone lucky enough to harness a Pfenix, that rare creature. The view was like a model of a city made with an impossibly deft hand—hundreds and hundreds of buildings, grand and humble, glazed with tile and black with soot. A city built on a gentle rise, he could now see: long slicing boulevards and curving promenades, a honeycomb of streets and canals, parks and squares, a thousand mews, ten thousand alleys, a hundred thousand windows blinking bronzely. A glowing organ, like the illuminated heart of Oz itself pushed through the flesh of the land, pulsing with its own life, tricked out with monuments, defaced with the graffiti of broken trees, the Palace of the Wizard a cancer upon the landscape, the dead center of it all.

In his grief at having missed a chance to save Nor, and his shock of the unanticipated flight, and the confusion about what to do next, he was more successively Liir with every breath.

He circled the Emerald City, afraid if he landed he would return to being slightly dead. How could anyone live without flying?

So the boyhood of Liir began—began in a new way, as if all that had gone before had happened to someone else.

But it seemed amazing to him that he'd had the courage to set out cross-country with that Dorothy. Was it courage? Perhaps it had only been sheer ignorance of the breadth and treachery of the world.

The broom brought him to ground on the cobblestoned quay near one of the smaller canals. The wind was strong, so itinerants were huddled face-front around brazier fires made of scrap wood and boards ripped from fences. No one saw him land.

Bravado was not what he felt; but he felt something, and that was rare enough. A cold sense of thrill: absorbing the news of Nor's escape, her being alive. Wounded, cursed, embattled—alive nonetheless.

He walked for a while along the quay but realized it was colder there, and ducked into an alley. The broom on his shoulder bounced as he walked and looked for a place to doss down. It bounced harder, as if thwacking him with congratulations, but this was silly: he was walking with a spring in his step.

After a while he just jumped, six, eight times in a row, in glee, like a kid playing Hoptoad Hoptoad Call My Hoptoad. He'd look a right idiot to anyone peering out a window, but he didn't care.

A GOOD NIGHT'S sleep under a rubble of marketplace hay neither dampened his spirits nor inspired him with a plan. Eventually he made it back to Lady Glinda's town house in Mennipin Square. Perhaps she could arrange another meeting with Commander Cherrystone, who might be able to find out what had happened when Nor had had herself secreted upstairs. Or maybe Lady Glinda had an opening for a bootblack or a son.

The houseboy who had first talked to Liir reported that Lady Glinda had repaired to Mockbeggar Hall, the Chuffrey country pile near Restwater, there to do good works among the rural poor. It pleased her to dispense largesse from time to time. It calmed her nerves and made her happier with her marriage. She'd brought her cabinet with her, hoping that some grouse hunting of a sunny afternoon would breed camaraderie and unity of purpose, or if not, that one or two of the more difficult ministers might be shot accidentally in a convenient hunting accident. More than one kind of grouse needs bringing down!

That was how the houseboy put it, anyway—with high knowingness. No, there was no way to say when Her Ladyship might return. In her absence, the household was investing in a pack of howling Bratweilers, which as a breed was not known for its docile disposition. And take off that suit of livery, by the by, lest the house of Chuffrey be besmirched by whatever smut you're about to get up to.

Liir was happy to oblige. His old garments, which had been placed in a bin for disposal, were dug out and tossed at him. Wriggling into them, Liir noticed an unfamiliar snugness. As if his limbs were lengthening after just one flight.

The rest of his life, and all its possibilities, were spread like a landscape before him, and he couldn't help taking in three or four breaths, keenly and quickly, to sample the day. The air was bracing and his blood quickened. He felt as lithe and full of ginger as that cunning Shell had seemed. Liir could commit a crime, or . . . or banter with fellows on the street . . . or wink at a girl and cadge a kiss. That's what people did. He could do that.

Soon. First he answered the summons of a carillon and presented himself on the broad steps of a church. He had a dim memory of mauntish prayers, but not of services, and this morning he felt worthy enough to feel humble. He would prostrate himself before whatever-it-was-inthere, and thank the Unnamed God for having brought him that close to Nor. And ask what next.

The doors were flung open and the service just starting. Was it a holiday, and he hadn't known? Or were churches in the Emerald City always this thronged? Peering between the unstooped shoulders of gentlemen standing in the vestibule, Liir caught sight of the wide, bright room, a preacher of some sort declaiming from a plinth to a sea of faces varnished with rapture or, at any rate, close attention.

"I'm sure our Unnamed God requires of us conviction and perseverance. I'm sure our Unnamed God grants us the privilege of obedience. In the face of uncertainty, the one thing we can be sure of is the value of certainty. And the Unnamed God bestows upon us the balm of certainty."

He's sure of a lot, thought Liir; how consoling to stand within the sound of such confidence. And the way he rolls "our Unnamed God" off his tongue—the *our* might as well be *my,* he's that well placed. People say "my God!" all the time, but usually they mean "oh shit." He means something better.

Liir stood on his toes. The homilist was an affable older man, neither handsome nor plain—rather forgettable, but radiant with the effort of explaining the Unnamed God to all these devout, and devoutly interested, people. He looked a bit like an animated puppet, tufts of hair behind his ears taking a red tint from the colored windows behind him. "Let us continue this celebration of Thanksgiving for our deliverance from the Witch. Our independence from the Wizard and our relief from the Witch bring all of Oz to a new chance for greatness. Miss Grayling will lead us in Anthem Eleven: 'One Truth, One Truth Alone.'"

He wasn't sure he'd heard correctly. The room was so very crowded, and now skirts rustled and scratched, boots scuffled, as people rose to sing. He didn't know the anthem but the refrain was simple enough.

> *"One truth alone we hear:*
> *Your secret holy plan.*
> *With so much yet to fear,*
> *We trust what truth we can."*

The choir sang an unintelligible verse and the chorus began again, and this time Liir tried to join in, but an usher grabbed him by the collar and sidled him backward over the threshold.

"I know what you're after," said the usher. "Any cash in these pockets goes into the collection plate."

"I'm not a pickpocket," said Liir.

"Oh? You didn't exactly dress for the service." The usher had a point. Compared to the pious at noisy prayer, Liir looked like a peasant. "Catch you inside again, I'll alert the constable, who's sitting in the back row on the ready."

"Sorry," said Liir. But he found he could listen from the top step almost as well, and the air was nicer outside anyway—not so clotted with perfume and incense.

At the base of the wide stairs loitered a group of urchins, the oldest at least four or five years younger than Liir. They looked up at him as if he were one of them. "You don't go in either?" he asked them.

"Never had a chance," said one; "Never wanted a chance," added another.

"What're you doing here?"

"Charity pennies when the service lets out, stupid."

"Oh. Right. Don't you get cold?"

"No," said a small girl missing some front teeth. "We fights a lot to keep warm."

"It's a good song," said Liir. "Can you hear it from down there?"

"Don't know hymny-singing."

He began to hum the melody and came down a few steps. "One

truth alone we hear," he said with bright enunciation, "your secret holy plan."

They liked the sound of a secret holy plan. "What is it?" said the gap-toothed girl.

"It's secret, stupid," said the older boy.

"Shut up," said Liir, happy to be bringing joy and religion to the masses. "Your secret holy plan . . . get it? Da da da something, we trust what truth we can. Now there'll be another verse and they'll start over. Everyone ready?"

"You're a ragamuffin cleric," said an older girl, but she sang when the chorus came around again, and the others chimed in with more gusto than grace until the usher came out with the constable, and they all had to scatter.

"Thanks," said the urchin leader, "now we got a song, but we got no breakfasts. Come on, looters; we'll go steal bread from the pigeons near the Ozma Fountains."

"Surely there'll be more food to go around," said Liir. "I mean now the Wizard is deposed."

The kids ran and laughed, as all kids can, even malnourished urchins. "What, because he's not around to eat his own portion? We'll see about that!"

Undaunted, Liir wandered about until he came to a small hostelry. A sign read SURGERY FOR THE SENSELESS, and beneath that hung a wooden image of scissors in the act of snipping off the heads of a bunch of daisies.

This time he knew enough not to go in the front door but to wander the alley behind till he found another entrance. A graceful young woman in a dotted purple cloak came to the door when he knocked. "I'm looking for an Arjiki girl, about sixteen, newly sprung from prison, and possibly in poor health. Would she have come here?"

"We tend the wrinklies here."

"Well, then," he ventured, "I'm here to offer my services."

"We have no budget for a houseboy."

"I don't need funds. Just a place to sleep and something to eat from time to time. I can help take care of the senseless. I had an old Nanny who needed all kinds of assistance, and I know how. I don't mind."

"When we're through with them, they don't need much help," said the woman. "They don't care so much what goes right or wrong for them anymore, and that's a blessing, don't you think?"

"I suppose so. I'm merely looking to be of service," he explained. *My life started today,* he wanted to add, but she looked too cross to take it all in.

"I wouldn't be surprised if the solicitor sent you to spy on us," she replied. "We doctor the patients, not their last wills and testaments. We've been cleared of suspicion any number of times. Why are you tormenting us? Isn't there supposed to be some relief of oppression now that the Wizardic administration has left the Palace?"

"I'm not from the Palace," he said, affronted partly, but also impressed: could he seem that old and competent already?

"If you don't go away I'll set the cat on you." She pulled down her sleeve; her left arm was raw with swellings and scabs. "Unlike some, he's not very nice since he's been neutered," she said ominously. Liir had the feeling that if there was a cat in the house, it was really a Cat. He backed off.

"I couldn't just come in and get warm?" he began, but she had shut the door.

DAYS WENT BY, and he was glad to have learned about the stale bread fed to the pigeons at the Ozma Fountains. He kept body and soul together there. Scrambling for food, he wasn't as nimble as some of the street dodgers, but his legs were longer, so he made out all right. At night he had the benefit of the cape as a blanket, so he was warmer than some.

He asked about Nor, but the City was filled with itinerant children, and to the good burghers of Oz, tinker children were anonymous when they weren't invisible. No one had noticed an Arjiki girl on her own, and push off, you, before we call the authorities.

He thought about Princess Nastoya, but what could he do? The famous Wizard of Oz, granter of wishes, wasn't going to stage a comeback just so Liir could beg for help for that old She-Elephant. And there was no one else to ask.

Determined not to be cowed, Liir took to hanging around the army barracks just inside the south gate, known as Munchkin Mousehole, a reference to the diminutive stature of Munchkinlanders. The Emerald City Home Guard was better fed than the poor under the bridges, that much was obvious. After a while Liir decided that membership in the Home Guard would relieve his hunger while he tried to decide what to do next. And maybe he'd find that devoting his life to service paid dividends.

Stuffing the old cape in a sack, pressing it as compacted as he could manage, Liir joined the throng of roughhouse boys on the parade grounds—the boys who played gooseball with soldiers at free exercise. The lads hoped to merit the gift of a cracker or a coin or a plug of tobacco, but Liir wanted more. He bade his time and steeled his nerve.

One afternoon a sudden hailstorm blew in from the Kells. Everyone scattered for cover. Liir ducked into a narrow archway hardly large enough to protect one. The soldier already there couldn't be more than a year or two older than Liir, and so they fell into conversation as they waited out the storm.

The soldier, proud of his stature as Petty Fife in the Guard's musical corps, told Liir where and how to apply, and what to say that would amuse the conscripting officers. "Don't tell them you don't know who your parents are," he advised. "The officers are a high-strung bunch. They think that all the orphans who apply are really sent there by their parents, infiltrating the Guard for an eventual insurrection. If you're really an orphan, lie. Tell them your folks can't keep from screwing and they just had their twelfth baby, and you were kicked out of the family sty. That they'd understand; they're screw-starved here, a lot of them."

In time, Liir followed the advice, and learned it was sound. Though eight other gaunt-cheeked boys presented themselves in the same audience, only Liir answered smartly enough to be signed up. He was given a number, a cot, a cabin, a chit for meals, a key, a position title—Second Scrub—and a job, doing just that: potatoes in the commissary kitchen, morning, noon, and evening. The Home Guard ate little but potatoes, it seemed.

Still, there he was! Here he was! It seemed too good to be true. A smart uniform—someone else's before it was his, for a few old stains hadn't entirely washed out, and one sleeve had been replaced with a new one cut from a cheaper weight of broadcloth—but smart just the same. It came with a cap sporting a stiff silly brim in front, and a cocky periwinkle-colored tuft up top. The outfiteer also located a pair of boots, down at the heel and splayed at the toe, but serviceable enough, for they were conveniently overlarge and could take an extra pair of socks in the toe, which kept out the cold.

Once in a while Liir caught sight of the chatty fellow who had befriended him in the archway, but that soldier was assigned to a different division. In any case, Liir was determined to maintain a comfortable anonymity, so he didn't go chasing for friends, neither in his own division nor beyond it.

One morning in the yard, when Liir was hauling sacks of potatoes from a delivery cart, he spotted Commander Cherrystone arriving in a brougham. The man appeared weary. Liir hung back and kept silent, but he invented reasons to linger in the area. He watched as the Commander spoke with a sergeant at arms. The Commander took a cup of coffee in a china cup and reviewed a construction site marked out for a new latrine or barracks or something. He then disappeared into a foreman's shed with a roll of schemes under his arm.

An hour or so later he emerged, a cigarette between his gloved fingers. Liir approached Commander Cherrystone and reintroduced himself, a new politeness and reserve hiding what remained of his disapproval. Cherrystone might still be helpful.

"Yes, yes," said the Commander, distracted. Liir wasn't even sure Cherrystone remembered him, but the commander listened politely and said he would try to find out what he could about the details of carcass removal at Southstairs. "You mustn't hold your breath though," he said. "I've a lot on my plate. There is much to be done for the defense of our city."

"There is? But we're not at war? I thought peace was at hand."

"Your highborn champion, Lady Glinda, thinks all is peaches and cream. She'd like it to be. But given the uncertainty of the political situation, the economy needs stimulus, and the threat of war is a great incentive to spend. Fiscal frottage."

Liir didn't know what this meant. But things did seem to be happening. For weeks, and then for months, he fed potatoes to the burly soldiers who dug and hauled the earth away from the building site, and eventually began the even harder work of setting colossal foundation stones in place. Liir was glad he was a slender thing, for he was better suited to kitchen work than transporting boulders. But slowly he deduced that, despite his nothing childhood in the nowhere mountains, he wasn't quite as obtuse as he'd imagined.

He had no reason for smugness about it, to be sure. He was a bumpkin when it came to national affairs. He'd had little schooling and less practice at rhetoric. He didn't venture an opinion about current affairs, for he hardly knew what they were. No one bothered to circulate news broadsides in the barracks, and the banter at mealtime boasted about whores and sores. Period.

What Liir discovered, rather, was that merely by hanging around in the company of Elphaba he had picked up—something. Not power, not intuition, which she seemed to have down to her very eyelash. Not understanding. But something else—a good ear, anyway. Would he could find a way to perform a spell! That was the ultimate competence with language, a skill Elphaba had had in spades, and that she used rarely and reluctantly. What is a spell after all but a way of coaxing syllables together so persuasively that some new word is spelled . . . some imprecision clarified, some name Named . . . and some change managed.

Despite his flight on the broom, Liir was sure he had no instinct for magic. It was the broom that had managed that feat: he'd gone for the ride, nothing more. If he'd ever felt the slightest tremor of intuition or capacity, he'd have pounced on it like a cat on a rat. No, he was duller than the other kitchen lads even about basic things. He couldn't even predict when he was going to need to use the latrine.

But he found himself rounding syllables like stones in his mouth, silently. He knew he was shy, and thought to be stupid; he was beginning to suspect, though, that he wasn't stupid. Perhaps not even slow. Merely uneducated. But not, he hoped, uneducable.

COMMANDER CHERRYSTONE DIDN'T COME seeking out Liir to answer his question about Nor. When several more weeks had passed and there was no sign of the Commander again, and no message passed on by his aide-de-camp, Liir began to press the issue to others in the Home Guard. Cautiously he started to circulate a scrap of gossip he had invented. A pair of Horned Hogs was slain in Southstairs—*because the Hogs were magic.* Their carcasses were removed before they could contaminate the other inmates with sorceric powers. Could it be? The kitchen boys, hungry for tales of enchantment, took up the story as if it were gospel. Liir hoped his invention would trip a rebuttal, turning up some useful information about the actual disposition of the Hogs—and by extension, suggest Nor's next whereabouts. But revelation was slow in coming.

The winter crashed in with icy spite. His hands turned red and chilblained from the water into which the potatoes dropped. At least he wasn't freezing or starving to death outside; snow was felling dozens. He bade his time. He was glad he got to feed the fellows who worked at the construction. They had finished shunting boulders onto the site, but even in this cold they were required to lift and set, plumb and point. They got little relief from the cold.

The Home Guard guessed they were building yet larger barracks, as if the numbers of the force might swell sometime soon. Or perhaps warehouses for the defensive artillery supposedly under development. During a thaw, a steep roof was framed and shingled; when the snows returned, the interior was roughed in at a rapid rate. Before long a unionist cleric, his ceremonial garments hidden beneath heavy fur robes, appeared on its steps. With smoking urns and hallowed gestures he signaled the Unnamed God, and the unfinished place was consecrated as a basilica.

The basilica was more or less functional by Lurlinemas. True, the pagan cult of Lurline, the sprite said by some to have founded Oz, was out of favor; few but illiterate country folk paid obeisance to Lurline anymore. But the celebration of that old holiday was still popular. Lurlinism had been quietly absorbed into the common culture, not least because the cash tills splashed with money during the festive season.

Lurlinemas made a welcome distraction from the anxiety about leadership that seemed still to grip Oz, even though the Wizard was now gone half a year. Holiday presents came in on all sides for everyone but Liir. He had prepared a story about his parents' fierce devotion to unionism and their rejection of the heathen custom, but he didn't need to lie: no one asked him about the absence of gifts by his bunk. His mates received parcels in gilt paper, silly trinkets, useful clothes, small wallets of cash scented with cloves. He remembered the time Nor had given him the tail of her gingerbread mouse, and his mouth watered, but he swallowed it down.

The basilica was large enough to hold nearly a thousand at a time, so everyone got to attend the strictly unionist service on Lurlinemas. Liir saw Commander Cherrystone in the front.

A visiting chaplain with an ungainly flapping lip pulled himself into the pulpit and intoned the beginning of a homily. The sung petition petered out into a tirade against the loose morals of the day. Most of the soldiers went instantly to sleep, propping one another up on the benches, but Liir still had had so little exposure to homiletics that he sat straight up and listened. The preacher, perhaps sensing that someone midway down the room on the left was actually paying attention, began to improve.

The minister gripped the edges of the lectern and swayed sideways. "At every stage, even in the decorous and seemly home that the army provides you here, weird rumors of magical uprisings spring up! Like weevils in the wheat, like maggots in the rump roast!" Either his raised voice or the mention of magic stirred the morning crowd awake.

In order to challenge the blasphemous apocrypha, the minister repeated some stories being told and retold about town. "Magic's appeal is sheer pfaithism: the pleasure faith that attracts by the glitter of its surface," he railed. "Change a fish into a farthingale? Or a feather duster? All distraction! All sleight of skin! But change a fish into a fish fillet and feed your hungry mother: now, that's a magic we can applaud: the magic of human charity!"

Liir *was* ready to applaud. Who wouldn't? But no one else stirred, so he settled his hands back in his lap.

"Urban legends; they spring up when times are grim," continued the homilist. "That Ozma will return to govern the humble! That little toast roundlets spread with herbed goat cheese will fall in the desert and feed the starving! That Horned Hogs, in sacrificing themselves, will confer a magical immunity to residents of Southstairs and help them to survive their confinement!!"

Liir nearly jumped out of his seat.

"No, no," continued the minister. "The Ozma kidnapped years ago is dead in an unmarked grave, and her bones are halfway to dust. Toast roundlets don't fall in the desert unless you're in the final delirium of starvation, and they don't taste of much even then. Horned Hogs, when they die in Southstairs, are carted to Paupers' Field, and their corpses burned. Nothing of them remains, not a jot of magical comfort for any of the denizens of Southstairs. Better that prisoners should turn their wretched hearts to the Unnamed God, and beg forgiveness for even imagining such a farrago of faith!"

Paupers' Field, then. Liir committed it to memory. But he listened to the minister's address to the end, in case there was more to learn. The words rolled on, sonorously and as buoying, in their way, as the winds had been, the one night that Liir had ventured on the broomstick.

At the close of the service, Liir bravely pushed forward and touched the minister on the sleeve. The man—older than he'd appeared from below—turned wearily to look at Liir.

They exchanged a few words. Liir asked for instruction in unionism. He'd been moved by the remarks. He wondered aloud if escaping Kiamo Ko the way he did, even at the cost of Elphaba's death, had been the Unnamed God's way of getting Liir's attention. But the minister said, a bit too sharply, "Why? Have you seen or do you know of magic being done? Here? On the premises perhaps? Are you being tempted by the wrong forces? Explain, boy!" Liir was alarmed and shrank back. Foolish to have identified himself so! Shaking his head, he excused himself from the conversation and left.

It was too cold to venture out of the Guard yard. But the weeks would pass, the sun would wheel. When the worst of the season had slunk by, he would think up an excuse to skulk out to Paupers' Field. Learn what he could.

THE DAY DID COME, though not soon enough, and Liir made the trip swiftly, and only a little illegally. (Initially he had invented an ailing mother and a crippled father, and after he'd been in the Home Guard six months, he was given leave to carry them a few coins and a loaf of bread.) Apparently, though, his invention of the story of magic Horned Hogs had worked too well. The legend had spread through the urban population like news of a scandal, and pilgrims had begun to mass at the pyre of the Horned Hogs. The crematorium at Paupers' Field had had to be abandoned and demolished. The squatters whose tents had sprung up on the dreadful spot knew little of what had recently gone on there, and nothing of Horned Hogs, or if an escaped convict from Southstairs had been discovered.

Still, returning to base, Liir found himself less than distraught. If Nor had really had the invention and courage, even after those years, to secret herself out of Southstairs sandwiched between two slaughtered Hogs, she'd have managed somehow to find a warm place for the winter. Their reunion was ahead somewhere, waiting for them.

He would have faith in the Unnamed God, who even now was probably ordaining the right time and place in some secret holy plan. All Liir had to do was bide his time, do his work, peel his potatoes, keep his nose clean and his eyes open, and the UG, as Liir's barracks mates termed it, would tell him what to do next, and when to do it.

As to his hopes for helping Princess Nastoya—it wasn't going to happen. You didn't learn magic in the army. He had nothing to say to her, no way to give comfort. Probably she was dead already, anyway.

THERE WERE NEW HABITS to examine in the privacy of his bunk. Self amusement was the least of it: operating solo beneath the rough sheets was risky business in a dormitory setting, and his mates were always alert

to the cues that one of their number was finding himself hot and bothered, and doing something about it.

No, his secret distractions were acts of memory, flights of doubt,
even at times a feeble attempt at prayer. (He wondered why the chaplain
spent so much time discoursing on the value of prayer to the enlisted
man, yet never gave instruction in how prayer ought to be conducted.)

Deep in the funk given off by a dozen young men dozing in nearby
bunks, Liir itemized his attributes, and considered how they were being
heightened and strengthened by life in the barracks.

Rectitude, for one. Propriety. Custody of the senses!—that was how
he (mostly) resisted masturbation.

Also, Liir found he was developing a capacity for respect. The mark
of a soldier, of course. Back at Kiamo Ko, he hadn't been respectful—
he'd been ignorant and scared. There was a difference.

The army thrived on its *regulae*. Precision, obedience, and rightness
of thinking. Had Elphaba possessed any of those virtues? When she'd
been sloppy with emotion, vivid with rage or grief—which was most of
the time—she hadn't kept to a schedule. Coffee at midnight, waking up
the others by slamming the larder door looking for cream! Lunch at sunset, bread crumbs on the harpsiclavier keys. Pelting through the gates of
the castle, in any weather, at any hour, no matter if Liir had just laid out
a couple of coddled eggs for her. Studying the night through, getting excited, reading things from that—that *book* of hers—out loud, to hear
how they went, to hear how they sounded. Waking Chistery on his
perch at the top of the wardrobe. Impetuous and selfish, totally selfish.
How had he not seen it?

She was obedient—yes—to herself. Though what good had that
done her—or anyone else? So far as he could remember—and he spent
some wakeful nights examining his recollections carefully—she had
rarely asked anything of Liir except that he keep himself safe.

And certainly she'd never asked him to be obedient. How was one
to learn obedience unless one was thwacked into line? He'd been left
alone, to roam the dusty corridors with Nor and her brothers. He'd
picked up reading almost by accident. He'd been clothed by Sarima's sisters, that clot of spinsters who had nothing better to do but brood and

bitch. Now, *there* was a group of responsible adults, he thought, though he found he couldn't actually remember their faces.

Still, he reminded himself, stiffly, to be kind. What did Elphaba know of child rearing? When he listened to his companions gossiping about their mothers—those cozy, pincushiony mamas, who never cuffed a child without a follow-up cuddle—he knew that nothing about Elphaba smacked of the maternal. Maybe this was all the proof he needed that she wasn't his mother, couldn't have been. She had had lots of power, in her own way, but she had no more motherly instinct than a berserk rhino.

Even a berserk rhino can bear a child, his deeper voice reminded him, till he told it to shut up.

MONTH AFTER MONTH, his days were spent in drilling. In learning to shoot. How to run holding a rifle without tripping on it and spearing himself. How to march in formation. (He didn't learn horsemanship, as the only soldiers permitted to ride were those who had brought their own mounts with them when they enlisted.)

How to wear his hair saucily, to thrill the maidens on the pavement.

How and when to salute, though not, precisely, why.

How to peel potatoes faster.

What was curiously obscure, Liir thought, was the nature of the menace that the Home Guard was formed to protect against. The commanding officers didn't reveal much about possible threats. When at ease in their dormitories or in the canteen, the enlisted men discussed the question.

Some felt the Home Guard existed to provide mortal comfort to the citizens of the Emerald City. Should the rabble ever rise up, should the denizens of Southstairs break free—hell, should a mighty comet thud into the Palace and burn it to blazes—the Home Guard would be right there, ready to restore order.

Others argued that the Home Guard wasn't a municipal police force but a defensive army. Before the Wizard's departure from the Palace, the province of Munchkinland had declared its autonomy as a Free State. Since the Emerald City's main water supply, Restwater, fell wholly within Munchkinland's borders—to say nothing of the great arable reaches that fed the capital of Oz—hostilities were conducted primarily on the diplomatic level. It was inconceivable that the EC would retaliate against the upstart government in Center Munch; a full-scale civil war in Oz would imperil both the water and food supplies of the capital.

But what if Munchkinland raised an army? If such an army invaded the Emerald City, the Home Guard had to be ready to toss them out on their asses. So the drills were constant, the defenses shored up, and it was said that spies were kept busy trying to find out just what Munchkinlanders were up to.

"Spies," said Liir. It sounded lovely and sexy and dangerous.

Still, he supposed that it was good policy for the enlisted men not to know the precise reasons for their constant drilling. The information belonged to those wise enough to interpret it, and Liir knew this didn't include him.

HE LEARNED A LITTLE MORE when he and five others were singled out of a lineup one morning and told to wash and clothe themselves in their dress uniforms. "Palace detail," said the commanding officer.

Palace detail! How smart! He *was* moving up. Nose to the grindstone, eyes on the prize: it worked.

When Liir and his mates reported for duty, he realized why he'd been chosen. The detail involved six trim young men of identical height and build: two blond heads, two chestnut, two charcoal. Liir was one of the charcoals.

They were to accompany Lady Glinda and Lord Chuffrey into the House of Protocol, said the commander. There, the well-placed couple was being inducted in the ceremonial Order of the Right. The Lady Glinda was being thanked for her period of service to the country, and her husband for his own contributions. It was a high honor for the soldiers of the Home Guard to attend this ancient privilege of the just getting their just deserts, said the commander. So smarten up, top form, eyes front, chin high, buttocks in, shoulders back. The usual.

With his riding crop he smacked one of the blond heads. "You think this is the stables, you dolt? Get rid of that chewy pulp or I'll knock your teeth out your behind."

It is something to be charcoal-haired, anyway, thought Liir. Isn't it?

He'd see Lady Glinda again. That much was for sure. If he had no further campaign with her, at least he had a little history. And who knew? As the throne minister of Oz, perhaps she followed all things; maybe she'd remembered his quest for Nor, and had information for him that Cherrystone had never heard.

At the Palace, Commander Cherrystone caught his eye and winked. Liir and his five mates made a sort of human wallpaper, dazzling in their white sartorials and whitened boots, gold plumes splashing from their half-helmets, standing at the head of the aisle.

Lady Glinda walked a step or two ahead of her husband, greeting the cheering crowds with a rolling movement of her scepter. Her skin was firm and her chin up, and her eyes dazzled as they had done the first time Liir had seen her. She wore antique mettanite struts, and a tiara of cobalts and diamonds, and she advanced in her own warm front of orange blossom fog. Her face was trained on the crowd, giving them love, and when her eyes passed over Liir and he gulped and willed her to recognize him, she didn't.

Commander Cherrystone followed, pushing Lord Chuffrey in a wheeled chair. The nobleman's head was fastened peculiarly on his neck, as if it had come unfastened and been reattached by someone inadequate to the task. Chuffrey drooled on his epaulets. Attending like a nursemaid with impeccable references, Commander Cherrystone discreetly wiped away the spittle.

The ceremony was abbreviated due to Lord Chuffrey's obvious ill health. Perhaps he was dying and they were rushing through this convention as a thanks for all the good he and his bride had done the government. Which in Lord Chuffrey's case, if Liir understood the testimonial talks correctly, seemed to be a canny invention in the field of fiscal accounting that had helped the government avoid bankruptcy some years back. In Lady Glinda's case, it was her dazzling throne minister-ship, over all too soon, but the rewards to be reaped for years to come, and so on, and so on.

Glinda seemed to have learned how to control her blushing in public, or perhaps she just wasn't listening to the speeches.

Toward the end, when Liir's green eyes had begun to glaze over a bit, a rustle and hush in the peplums and fozzicles of the gentry caused Liir to turn ever so slightly to a side door. Supported on both sides by a pretty maiden, in came the Scarecrow himself. He looked greatly inebriated, or troubled by muscular atrophy; his limbs were akimbo and his eyes rolled like hard-boiled eggs on the spin.

At first Liir thought it was a joke, like a Fool at a sacred pageant. But the cornets trilled, and the great and good deigned to applaud. The Scarecrow gave a genuflection of such profound clumsiness that several of the Home Guard snorted. The Scarecrow said nothing, just waved, and Lady Glinda curtseyed, a cataract of tulle bunching in front and frothing around to the back.

The Scarecrow retreated. Liir felt cold and mean. The Scarecrow had been an obvious imposter—nothing like the Scarecrow Liir himself had walked with along the roads from Kiamo Ko. Couldn't they see it? Or were they complicit? Or maybe, in their eyes, one Scarecrow *did* look like every other Scarecrow.

The whereabouts of the real Scarecrow hardly bore imagining, now that Liir had seen the depths of Southstairs. Or perhaps, just perhaps, cannier than he'd ever let on, the real Scarecrow had managed to disappear himself somewhere. Good luck to him, in prison or in hiding.

Liir didn't pay attention to current affairs, generally, or not those beyond the intrigues within the barracks; he thought it beneath him to follow the details of how the civilian world amused itself. Was Lady Glinda stepping down willingly or had she been crowded out by some coalition of antagonists? The question occurred to him, but in dismissing it as meaningless, finally, Liir felt the first flush of adult apathy. It was welcome. About time.

At any rate, to be invisible to Lady Glinda and unrecognized by the next hollow head of Oz—it brought back to Liir the truth of his isolation. He wouldn't approach Glinda for news of Nor; he wouldn't stand the insult of having to reintroduce himself.

At length, the soldiers were shown a side room where they could nibble at dry crackers while Lord Chuffrey and Lady Glinda were received at a luncheon. To avoid possible stains on their dress sartorials, the soldiers were forbidden to drink anything but water. Liir was pissed at serving as a pretty accessory for Lady Glinda. He refused even the water.

When they saw the couple back to its carriage, Liir didn't even bother to let his eyes sweep over them. Should her eyes pick him out, now that the job was done, let her address him. But she didn't.

A YEAR PASSED, another. Nothing was the same, year by year, but little was different, either.

He found himself watching how the men consorted together, realizing long after it had begun that this was effectively his first experience of male behavior. Kiamo Ko had been unrelievedly female, at least in the adult generation; the shadowy presence of Fiyero, long lost husband and lover and father, was real but indistinct. Liir had learned nothing of how men speak, or joke, or trust, or fail to trust one another.

In the service, there were games, and Liir played hard and well. Formal clubs and socials, and he attended—stiffly. His work assignments gave order to his days and brought some satisfaction. He became known as a good listener, though this was mostly because he was unwilling to spill the beans about his quirky upbringing, and listening was easier than chatting.

Liir grew accustomed to his privacy. When furloughs were granted, he chose not to take advantage of them. Once he was invited to join a fellow cadet on a trip home to the family farm somewhere north of Shiz, in Gillikin. Liir had been tempted to accept. But the night before they were to leave, the cadet had a few too many. He began to carol about his doddery old daddums and the good little woman who'd married him and on and on and so forth.

"They're so proud of me. It's the best thing anyone in the family has ever done—to be selected a member of the Home Guard!"

Peculiarly undistinguished lot, Liir supposed.

Oh, said the cadet, but his mother's apple trickle could bring tears to the eye! Indeed, it brought tears to his, but Liir's eyes were stones. The next morning he told the headachy cad to go on without him; he'd changed his mind.

"You don't know what you're missing," said the cadet.

"I'd like to keep it that way."

The fellow returned with a sizable chunk of apple trickle wrapped in a checked cloth, and it was good. Too good, in a way; Liir had never tasted anything so wonderful. He resented every tasty crumb.

A few weeks later, when a commander's rifle had gone missing from the rack, Liir made an appointment to see the commander privately. He said he knew that the code of honor required him to speak. Deftly Liir laid suspicion on the shoulders of the Gillikinese cadet. The lad was hauled off into solitary for a few days. When he had not confessed in a week, he was stripped of his uniform and excused from service, dishonorably.

He never made it home, someone said later; he killed himself on the way. Hung himself in someone's back field, strung up on a black-trunk elm.

Nonsense, thought Liir; that's just army gossip. Who would bother to learn such specific details of a suicide of someone so patently soft and regrettable?

He sat in chapel. "Nothing convinces like conviction," thundered the minister, warning against softness, which when you came to think about it seemed like the UG's way of approving of Liir's maneuver. His own lack of remorse about it seemed authoritative in and of itself. When the rifle was found elsewhere, merely misplaced in the wrong locker, the entire company simply avoided the subject. No one came after Liir to ask him to justify his previous statements. It seemed no one wanted to be caught in the wrong.

A capacity for interiority in the growing adult is threatened by the temptation to squander that capacity ruthlessly, to revel in hollowness. The syndrome especially plagues anyone who lives behind a mask. An Elephant in her disguise as a human princess, a Scarecrow with painted features, a glittering tiara under which to glow and glide in anonymous glamour. A witch's hat, a Wizard's showbiz display, a cleric's stole, a scholar's gown, a soldier's dress sartorials. A hundred ways to duck the question: how will I live with myself now that I know what I know?

The next time Lurlinemas rolled around, Liir volunteered for solitary guard duty in the watchtower that capped the great chapel. He wouldn't agree to being spelled so he could spend an hour at the holiday dinner. "I determine my own duty and I perform it," he said to the cadet assigned to replace him. The cadet was only too happy to sidle back to the festivities. Liir took pleasure in dumping out, untasted, the tankard of ale snuck in to thank him.

ANOTHER YEAR, or was it two? At length the day came when Liir's company learned it was shipping out. But to where?

"You don't need to know," said the sergeant from Detail Desk, looking over his notes. "Your mail will be forwarded."

"Is this a . . . military moment?" asked someone, trying to speak stoutly.

"You get a night on the town before you go, six chits each. A courtmartial for you and a fine for your family if you don't come back by the morning call of the roll," they were told.

Liir had no family to be fined, and no one to shame with a courtmartial, but he was beginning to have enough of a sense of propriety not to want to be ashamed of himself. And since the months had become years, and the Home Guard was an institution that honored tradition and resisted innovation, he had lost sight of how much he had grown up. He was old enough to have a couple of beers, goddamn it. Because who the hell knew what was coming next?

He had to borrow civilian clothes from mates—a pair of leggings, a tunic, a waistcoat—for he'd long outgrown the rags he'd arrived in. He'd outgrown everything but the old cape, in which he had no intention of swanning about, not in front of his mates, nor anyone else.

He kept the broom and cape in a locker, away from prying eyes. He no longer put his face in the musky pleats of the cape's broadcloth, to harvest piercing memories. He didn't want to think of the past. Memories of Nor were pressed flat as envelopes, juiceless, between the folds of the cape, interleaved with memories of Dorothy, Chistery, Nanny—and oldest, Elphaba. They were of no use to him now. Indeed, they were a hindrance. Neither did he dream of his old associates—he could scarcely call them family, or friends—nor of anyone else.

The fellows who made it a habit of jolly-follying knew where to head for a good time. A tavern, they said, in Scrumpet Square: known for cheese-and-bacon temptos and even cheesier women. The floor was sawdusted, the beer was watered, the elf who served the drinks was neutered, and the tone agreeably disreputable. The place proved to be as advertised, and packed to the rafters, as the news of a Mission had spread. Common knowledge held that departing soldiers were good at loosening their wallets, their trousers, and sometimes their tongues, so an assortment of bamboozlers, shady ladies, and spies were fighting the buckos for the attention of the barkeep.

After so long in something like solitary confinement—solitary because he *was* solitary now, by choice and by nature—Liir found the exercise unsettling but not appalling. He tried to relax. He prayed to the UG that the spirit of relaxation should break the yoke of tension that rode across his shoulders here and now and, come to think of it, always.

Everyone wanted to know where they were going, and why. In all the theories that were shouted from table to table, one of them had to be right, but which one? An uprising among what remained of the Quadlings down there in Qhoyre? No—a final decision, and about time too, to invade Munchkinland and reannex it? No, no, nothing so exciting—only a boring public works project, building a dam across one of the vales of the Scalps, to create a reservoir deep enough to supply the Emerald City and decrease its dependence on foreign water. Or yet again no: no: no: no: something more wonderful than that. The cave of Ozma has been discovered, and she is to come back and rule our Oz, and the idiotic Scarecrow can go stuff himself. Hah! Good one: a Scarecrow stuffing himself.

Liir hunched into his borrowed jacket and tried to look as if he was expecting someone. His mates weren't avoiding him, exactly; they knew they'd be stuck with him for some time to come. They were spilling over with chat and banter on all sides, from all comers. Liir watched pockets being picked, groins being stroked, apron strings unraveling, beer spilling, candles guttering, mice cowering in the shadows, and the elf scampering almost weightlessly about with trays of beer glasses.

When he came to whisk away Liir's glass for a refill, he said, "Three Ozpence, guv; and how've you been keeping since Southstairs?"

Liir's head whipped. When Glinda hadn't recognized him for anything but his function, he had hated her for it. Now he hadn't recognized this elf—and he'd only ever seen one before! Or was that a good enough excuse?

He found the name on his tongue. "Jibbidee?"

"The same. Can't stay to chew the fat. Money's sloshing in the till."

"How'd you get out? I thought no one got out—"

"No one? Hah. You did, didn't you? You weren't meant to, I think. And so did that girl you were looking for, if the stories they told were true. Folks gets out, boy-britches. Many different ways. Sneaks out, flies out, folks their way out. Myself, it was bribery. Once upon a time I recognized a ring too unique to have found its way to the Under-mayor legally. Chyde would've slaughtered me, but elves are hard to pin down." He leaped up in the air like a figure filled with helium; it was true. Elves had little weight. It's what made them so easy to kill, if you could catch them. "So now I'm Upside, enslaved here to the shackles of righteous employment, too tired to think straight, and Chyde is free as a bee down Southstairs, out of mortal company, light, and beauty. Which of us wins the liberty sweepstakes?"

He skirled away without waiting for an answer, but when he came back to drop the next beer on the table, he added, "You're not one I'd have spotted for the military, you."

"Hidden depths."

"Hidden shallows, I think." But Jibbidee wasn't being mean. He grinned. Elves were like house cats that knew how to smile; the effect was unnerving. "That beer's on me."

"I inshist—"

"Don't bother. You've got the welfare of the land on your shoulders. All I have to do is keep awake till last call, and then mop up the vomit." He twitched his ears—which looked in considerably better shape than they once had. "I heard about how the girl you were hunting for was said to have escaped, but not how you did. They're still talking about it down there. Confounded 'em all."

Liir scowled; he didn't like to remember flying. The experience had been grand, and a sense of airsickness had obtained only after the fact.

"Did you ever find the girl?"

"I found out how to mind my own business."

The elf didn't take the offense Liir had intended him to. Cheerily enough, he riposted, "You're the rare one, then, who knows so well the line between your business and anyone else's." He bounded off.

Liir drank up and felt the beer rise in him—an agreeable and uncustomary heaviness. He imagined he could sit there all night, shoulders hunched, watching the circus of human life at a high pitch. After a half an hour, though, he had to go piss it out.

On his way back to the table he lurched against a soldier, who turned at the thump. Liir recognized him. It was the guy who had told him how to apply to the Home Guard all that time ago—the fellow on the gooseball pitch who'd sheltered with him during a hailstorm. Imagining Liir had approached him intentionally, the soldier said, "Oh, it's you."

"Well, it is," said Liir. "All these years, and never thanked you for the skinny on how to get in."

"If you're looking for advice on how to get out, I'm afraid it's too late now," said the fellow. He was sleek and rangy both, with hair the color of clarified butter, swept long across the brow and clipped at the nape. Even in this welter and swelter he was wearing officer's code stripes on the shoulders of his smart civilian tightcoat. A Minor Menacier, by the look of it.

"Liir," said Liir.

"Some do. They can't help themselves," said the petty officer. "*Leer*," he explained. "How much have you had to drink?"

"Not too much enough of."

"You ought to sit down. You don't want to throw up on my threads."

The Menacier commandeered a small table from a couple of floozies. "Trism," he said, by way of introduction. "Trism bon Cavalish."

"Liir." He never said "Liir Thropp," though that was his closest approximation to a real name. Formally he'd enrolled as Liir Ko—taking the second part of Kiamo Ko as his surname. Now, though, he didn't offer even that. The Minor Menacier seemed not to notice, however.

"Do you know where's we're going?"

"I'm staying put. But if I knew where you were going and I told you, that'd be treason." He took a long pull on his beer. "No, I don't know."

They studied the crowd in a complacent silence as if they'd been friends for years. Liir didn't want to ask questions of Trism's origins, lest Trism ask him the same. So he asked Trism what a Minor Menacier's duties consisted of. Maybe he'd one day get to be one. Day. A Minor Menacier. Someday. Pluck a duck, the beer was telling.

"Development of Defense," said Trism. "That I can tell you."

"Which means what? New sword technique?"

"No, no. I'm in husbandry."

Liir didn't know what to say to that; he wasn't sure what husbandry was.

"Animal husbandry," Trism explained, though in the noise of the bar, Liir couldn't tell if he said Animal or animal, the sentient or the nonsentient creature. "Training for military uses," said Trism at last. "Are you slow, or are you falling in love with me?"

"It's the beer," said Jibbidee, swooping down again. "I'm not sure I'd fill him up with any more, begging your pardon, unless you want to husband him home."

"Sorry; it is the beer," said Liir, suddenly queasy. "I think I need some air."

"Can you manage on your own?" By the tone of Trism's voice he certainly hoped so but courteously he helped Liir up and loaned a strong arm. "Make way, make way; hail hail, the prince of ale," he cried. Liir felt like that old weevily Scarecrow he'd seen at the Palace. His legs had contradictory intentions.

More or less tumbling out a side door, they were almost plowed into by a carriage careering down the alley from Scrumpet Square. It pulled up to let out more custom. "Whoa, your country needs you, don't go slipping under the wheels of this fancy rig," said Trism, hauling Liir back and holding him up.

The door flew open and a man in a fashionable dark brocaded vest jacket descended. "All my small life that stays small and separate comes out now's time to see me drunkish," said Liir, "not fair play, that." The smart figure was Shell.

"Oh ho," said Shell, in a merry mood. "I knew you'd turn up one day! So, laddio, you're doing the town? Out soliciting officers, by the look of it? That's my boy."

"I'm a Guardsman," said Liir, straightening up more or less successfully. "Ow."

"Watch your head. You may need it one day. I wondered where you'd gone! Wicked old Chyde was absolutely flummoxed. He'd no idea what happened to you. Assumed you'd slipped and drowned in one of the canals, but then suicides and other such big shit usually silts up against the grates at one end of the line or the other, and you never did. Somebody said you'd melted, and sifted right through the sieve! Ha! That was a good one."

"I was looking for Nor," said Liir, trying to hang on to any small knot of reality he could pinch.

"Sure, and I remember that well. She'd snaked her way out somehow, hadn't she? And then word of her turned up, now where was it—?"

"I shall leave you to your reunion," said Trism, starting to detach himself.

"Oh, I wouldn't dream of parting chums," said Shell. "We're only young once, lads; make the most of it. And tomorrow you go toodle-oo, I hear. No, I can't stay and chatter; I've work to achieve in the next hour, now that lips are oiled enough to speak what I want to hear. But I'm talking strategy to the armed forces: I'll save my breath for kissing, or kissing up. Off you go, boys. If you want to borrow my trap and get home in a hurry, just see it's sent right back. I was young once, I remember. Go ahead."

"Sir!" snapped Trism. "I am an officer of the Home Guard!"

"And I'm the wicked snitch of the west," said Shell. "Oh well, I was trying to be useful. Not my strong suit. Driver, an hour, and don't have too much yourself; I don't want to end up in hospital. I'm to be back at the Palace by midnight for fun and frolic if I can pay with the coin they require."

"Nor!" said Liir. Saying the very word, after all this time, had made him come round. "Where is she?"

"Am I your personal secretary? I don't know. Was it Colwen Grounds in Munchkinland?"

"Couldn't have been; that's a hostile state," intervened Trism, bulking up.

"*You're* in a hostile state, by the look of it. Don't sneer at me, Minor Menacier. I get around; that's my job. But no, it wasn't there. Maybe it was Shiz. Was it Shiz? I can't remember exactly where. Don't pester me, Liir: I can see you're going to pester me. I have to go."

"Shell!" said Liir, but the man was gone in a snap of cloak and a slam of the door.

"Well," said Trism. "I'm not seeing you home, if that's what you're thinking."

"I am thinking no such thing. Though that coach would have been useful right now."

"I wouldn't take the loan of a boot from the likes of him. Bounder. I'll hail a cab or a street chair for you."

They walked to the front of the pub. Scrumpet Square was bright with torchlight. While Trism hailed a driver, and the cab was being brought round, Liir trained his eyes on some scraps of graffiti written with drippy paint on a public wall. He tried to bring them into focus as a way to sober up. In four different hands, applied at four different opportunities, to judge by the aging of the text, the wall read

ELPHIE LIVES!

OZMA LIVES!

THE WIZARD LIVES!

And then

EVERYONE LIVES BUT US.

Trism dumped him in the cab and paid for it, and gave the driver directions. Then Trism disappeared back into the pub before Liir could even thank him. So Liir settled back against the moldy cushions.

Everyone lives but us.

Nor was somewhere in Shiz. Shiz. Where was that?

He would find her. He should find her. He should leap from the cab right now and go find her. He tried to sit up, but the world beyond the isinglass windows was unsettled and rolled about as if on the backs of a school of earthquakes. When he was deposited at the barracks, his feet found their way to his bunk while his head tried not to hurt, and also tried to remember what was so important.

HE WAS HALFWAY PACKED next morning when he recalled Shell's comment about Nor. Through the sawteeth of his headache he grappled with the question. What to do? Packing, he paused over the cape—leave it behind, leave all the past filed in its pleats? He didn't want to deal with that decision now, while his head hurt. Easier to pack the old thing. Easier to bind the broom's head in a cloth so it would look less womanly, and tie the thing to the satchel laces. Postpone chucking these things out for good. Any minute now inspiration would strike. An idea would form, and as if by magic the courage to follow that idea would flare up. If only his head wouldn't pound so!

Now's a good time for an idea, he said, as he joined his mates in formation to receive orders.

Commander Cherrystone had not been informed about his own new assignment, it appeared, until that very dawn; he arrived at the head of the transport column with an unpinned collar and crumbs in his trim, silvering beard. His expression was thunder. He delivered his instructions in a throttled tone. No one dared ask a question. When the chaplain arrived, Commander Cherrystone didn't join in the public atonements delivered under open skies to the Unnamed God, in exchange for the success of their mission. Whatever it might turn out to be.

"We leave in an hour," said the Commander.

So, oh, what next? If only he had more oomph this morning! Or if he had a place to rest his head till the screech of today calmed down.

He finished clearing his trunk. Unlike all the other men, he had no private books, no mezzotints of family grandees, no clutches of letters from admonitory father or teary mother or whispery girl back home. He was bereft of the more traditional impedimenta, and determined to be proud of it.

He waited in the yard beside the basilica. What did he take of his mock parents? If Fiyero had been his dad, really, Liir had got nothing from him but a possible half-sister. No model of comportment, no word of wisdom, no wallet fattened with funds, no blessing.

If Elphaba had been his mother, he got something more—that much was sure. But what? She had acted to pervert fate, to interrupt and bludgeon history into shape—to topple the wonderful Wizard of Oz, no less—and what good had it gotten her? She was fierce and futile at everything she attempted. What kind of a lesson was that?

She hadn't talked to him much. Only in a cast-off manner. One lunchtime she'd seethed, more to herself than to him; "It isn't whether you do it well or ill, it's that you do it all," she'd said, dumping her attempt at poached eggs on the floor and hurrying back to the books and charms in her tower. That was her legacy, and it didn't add up to much.

So perhaps he should consider the absence of good advice a kind of direction from the universe: Follow where you are led, and take it from there. Maybe fate intends to lead you to Nor. It's gotten you this far, hasn't it?

It was easier to be passive, easier on his brain anyway. His cohorts gathered for departure while he congratulated himself for sorting this out.

And it was indisputably thrilling to fall into formation to the punch of snare drums. The men squared their shoulders and became Men. The wind obliged by whipping the banners and emblems: it was all so glorious and immediate.

The four departing companies of the Home Guard were now colloquially named the Seventh Spear, after some magic weapon in a children's fable that Liir had never heard told. The convoy marched in formation through the smell of sweet morning loaves, as Emerald City shopkeepers were unshuttering their windows and washing down the paving stones.

What a joy there was in movement! Liir hadn't realized how petty he'd become, worrying daily about the gloss on his boots, the snap in his retort. The Guard's culture had trained him into thinking that a well-brushed smile and a groomed chin were somehow vital to the preservation of the nation.

He saw the Emerald City—perhaps for the last time?—as if for the first. And how fitting it seemed that the Seventh Spear was shafting its way through the capital toward Westgate, the portal through which Liir had first made his approach. They marched past the polished half-domes and buttresses of the Wizard's Palace—still called that, even now. The sun came out and glazed the marble; one could hardly look at it. A giant broody hen. From this angle, a distance north: the grimmer spectacle of Southstairs, lurking behind the hunched shoulders of its walls.

Everywhere else—on this boulevard, anyway—the allure of healthy commerce. Cafés catering, at this hour, to merchants on their way to their warehouses. Stalls of books, pottery, feathery remnants to adorn hats and hems. A display, arrayed under a bentlebranch arbor, of several dozen tribal carpets imported from the Vinkus, suggesting that the West was trading with the capital these days. And floral silks from Gillikinese artisans, sprays of lavender and lime, to upholster furniture in better parlors. One merchant had hung an entire chandelier, chase-worked mettanite with crystal pendants, from the bicep of a healthy oak, and he had arranged below it a dining area for eighteen—table, chairs, Dixxi House porcelain settings and silver service, with linen napkins folded to look like swans, one at each place setting.

That those who headed the nation could enjoy their meals in such luxury!—the men marched with firmer step. The vitality of the capital gave life to their cause.

The Seventh Spear turned a corner, continuing toward Westgate. Liir recognized the warehouse district through which he'd passed with

Dorothy and her friends. The convoy paused while Commander Cherrystone negotiated some last-minute business with a wine merchant, and the soldiers were allowed to fall out of formation. Bleary from last night's mistakes, Liir wandered to the brighter side of the street. He propped himself against the wall of an abandoned granary of some sort. Putting one heel against the wall, he closed his eyes and lifted his face to get some sun.

The warmth of the walls behind him, the pleasure of being between moments of his own history . . . his skittery mind indulged in a waking dream. His thoughts wandered up the cracked plaster walls of the cornhouse. It was as if he were looking down at himself from the window on the second level. That's me down there, that young soldier, anthracite-haired, trim, smart enough, having his moment of rest . . . How handsome a figure he managed to seem, from this vantage point: shoulders acceptably broad, the windblown hair on his scalp, the knee thrust forward. A soldier doing the work of the empire: a good guy.

Then the focus of his attentions backed up—for that fragment of an instant in which a revery implies eternity—and Liir had the sense that the young soldier at street level was out of sight again, and out of mind; and the two people who might have been looking out at him from some private aerie above had turned their attention back to each other, lovingly.

Must be the sun! Must be the beer! Filthy slutty mind he had, after all.

"Straighten out!" barked Cherrystone, and they did, and he did.

THROUGH WESTGATE, they turned to the south. The lads knew the habits of the sun enough to be able to tell that much. They marched as suited the Commander's whim—more relaxed when in the rural outback, in parade formation when passing through villages. The companies tented at night, found the dried lentils and local celery exotic and filling, alternated hymns of patriotism to Oz with anthems of devotion to the Unnamed God, and didn't bring out the bawdier ditties until Commander Cherrystone had retired for the night.

Fording the Gillikin River, they came to a broad sweep of pebbly waste, marked here and there by stands of scrub maple and pencilnut.

Once they stopped for water at a kind of oasis, a mauntery of some sort, hoping that some novices would come scupper for them—lean down to reach the bucket, and show evidence of some lovely curve beneath their voluminous habits. But the maunts who supplied some succor were desiccated old biddies who had no curves to flaunt.

Liir waited to feel some frisson of recognition—could this have been the place where he and Elphaba originated? He couldn't decide. Maybe one mauntery looked just like another. Certainly one maunt and the next seemed identical twins.

"If we're going south or east again, wouldn't the Yellow Brick Road give us better speed?" some wondered. But perhaps the Free State of Munchkinland hadn't granted the necessary license.

Another opinion held that since most of the Yellow Brick Road leading south and east fell within the boundaries of Munchkinland, perhaps the final destination of the Seventh Spear was the mysterious west—Kumbricia's Pass, or the Thousand Year Grasslands, or Kvon Altar—romantic locales, full of intrigue, exoticism, magic, sex. Everything over the horizon beckoned more temptingly than anything near.

Crossing into the eastern Vinkus, they continued through the oakhair forest between Kellswater and Restwater. Fording the Vinkus River, too, they paused on the escarpment of its southern bank. A dozen miles or more to the southwest, the Great Kells gave off a faint but redolent breath of balsam and fir. Nearer, scatterbirches in the lowland meadows shimmered in their new leaf, like chain mail on skeletons. Several hundred small grey birds flew by, brazenly low, singing their throats sore.

It felt as if the world itself were blessing the endeavor when Commander Cherrystone gave the signal not to head west toward Kumbricia's Pass, the main route to the vastness of the Vinkus, but instead to the southeast. They would skirt the mountains and, rounding them, head south into Quadling Country.

The where, then, but not the why.

Why Quadling Country? When the Seventh Spear paused to make camp, the soldiers shared what they remembered about the southernmost province of Oz. Quadling Country was your basic muckland. An undifferentiated waste of bogs and badlands, once widely populated by the

Squelchfolk, a marsh people known for their ruddy complexion and fishy odor. Hadn't they mostly been eradicated when the Wizard had drained the wetlands in the hunt for swamp rubies? In the Emerald City you could see Quadling families from time to time. They were clanny, silent in public, making little effort to integrate. In the Emerald City they'd cornered the market on trash removal—all the funnier: trash hauling trash.

But the two larger cities of Qhoyre and Ovvels: surely something of them remained? The southern arm of the Yellow Brick Road ended in Qhoyre, and Ovvels was a nearly impassible distance beyond. A town built on stilts, Qhoyre. A town whose streets were silted with mud, Ovvels. No wonder the Seventh Spear's administration had obliged them to include gum-rubber boots in their packs.

WONDERFUL WEATHER, bracing light, cheery companionship. Now and then a free-held farm or some nobleman's country estate would welcome the convoy. A whole stable of milk cows at one, and they had milk to drink, to pour in their coffee, to splash on their faces; they had milk puddings, cheese temptos, creamed curd, lake lobster bisque. Who needed that fancy dining ensemble for sale under the trees in the Emerald City? The soldiers ate like kings and nodded off under the willow fronds, sassy and satisfied.

One day Liir and a couple of pettys were sent to collect fresh water at the foot of a wooded dale. They paused to rest before starting back with the filled jugs yoked to their shoulders. Other topics of conversation having been exhausted, Liir asked his mates, Burny and Ansonby, about the place of husbandry in the development of new defensive systems for the Emerald City.

As it happened, Ansonby and Burny had both flirted briefly with defensive husbandry. Ansonby had worked in the veterinary arts, and Burny had helped copy some legal contracts with farmers outside the Emerald City.

"It's supposed to be hush-hush, but everyone talks about it," said Ansonby.

"Not to me," Liir said pointedly.

"Well, then, I'm not sure it's my place—"

"Dragons," Burny interrupted. "Smallish flying dragons."

"Dragons!" said Liir. "Nonsense. Aren't dragons mythological? The great Time Dragon and all that?"

"Don't know where the stock came from," said Ansonby, "but let me tell you: I've seen 'em with my own eyes. They're about yea big, wingspan the length of a bedspread. Vicious things, and hard to control. There's a team been breeding them for a few years now."

In the course of their military careers, Ansonby and Burny had both come across Minor Menacier Trism bon Cavalish. They had no opinion one way or the other, except that he was remote and a bit uppity. Good at his job, though.

"Which job is that?"

Ansonby said, "He's a kind of—what would you call it? An animal mesmerist, I guess. He's got a silky voice and is real calm. He can woo an agitated dragon into a sort of trance. Then he takes the dragon's head in his palms. This is seriously risky, you know. The notched beak of a dragon can puncture the skin of your forearm, hook your vein, and unspool it out of your arm with a single jerk. I've seen it happen. No, I have. Really. Not to bon Cavalish though; he's smooth. When the dragon's purring, the dragoneer does something suggestive to the beast. I guess it's about overriding the creature's internal gyroscope, or navigational mechanism. Or just being persuasive and chummy with an attack beast. When he's done, the dragon is directable by voice, at least for a while. Like a falcon with its falconer, a sheepdog with its shepherd. Go, come, round, back, stay, up, dive, lift, attack."

"Retreat?"

"Dunno about retreat. They're attack dragons."

Liir closed his eyes. "I can't picture a dragon, try as I might, except for something fanciful in an illustrated magazine, or a stage prop. And a flying dragon!—sounds effective. Also a little scary."

Ansonby remarked, "Trism bon Cavalish thinks that someone came up with the idea after hearing about those flying monkeys organized by old what's-'er-face out west. The witchy witch. What was her name anyway?"

Nobody spoke. The wind soughed and the leaves scratched against one another. "Come on then, better get on," said Liir nonchalantly. "The water's heavy, and it'll be a bitch to haul. We're rested enough."

"Who made you boss?" said the other fellows, without offense. They dusted themselves off and began to press back to camp.

THERE'D BEEN NO SIGHT of settlement nor even of a solitary hermit for days. No border marking, either, but they knew they'd reached Quadling Country by the change in landscape. Little by little the land was sinking, a series of overgrown meadows stretching for days, every few miles another half inch lower. The grasses went from emerald to the yellow of pears, and then to a ghastly sort of white, as if the fields were being tinged with hoarfrost in the height of summer.

At night they slung hammocks in stunted sedge trees, and tried to sleep, though a zillion mosquitoes emerged, and there was little protection against that. Also a soft, thumpy sort of airborne snail would constantly blunder into their faces at night, perhaps drawn by the steamy exhalation of human breath. The camp echoed with a night-long chorus of stifled girlish screeches or curses as the worm-clods landed wetly across noses, cheeks, mouths.

"No wonder this place is uninhabited," said Burny once.

"It didn't used to be. The Quadlings lived here," Liir pointed out.

"It's one huge stinkhouse. Any locals still preferring this to the rest of Oz must be cretinous. Or subhuman. En't our old Wizard done them a favor to clear them out?"

BUT WORM-CLODS AND MOSQUITOES were hardly enemy combatants, and the Seventh Spear knew things could get worse. It *had* to get worse, or why were they being asked to suffer the indignity of this climate?

They gained an uncharacteristic hummock of land, a half mile across, from which the ground water had drained, more or less. Commander Cherrystone gave them permission to peel off their boots and air their feet. Eighty men scratched between their toes, where the itch was most maddening; flakes of wettish skin billowed before being borne away. It almost looked like snow.

Commander Cherrystone spoke about their mission.

"By my reckoning, we aren't far from the outskirts of Qhoyre," he said. "Common talk in the City treats Qhoyre as a provincial backwater, and compared to Oz's capital, it is, of course. But it has a distinguished history of its own, predating annexation by northerners. In the modern times, there's usually been a Viceroy stationed here to oversee. Not now. Were things calmer, we would have expected someone dispatched from Government House to serve as a translator of the native tongue, Qua'ati. We'll do without, I'm afraid. Unless I have a secret linguist among my fine young men?"

No one volunteered.

"As I thought. It's an ugly tongue but not hard to pick up, I'm told, if you work at it. I'm sure some of you will find yourselves fluent in a matter of weeks, and that will come in handy in due course."

The *matter of weeks* stumped them. Also, *in due course.* Was this some sort of permanent billeting? To what end?

Commander Cherrystone explained. It seemed that the Viceroy had been abducted, and his wife had disappeared, too. No one in Qhoyre admitted to knowing who was responsible, but the indifference of the natives to the situation was unsettling to the Scarecrow's cabinet back in the Emerald City. Quite offensively the Quadlings behaved as if life ought to go on much as normal, whether with a Viceroy or without one.

The job of the Seventh Spear was to befriend the locals, keep the public order, and—best-case scenario—identify and punish the perpetrators. If the Viceroy and his wife could be found and rescued, all the better, though he wasn't an indispensable civil servant, apparently— otherwise he'd not have been saddled with such a hardship assignment. In any case, the brief of the Seventh Spear didn't extend to recovery of the Viceroy; showing some muscle, however, was paramount.

"We'll move into the city, reclaim Government House, and restore order," he said. "There may be some bloodshed, men."

They nodded and clutched their weapons.

"Let us bow our heads and put our holy mission of right governance in the sight of the Unnamed God."

This, so far as it could be said for a fact, they did.

DISAPPOINTINGLY, THEIR RECLAIMING of Government House involved no bloodshed at all. The toothless old woman who had set up a loom in the eastern verandah merely handed over a rusty key that had been dangling on a string around her neck. For one so plump and wrinkled, she took off at a jaunty trot. Before nightfall a cohort of youngish teenagers, possibly grandchildren, appeared in the street to haul her loom away. They left a large tray of aromatic rice, still steaming, and they tossed red blossoms on the verandah floor that, in the moonlight, looked like splashed blood.

Thus a military skirmish fizzled into a social call. The establishment of dominance proved all the more elusive because the native culture was one of deference, hospitality, and bonhomie. "This is going to be harder than I thought," said Commander Cherrystone.

Being built large enough to be pretentious and commanding, Government House could just about domicile the entire company of the Seventh Spear. There was a lot of work to be done in terms of general upkeep, however. Cracks in the plaster, mildewing whitewash. The garden had run to seed and was a total embarrassment. How long *had* the Viceroy been gone? Or had he simply been a hapless steward of government property?

For a good price, the locals supplied acres of mosquito netting, which the men slung from hooks in the ceilings in the local fashion, cocooning each small grouping of cots. For extra protection, lengths of netting were nailed up at the windows, and a webbed arcade was erected from the kitchen door to the latrines at the back of the garden. In their smalls the men could walk to relieve themselves at night without fear of being bitten alive.

Some of the soldiers picked up Qua'ati, as Commander Cherrystone had predicted they would.

IT NEVER SNOWED in Quadling Country. The swamp forests held in the heat. Time seemed languorous and unchanging. How many years had they been there? Three? Four? They'd reopened a school and built a kind of surgery to augment the work of the local doctors. Some of the men had moved out of Government House, informally, and were consorting with Quadling women. This was forbidden during a campaign of occupation, but Commander Cherrystone looked the other way, for he had a common-law wife of his own by now and he hardly cared to enforce an inconvenient standard.

Liir worked mornings in Commander Cherrystone's outer office. He copied documents, he filed, he recommended which of his peers needed punishment for various minor infractions. As often as not Commander Cherrystone was absent from the inner office. Liir could go in and smooth down the crinkled months-old newspapers in which the shipments of Gillikinese wine came wrapped. He read about the Scarecrow's unfortunate accident involving that beaker of lighter fluid—what a horrible twist of fate, that it was *right there*!—and the subsequent elevation of the Emperor. "Would've liked to be invited to *that* investiture," said Commander Cherrystone, coming in on Liir as he jerked upright from his perusings.

"Old news is better than no news," Cherrystone remarked ruefully, about once a week. "Still, maybe it's better to be marginalized. You don't get noticed, and there's a liberty in that, eh, son?"

"You'll want a bottle of the Highmeadow blanc in the water well, sir, if you're having guests at table tonight."

"You remember everything. I'd be lost without you. Can you see to it?"

"I will." He already had.

Once a small crate of perguenay cigarettes arrived. "Bless my sweet bankers, I must've made another killing," said the Commander, reading a note. "Those Shizian accountants are wizards; they can make money out of a massacre of mice. Try one, Liir, you won't find better."

"I've no skill at that, sir."

"It's not much fun to smoke alone. Put down those charts till later and join me on the verandah." It sounded like an order, so Liir obeyed, willingly enough.

The smoke of dried perguenay was nutty and gamy both, hardly disagreeable, though taking perfumed heat into his lungs made Liir cough. "Ain't it grand, the life," said Cherrystone, propping his boots on the seat of another chair.

"You could get used to this if you were an ironsmith. Bit roasty for me, though."

"You learn to love it. So. Liir. What do you hear from home?"

Liir was unused to personal conversations with his peers, and this blunt question from his boss unnerved him. He was glad to have smoke in his lungs; he held it there while he thought what to answer. "Precious little."

"Sometimes the less you hear, the more precious it becomes."

Sentimental math problems were beyond Liir. "I follow my work day to day, breakfast to bedtime, sir. That's my life, and it's enough."

"You're a good lad. You're shaping up. Don't think I don't notice." Commander Cherrystone closed his eyes. "I would've been happy for a son like you, but my fond Wendina only gave me girls."

"You must miss them, sir."

"They're girls," he said neutrally, and his point was beyond Liir. *They're girls, so why bother?* Or *They're girls, so of course I miss them, don't be daft.*

"Since we're chatting, I wonder if it's bold to ask a question of you, sir."

"Ask away."

"If you had children, how could you stomach storming the castle of Kiamo Ko and carting off the widow and children of Fiyero?"

"Oh, back to that! Fair enough; you've earned the right. It was another time, another country—perhaps another me, Liir. When you're off on a posting and your family is left behind, they loom in your daily reflections with a . . . a size, a significance . . . and the thought of them gives you courage in times of doubt. I didn't like the maneuvers at Kiamo Ko, I'll have you know that right now. But I like being a man of my word. I like doing my duty. As I see you do, too.

"Besides," he added, "I did my best to delegate."

"Do you remember seeing Nor? The little girl?"

"She wasn't a tyke, she was growing up. I saw her. She was brave, if that's what you're asking. Quite possibly she didn't understand what was going on."

"Quite possibly." What a phrase. Of course she didn't understand it: how could she? She'd been raised on a mountaintop by a widowed mother and a half dozen spinster aunts. What could she know of military maneuvers?

"I see it still gives you pause."

Perhaps less pause than it once had. Waiting for fate to intervene was hardly taxing, Liir realized. "I think of her from time to time."

"You probably harbor a youthful resentment against me. It's all very normal, my lad. You were young at the time, and what could you know of duty and honor?"

"I am not sure, even now, I know what honor is."

The Commander was silent for so long Liir felt perhaps he'd been rude, or that the Commander thought his remark was rhetorical. But finally he opened his eyes and said, "How would it seem to you to be promoted to the rank of a Minor Menacier?"

Liir felt himself blushing. "I don't deserve it."

"You deserve it, son. You deserve the honor of it. I'm not a wordsmith, I can't define the concept of honor. But I know it when I meet it, and I see by the look on your face you do, too." He grinned almost sheepishly at Liir. His teeth were yellowing in this climate.

WORD ARRIVED THAT THE new leadership in the Palace was displeased with laxness at Government House, and requested the prompt execution of the Seventh Spear's original mission.

Commander Cherrystone turned to Liir. Although chilly politeness often still marked their exchanges, there had come to be some measure of regard on both sides. Liir was often disdainful of Commander Cher-rystone for his complicated moods—now a front for the Palace, now a critic of the system—but Liir practiced loyalty and obedience, virtues the Seventh Spear espoused and he shared. And he was grateful for the pro-motion, and the smarter braid on his dress habillard.

Some of the fellows resented the promotion, but they saw the point. Liir was unusually circumspect for a young man. Not in any obvious way a dangerous loner, Liir kept to the margins, befriended other soldiers only so far as was fitting, and he didn't consort with the Quadlings be-yond what the work required. He was the model of a military man at the start of his career, so far as anyone could tell. And since he had no social links with Quadling circles, he was a natural to enjoy what confidences might arise working in the Commander's office.

"Sit down and let me rehearse an idea with you," said Cherrystone one afternoon. Liir remained standing.

Bengda was a small community twenty minutes southwest of Qhoyre on the broad flat river known as Waterslip. In the days before the Wizard had mucked up the water table and wreaked havoc with a centuries-old way of life, the Bengda district had thrived in one of the few dry areas, humps of sandy hill on either side of Waterslip. A bridge between the cliffs had spanned the river. Over the years, with the har-vesting of trees, the soil eroded, though. The hills lost height and sub-sided into the muck. Little by little the Bengdani villagers either left or took to the bridge. Now the hamlet of Bengda supported itself by ex-acting a toll from the ferries and commercial fishing vessels that used Waterslip as a highway between Qhoyre and points south.

"Entirely improper, of course," said Commander Cherrystone.

"Surely they'll stop if you threaten them with a fine?" asked Liir.

"They might and they might not. I hate to give them a chance to knuckle under, for it's worth more to us if they resist. Can you sniff around and find out if they would?"

"I'm not the man for that job," said Liir stiffly. "Begging your par-don, sir, you have more pull in that department than I do."

"If I start talking, I'll plant ideas in their heads." The Commander spoke wearily. "It'll work much better if it happens below ranks. Your expertise is needed, Liir. Can you put it about among the men that this information is of interest to me?"

Liir did, and came back a week later. The residents of Bengda were stroppy, at least by Quadling standards, but they would probably cave if presented with an order of prohibition or a bill of tax.

"That's no good, then." The Commander rubbed his elbows. "What they're effecting is a kind of extortion of river merchants, really. Perhaps I could charge them triple all that they've collected since we've been here. That would beggar them and they'd have to resist. Find out, will you?"

Liir returned and said that, begging the Commander's pardon, he couldn't really learn the answer to so specific a question without tipping the Commander's hand. "Tip, tip, that's the point!" roared the Commander, so Liir tipped.

The reply came back that the extended families of the Bengdanis would manage to come up with the triple penalty and that the bridge dwellers would stop levying the toll.

"Damn," said Commander Cherrystone, and he had Liir send out a formal censure of the Bengda bridge dwellers with a public declamation and a request for a penalty twice what had already been posted as the triple penalty.

Bloody hell no, said the Bengdanis, in Qua'ati, of course. At least not yet.

They paid up what they'd collected and made no promise as to when the exorbitant balance could be expected.

"That's that, then," said the Commander. "Make sure the whole district knows about their resistance, Liir. This has to get back to the City or my reputation is, like everything else in this Quadling quagmire, mud."

Liir did what he could, talking against the Bengdanis at the mess hall, the local gin pavilions, in the latrines even. It was uphill work now, for the Seventh Spear had become lax, and many men tended to think their Commander was getting high and mighty, not to say unreasonable. "He could just fork over a third of his own salary to his concubine, and she could find a way to get it to the Bengdanis," they said. "Why scapegoat those poor buggers? Why make life so miserable?"

"It's not ours to make life miserable nor to avoid misery when it's required of us," said Liir. "Have you whole lot gone to ground here? That says little about the military discipline we learned."

"Lighten up," they answered.

COMMANDER CHERRYSTONE TOOK LIIR under his arm and gave him the assignment to burn the village right into the river. "Tonight," he said.

Liir's face was stony. "Sir," he said, "you know as well as I that it's almost impossible to set anything alight in this climate. The moisture seeps into everything."

"I've sent to the Emerald City for provisions to help," said the Commander. "I've got six buckets of the tar of pulped Gillikinese maya flower, which would burn in a monsoon. Once night falls, you can paint the struts and supports of the bridge with it. Begin with the beams nearest the ends of the bridge, and paint high. Toward the center, paint low, closer to water level. Light the ends first—simultaneously—to create walls of fire on each approach, so the Bengdanis can't escape that way. They'll be crowded toward the center, and there'll be time for them to consider what to do, to call for help, before the lower-lit struts burn up enough to imperil them."

"Who will come to their aid?" said Liir. "They're twenty minutes from Qhoyre."

"In twenty minutes someone will hear them and, just as important, someone will arrive in time to witness their distress. That's the important bit. I'll see to that if we synchronize our timepieces."

"Arrive in time to witness? Not to help?"

"Liir, it's a bridge. They can jump into the water."

"Commander. Begging your pardon. No one swims in Waterslip at night, and rarely during the day, either. There are deadly water eels in the depths, and alligators that feed nocturnally."

"I didn't settle them there," said the Commander. "Do I detect a note of insurrection in your voice, soldier?"

"I don't believe so, sir," said Liir. He was troubled, though, as he turned away.

So that there could be no possibility of a warning leaked to the

Bengdanis, the campaign would have to commence at once. Liir conscripted Ansonby, Burny, and several others. Learning a trick or two from the high command in the Emerald City, Liir didn't tell them the nature of their mission. They were to dress in dark clothes and to wear mosquito-netted caps, to smudge their faces with mud, and to tell no one what they were doing.

"It's about the kidnapped Viceroy, I think," Liir invented, when someone pressed him. "There's been a lead. We're going to smoke out the kidnappers. But we can't give them a lick of warning or they'll scarper."

Sunset, with its usual caramel-orangey smear, was quick. The night creaked in on the wings of countless wakeful insects churring. An audience of billions.

"DETAILS TO FOLLOW, fellows, but first things first: This is a secret mission." Liir and his companions huddled by the flatboats he'd commandeered for the exercise. "You've been chosen because you have girlfriends here. You'll want to get back to them quickly as possible and hop into the sack with them. My advice is to try something new tonight. Make it memorable for you both, so if there's a call for alibis, you'll be prepared."

"But fraternizing is frowned up," said Ansonby.

"I mean if the Quadlings cry for scapegoats, you'll be covered. Anyone needs advice in the sex department, ask Ansonby. Tell them about position six, Ansonby." Liir winked. "It's known as Choking the Mermaid in some quarters."

He wasn't fooling anyone. Liir was suspected of sexual ignorance, and he had a reputation for an old-fashioned reticence about such matters. The fellows looked unhappy.

"If we're supplied with alibis," said Burny after a while, "what about the fellows who en't?"

"Tough luck hits us all," said Liir. "Sooner or later. Maybe they'll duck it this time. Maybe we will, too. Come on, we're moving out."

Once it grew dark, the mosquito problem drove most Quadlings into their stilted huts, though the odd canoe or flatboat sidled along. No one paid much attention. With the sky moonless at this time of the month—no doubt the Commander had already figured on this— visibility was reduced, helpfully.

A half mile north of Bengda, Liir signaled the boats in. He gestured at the rickety community cantilevered over both edges of the bridge, a hive of windowed light and the noise of supper and chatter. Then he explained the mission.

Burny was the first to speak. "Folks might die," he said.

"Not sure on that score, but I believe that's taken into account. Regrettable, but there you are."

"But women and—and children," said Burny. "I mean, what's children got to do with tolls or paying taxes, or refusing to pay them? En't they blameless an' all that?"

"Are children still blameless if they're going to grow up to be the enemy? I'm not going to discuss this. We're not taking a class in moral philosophy. We're soldiers and these are our orders. Ansonby, Somes, Kipper, you do the far end; we rest will start on this side. Here's the supplies—tar, brushes, a flint when you're ready. Knives."

"What're the knives for?" asked Burny.

"Carving your initials in the supports. You moron, what do you think the knives are for? Use them if you need to. Are we ready?"

"I can't do this."

"We'll ask the Unnamed God for the successful completion of our mission." Four seconds of silence. "Let's go."

They poled the flatboats forward and then nudged their way among the villagers' fishing boats, which as usual were tied in a long barricade beneath the bridge to prevent night traffic from sneaking through toll-free. The soldiers got a shock when they roused an old Quadling grandfather from the bottom of his boat, probably avoiding his scold of a wife. They clapped their hands around his head and bound his mouth tightly. Then they tied him in a burlap sack and dumped him into Waterslip.

Commander Cherrystone had chosen the hour perfectly, for the children of the settlement were fed but not bedded down, and as the soldiers set to smearing the tar pitch, they could hear the shrill laughter, the tired crying, the occasional lullaby filtering down through the rush-matted floors above their heads. The noise made a suitable cover, were any needed, for the quiet work of arson.

Their retreat would have to be swift, Liir knew, not only so that they would go unnoticed by fleeing Bengda villagers, but also so that his men would be spared the witnessing of what was bound to be ugly. All tyrants were harsh, but fire was more ungovernable than most.

He mouthed, "Set. Right. Light." With trembling hands both teams reached for the oil-soaked rags, which were balled by net wire. The men impaled the rags on the end of their swords, and struck their quickflints. The length of the sword allowed each soldier to reach high enough to light the tar his mate had already smeared into place.

One team finished faster than the others, since Ansonby in his haste whipped his sword too swiftly around. Perilously, the clot of burning rag dislodged early, but Ansonby ducked, and the rag hissed into the river.

It was neat, a job well done, and both flatboats were eighty feet back before the timbers truly caught and the night became annealed with the light of hell. The river reflected the crackling timbers, the shuddering bridge, which almost at once seemed to be gateposted with pillars of fire thirty feet tall. Good strong stuff, that maya flower tar! Then the screams, the dropping timbers, the burning water.

They were to have been fully away by now, and some other contingent to come upon the sight, to report it objectively. But the flatboats got snared bankside in the knotted roots formed by ancient, shadowy sedge trees. Besides, the men couldn't stop looking. They could see Bengdanis running from window to window, house to house, and climbing up the mildewy thatch of their roofs. Some threw furniture in the water and tried to leap upon it; a few were successful, though Quadling furniture, mostly woven rush, was known neither for its strength nor its buoyancy.

One clump of thatch fell lazily through the blackness, like a falling star extinguishing itself, or a burning alphabetic vowel swallowed by watery silence, or a firebird plunging into a suicidal dive in a dark nameless lake.

Drunk on metaphor, thought Liir: that means it's time to scamper.

"Guess we better go. We mess up this part of the job, guys, we've messed up the whole thing."

"What *was* the point of this?" asked the one called Kipper.

"Campaigns are devious; that's why they're called campaigns and not ballroom dancing lessons," said Liir, but his voice sounded odd. He leaned his whole weight against the barge pole and began to move out. "The beds of your lady friends are cold tonight without you, lads, and if you're not back in time there'll be someone else to take your place before dawn. You know it better than I. Look sharp—"

He himself looked sharp, casting an eye around to make sure nothing was coming upriver from the Bengda bridge. How could it, unless it was a river monster disturbed by the conflagration and rising in rage? No boat would ever leave from that bridge again, nor be prevented from passing under it, either; it was falling, timber by burning timber, and its population with it, as he watched.

A man and a woman on the near side, which was collapsing haltingly into the burning water, had grabbed a child between them. Her clothes were aflame and the parents or neighbors tore them off. All their mouths were open, though Liir couldn't distinguish one human scream from all the others. Then the parents braced themselves as upright as they could against the sloping structure and began to swing the girl, arms and legs, to fling her free of the burning.

Liir was reminded of a game he'd played when he was what, seven, eight?—when Irji and Manek had swung little Nor like that, and then swung him, too. But it was into a bank of snow in the wintery heights of the Great Kells, at Kiamo Ko; it wasn't to save his life, or hers. It was for fun.

The girl twisted as they let go, and her arms reached back, as if she could will herself to swim through the night air and return to the arms of her parents. The fire behind them caught up with their legs and ran up their backs as she hovered like a naked girl bird, gilded red-bronze in the light. Then she crashed into the water. The efforts of her parents had worked this much: she landed beyond the pools of burning oil in which everyone else had fallen.

Liir leaped from the boat, hissing over his shoulder "Back to base!

That's an order!" He didn't turn to see if he was obeyed. In vain he looked for the girl. He didn't see her. He didn't see if she had swum ashore, or if she had sunk, or if she had swum back into the fiery liquid to join her parents in their immolation.

GOVERNMENT HOUSE WAS LOCKED down with tighter security than he'd ever seen it, but Liir had no trouble signaling to the night watch and getting in. Despite instructions to the contrary, Ansonby and Burny and the others weren't out canoodling with their local girls; they'd taken refuge in the barracks. The company of their mates must seem more consoling. And Liir observed that *no* one was off the premises that night. The other soldiers must have been alerted not to stray. For defense of the post? For their own safety? That meant the guys assigned to the mission would have been the only ones outside of military protection. Liir saw it now. They'd have been sitting ducks, isolated from each other, naked in bed with native women when and if the news spread and a retaliation was launched.

"The hero of the hour! Where've you been?" asked Somes.

Liir started to say something about the girl. He hadn't been able to find her, partly because it had been hard to train his eyes on the scene. It seared too brightly to be able to read.

"We've been fortifying ourselves with whiskey and patting ourselves on the back. The bridge is history! Come in for a rousing welcome."

"History. History. In a flash," said Liir. "Need to get something first."

He ducked along the upper verandah that looked onto the central courtyard, keeping back in the shadows and out of sight of men lounging by the fountain below. It only took him a moment to grab his satchel, the few things he'd stored in his trunk at the foot of his bed. He put his dress boots on the windowsill: a kind of symbol, he supposed, that he'd jumped. Everyday boots would serve well enough. Then, the old, mildewing cape and the broom on his back, a corked flagon of fresh water slung over his shoulder, he made his way lightly down a back staircase and through the dry goods pantry. Then over the wall, literally and figuratively.

WITH THE WITCH'S BROOM, he had the means to travel swiftly, but his heart was so heavy that he couldn't imagine lifting off the ground—or if he did, only to reach a height suitable for throwing himself from his perch.

He walked, and took no pains to conceal his tracks or silence his footfall. North, as far as he could tell. He corrected his trajectory by checking it against the movement of the sun, and if one day he wobbled too much to the west, the next he would likely wobble easterly.

It was early spring when he left Qhoyre—spring by the calendar, not by the growing season, for in the marshlands, rot and flower and fruit and seed and rot happened simultaneously all year. Long ago the climate had become a second skin from which he couldn't extract himself until, weeks on, his path began to climb, and now and then his foot landed on a hillock of dry grass.

He'd expected some crocodile to snap off a limb while he slept, a marsh cat to take a swipe at him, but the only creatures that seemed aware of his presence were the mosquitoes, and he yielded himself to them without complaint. He imagined them bleeding him dead, a thousand bites a day for a thousand days, until from the inside out he would have dried up entirely. Then—another way of flying!—a strong gust might come along and begin to worry a fleck of skin, and his whole being might toss itself like a scatter of midges in the air and disappear.

Weeks of walking, resting, walking. He didn't look for food, but the amoral landscape threw succor in his path. Thrashes of greenberry bush, ground nuts, the occasional swamp apple, porcupine root. He grew leaner than ever, though his diet seemed sufficient, for he suffered neither from dreams nor dysentery.

His sense of the geography of Oz was limited, but its most salient feature was the scimitar-shaped spine of high mountains that curved up from south central Oz to the northwest. He needed to get through the Quadling Kells—either by the Yellow Brick Road or not. Once he was northside of the mountains, he'd turn west and keep them on his left. Sooner or later he'd come to the gorge known as Kumbricia's Pass, the

best route to the vast grasslands of the Vinkus. But he'd move on, until
the Great Kells raised their ice-sheathed peaks on the west. He'd have to
hit the Vinkus River, and he'd follow it north to where it emerged in a
dazzling waterfall from a hung valley in the central Kells. Up the side of
that waterfall, tracing the banks of the rightmost branch of the higher
Vinkus, and still higher up the middle ridge of Knobblehead Pike, and
he'd be back.

Not home. There was no place like home. Just back. Back at Kiamo Ko.

As he walked, he thought of nothing, when he could manage that.
The world in its variety had no appeal, and seemed mocking and vain.
Clearing the Quadling Kells with relative ease, he'd come out into an
easy summer on the northern slopes, wherein fruit trees sported flocked
yardage of blossom, and bees sawed the sunny afternoon with their industry. It was not music, but noise. He stole some maple sap from a hermit's storehouse in the woods, not to savor, just to feed the gut.

In time there was evidence of human habitation again—a home-
stead here or there, a shrine on the road—to Lurline or to the Unnamed
God, he couldn't tell and didn't care, and didn't stop to pay homage. He
avoided people when he could, and when he could not, he was stone-
tongued enough to be alarming. The kinder of the farm folk might offer a scupper of milk or a blanket in the hay loft, but they wouldn't
welcome him in to their table. Nor would he have accepted.

Once he came upon an old woman driving a four-horned cow before her with a switch. She was accompanied by a kid, a boy by the looks
of it, who seemed frightened of his granny, and shot Liir a desperate,
pleading look. The woman turned her switch on the child and hissed,
"There's nothing to look at in him, Tip, so mind your eyes or the road'll
trip you up, and you're not riding the cow so stop thinking about it. We
didn't come all this way for a prize specimen so you could mope and roll
your eyes."

"How far is all this way?" asked Liir—not that he cared, but he
thought if the woman would talk to him, she'd have less breath for
smacking the boy.

"Gillikin, and we aim to get there before the snow flies, but I have my doubts," snapped the woman. "As if it's any of your concern."

"That's a long way to come for a cow," said Liir.

"A four-horned cow gives quality milk, useful for certain recipes," said the woman.

The boy said, "You could sell me to this soldier, and then you could ride the cow home yourself."

"I wouldn't dream of selling a boy as useless as you," she answered, "the good burghers of Gillikin would have my license for passing on damaged goods. Keep your mouth shut, Tip, or you'll regret it."

"I don't buy children," said Liir. He looked the boy in the eye. "I can't save anyone. You have to save yourself."

Tip bit his lower lip, keeping his mouth shut, but his eyes stayed trained on Liir's. The rebuke seemed to Liir to say: *You have to save yourself? And what proof of that are you, soldier?*

"Although if you were to offer that besom of yours," said the woman, "I suppose I might risk my professional reputation. It's a handsome item."

Liir passed on without replying. A mile or two later, he stopped to tighten his bootlace, and in looking back he saw that the woman, the cow, and the child had veered a bit northward across some meadows. The best route to the Emerald City, and Gillikin beyond, led between Kellswater and Restwater, through the oakhair forest, so now he could guess he wasn't far from Kumbricia's Pass. This proved to be true.

High summer, then, on the banks of the Vinkus River. He bathed in it. The mosquito plague was behind him now, kept away by a steady breeze sweeping down off the flanks of the Great Kells, which like transparent slices of melon were beginning to hover insubstantially to his left. The Vinkus River ran broad and shallow here, and icy cold even in the hottest sun, for it was fed by a thousand rills cascading down the piney slopes of the mountains.

Still, no animals. No herds of dancing mountain ponies, no turtles spending a decade or two in the middle of the path, very few birds even, and those too far away to identify. It was as if he gave off such a stink that the animal world was retracting from him as he moved north and west.

One evening he tried to cut his own hair, for it was falling in his eyes. His army-issue knife had become blunt from peeling porcupine root, and his efforts to sharpen it on a stone had come to nothing. He made a pig's breakfast of the haircut, finally dropping the knife and pulling at his hair, yanking it out by the roots till his scalp bled into his eyes. He thought the blood might refresh his broken tear ducts, and for an instant he imagined something like relief—relief—but it did not come. He dried his face and tied his hair back, and endured the sweat and damp of a heavy burden of hair.

The mountains, nearer now, loomed as a kind of oppressive company, their aroma of granite and balsam unmistakable, unlike anything else, and as unconsoling as anything else. Their million years of lifting their own heads was just a million years, nothing more than that. The summer was going, the sun was sinking earlier, he caught the tang of a fox one day on the wind, and felt the bite of an appetite—to see a fox. A simple fox darting past, out on its own business. He saw no fox.

The world seemed punitive in its beauty and reserve. Sometimes, thought Liir—his first thought in weeks and weeks—sometimes I hate this marvelous land of ours. It's so much like home, and then it holds out on you.

THEN HE CAME to a place where the Vinkus ran by a series of small lakes—none more than a mile or two long, and all of them narrow. Clearly they'd been formed by the same compulsion of landscape, for there was a family feel to them. The water was fresh and moving, and though he could see no fish, Liir imagined there were schools out of sight. Larches and birches and the thin growth known as pillwood made a pinkish fringe on the far shores. For the first time since leaving Qhoyre, Liir aborted his slow tromp north. He took a day to look around, for the landscape seemed obscurely pleasing, and he wasn't used to being pleased anymore.

The middle of five lakes was more fan-shaped than the others, and from the pinched point to the south it opened up to a wide vista of low hills—basket-of-eggs country—that caught the light and made patterns of shadow, one hill to the next. He explored the lake's southern shore and found there a smoothly rounded hill not much larger than a pasture or two, overgrown with pillwood trees, and slashed through with horizontal outcroppings of granite or trusset, he couldn't tell which.

The grass beneath the trees was evenly cropped, and pelleted with droppings, so some ruminant herd loitered nearby, keeping the sward neat. This gave the place a domestic look.

Liir sat down with his back to a tree and looked out over the water, which was lipped by the wind coming south, and striped with light catching on the wave tips.

It could make a home, he thought; pretty enough to tolerate, and no one around. The beyond of beyond. Nether How, he named it, *how* being a useful old word for hill. And how pompous that is, to name a place just because you rested your own *nether how* there for a while!

But he closed his eyes and drifted into a sort of waking dream, as he'd done once or twice before. He saw himself sitting there, almost nodding off, more of a man than when he had started out, but still lost, like most young men, and *more* lost than most. With no sense of a trade, no native skill except to make mistakes, no one to learn from, no one to trust, and no innate virtue upon which to rely . . . and no way to see the future.

He rose to the height of the leaves of the pillwood trees, which were beginning to turn amber, a first hint of autumn. He saw himself below, the ill-cut hair—what a botched job!—and the knees, and the feet turned out as if planted there. If he could just stop breathing, he'd become part of Nether How; sink capably into the grass. When his offensive spirit had left his body, the mountain sheep or the lakeland skark or whatever animal fed here would eventually overcome its fear, and nibble the grass right up to his limbs, keeping it shorn around him.

Then his attention turned to another figure, distantly apprehended though near enough. It was a man in a cloak of purple-rose velveteen, holding a staff and a book of some sort. He was emerging in the air as one seen coming through a fog. He seemed to be off balance at first, and tested the ground with his staff until he found his feet. Setting his funny hat straight on his brow, he pulled at his eyebrows as if they bothered him, and he began to look around himself. Liir imagined he was speaking, but there was no sound, just the apparition of a funny old man, sober and crazed at once, making his way along the brow of Nether How.

The old man passed close by the body of dozing Liir, down below—the Liir-shade in the tree branches saw it. The old man, maybe a scholar of some sort, paused as if curious, and looked at the tree against which Liir was leaning. Then he looked up into its branches. But his eyes could not focus on Liir at rest, nor Liir aloft, and he shrugged and began to make his way down the hill.

A good way to avoid company, if I want to avoid it, thought Liir, as his spirit began once again to settle down into his body, or—put another way—as his little dreamlet ended and the sorrier sense of the world, even this pretty corner of it, flooded back in.

He had left Nether How and was well along the lake's rightmost flank, continuing north, when he remembered the revery and saw something in it he hadn't noticed at the time. He had recognized the book that the old fellow was hauling about with him. It was the Grimmerie, the book that the Witch—that Elphaba—had used as her book of spells.

He had looked for the Grimmerie once, hadn't he? But that was before he'd set out from Kiamo Ko with Dorothy. And met up with that old she-Elephant, Princess Noserag or something. Who had promised to try to help find Nor, or to share what she could learn.

Proud and confident as only the truly stupid can be, he'd set out to find Nor on his own. Smart move, Liir, he said to himself. Good one, that. Just look at where you got to by keeping your own counsel.

Well, that was something, though. At least he was talking to himself—instead of giving himself the cold shoulder.

IT TOOK TWO MORE months to finish the journey. He was in no hurry.

Once, as he rejoined the Vinkus River, he spotted a single stag. It stood alert in the middle of a long line of mature beech trees that ran the crest of a ridge, half-lit by an effect of late afternoon sun and cloud. Knee-deep in dried grass, the stag watched him as he passed. It did not flinch or flee. Nor did it attack him.

AT LAST, something familiar: the small settlements that clung to the slopes of the Kells. Arjiki villages, some with names, some not. Fanarra, and Upper Fanarra, and Pumpernickel Rock, and Red Windmill. It was late fall, early winter; the flocks were down from the heights, noisy in their fold; the summer cording was done, and skeins of dyed skark yarn were knotted and hung out to dry on pegs. The smell of vinegar used to set the dye tightened the skin in his nostrils.

The Arjikis regarded his progress along Knobblehead Pike without comment. If some of them recognized him, they didn't let on. It had been almost a decade since he'd left with Dorothy. Everything had changed within him—he'd broken out of his shell to find himself wanting—but the Arjikis looked stolid and eternal.

He recognized none of them, either.

As he walked the last mile, looking up, the old waterworks towered high from the strong thighs of the mountain. It loomed overhead with impossible perspective, and the clouds above it whipped by so quickly that, as he stood with his head thrown back, he became dizzy. To see it again!—the old pile, once the family home of the prince of the Arjikis, then the castle refuge of the Wicked Witch of the West. Kiamo Ko.

Its stones were streaked with the water from snow melting off the battlements. (Harsh weather sometimes hit the higher mountains as early as Summersend.) Its roofs looked to be in a serious state of disrepair. Crows shot from the eaves, and an oriel window seemed to have collapsed, leaving a gaping maw, but smoke was issuing from a chimney, so someone was in residence.

He hadn't spoken a word since meeting the woman on the road, the crone with the four-horned cow and the child. He wasn't sure he could still talk.

The bartizans were deserted, the ceremonial drawbridge of the central gate was up, but the gatehouse door was wide open, and snow drifted within. Security wasn't the top concern of whoever lived here now.

He gripped the broom in his hand, and tightened the Witch's cape around him—he'd worn it several weeks now, glad to have carted it all these seasons, as it was helpful against the chill. Mercy, mercy, he thought, I'm home from the wars, whatever that means. He climbed the steep steps to the gatehouse and went in to the primary courtyard.

At first he saw no change at all; but he was looking through the eyes of memory, and those eyes were blurred with tears. She might have come back here, he thought at last. Have I been hoping this all along, step by step—is this hope what has kept me from dying? If Nor really had survived her abduction, she might have made her way back here as I have. She might even now be slapping a meat pasty into a hot oven and turning at the sound of my foot on the cobbles.

Then he wiped his eyes with the heels of his hands. The place had gone from rack to ruin, and some of the hard edges of its utilitarian design had become softened by neglect. The cobbles were covered in dried leaves, and a dozen or more saplings like party guests stood here and there, human size or even a little taller, twitching their thin limbs in excitement at a new arrival. A shutter banged overhead. Ivy clawed up the side of the chapel. Several windows were broken and more young trees leaned out.

It was silent but not still; everything rustled almost without sound. He could have heard a baby cry in its sleep down in a cradle in Red Windmill, had some baby needed to cry just then.

He turned about slowly, his arms open, pivoting on one heel. Allowed a torrent of emotion to batter him from within.

When he finished his revolution, the monkeys were there under the trees, on the outside steps, peering out through the yellowing foliage in the windows. They had come from nowhere while his eyes were misted. Some of them trembled and held their wingtips; a couple shat themselves. This breed had never taken to personal hygiene with any conviction.

"Liir?" said the nearest one. He had to walk with his knuckles on the ground; had the years of living with heavy wings curved his spine? Or was it merely age?

"Chistery," said Liir, cautiously; he wasn't sure. But Chistery's face had broken into a grin at being recognized.

He came up and took Liir's hand and kissed it with gummy affection.

"Don't do that, don't," said Liir. He and Chistery then walked hand in hand through the warped door into the ominous, plain, high-ceilinged staircase hall, just as they had done fifteen, eighteen years ago, when for the first time they'd arrived together at the castle with Elphaba Thropp.

It didn't take him long to figure out that Nor wasn't there. The sudden lurch of thought about her, though, crackled almost aurally through his apprehensions of Kiamo Ko. It was as if he could just about hear her childish squeals and pattering feet.

Still, he couldn't indulge in moodiness even if he wanted. For one thing, the skanky stench of monkey ordure cut through the complicated memories of childhood. He had to watch where he stepped. Public health hazard.

He was hardly surprised to find Nanny still alive. She'd be in her ninetieth year now, or more? Surely. Her olfactory senses had long fled her, so she seemed unbothered by the fumes, and her own bedding and day gown were in a less-than-pristine condition. Sitting bolt upright in bed with a bonnet on her head and a beaded purse clutched between her hands, she greeted him without much surprise, as if he'd only been down in the kitchen this past decade, getting himself a cup of milk.

"It's hizzie, it's whosie, yourself in all your glory, if you can call it that," she said, and offered her cheek, which had sunk dramatically into a hollow of greying crinkles.

"Hello, Nanny. I've come to visit you," said Liir.

"Some does and some doesn't."

"It's Liir."

"Of course it is, dear. Of course." She sat up a little straighter and looked at him. Then she picked up an ear trumpet from her bedside table and shook it. A ham sandwich fell out, the worse for wear. She regarded it with disapproval and took a healthy bite. She put the trumpet back against her head. "Who is the whosie?"

"*Liir*," he said, "do you remember? The boy with Elphaba?"

"Now that's one as never visits. Up in her tower. Too much studying and you'll chase the boys away, I always said. But she had a mind of her own. Are you going up there? Tell her to show some respect to her elders and bitters."

"Do you remember me?"

"I thought you might be Grim Death, but it's only the haircut."

"Liir, it is. Liir."

"Yes, and whatever happened to the boy? He was a funny noodley one. It took him forever to get trained, as I recall. Still, he'd fit right in now." She rolled her eyes at Chistery, who stood fondly by with his hands folded. "He never writes, you know. That's all right, though, as I can't read anymore."

Liir sat down on a stool and held Nanny's hand for a while. "Chistery, is there anything like sherry around?" he asked suddenly.

"Whatever hasn't evaporated in its bottles. We don't touch the fumey stuff," said Chistery. That's a bit righteous, thought Liir, and realized, too, that Chistery's language had improved hugely. Now that everyone had stopped trying to teach him.

Chistery returned in time with a dusty bottle. It was ancient cooking brandy, and a B grade at that, but Nanny's palate had clearly deteriorated like some of her other talents, and she sipped it happily, goofily.

After a nap that lasted only a few moments, she was awake, and more alert. Her eyes looked as they once had: less swift to track, perhaps, but no less canny.

"You're the boy, grown up some," she said. "Not enough, I see, but there's time."

"Liir," he reminded her. He wanted to work fast while she was attending. "Nanny. Do you remember when we came here? Elphaba and I?"

She screwed up her face and settled on an answer almost at once. "I do not, Liir. Because I came later. You were already here when I got here."

Of course. He had forgotten this. "Elphaba was your charge, wasn't she? You were her nanny. She told you everything."

"She hadn't much to tell," said Nanny. "For an interesting life, you wanted to listen to her mother. Melena. Saucy little thing, got around the parish, if you know what I mean. A trial to her husband, Frex. Now *he* was a good man, and like most good men, a crashing bore about it. The hours he spent trying to convert me to unionism! As if the Un-named God wanted to take an interest in Nanny! Preposterous."

He didn't want to talk about religion. "I want to ask you something directly. If you know the answer, you can tell me. I'm grown up now. Was Elphaba my mother?"

"She didn't know," said Nanny. Her mouth took the shape of an O—*O!*—as if startled all over again by the ridiculous conceit. "She suffered some terrible blow, and lapsed into a dreamless sleep for months on end. Or so she said. When she came to, and was suitably convalesced, she stayed on to work for some maunts. Then she left them to come here, and they gave her you to take along. That's all she ever knew. She supposed she *could* have given birth to you in a coma. It is possible. These things do happen." She rolled her eyes.

"Why didn't she ask about me—and her?"

"I suppose she thought the answer didn't matter. There you were, one way or the other. It hardly signified."

"It matters to me."

"She was a good woman, our Elphie, but she wasn't a saint," said Nanny, both tartly and protectively. "Leave her her failings. Not everyone is cut out to be a warm motherly type."

"If she thought I *might* be her child, wouldn't she have mentioned the possible father?"

"She never did what another person might. You remember that. Now, I *did* know that fellow named Fiyero, once upon a time, and you don't look much like him, if that's your game. Frankly, you could more easily pass for a child of Nessarose. Elphaba's sister, the Wicked Witch of the East as they called her behind her back. If you *were* Elphie's there'd be the green skin, wouldn't there? It's a puzzle. Is there any more of that juice?"

He poured a small sip more. "Did you raise Nessarose, too? And their baby brother? Shell?"

"Their father, Frex, thought I was too pagan to be over involved with *Nessarose*. Me with my devotions to dear Lurline, our fairy mother. Frex wanted a godly child, and it was clear, with her alarming hue, that Elphaba wasn't it. Nessarose was born a martyr—that unfortunate disability! Revolting, really—and she lived and died as a martyr. If she had even a second or two to understand that a house was about to come and sit on her head, I'm sure she died happy."

"I never met her."

"In the Afterlife, my boy, count on it. She'll be waiting there to improve you some more."

"And Shell? I've met Shell once or twice."

"Oh, *that* lad! The high jinks of that one! He was in and out of trouble like tomorrow's stitches in yesterday's britches. He led poor Frex a merry chase! Shell was hopeless at school, a good-joke johnnycake, in trouble with the masters and in the skirts of the misses. And he grew to have a smart mouth for wine, they say. He used to lie to his father so well that you'd've sworn he was born for the stage. Of course in his line of work, later on, all that came very much in handy."

"What work was that? Medicine?"

"Never heard it called that. I think the term is espionage. Snooping, settling scores out of the public eye, selling information, and if the tales have any truth to them, sexing up the ladies from Illswater to Ugabu."

That made some sense, then, of Shell's activities in Southstairs. He was ferreting out information from political prisoners and getting laid in the bargain.

"I know she's dead," said Nanny flatly, looking out the window. "Dead and gone. At least once a day I remember that much. You could be her son. Why don't you just decide you are?"

"I had nothing from Elphaba but misery," he replied. "It was a happy sort of misery, since children know no better. But she left me nothing—nothing but a broom and a cape. She left me no clues. I have no talents. I haven't her capacity for outrage. I haven't her capacity for magic. I haven't her concentration."

"You're young yet, these things take time. I myself couldn't cast off until I was well into my sixties, but then I could do it so enthusiastically I once fell right out of my chair."

"I think you know if you're different," he ventured. "I think you know if you're gifted. How could you not?"

"You know if you feel set apart," said Nanny, "but who doesn't feel that? Maybe we're all gifted. We just don't know it."

"Does no good to have a useless gift."

"Have you tried? Have you even tried to read from her book of spells? From what I remember, Elphaba had to learn. She did go to school, you know. She was a scholarship girl at Shiz."

"Chistery's learned to talk well," he said, after a while.

"My point exactly," she said, draining her glass. "He had to try for years, and it suddenly clicked."

He walked around the room. The windows were shuttered against the early autumn gale—how well he remembered the way it blew up the valleys, sometimes forcing the snow back up into the clouds that had dropped it. "You have a good life?"

"I have *had* a good life," she corrected him. "Chistery comes from time to time, and the filthy peasants bring their filthy food, which I'm expected to eat as my part in community relations. I do as I'm bade."

"Anyone else?"

"Not in a dog's age. Not since that Dorothy. And you and the others. Did Dorothy ever stop whimpering so? She'll grow up to require the convent, mark my words. Or a husband with a good strong backhand. Her fanny wants spanking badly."

"Dorothy came back?"

"She did?" Nanny's clarity was ebbing.

"If I go up to Elphaba's room," said Liir carefully, "and if I find something of hers, may I take it?"

"What, you're looking for precisely what?"

"A book, maybe."

"Not that big thick thing she was always poring through?"

"Yes."

"Much good it would do you even if she would let it out of her sight. She could hardly ever get those recipes to work. I remember once she was trying to work a spell on a pigeon she'd caught. She was trying to teach it to be a homing pigeon. She let it loose from her window. It zipped away from her as fast as it could, but when she called 'Come back now,' the thing turned and dived like a suicidal lover, and impaled itself on the weather vane." The old woman sighed. "Actually it was kind of funny."

"I'll leave you for a while, Nanny, and I'll come back. I promise."

"I never cared for pigeons except in pies. Poor little Nor, though, was heartbroken."

"Nor," said Liir cautiously.

"The little girl who used to live here. You remember. With the others." But Nanny grew vague now and she could be made to say no more about Fiyero's three children.

"What if I find that book?" asked Liir. "If no one has taken it away, may I have it?"

"You'll have to ask Elphaba."

"If she's not there to ask?"

"Where would she be?" said Nanny. "Where would she be? Where is she? Elphie!" she suddenly bellowed. "Why don't you come when I call you? After all I did for you all my life, and your slut of a mother before you! *Elphie!*"

Chistery came flying from the corner of the room where he had been folding a basket of laundry. He made shooing hands to Liir, who backed out of the room, shaken.

LIIR SPENT THE FIRST few weeks helping put Kiamo Ko to rights. He reminded the monkeys about sanitation, first and foremost. Under his help, the monkeys set to work closing up windows that had blown open, and repairing the roof when the wind didn't imperil them. Liir began to weed the forecourt of its convocation of trees, sad as he did so, for even in their autumnal twiggery they provided some semblance of company. But then he decided to prune and thin rather than remove the trees entirely. Under its ivy and moss and tiny domesticated forest, the place might as well succumb to green. It seemed a suitable memorial for Elphaba Thropp.

He couldn't bring himself to go up to her tower rooms, though. He was afraid he might throw himself from the highest window if the grief took him unawares, like a demon lover.

He visited Nanny and made her conditions comfortable and more sanitary. In a sideboard in the dining room he found a magnifying glass and some dusty old novels written decades ago. *The Curse of the Admirable Frock* was one; *A Lady among Heathen,* another. "Trash," decided Nanny at once and set to reading them with gusto. It turned out she had not forgotten the skill; it was merely her eyes giving her trouble, and the lens helped.

He watched the autumn go golden, then spare. He took care not to get too friendly with Chistery and the others. Isolation was one thing, but forming an unseemly attachment to a Flying Monkey might be quite another. The monkeys kept to their quarters—the old stables, the hayloft and granary—and he slept in the room that Nor had used as a little girl. The days darkened earlier, and when he went to bed in the gloom, he hardly knew if he was twelve or twenty-ish.

A few days after the autumn rains began, a Swan was driven into the forecourt, and huddled for four days under a set of steps. He brought her milk and meal, and helped her wash her bloody breast, for she'd been attacked. She couldn't give a name to the predator; she didn't know what it might be called. She lived long enough to say that she had summoned a Conference of Birds to convene in Kumbricia's Pass, but she'd gotten blown off course in some nasty weather.

"What's the Conference about?" asked Liir.

She wasn't accustomed to talking to a human, and resisted saying more. As her death drew nearer, though, she relented. "The rising threat. Can't you see it? Being creatures of the wing, we have largely escaped the harshness that has befallen the creatures of the soil, but now we are paying for our isolation and pride."

Before she died she said more to Chistery, perhaps feeling that as a winged creature he was more deserving of her confidences. Despite a blinding rain, they buried her beautiful downy carcass deep in the orchard. Out of respect Chistery and Liir didn't rake her plumage for feathers to improve the household bedding, though Liir guessed that they both considered it.

SHE HAD BEEN A PRINCESS among the Swans, said Chistery. Her last wish was that, as a Flying Monkey, he should take her place at the Conference and deliver her opening remarks to those assembled.

Chistery said them carefully, trying to remember.

"She said that the danger imperiling members of the Yunamata and the Arjiki clans, the Scrow and Ugabusezi, and the other tribes of the Vinkus, is related to what threatens Munchkinlanders in their fields and Scalp dwellers in their caves—it is a related sorrow, or the same trouble under different names. Trouble, sorrow, danger, peril: the Animals suffer no less than the Quadlings; the Birds are merely the latest, and neither the least nor the last—but only the Birds see everything, and they are coming together to share their information, to tell what they see, and to sound an alarm."

"I can't make out what you mean, Chistery."

He moaned. "I'm trying to say what that Swan Princess said. Don't ask me what it means! My head! She said, 'It isn't a matter of each generation taking care of its own, each species protecting its own young, each tribe its own kind. It is not a matter of that.'" Chistery's head looked as if it were going to explode. These were not matters he was used to discussing. "The parvenu Emperor is the First Spear of God— that's what he calls himself. He aims it against the whole world; no discrimination left. We have no choice but to resist.'"

"Are you going to go to the Conference? Where is it?"

"The eastern mouth of Kumbricia's Pass. No, I'm not going." Chistery spat. "I'm not a Bird, and I'm hardly a Monkey—more a monkey, really. Besides, my wings wouldn't manage that distance anymore. I need a nice perch and a hot cup of cocoa before sleep, and a good private scratch in the morning, or I can't answer for myself. It isn't pretty."

Liir couldn't force Chistery to put himself in danger. He was the chief of his tribe, after all; the others had never advanced in language or understanding quite as he had. Well, he'd had Elphaba's tutelage.

What would the Witch have done? Liir didn't know. He pestered Chistery until the Monkey cried, "Leave me be! How would I know what she'd do?"

"She always liked you better than me," Liir snapped at him.

"Frankly, Liir, I'd rather be cleaning the chamber pots than having this chat." Chistery left. Liir noticed he hadn't contradicted the assertion about the Witch's affections. Weasely beast.

Liir started up the stairs to see if Nanny was in one of her sharper moments. But she was asleep with the port bottle nestled between her fingers, so he kept going, up and up, at last, to the rooms in the southeast tower, the suite that had been the Witch's study, her home and her hermitage.

The place was much as he had left it a decade earlier, though furred with a cold and clammy sort of dust. The one broad bank of windows looking east was shuttered, enshrouding the chamber with shadows. Mouse droppings littered everything, but that was expected in a castle without a cat.

He had to put his weight against the bar that kept the shutters closed, but at length the thing trembled and gave way. He only opened a segment of the window, so that enough light could come in and save him from barking his shins. As it was, he stumbled over a low chest of drawers, shattering a range of baby roc wing bones that the Witch had been drawing shortly before the end.

The room was a wheel, and he imagined it spun around him, but then that was him turning, wasn't it, turning so his eye could fall on everything at once. He had looked unsuccessfully for the Grimmerie once before. Now he was taller, and his eye better trained: perhaps he would make it out lying slumped on some shelf, or stashed on top of a cupboard.

He didn't see it. Maybe he just didn't want to see it, for it would only reinforce the murkiness of his origins. Elphaba had been able to read that book, to decipher its skittering language somehow, but few else had—maybe no one else. He didn't know. He had been good at Qua'ati, but to master a foreign language of magic was another business entirely. Hell, he hadn't even been able to tie his own shoes until he was ten.

Expecting little, he pushed aside furniture, looked under the mildewed cushions of the window seat. The wardrobe was locked, but he found a skeleton key in a chipped teacup and worried the latch open.

Inside hung a few dresses, mostly in the black that the Witch favored. There were no shelves, and no Grimmerie hidden beneath a secret floor. Just a pair of boots. He pulled them out and looked at them.

They were expensively cut and pieced, made of some supple leather that had been well treated. Where the boots had folded a bit, there were only eyelash cracks. A gentleman's boots, Liir realized. Elphaba kept a pair of men's boots under lock and key?

He felt inside them. One was empty. The other yielded a piece of curling paper about eight inches square. He took it to the window and flattened it on his knee so he could make it out.

A sketch of Nor. No mistake about it. The chin was all wrong, and the eyes too close together, but the joyful tilt of the head, the way the hair whipped off the brow—it could be no other. Liir could see the artist's tentative first lines corrected by definitive cross-hatching in a kind of drypoint, with highlights of coffee-colored wash. Maybe the artist had spilled some coffee on purpose and rubbed definitions in with a finger. Elphaba?

He turned the paper over. On the back, in a crude, distinctive hand, was scrawled

Nor by Fiyero.

This is me Nor
by my father F
before he left

So Elphaba had kept it—as another token of Fiyero, maybe, something from his hand. And perhaps also because she had admired Nor a little, in her own way—to the extent Elphaba could admire any child. Nor had had spunk.

He turned his head to avoid any more of that kind of thinking. The light from the window worked a glint upon a kind of bowl of glass. A ball, really. He rubbed the dust from it; it played like a bright spatter of sunlit rain as he cleaned it.

He found a low stool with five legs, each carved with its own representative foot: a dwarf, an elf, a human, a bird, and an elephant. He drew the stool close and sat down with his chin in his hands.

Lifting his chin this way and that, looking at himself slantwise. Did his chin have a sharp line to it, was his nose sloping and stabbing as Elphaba's had been? Was his skin the color of her brother Shell's? Whatever efforts or accidents had brought him into the world—was he worth it? And if so—worth it to whom? He was poised as a girl preparing for her first party, trying to see her own loveliness. He didn't care for loveliness, one way or the other: but he looked for something that might stand in its stead. Something like merit. Capability.

If only she were still alive to tell him something, anything.

A cloud passed before the sun. The room shook a little, adjusting its outlines. The ball darkened and brightened again. He took it in his hands, the old thing, scratched and crazed, and cracked along several seams. It looked as if it had once been a flat bit of glass, and someone had heated it, thinned and curled and patched it into this makeshift gazing ball. A miracle it hadn't fallen apart. The shapes within shifted as he tilted it this way and that, to try to surprise himself by a new aspect. Catch a new angle, learn a new regret. Anything.

He leaned down and breathed against it, and quickly wrote his name with his finger in the condensation. It dissolved into shapes, his reflection no longer sharp-lined, but foggy. Colored blobs like tossing petals. Then they resolved. The lines he saw were not the carved cornices of the wardrobe or the line where the ceiling met the walls. Instead he saw a skylight, and walls of old cracking plaster, and a white cat observing from the top of a crate. A man moved out of the margin of the mirror, turning his tunic inside out in his haste to remove it. He was dark and beautiful; Liir knew enough about the beauty of men to tell this. He circled an arm about a woman and drew her toward the wall, where he leaned down to kiss her. Then the man turned to open a wide double-doored window, and a flood of light that was never seen in the tower at Kiamo Ko burned into the room in the mirror. *(Liir the young soldier was outside, heading for Quadling Country, daydreaming in the sun.)* Their forms were indistinct in the sun flooding around them into the room. The woman pulled back, away from the window frame, and raised her arms around the man. Her face was hidden. Her arms were green.

Liir set the mirror gently down. He turned as if to say to the white cat, *Hush, that's private*—but the white cat was in the mirror, of course.

Elphaba. Elphaba and Fiyero. Elphaba once upon a time, maybe not much older than Liir was now. And Fiyero, Fiyero for sure. In the light of that distant memory, captured somehow in a looking glass, one couldn't mistake the pattern of blue diamonds that had been incised into Fiyero's skin. Liir had envied how Nor had spoken so affectionately of her father's blue-diamonded skin.

Liir didn't want to see more. He was too constricted for prurience of any sort, much less this kind. But he was young and normal—too normal—so of course he had to look again. He was relieved to find that the circumference of the ball was misting up, and in any case the picture was different. It was the Witch now, the woman he had known so well—fiercer, less forgiving, more impatient, more focused. She was slapping the pages of the Grimmerie, looking for something she couldn't find. Then she closed the book with a *whomp* so hard the globe almost rocked on its stand, even now, at the memory of it.

She turned and raised a crooked arm in the air above her, and her mouth was open, but he could hear no sound; and the broom came rushing forward, dragging its hems across the floor. The Witch wrenched it with one strong hand and settled her rump firmly against the tied top of the brush. They rose as a single instrument and left the room through the broad window. The Great Kells—as they were a dozen or so years ago, as they were today—seemed like fans of lavender and ice in the distance, and he could make out her path for a few more seconds, trading on the currents of the wind, after an impossible prize.

He said his good-byes to Nanny, though she seemed mercifully vacant this afternoon. "Tell 'em all to go to hell," she advised. "And save me a good seat by the racetrack when they get there."

Chistery saw him out. "You've no need to take this on yourself," he repeated.

"She would," he said.

"You aren't her; you can't be, and shouldn't try."

"Try to be her, or try to be me? There is a difference. Of course there is. But I've got the broom now, haven't I? So who else should do it?"

Chistery shrugged.

"If the Princess of the Swans was presiding over a Conference of the Birds, so that the flying creatures of the world could share what they knew about the trouble ahead, you know who would be there. She would. She flew on a broom. She qualified. So I'll go in her stead. I may not have her blood, but I have her broom. I'm all there is."

"Go with the winds," said Chistery. "Shall I save supper?"

Liir put on Fiyero's boots. Hadn't he earned them?

Or perhaps not. He took them off again and replaced them in the wardrobe. But he did take the drawing of Nor, and fold it up, and tuck it in an inside pocket of the cape, from where it could not blow away.

He climbed to the windowsill in her old study and threw himself out, trusting that the broom would remember its mission. His eyes closed against the fall, and the crows sheltering under the eaves screeched in shock and terror. The broom stumbled and pitched, rolled and yawed, but Liir kept his boots kicked firmly in the straw and his hands iron-tight around the pole. When after the first few seconds he had not yet whumped into the side of Knobblehead Pike, he opened one eye.

The landscape was a broken thing from this high up. The mountains looked like mud, swept into ridges and painted white and brown and grey and green. Thin flat lines of polished silver: rivers threading along the valley floors. Almost as far as the eye could see, the Kells curved north. The horizon beyond them was white as sugar crystal where the sun made some fun of its own.

To the south, Kumbricia's Pass was out of sight, hidden by the shoulders of mountains between, but it wouldn't be hard to find from this height.

He wheeled about, vaguely southward, leaving Kiamo Ko for the second time in his life. He didn't look back, for the whipping black cape would interfere with his view anyway. To the east, invisible still, the Emerald City, and all that went on there. To the south, a flat plate of greenish brown. Maybe Kellswater in the distance already? That would put Nether How beneath him, and the five lakes west of the Vinkus River. He hadn't the nerve to look down, however; looking out and across was just barely tolerable.

He saw the first sign of the moon, and the weird hump of a snout it had. The jackal moon, Nanny had told him; she'd hoped to get another jackal moon in her long life. There it was, his first, or the first he could remember anyway. It lay on the horizon to the southeast like a dog with its nose on the threshold, barely obeying the instruction to stay outside. It had a cold and a personal look to it.

The wind played tricks in his ears: now a soughing like the breath of a man in distress, now an indistinct glissando almost as of fingers on purely tuned strings. From here one could see nothing of the works of man in the world, and it was the more beautiful for it: how odd, then, that the wind should still sound like human music. Or was it that human music sounded more like the wind than people could possibly know?

On his right, coming over the Kells from the west, three or four clots of dark matter, indistinct because of the light and the wispy streakiness of the skies. He paid the flotsam no mind until a skein of cloud parted and they were nearer. Larger than he'd guessed; now he could see they were still rather far off. But gaining in speed; and gaining on him, slicing toward him in a wide curvet like hounds let loose on the side of a meadow, and he the fox already moving broadly down its middle.

He used the force of his thumbs to press the wood of the broom pole down, and as if possessed of a mind, or as if it had become part of his own body, the broom obliged, and he lost altitude in a hurry. The larger creatures would have a hard time adjusting their speed and height, he thought, and he was right; they were less nimble. But the air below was thicker with the water vapor and breath of forest. What they'd lost in maneuverability, the hunting birds made up in greater weight; they plunged toward him.

Farther, and he dropped farther still, each time catching some small advantage, to lose it within a few minutes. The four birds now penned him in the air: two keeping slightly forward and below, one coming on his left. Above—he could feel it with his peripheral judgment rather than see it—the final one. And closing in fast, to judge by the pair of shadows that he could see racing along the flatlands below: his shadow and his pursuer's.

There was nothing to lose by an attempt to buck sideways and zigzag; with luck two of the dedicated missiles might collide, and each one knock the other unconscious. But the broom didn't seem responsive enough. A small amount of jerking up and kicking back made little difference. The farther the drop, the slower the broom's response: the more resistance put up by the moods of the climate.

Now above the horizon the jackal moon was staring. It had risen as Liir had descended, and their relative positions were reversed. It was the head of a predator on the crouch, and he was the prey trying lucklessly to make it to a mouse hole of one sort or another.

The first attack was of talons, so Liir thought, eagles? Massive eagles—and the second attack was by a tooth or a beak, which might have meant anything. It ripped off the cape as if calmly unknotting it. Then Liir turned to beat at the creature with his arms, since encounter was inevitable, and he came face-to-face with a flying dragon. Roughly the size of a horse, with wings of black and gold, and a venomous eye of gold shot through with black where red should be.

The other dragon neared, and the two of them made their nab neatly, tossing Liir between them as his clothes shredded and his voice raveled. Then, having worried him at last from the broom, they let him fall, and retired with their spoils.

The
Emperor Apostle

One Plus One Equals Both

HE HAD HAD EVERY INTENTION TO DIE, and music had forbidden it. He'd been netted by melody not so much beguiling as nagging. That's what he thought, when he could think about it. Though it was another few hours or days (he couldn't count either) before even this much came clear to him.

What he remembered from before his fall from the sky was imprecise at best, and its emotional character muted. Panic over the sight of a girl being slung from a burning bridge . . . disgust at realizing what Shell had been up to in those cells at Southstairs. Consolation at seeing a stag at the far side of a field in early autumn. Panic, disgust, consolation—cheap souvenirs from a holiday. Emotions were portable and obvious: small savories of a life, suitable for kicking his mood upswing or down as the moment required. False, somehow.

But he and his memories alike had awakened into a new capacity of pain and grief. He had awakened to find himself alive again, damn it. Couldn't he even fall from a great height and expect the comfort of a quick death? Need Feckless Liir march on yet again?

Though marching was hardly what he was doing, in literal terms, as he tossed, and kicked the sour blankets in this abandoned mill building or industrial outpost, wherever it was she had taken him.

The girl was named Candle, she said. She spoke to him colloquially in Qua'ati.

She brought him water from a well outside. He could hear the squeak of the pulley as the bucket went down, came back. She brought him nuts and moss apples, which gave him a stentorian diarrhea at first, but cleaned him out and started him up again, and before long he was able to sit up. Then get up and piss in a pail. Then walk to the window and rub a shaky hand against the dirt on the glass, and circle a clean space with his palm, and look out.

His resting room was off the kitchen of a small compound: a few stone domestic buildings connected to dependences built at right angles to one another. In the yard he saw the laundry cart to which Candle and that ferociously old maunt had dragged him. Now the donkey was un-hitched and was grazing nearby in an overgrown orchard, braying opin-ions about nothing in particular. Within a couple of days, out on her scouting adventures, Candle had come up with a hen, too, and once the hen grew familiar with her new home, there were eggs in the morning.

"Is it a farmhold?" he asked her.

"It was once," she said in her half-a-voice. "Old apple trees in the woods, and dozens of barrels in a shed. I think it had been a cidery. But it seems to have been fitted out for industry of some sort since. I've found a . . . a heap of machinery standing in the high main barn. It's been hacked with sledgehammers and I can't guess what job it was meant to perform. When you can get around better, you can tell me what you think."

Beyond the orchards and a few overgrown pastures, as far as he could tell, they were surrounded by a forest. By day it was the color of a hun-dred fawns, every afternoon brighter as more leaves fell and the light sank nearer to the ground. By night, owls hooted, and in the ceaseless wind the branches made sounds like coughing.

He dozed much of the day and lay awake next to her much of the night, when she fell into a sound sleep. She showed no sign of restlessness. But then, he couldn't play an instrument to trouble her dreams. The domingon, if that's what it was called, hung on the wall like an icon.

"Why did you rescue me?" he asked her. She couldn't answer the question; she seemed not to understand the concept of rescue, though the word in Qua'ati could mean nothing else. "Who are you?" he tried, another way of posing the earlier question. The reply, "Candle," nothing else, gave him something close to comfort, but it was not comfort, quite.

Another time he asked, "Why did we flee that place?"

"The old maunt told us to go. She said they would hunt for you sooner or later."

"They? Who?"

"Perhaps I misunderstood. Anyway, she said you were in danger. She had heard tell of this abandoned place and gambled that the donkey would find the way. Indeed, it did."

"I am still in danger? Then I'd have been safer if you'd let me die."

"I didn't cause you to live or die," she said. "Don't give me credit for skills beyond me. I played music; you remembered. Music will do that. What you remembered—that was within you, and nothing to do with me."

But he wondered, as he grew stronger. So many of his memories included an offstage trickle of melody, like marginalia embroidering a page of manuscript. He hardly recognized himself in the glass of the window, when at night he took a candle to the black pane to see who he was now. Gaunt, and stubbled, almost palsied with the weakness of the infirm. Had her playing helped him to remember his life as it had been lived, or had she enchanted him with music and given him a false past?

He could be anyone, this could be anywhere. He might be mad, and not even know it. There might be no Emperor, no dragons, no broom— no castle of Kiamo Ko before that, no Nor abducted from it a half a lifetime ago. No occupying force in the provincial capital of Qhoyre. No parents slinging their daughter clear of the burning bridge. Candle might have riveted his comatose mind with a battery of pretend memories so as to distract him from something more important.

Though she spoke Qua'ati, and so did he. She wasn't likely to be that skilled a player that she could have taught him a whole new language in his coma.

• 2 •

THE FIRST NIGHT HE COULD MANAGE IT, they pulled two chairs into the open doorway to watch the stars come out. "Tell me about yourself," he said.

She lit a candle, charmingly. Even more wonderfully, she pulled a bottle of wine from out of nowhere. "Mother Yackle gave it me, along with a few other things filched from the mauntery's pantry," she admitted. It took some ingenuity to remove the cork, but when they'd succeeded, they sat with their legs entwined, and sipped from old clay mugs with broken handles.

She told of her past. He tried to listen. After a while he realized that he was waiting for clues to prove that he had been comatose for several years, not merely weeks. He wanted her to be the Quadling girl tossed from the bridge at Bengda, grown up and magically restored not just to life but into *his* life. How he wanted to provide for her—to begin the impossible task of reparation.

It was hard to shake off this hope, but in order to hear of Candle's real life, he had to try to still his own rackety guilt.

Candle was raised in Ovvels, in all of Oz the southernmost town of any size. Well, hardly a town, as she described it: a network of cabanas built in the rubbery limbs of suppletrees above the salty damp of flooded groves. As a child she hunted charfish with her spear. Like most of Quadling Country, her settlement had become economically blighted in the decades of the Wizard's ascendancy. She thought prosperity must once have been possible here: great tiers of granite blocks, eighteen feet at their highest, were set together in long broad curves. One could have driven a horse along the top for nearly a mile. Nobody alive could imagine what such massive structures had been used for, nor how they had been erected; there was no granite anywhere nearby. The locals used the place for fixing their marsh nets and for drying fish.

Beyond that, Candle had little else to say. Her father had lit out long ago, her mother being rather wiftier than was useful in a wife. Food had grown scarce, and some of her relatives had set out to try their luck as itinerants. She'd learned to play the domingon while traveling with her uncle.

"But how did you come to stay in a mauntery?" asked Liir. "The Quadlings aren't unionists."

"In general, Quadlings are inexpressive about holy matters," said Candle, "which means they're not easily offended by other traditions. However, you're wrong about southern Quadlings. A whole passel of Quadlings from Ovvels converted to a kind of unionism several genera-tions ago when a missionary and his entourage came through. I heard my great-grandmother speak of it once. A sickly group of do-gooders, prone to being afflicted with mold in our climate. Frankly, it's a wonder they had any effect. But they did. I was raised on a cushiony variety of unionist thought, so I don't mind the chapel and the devotions that the maunts engaged in. Nor the custom of caring for the sick, either. It seems a decent way to spend one's hours."

"You played for me on that—domingon. Where is it from?"

"It was a gift of my uncle," said Candle tersely, and would answer no further questions on the subject of the instrument or her uncle, either.

"You cared beautifully for me." Liir noted the rue in his voice. "I re-member what it was like to fall through the air and see the ground rush up with a speed you can't imagine. It was all a brown blur of wind and earth."

"I couldn't have saved you if you had fallen very far," said Candle. "Likely you imagine it worse than it was."

"But my bones are healed. I can move," he said. "I didn't bleed to death."

"The maunts who tended you first were more capable than they let on. In any case, I am still not clear on why you came to be airborne," said Candle.

He ripped the skin off a wild winter orange she had found in the woods somewhere. The pungency stung his nose with eclipsing sweetness. "With all I seemed to relive in my dead sleep, there's a lot I can't remember," he said at last.

"Do you remember what happened to your broom?"

"I suspect it fell to the ground. I'm not sure. Or maybe the dragons took it, though why they'd bother I can't imagine."

She didn't press him further. It was Liir who did the asking. "Why did you take me away from there? Why did that one you called Mother Yackle lock us in the tower together, and release us when she did? What did she say to you about it?"

"Mother Yackle is well known to be wandering in her mind. In the short time since I arrived at the mauntery, I never knew her to cause trouble nor even, often, to speak. Somehow your arrival engaged her, though whether it was into a further madness or a mysterious clarity, I can't say. Perhaps we were locked in so . . ."

"Finish your thought."

She couldn't, or wouldn't. She merely smiled at Liir. "It's nice to speak Qua'ati again. They thought I was simple at the mauntery. I didn't mind that, really; I suppose I am simple. And my small voice doesn't lend itself to public utterance. But I find it is nice to speak with words again, as well as with music."

"How did you learn your skill with music?"

"We all have skills," she said. "I mean the Quadlings from Ovvels do. They emerge in different ways. We can—see things—is that how to put it?"

"Can you see the future?" said Liir. He gripped her hand. "What is our future?"

She blushed a little; he hadn't known a Quadling who could blush. "It isn't like that," she answered. "I can tell you—I suppose—a little bit about the present. It's not the future."

"Tell me about the present," he said.

"I did already." She pouted, a jest only. "I sat by your side for days and days and played the domingon to you. It gave you your present."

"You gave me memory. That's the past."

She corrected him. "Memory is part of the present. It builds us up inside; it knits our bones to our muscles and keeps our heart pumping. It is memory that reminds our bodies to work, and memory that reminds our spirits to work, too: it keeps us who we are. It is the influence that keeps us from flying off into separate pieces like"—she looked around— "like this peel of orange, and that clutch of pips."

"Play for me again."

"I'm tired of playing," she said. "For now, anyway."

Before they went back inside, they explored the high-ceilinged barn. "I'll look again in better light tomorrow," said Liir after poking around a bit. "But I think this was a printing press."

"Out here in an old farmhouse in the middle of nowhere?" said Candle.

"Maybe it printed seditious tracts," said Liir. "Someone didn't like what it was being used for, and expressed that opinion with an ax and a hammer."

"From pressing cider to publishing broadsides."

"Both are presses. This is Apple Press Farm. I'm naming it."

They retired. Candle fell asleep quickly. Liir rolled up against her for warmth. I am not a soldier any longer, he said to himself; this is not my Qua'ati girlfriend. He stiffened, as a man will, but took pains to govern the appetite. She was his rescuer and not his concubine. He might be infected with something contagious, and he wouldn't endanger her that way.

When it seemed that the sweet lettucey smell of her breathing, the roll of her breast in the moonlight was too much to bear—that he would sink his mouth upon it—he turned onto his side. A minute or two of envisioning the burning bridge at Qhoyre was all it took to restore him to the sadder state in which he'd spent most of his life.

✦ 3 ✦

IN NOON LIGHT, the mess in the main barn proved more severe. Dozens of trays of letters used by compositors in a back room—once a milking stall maybe—were overturned on the floor. The wheels and weights and great drum of the press proper, cabineted in well-oiled oak and well-blackened brackets and footings of iron, had been gashed, and fairly recently, by swords or axes. The metal cuts gleamed with as yet untarnished brilliance.

They saw no sign of blood. Perhaps the obscure printers had gotten wind of an assault and cleared out in time.

Liir poked about in the charred rubble of the barn hearth. He managed to dislodge a few scraps of a broadsheet. He pointed to the words, but Candle said that she couldn't read the script.

" 'Pieties of the Apostle,' " Liir told her. "That's the heading. Here, beneath, it says 'The Virtue of the UGLY.' "

"I didn't know the ugly had special virtue," said Candle, "just a sort of misfortune."

The print was small and Liir had to carry it to the open door in order to make it out. "It seems a blameless sort of religious tract, near as I can tell."

"Perhaps the press was used for more incendiary publications, too."

"Maybe." He rubbed away char and declaimed from the parchment: " 'The Apostle boasts no special skill. For his humility the Unnamed God has blessed him with the reward of untroubled conviction.' "

"I told you," said Candle, "we're already converted. I don't need a further catechism."

She left to gather firewood, and when she returned a few hours later leading a goat, Liir said, "You are systematically raiding some nearby farm, aren't you? Is that why you have been carrying your domingon with you?"

"There are a few holdings in these hills, farther up," she admitted. "Mostly they're abandoned at that time of the morning, but it's true: the instrument helps lull any resident grandfather into his morning nap."

"I hope you're not beggaring them."

"Should I bring it back?"

Milk. Cheese, in time? "No."

But what were they doing here? Resting up—for what?

"I've been scrutinizing such flecks of pages as I could salvage," he told her. "I've come to think this circular was not a missionary tract. I think it's oppositional. You just don't see it at first—you read some ways down and begin to find resistance to the notions of the Apostle. It's a clever rhetorical device, in its way; it may have fooled some readers, or convinced others to join a resistance to—this Apostle, whoever he is. It's seditious, this paper, that's what it is. And whoever didn't like it traced its origins here, and made their sentiments known."

"I hope they don't come back."

"What're they going to come back for? The goat?"

She rolled her eyes. "Do you know anything about milking goats?"

"I learned to fly on a broom," he said, rolling up his sleeves. "I can learn to milk a goat, I bet." Though flying on a broom proved to be the easier task, he found.

• 4 •

CANDLE SAID EVENTUALLY, "The weather is steadily chilling. If we're going to be here all winter we're going to need to get in some firewood. Are you feeling well enough to begin to collect some?"

He was, and he did. In finding his way around the browning dales and hollows, he realized that the press had been set up in a farm that most likely had been abandoned a generation ago. Rangy teenager trees were colonizing some of the pastures, and deeper in the woods, the criss-crossing of stone walls suggested that these had been working meadows not all that long ago.

At suppertime he told Candle what he'd seen. "I don't know much about how land is used anywhere but Ovvels," she admitted. "I have seen those walls among the trees, and I thought perhaps they grew there like lichen."

"The influence of pebbles! To grow stone walls. Wouldn't it be nice if you could plant a farm that way! Drop the seeds of a barn here, drip a tincture of millpond in an eyedropper over there. Plant an egg and get a whole henhouse, complete with cockcrow and breakfast omelet."

"What would make a sheepfold?"

"All you need is a lamb's tail."

"How horrible!"

"Not really. To avoid fly strike, shepherds often dock the tails of lambs."

She didn't like this line of play. She got her domingon—Liir guessed as much to change the subject as anything else. He needled her anyway. "To grow a mauntery you'd have to plant a . . . a what?"

She struck up a tonic depressive and then played it backward. "Plant a prayer," she said, despite herself. "To grow an army . . . ?"

"Touché. Well, the story of the Seven Spears says you plant dragons' teeth." He'd heard the folk story eventually, the one that had given the company of the Seventh Spear its name. A bit close for comfort, that. "To grow a melody?"

"You can't grow a melody on purpose," she said, and slyly added, "you have to plant an accidental." This seemed a musical reference, and it went over his head. "To grow a memory. Tell me that one, mister magic farmer."

"To grow a memory. To grow a memory, one must plant . . . I'm not sure. Who wants to grow memories, anyway?"

"I'll make it easier. To grow a good memory. A happy memory."

He shrugged, indicating, Go on.

"It doesn't matter what you plant," she concluded, "but you must plant it with love."

Then she whipped up a scale and finished with some splay-handed chord clusters. The sounds hung in the air like prisms suspended from the trees on invisible strings. The donkey brayed in an altogether more accomplished voice than usual, looking astonished at himself. The goat cocked her head.

Candle added a few grace notes in a complementary modality.

The hen stepped closer as if surprised, at her age and station, to receive an invitation to dance. She let out a squawk that turned into a nightingale's sonnet, line after line after line, though Liir couldn't imagine what it meant.

Candle added a hedge of bass notes, tense as the girders of a bridge.

The goat opened her mouth and provided an alto obbligato line—rather huskier than would work for a paying audience, but entirely serviceable in a barnyard.

Then the Quadling girl sang something in Qua'ati—some rural advice; Liir had to struggle both to hear her and to translate. He guessed she was singing, "No one can sing unless they can remember." The trio of animals attempted a big harmonic finish, but it was beyond them, and the moment passed.

"You can make the animals sing," he said. "You are a wonder."

"I can play a wonderful instrument," she corrected him. "To grow a song, you must plant a note."

THE NEXT DAY he went for more kindling. His strength returning little by little, he scaled another rise, a higher one than before. He saw in the distance a blurred line of tree heads a different shade of brown. The oakhair forest, in that direction, and, when he turned to see, the suggestion of the Kells in the other.

He collected what he could comfortably carry, not yet having regained full strength, and put off what needed to be said another day or two. Before he could bring the matter up, though, Candle got there first.

She said, "It's a month now since we left the mauntery, and you dropped out of the sky perhaps two weeks before that. I've been nursing you as best I could, and I've assumed we'd winter here together. But is that a false premise? You ought to let me know. I must decide if I want to try to stay here alone through the winter, or return to the mauntery."

"Why would I leave?" he asked, looking for a reason.

She tried to lighten the mood. "To grow a man, you must not only plant a child, but harvest it," she said. "You're not done yet. Are you?" When he didn't answer her, she added, "You ask why you would leave. But I ask, why would you stay?"

"I owe you that much."

"You owe me nothing." She looked as if she meant it, seeming neither combative nor proprietary. "I did the job that was set me by the Superior Maunt, that's all. Though maybe in evacuating you from that keep and bringing you here I exceeded my charge, and endangered you the further."

"I can't be in danger here. Look, what? Are the very elm leaves going to wreathe up by magic and smother me?"

"Something attacked you six weeks ago, and for a reason," she reminded him.

"I had a flying broom. Of all things. No reason more than that."

"You had the power to fly on it, too."

"Any ant has the power to wander aboard an eagle."

She demurred, but didn't want to argue. "You were going somewhere. Surely you remember by now?"

"A Conference. A Conference of Birds in the eastern entrance to Kumbricia's Pass. Though I have no way of knowing exactly when it was formally opening, nor how long it would last. It could be over already."

She sat down. "If I understood what I picked up in the mauntery, we aren't that far from the eastern edge of the Kells."

"No. A few hours by broomstick, I guess. A few days, maybe, on foot."

"There's the donkey."

"Two weeks on the singing donkey. He seems very lazy."

"You're still weak. You ought to ride."

"You're pushing me out of the nest?" He was relieved, in a way: someone was making a decision for him. Or perhaps she wanted to hear from his lips that he wouldn't abandon her, he wouldn't consider it.

Her thinking was further along than that. "I don't know if you want to stay with me for a day, or for longer, or at all," she admitted. "But you should choose what you want and not just fall into it. I abducted you, after a fashion. I will not keep you."

"I'll give myself permission to stay here."

"You'll settle your curiosity first," she told him. "You don't know why you were attacked, really. You don't know what the Conference was for, nor what it might mean to the Birds that you didn't arrive. You should find out that before you make any other decisions."

"I'm not that selfless anymore. Anytime I try, I fail. I learned failure early, and mastered it."

"Be selfish then. Ask those Birds if they have seen your friend. That Nor."

He could hardly believe her generosity. He loved Candle already but didn't have the perspective to know if it was as a savior, a woman, a friend, an alternative to loneliness. Or all of those together. Or if any of those were the right reason to love someone. Well, what personal experience of love had he ever had? And what testimony of love had ever been paraded before him? Precious little.

He knew in many ways Candle was right and that, also, she was giving him a way out.

"I need firewood. If you help me with firewood," she said, "I'll stay here the winter and not leave till spring. Between the fruits and mushrooms I've been drying, the potatoes growing wild in the sunny patch yonder, and what the goat and the hen can provide, I won't starve. If I'm turned out by some landlord, or if trouble chases me away, I'll return to the mauntery. I can be found there, by my uncle if he comes to claim me, or by you. Or there I'll stay, maybe; it's as good a life as most, and they're kind women."

He helped with the firewood, redoubling his efforts to build up the stockpile, and in so doing restoring mass to his muscles and strength to his step. By the time the first hard frost came, and the chimney was issuing its thin braid of smoke all hours of the day and night, he was ready to leave.

He wouldn't take the donkey. She might need it.

"For what?" she asked.

"He's better company than the goat," said Liir at last. He took Candle in his arms on the final morning, and kissed her fondly for the first time. "I do not need to hear about goodness from any Apostle," he told her. "You have given me more to admire than almost anyone I have ever met."

"It's very clear you haven't traveled the world," she chided him, almost lovingly. "Be safe, as safe as you can, dear Liir: and be brave."

"Are we a couple?" he asked, bravely enough.

"We are one and one," she said. "In Quadling thinking, one plus one doesn't equal a single unit of two. One plus one equals both."

For a long time, turning back, he could see the soft curl of smoke hovering over where Apple Press Farm must stand in its encroaching forest. The fire's breath hung like a question mark above the place that she had planted herself, already, to wait for his return.

The Conference of the Birds

WHILE THE TREK FROM the farmstead in the woods to the start of Kumbricia's Pass was short, comparatively speaking, every step he took bit at his bones and taxed his joints in a way that none of the long forays across country had seemed to do before.

Well, he was older. Hardly *old* yet—twenty-three, was he, or twenty-four? Something like that. Not old enough to feel like an adult, really, but old enough to look like one, and to know the distinction between being carefree and careless.

So he took care. Any little scatter of stones might shift beneath his weight, any patch of grass might prove more slippery than it ought. He latched his eyes to the ground. Confidence and stamina returned all too slowly.

But return they did. Eventually he was walking two hours at a stretch before pausing to rest. He fixed his gaze to the horizon and willed himself forward by setting himself serial destinations. That tallest blue pine, that nubble of grasses in the upland meadow, that outcrop of granite. Before long, the prospect grew grander, as the Kells swam into clearer focus, and the steep cut between them said KUMBRICIA'S PASS: enter if you dare.

He remembered his childhood journey with Oatsie Manglehand and the Grasstrail Train, and how the travelers had traded tales. Fierce Kumbricia, the witch from the oldest tales of Oz! Kumbricia was so ancient a figure of lore that she seemed freed from the limitations of any particular moral position. She was not exactly the demon crone from hell, intent on the destruction of mortal souls, nor was she the nodding grand-tit of the world, providing succor in times of trial. Or perhaps, more truly said, she was both. One plus one equals both. Like the most insouciant and playful of earthquakes, collapsing villages and crushing populations, Kumbricia's actions followed her own secret intentions. To a human, what might look like luck one minute was disaster the next, but what meant luck to Kumbricia, or disaster either? In the stories she was fierce, amoral, wholly herself. Unvanquishable and incorrigible.

And unknowable, really.

Like the Unnamed God, when you came right down to it.

Occasionally, Nanny had singsonged, as a nursery ditty, something probably derived from the Oziad or some other baroque history-legend.

> Kumbricia stirs the pot, and licks the ladle,
> Sets the table, pours a glass of tears.
> Waits beside the ominous vacant cradle.
> Waiting still. She can wait for years.

Yes, just like the Unnamed God.

◆ 2 ◆

THE CLIFFS OPENED BEFORE him and then closed behind him, for the track into Kumbricia's Pass took several quick turns along the valley floor before it began to rise. The ground breathed different vapors here, and the season was delayed: the browning leaves of the trees hadn't fallen yet. Not enough wind could wend through to tear them away.

The brightness of the sky was shattered into glazed mosaic bits by the fretwork of branches and foliage. This high-slung canyon went on for days, didn't it?—wasn't that his recollection? Until it opened on the western slope of the Kells, and the Thousand Year Grasslands spread out as broad as the imaginary sea from children's stories? How would he ever find traces of a convocation of Birds in this secret haven?

But a good place to gather, he had to concede. The mountains served as ramparts, and the ravine was helpfully overgrown. Here the Yunamata made their home most of the year. And here Elphaba and Liir had picked out their way all those ages ago, pressing on toward Kiamo Ko and the hope for sanctuary.

He had all the time for rumination he needed—and then some. What had he understood, then, of Elphaba's drive? Her need? The force that pushed her around? Precious little. But he remembered the day she had saved the infant Snow Monkey, who would become Chistery. Her native—talent? power? skill at concentration?—or maybe, merely, compassion?—had caused a small lake to ice over so she half walked, half slid across it to collect the abandoned, fretting monkey baby.

That's what his memory said. *The very ice formed under her heels. The world conformed itself to suit her needs.* But how could this possibly be true? Perhaps it was the unreliability of memory, the romanticking tendencies of childhood, that made Liir remember it this way. *The lake went ice. The baby monkey was saved.* Maybe, really, she'd waded. Or maybe the lake was already iced over.

Maybe all that really mattered, as to her power, was that *she saved the baby monkey.*

At the shores of a small tarn, he paused, and became aware of a new variety of silence. It was the sound of everything holding its breath.

At the farther side of the tarn was a small island. A spinney of knot-branch trees grew in the center of the island, their five or six tree trunks so close as to resemble the uprights of a series of doors, all leading to the same interior space among the trunks, some dozen feet in diameter. The trees held what was left of the Conference of the Birds, and the Birds were holding their breath.

He stood, not ready to call out, for he didn't want them to scatter. But they were aware of him, he was sure. How many hundred pairs of eyes blinked or unblinked at him from those ring-coiled leaves? They neither approached him in sortie nor twittered in fright. Perhaps, he guessed, they were stupid with fear.

Finally he thrashed about along the bracken and located a fallen tree trunk substantial enough to bear his weight. He hauled it to the water's edge and pushed it in. No conjuring up an ice-walk for him. With the help of a staff, he balanced himself and began to draw his way across the water. He could have swum, he knew, but that would require his undressing either before or after the swim, and it seemed an undignified way to approach a Convention.

The Birds seemed patient, and as he got closer he thought: It's as if they have been waiting for me.

This was so, according to the hunch-hooded Cliff Eagle who bade him welcome.

"You're the boy-broomist," he said. "The fledgling. We knew you'd been downed. A Red Pfenix got far enough through enemy lines to cry out that much information before being wounded and having to turn back. We trusted you would come. You've come."

The Cliff Eagle paused smartly, puffing out his breast feathers.

"I almost didn't," said Liir. "It wasn't even my idea, really."

The Eagle made a mouth gesture as close to a sneer as he could manage. "Humans are fickle. We know. But you're here. The boy-broomist."

"I'm without the broom." Liir put his staff down on the ground so the Birds could see. "I walked. Have you a name, by the way?"

The other Birds hopped a branch or two closer to see if the Cliff Eagle would answer. They were the larger creatures, mostly—a few random Finches and Fitches, some Robins, and a busy preening department of Wrens—but mostly Eagles, Night Rocs, a youngish Pfenix in its glowing halo. Nine Swans still waiting for their Princess. A blind old Heron with a twisted left leg. Others.

"I know what happened to the Princess of the Swans," said Liir, and told them how he had buried her—and, in a dim sense, come in her stead.

The Cliff Eagle took the news unflinchingly, though the Swans bowed their heads until their necks were white hoops, and their wings shuddered with an airy sound, as of an industrial baffle.

"I am the President of the Assembly," said the Cliff Eagle. "Thank you for coming."

Liir had no use for honorifics. "Am I to call you Mister President? Or just Birdy?"

The Cliff Eagle bristled, and then said, "General Kynot is my name, though my name isn't important. And yours isn't either. We're soldiers at strategy, not a military tea."

"Well, I've been a soldier and I'm not going back to it. I'm Liir, for what that's worth, and I use my name. I'm not Broom-boy."

Kynot ducked his head and bit at a nit under his wing. "Sorry, the place is crawling with nits," he said. "Liir." It was a concession, and Liir relaxed. He was about to ask permission to sit down, and then remembered he didn't need it. So he sat, and the Birds came farther down from the branches, and most of them settled on the hardscuffle with the sound of small loaves of bread falling to a floor.

Kynot made quick work of their concerns. The Conference seemed to be comprised of seventy or eighty Birds who were now afraid to leave. They had met to convene about the threat in the skies, but that very threat had cornered them and grounded them. It would take a talent and a cunning greater than any of their skills to make the skies safe for travel.

"You've come to the wrong beak if you want talent or cunning," said Liir.

"Don't be absurd," snapped Kynot, and continued.

He beat out every point of his argument with a hard flap of his wings. *Whereas* conditions of life under the Emperor had become intolerable, *whereas* his airborne army of dragons had systematically disrupted air travel, unsettled populations of Birds and birds, and interfered with the natural rights of flight and migration and convocation, *now therefore* a Congress of the Birds had been summoned, if sadly beleaguered by aforementioned hostile army, and such delegates as had managed to sneak in had concluded *thereby* that they were singly and in unity incapable of combating the enemy fleet. *Therefore* they needed help. Fast.

"I came to tell you of the death of the Princess of the Swans," said Liir, "because it is what Elphaba would have done. Beyond that, I can't be of much use. If I'm the only hope around, you're in a heap of trouble."

"Unlike Animals, we Birds haven't often lived wing by jowl with humans," replied the general. "The human prohibition against eating Animal flesh being subject to abuse, think how much less strict is any taboo against eating the Bird of the air. We must be shot at and brought down before we can be interviewed to learn if we are talking creatures. Few hungry farmers are willing to extend Birds that courtesy, so those of us who talk tend to congregate in areas less frequented by human scum. My apologies, that was crude of me."

"Don't apologize too fast, you don't know me very well," said Liir. "But still, why ask me for help?"

"You have flown, as most humans have not," said Kynot simply. "You have powers unique among the humans we've met . . ."

"I can keep my balance. So what. It's the broom that has powers. Elphaba's broom."

"The wing doesn't work separately from the feather, Liir. They work in tandem."

"Well, I haven't the broom any longer, or haven't you heard? So I can't fly—which means this hardly concerns me."

"You were attacked by the dragons yourself. Weren't you? Or have I been fed misinformation?"

"Well, I was. But that's between me and the dragons. It has nothing to do with you."

"And they call us birdbrains." Kynot was livid. "There is a common cause among our kind and a flying boy, you dodo."

"I object," said a Dodo, just waking up from a nap.

"Sorry, that was uncalled for. Listen. Liir. You must have been intending to help us, or why did you come here at all?"

He thought of Candle. "It was the suggestion of a third party."

"A suggestion of what? That you deliver your tragic news, and then stay to laugh at us in our plight? That you see your fellow creatures chased, tortured, kept from associating freely, just as you were chased, robbed, and nearly killed, and then you—what? Walk home and retail the event for amusing dinnertime conversation?"

"Don't paint me so bleakly. I'm capable of doing that for myself. Look, it's occurring to me that I might ask something of you. On and off over the years, I've been looking for someone. A girl-child. Perhaps you could help. On your various migrations and such."

"We can't fly freely, or haven't I put that clearly enough, you cretin?" Kynot was apoplectic. "How can we serve your private needs when our numbers are being diminished by the day?"

"Well, then." Liir shrugged. "It's a no-go. I guess I didn't really understand much about this skirmish involving the Birds. It's sad, but it hasn't anything to do with me. And even if it did, I'm powerless . . . I'm not Elphaba."

A small Wren hopped forward and said to Kynot, "If you please, begging your pardon, General . . ."

"Do not beg my pardon! Do not *beg* at all! How many times have I to drill this lesson into your brain, Dosey?"

"Sorry, Gen'ral. Begging your pardon for that one, too. It's just that the young man might want to think on this bit somewhat." Dosey turned to Liir and cheeped. "It ain't just us Birdys, mister. Those dragonfings are bad cess for human beings, too. Scraping the faces of defenseless women in the wilderness! Have they no shame? Have you? If you cain't help *us* out of the kindness of your liver, surely you could work to keep such things from happenin' to your own kind?"

"Well said, Dosey." Kynot sounded less apologetic than surprised.

"Those were unionist missionaries, I'm told," said Liir, his shoulders slumping. "It was horrible to hear about. But I'm not a maunt, and I don't even know if I'm a unionist."

"So what next? They'll kill your brother in his stockings, and you'll say, 'He had grey eyes and I have green, so it weren't really about me a'tall'?" asked the Wren. "They already attacked you, duckie, so's I heard. Ain't you rememberin'?"

"Maybe I deserved to be attacked."

"Oh, save us," muttered Kynot. "Somebody save us. But it's not going to be this nutter."

Dosey wasn't ready to give up. "Mebbe you did deserve it," she snapped. "But that's giving those dragons an awful lot of credit for knowing the insides and the sinsides of your soul! So what if they fly out of the stables of the Emperor! They're not Talking Dragons! They're in the pay of the Emperor of the Ugly! And you cain't be sartain those young maunts deserved what they got, can you? Their faces so scraped! It's hideous is what it is!"

"It's not for me to decide whose faces get scraped or not . . ."

"No," said Kynot. He reared up and looked as if he wanted to peck Liir's eyes out. "No. Leave it in the beak of the Unnamed God, or his mortal avatar, the Emperor. Leave it to the agents of the Emperor, who run the Home Guard for the security of the Emerald City at the expense of all others who live in Oz. Or leave it to the underlings who follow the orders of their superiors. Leave it in the beaks of the dragons themselves. Dragons don't kill people, people kill people. They kill themselves by walking unprotected in a world where there are dragons. You make me sick."

"I don't have any idea why the dragons attacked those maunts—"

"It is increasingly obvious that you don't have any ideas at all. The dragons attacked the maunts to stir up trouble between the Yunamata and the Scrow. Those human populations had finally positioned themselves to be ripe for treaty making, after ten hundred generations . . . They had been learning to trust each other. With random attacks on isolated humans, the dragons could keep the tribes suspicious of each other. Tribes are easier to intimidate when they are not united. You said you were in the military: didn't you learn anything about military strategy?"

Liir thought about the burning bridge. He could see again the letter of burning straw, changing shape as it fell, spelling something fiery and illegible into the vanquishing water.

He thought about Candle, waiting for him to return—having done something. Having completed some action. If Liir assumed he wanted Candle, and how could he know that yet?—he couldn't have her. Not until he had an alternative against which to make a choice.

"Look," he said. "Flattering, all this. But I can't fly anymore. My broom is gone. I risked having my face scraped by coming solo across the Disappointments as far as Kumbricia's Pass. I came for the wrong reasons—as usual. There's nothing I can do for you, even if I am a human. I have no talent. My broom had great talent!—if it even was my broom. But it's gone. Either the dragons took it, or it's lost."

"Listen. Keep listening. Wipe that squawky look off your faces. Please. Why don't you band together to fly out of here? A huge clot of you? The dragons couldn't take you all out—some of you would be bound to get through."

"Nice," said a small Barn Owl. "Very nice. I have an irregular left wing and I tend to fly in loops, which slows me down. I'll be one of the first to go. Gladly shall I sacrifice myself for the great Conference of Birds!" He didn't sound as if he meant it.

"While there are grubs to eat here in Kumbricia's Pass, and the dragons can't see into our hideout, we are imprisoned here," said Kynot. "But to leave would be to risk even one of us—and that is a risk we don't take. We won't. The least little Sparrow that falls diminishes us all. I thought you knew all about that."

"Yeah, well, my religious instruction was pretty feeble."

"I wasn't speaking metaphorically, but of military strategy. You could get to the dragons, couldn't you? A witch-boy passing as a soldier? You could see if they had your broom, for one. You could get it back. You could be our voice—our ambassador. Our human representative, our agent, our proxy—"

Liir interrupted. "If I could get my broom—what good could I do? They would just attack me again. Last time they were satisfied with my broom and my cape. Maybe this time they'd scrape my face."

"You just said it's not up to you to decide whose face gets scraped or not," said the Cliff Eagle. "If you believe that, put your face out there and deal with what happens."

"This isn't going to work," said Liir. "I can't do anything for you. I'm not a Bird. I'm not a witch-boy. I don't even have a broom anymore. And even if I had it, maybe I wasn't meant to fly. Maybe I shouldn't even have that liberty."

"Maybe none of us should have the liberties we have. We keep going as we are, we'll find out soon enough. But if you help us squelch the dragon threat, we'll do what you ask. We'll hunt for that human female you're seeking."

The Wren hopped forward again. "You're going to do it," she said to Liir. "You're going to try, ain't you. I kin tell."

"You read the future, Dosey?" said Liir.

"Begging your pardon, sir—"

"Dosey!" interrupted Kynot. "No begging!"

"Ooh, sorry I'm sure," Dosey continued. "No, Mister Broom-boy. You're going to do it for a perfectly selfish reason—our looking for your lost girl-fing—and that's okay. Why not? Long as the job gets done."

The Birds were silent.

"You've had a taste of it," she said in a softer voice. "Not many has, but you has. You've tried flying, ain't you. Now try giving it up."

She came nearer. "Try giving it up," she said. "Begging your pardon, sir, you cain't."

The Birds began to flap their wings and, one by one, to lift up, making their final argument. They swept counterclockwise around the dead little lake, perhaps in deference to the Owl whose wing anomaly made him list in a particular direction. There were more Birds than Liir had first perceived. Several hundred. The more timid ones must have been hiding higher in the branches, but listening intently: all listening. Now they flew, and as they flew, there could be no leader, no follower: they traced the same track in the air, faster and faster. The very force of their rhythmic pumping made the surface of the lake stand up in waves of its own, higher and higher, till wingtips of white froth were beaten up, and then the clots of pale spume lifted and circled beneath the vortex of birds like a second population, like ghost Birds, like the relatives of the Conference who had been slain. But what were ghosts without voices?

The birds were silent—none of them, even the Geese and Ducks, who liked to honk in flight, dared risk attracting attention to their stronghold.

"Stop," cried Liir and held up his hands—not out of pity, nor fear, nor a new moral conviction: simply out of the lack of any further reason to resist.

The blind, gimpy Heron hobbled forward and pecked at Liir's leg to locate him. "I can't fly either, now my sight's gone," the Heron said. "Makes me no less a Bird, though, do it?"

Kumbricia's Cradle

THE WALK BACK WAS FASTER. Now that his bones were knitted, all this trekking was building up muscle again. He hurt, but solidly, recuperatively.

The Disappointments afforded little by way of a blind, so he traveled by night as much as he could, hoping that dragons wouldn't be abroad then. He tried to keep to clearly marked tracks, goat paths, stream sides, where the going was smoother, though the cover less useful.

Arriving back at Apple Press Farm an hour shy of dawn, he was unwilling to frighten Candle by approaching in the dark. He found an old tree on the edge of the orchard still forcing out small, deformed fruit, and he made a breakfast for himself, shivering with his hands in his armpits. He tried to feel the day warm instant by instant as the sun rose over the horizon, but his apparatus for appreciating such subtlety was too crude.

Then the donkey brayed, and a cock cried out his serrated *Confiteor* through the rising mist. Where had Candle got a cock from? She must still be roaming the province, releasing creatures from homesteads with impunity. She was lucky she wasn't caught, as the donkey and the cock weren't exactly keeping their whereabouts secret. The cock sounded like a tenor.

With all that noise, she'd be stirring by now. Still, he waited till he saw the smoke from the kitchen chimney roll up, and he heard a window shutter bark against the stone. He came toward the house ready to call out, but she was standing in the doorway on one foot, the other foot rubbing against the back of her calf. "What have you been waiting for?" she asked, her head tilted forward. "Isn't it cold out there in the orchard?"

"You've been clearing the undergrowth."

"The donkey has. Makes my life easier; he's done enough for a kitchen garden. If we remove a few more trees, we'll have a good open space, and fertile, by the look of it. But we'll need fencing against the donkey and other comers. Why do you loiter, come in, you must be ice."

He was about to say *I was afraid I'd frighten you,* and then he remembered: She possessed some sort of a talent for reading the present. She'd probably known he was there; and indeed, she admitted as much when asked.

His fists clenched and opened at the notion of touching her sleep-warm body, of wrapping his arms around her, diving his cold fingers into the folds of her simple broadcloth sleeping tunic. But she ducked into the shadowy doorway before he could embrace her, as if his time away had made them strangers again.

The place was that much straighter, simpler, more pleasant. She'd been busy. Dried flowers set round in cracked terra-cotta pots. Tassels of herbs drying from strings, spooling their fragrance across the kitchen. In the fire nook, the andirons had been polished, and from the trammel hung a fine bulbous kettle with scented water roiling in it. "How did you know I'd be back today?"

"The cock crowed more self-consciously, so I guessed he must have an audience. Anyway, I sensed it would be you. Or maybe that was just hope, who can tell the difference? You must be weary. Rest your bones, Liir, and I'll fetch some rennety milk pudding from the cold room belowstairs."

"Don't move about so. Just sit—here." He patted a stool near him and smiled. Her hands flexed and met his at the fingertips, and their fingertips bounced gently against one another. Then she took herself off to get the pudding.

"You'll eat first, and then you'll sleep," she said, like a mother, "for I don't need the skills of divination to know you've been walking most of the night."

She would hear of nothing else. He had to content himself with watching her flit across the kitchen, into the sunlight and out of it again. How is it that she is like a bird, too, he thought, and felt he was on to something, but then the food settled him, and Candle had proven right, for his head was nodding on his spine. She helped him to the room where they had so chastely slept, and after she had taken his shirt off and lightly run a damp cloth under his arms and behind the lengthening mane of hair at his nape, she dropped the cloth on the floor and pressed her hands against his bare chest, as if trying to interpret the arcane language of his heartbeat.

"Later," she mouthed at him, and kissed the space where his lips would have been if he hadn't just then begun to keel backward against the pillow.

The sleep was devoid of character. A good sleep.

He awoke well into the heat of the day, such as it was at this time of year. She had set out a tunic and fresh leggings. What a capable scavenger she was. The trousers, cut for a slenderer man, cinched too tightly at his thighs, but they were clean, and the tunic scented of pomander. In new garb he felt a new man, and looked out of the window to find her.

She was hard at work in the patch she'd mentioned. Using a sharp segment of the printing press's broken iron wheel, she was levering aloft a resistant root of apple tree. Smudged now, where he was pristine, she wiped her face with the back of her hand and in vain tried to scatter a late population of midges who found the smell of her sweat enticing. He called to her, and she waved and fell heavily to her knees as the root chose that moment to yield.

"Let me do that," he said.

"Done now. But I'll rest a spell. Come down."

They walked to the edge of the orchard, by turns sipping sweet well water from a single pipkin. "You've done good work here," he told her gravely.

"I've had good reason." With her little finger she picked at a bit of wax in one ear. "You're back, now, and there's one on its way."

He arched an eyebrow, feeling very Commander Cherrystone-ish. "Company's coming?"

"You could put it suchly."

What was she reading out of this sunny hour that he couldn't see— oh, he couldn't, but then he could. "It's not so. You're not old enough."

She said, "Though like you I can't exactly say how old I am, apparently I am old enough, Liir." Her tone was easy and a bit bored, but he thought he knew her well enough by now to suppose that she was at least a little frightened.

Many of the fellows in the unit had talked about this. They'd shared their observations. Women always knew, and a preternatural calm swept all other earthly considerations aside when it happened. But Candle was hardly a woman!—and not inaugurated into those mysteries. Or not by him.

"I've been gone only a few weeks," he said, trying not to sound cold. "Or had you already charmed a local farmer with your domingon even when I was still recuperating inside? Is that how you got the goat, the cock, the hen—a bartering for your farmyard needs with your farmyard skills? Is that why you encouraged me to leave on a wild Bird chase?"

"You needn't fuss so." She bit her lip and looked at him levelly. "It was no other man, Liir."

"It is not by me. Candle!" He slipped out of Qua'ati for a moment, to spew expletives in the orchard air. "I am a fool and a naïf and a monster, all at once, but I am not stupid about how a girl becomes pregnant. It is not by me. Don't embarrass me with a hopeless ruse. Do you think I would abandon you over it?"

"I don't think—"

"Or maybe you want me to? Well, I won't. I haven't that crooked a soul. Just don't lie to me, for that's intolerable. Candle! The whole thing is beyond belief."

"Liir. I ask nothing of you. You're not married to me. You didn't choose me. I didn't choose you."

"You chose to save me," said Liir despondently, "when I might have slipped away, and a good thing, too."

"I chose to try to save someone. Someone sick in an infirmary, that is all. I didn't know who it was. I didn't know it was you. I didn't know you yet. I don't know you yet."

"I am *not* the *father*," he said. "Am I required to remind you how it works? I kept my distance, Candle. I never slept with you; I never buried myself in your trove. I thought about it, yes, but thinking's not doing, and no child is begat by the midnight thoughts of an adult sleeping alone."

"But you did," she said. Her shoulders slumped. "It would be easier to pretend you hadn't, but it doesn't matter one way or the other. The infant grows. I won't turn it out of its nest now."

"I didn't!" he insisted, and then she told him how he had, and when, and why.

A small rain came up over the orchard, and in an eddy of chill, the drops turned to snow. The season turned several more notches in an instant, as can happen.

They made their way inside without further remark, and Candle put herself to kitchen tasks. She measured two handfuls of coarse flour and shook it through a boulter of cloth. The light greyed, and faded, and he pulled the shutters tight, and built up the fire. There were the cock and the hen to bring in, and the donkey to stable, and whatever else he could think of to do, he did: shifting firewood, scattering clean straw for the floor, arranging things on shelves. Things with handles and spouts, items with purposes he couldn't imagine. He couldn't imagine anything.

They ate, and after eating she said softly, "This is a good thing, Liir."

"Then it couldn't have come from me."

As she prodded, and because it made a distraction if nothing else, he told her about the Conference of the Birds and the charge under which he was laboring—or had so labored, up until this morning upon his return—to find his broom.

She had always seemed unshaken by the notion of flying dragons. When he asked why, she told him that she'd heard rumors of such creatures a few years back. They were involved in an action in the provincial capital.

"Qhoyre," he filled in. "It figures."

"If there were going to be troubles, you'd expect them in Qhoyre," she concurred. "It began as a tax revolt or something. The garrison of the Emerald City military was stormed by Quadlings, and more or less annihilated."

"I don't believe you can be more or less annihilated. You either are or you aren't." He thought of the suave, genteel Commander Cherrystone, and hoped that he had been one of the ones who had been killed.

"Don't look to me for accuracy. I'm a simple soul. I'm merely telling you what I heard my uncle say. Some of the reasons we left." Candle continued. It was calming for both of them to avoid the matter of her pregnancy. "He said that the Emerald City flared up in reprisal. Overreacted. A small fleet of flying dragons was unleashed against the Quadlings at Qhoyre. It was pretty terrible. There were only a few survivors, and who could trust what those poor traumatized loons said? Flying *dragons*? Quadlings are so superstitious. No one knew what to believe—so let's get out of here, said my uncle."

She folded her hands in her lap. "So I'm not surprised that it has turned out to have been true."

He put his head in his hands. The other fellows in his squadron. Had any of them survived? Ansonby, Kipper, Somes? Burny, Mibble? The one they called Fathead? Or what about their girlfriends—were they tarred as collaborators?

It wasn't just the girl slung from the burning bridge—it was all of them. Her parents, their neighbors, the countryfolk. The occupying forces, the officers and the infantry, the support teams, the ambassadors. The repercussions seemed endless and only to grow in force and significance, never to recede.

Candle saw his expression. She took his hand, and he had to work hard not to snatch it away.

"Remember why you went to the Conference," she said. "Before you save anyone else, you have to save yourself, Liir. Otherwise you're just a bundle of tics, a stringed puppet manipulated by chance and the insensible wind."

"I will stay here, whether you've been sleeping round the country-side or not. We are called to be as limbs of God," he said.

"That piety curdles on your tongue, and you know it. If you don't rescue yourself, Liir, you might just as easily be a limb of evil."

"One has to admit one's destiny."

"Naming your destiny the will of the Unnamed God doesn't make it so. And self-glorifying, besides."

They lay down in the same bed that they had shared before. Neither of them slept, though not this time from being racked with desire.

◆ 2 ◆

THEY AROSE WHEN IT was still dark, besting the cock at his own business.

Tea in a cup with a crack in the glaze; small beads of tea lined up vertically. He stared at it, wishing to learn a new language.

"Whom will you choose to save?" said Candle, when the sun made an effort to lighten the room. "I am not that girl, you know. That Quadling girl you saw pitched into the burning river. You cannot make me her by beggaring yourself for my needs. You can't choose me in that girl's place."

"Maybe I can't save anyone," he said. "Since Elphaba died, how many times have I set out to try? There was Nor, who was in prison. There was Princess Nastoya, in medical extremis. I make no headway in either direction. Even some miserable boy I saw on a road, whose granny was willing to sell him in exchange for my broom—I just walked on by. Why should I be beholden to those Birds? Find the old broom! Speak out danger to the world! I'm not a spokesperson for myself; how could I be for them?"

"You can do what you choose to do. You're hardly on death's door," she reminded him. "I mean, not anymore."

"And you'd have me believe that I have lost my virginity, and I don't even remember it. Life in a coma. Well, it figures. It's consistent, isn't it? I'll give you credit for that: you've read me correctly."

"You owe me nothing." Candle stood up and put her hands on the small of her back. "There is enough food and firewood here to see me through my months. It'll be spring before the baby comes. The goat will provide backup milk if I run dry. Or I'll take myself back to the maun-tery for the final lying-in. The maunts will know what to do. It's not the first time the maunts have seen such."

"If I owe *you* nothing," he said, "no one owes *anyone* a thing."

"Maybe no one does."

"Except the Unnamed God."

"Maybe we don't owe the Unnamed God anything," she said. "Maybe not allegiance, maybe not gratitude, maybe not praise, maybe not attention. Maybe the Unnamed God owes us."

He sputtered at her impiety, but she looked queasy: a touch of morn-ing sickness upon her, no doubt. She hurried away to take care of it in private. The yard outside the house was rimy with hoarfrost, and the new sun shone upon it harshly. He had to squint to watch her cast herself away from him.

She was shivering. As the winter came in, she'd have to go more slowly to the outhouse, what with ice on the ground, and a weight in her belly. He would try to tie some straw to a pole, leave her a makeshift broom to sweep away the snow, if nothing else.

He gathered the straw and threw it on the floor while he hunted for cord with which to bind it. In the splayed angles in which it fell, it spelled the burning letter again, a letter he couldn't read.

Dragonfings

WAS IT THAT he was better traveled now—or just that he was older? Had the Emerald City actually changed, or just his ability to apprehend it?

The Big Itself had never seemed shy of self-regard—Liir remembered that much. Now he became aware of how everything flourished on a hefty scale. Architectural metastasis. The chapels were like churches, the churches like basilicas. The government houses out-bloated the basilicas, with bigger columns, more imposing flights of steps, higher spires. Private homes were nothing shy of palaces-in-training.

In his absence, the Emerald City had undergone a makeover. Oceans of whitewash had been splashed to obliterate the grattifi. Along the canals, trees had been pollarded to force full head, and ringed with liquid lime to prevent disease. The strip he'd called Dirt Boulevard had been replanted and it served again as a promenade, with well-raked tracks for military drill, and meandering paths among bushes and fountains where the plutocrats might see and be seen.

He supposed it came down to this: The Emerald City was no longer the capital of Oz. It *was* Oz. It survived for the sole purpose of insuring its own survival.

Maybe it always had done so, but now there was no pretending otherwise. Were there always so many ministries, or were they simply better marked? The Ministry of Comfort—that was aid for the indigent. The Ministry of the Home Guard. The Ministry of Sincerity (the sign beneath read FORMERLY THE PRESS BUREAU).

The Ministry of Artistic License. Apparently now you had to apply to be an artist.

Obelisks, cenotaphs, marble statues, fluttering banners and pennants. Souvenirs in kiosks: Everything OZ. I love OZ! A keychain, a whistle, a reticule, a letter opener, a lorgnette case: OZ, OZ. A military band every half mile, performing gratis for the residents of the emerald hive. The City seemed to have its own theme song.

But for what, wondered Liir. For background? For show? Everyone seemed in a hurry, more so than he'd remembered. The cafés were thriving, the public trams dripping with riders, the piazzas clotted with tourists, the museums thronged. "Apostle Muscle," an exhibit showing at the Lord Chuffrey Exposition Hall, was advertised in broadsheets plastered on all the public notice boards. The graphic was brilliant, Liir thought: a male foot in an open, leather-strapped sandal stepping out of a cloud. The painted landscape receding to the horizon showed that wherever the Apostle had already set his foot, communities like miniature Emerald Cities sprung up within the precise outline of his footly influence, from the heel to the sprawl of toes.

Liir turned his back on Southstairs, but it wasn't all that hard to do. The Emerald City had grown taller, more prosperous. Southstairs was more hidden now, though some edict or other must be keeping the land around the Palace relatively low built, so its stately domes and minarets could still dominate the City center.

◆ **2** ◆

AS FOR THE citizens of the Emerald City, business seemed to be profiting them very well. Skirts were thicker, hems were longer, fur trimmed everything, from ladies' hats to brougham bedeckings. Men's waistcoats were cut fuller to accommodate bigger bellies. The dry goods used by clothiers looked overdyed: the colors richly saturated, as if intended to be seen from a distance, as on a stage. The effects would have been comic but for a costive sobriety that seemed to have swept the City like an infection.

It'd be comfortable to be here, Liir decided. Everywhere else, ordinary folks laugh so much because they're nervous. Being stationed in Qhoyre, we laughed like morons: it helped us deal. It also made us friends. But perhaps you don't need to laugh if all your deprivations have been alleviated, your anxieties relieved. You can afford to be judicious, keep a civil tongue in your head, and speak in a lower tone of voice.

There were riffraff, as before—and a good thing, too, or he'd have stuck out even more than he did. Not so many Animals, still. A few in the service industry. An aproned old Warthog Governess, pushing a pram, some Rhino security guards.

And kids. Kids looking terribly old. Probably alley-cat thieves among the younger of them. Older kids, sloe-eyed teenagers, who cast him sly looks, trying to make out if he was an easy mark, competition for trade, or a possible ally.

Ruddy Quadlings in their huddles of family, clam-colored Yunamata indigents surviving on handouts and ale. Dwarves looking uppity, and why not?—dwarves looking shifty, and so what. Munchkins, in sizes small, medium, or grande, who'd emigrated from their own Free State. Or maybe they were turfed out for passing secrets or engaging in black trade. Dirty-looking polybloods in tatters of blanket, stepping on hardened bare feet across raked gravel forecourts, holding out their hands until some welcoming committee came out with a cudgel.

Elphaba had come to the Emerald City once, as a young woman. Maybe even his age—he didn't know. She'd never said much about it. "Pimps and Prime Ministers, and you can't tell the difference," she'd growled once. Had she stuck out like a green thumb? Or were people more accepting back then? For better or worse, he was able to pass.

He guessed by the end of the day he might be imprisoned in Southstairs himself. He thought he was ready for it, and perhaps he deserved nothing better. Still, if that were so, why was he taking care not to stand out? Skulking where he needed to skulk, striding confidently when the streetscape required it? A deeper intention at work, he guessed: that old beast-in-the-bear-trap thing that humans did so well? Even the reprobate who knows he's a moral coward wants to keep drawing breath.

Despite the building boom that the new prosperity allowed, the Emerald City remained familiar. Liir found his way more or less correctly to the Arch of the Wizard and along the Ozma Embankment, through the tony district of Goldhaven right to Mennipin Square, at the far end of which the house of Lord Chuffrey presided.

He wasn't exactly sure what he could accomplish, but he had to start somewhere. The Lady Glinda, née Upland, now Chuffrey, was his only contact in the Emerald City. Even retired from public life, surely a former throne minister would have access to the army, yes? To its barracks, its dragon stables, the lot. Could she be convinced to come to his aid again, after a whole decade?

Mennipin Square hadn't suffered any loss of prestige in the years since he'd been here. The house fronts were decorated with swags of green and gold. Lurlinemas was coming, of course. Ceremonial greens and garlands of winter golds were woven through the uprights of the iron fence that surrounded the square's private gardens.

In order to get to the kitchen yard where he had once presented himself, he had to pass the mansion's front entrance and turn a corner. When he reached the approach to the front door, he paused. Beyond the gravel of the carriage drive rose a flight of granite steps. At the landing, in front of the carved double doors, stretched a huge tiger in the act of licking its balls. A chain around its neck locked the tiger to one of the marble pillars supporting the portico, but there appeared enough length in the chain to allow the beast room to stretch and lunge. Sensibly Liir kept his distance. He looked, though. He'd never seen a wild animal chained in such an upper-purse locale.

The creature paused an instant and shifted its eyes without lifting its head, looking out from beneath tiger brows. "What are you looking at?" he growled softly.

A Tiger. A talking Animal, tied up like a farm dog, to scare off intruders.

Liir wanted to rush on, but to ignore the Tiger's belligerent question was to suggest a condescension he didn't feel. And Elphaba would have taken it all in stride. "I'm looking at a whole lot of Tiger," he said at last.

"That's the right answer," purred the Tiger. "You're either smart or lucky."

"I'm just brave," said Liir. "Have to be. I'm coming to see Lady Glinda."

"Well, you're *not* lucky, then," the Animal answered, "because she's not at home."

Liir's shoulders fell.

"She's off at Mockbeggar Hall. The Chuffrey country estate, down Kellswater way. A month in mourning."

"Mourning?"

"You just rolled off the cabbage cart? Looks like it. Her husband died. Didn't you know? Lord Chuffrey. He made a big donation to the Emperor and the banker's cheque had hardly cleared the First Accountant's office when Lord Chuffrey breathed his rummy last. Perhaps he thought he'd never be in as expensive a state of grace again, and might as well take advantage of it. Lady Glinda's bereaved."

"I'm sorry for her," said Liir.

"Don't be. She's not exactly a pauper widow. And she wasn't much more than a paper wife to him, anyway, so I hardly think she's fussed. She'll miss him, no doubt—we all will. He was a good sort in his way. Supports my family upcountry. Or he did."

Liir slumped against the stone gatepost. "Great. So what next?"

"I wouldn't come too close if I were you," said the Tiger. "I may be chatty when I'm bored, but if I chat too much I might work up an appetite." He winked at Liir, who moved back a few feet.

"Why do you stay?"

"Well, it certainly isn't the chains, is it? I sport these for effect," said the Tiger. He tossed his head and his eyes flashed in anger. "I mean, it's a statement of style, isn't it? Or are you *really* only a cabbage-head?" He was on his feet, and he roared. The gate shook on its pins, and Liir was halfway through Mennipin Square before he realized he was running.

So much for his first idea. Well, he'd have to work without the help and blessing of Lady Glinda, Society Goddess. And he'd hoped for a square meal to set himself up for harder campaigns. He had only the small scraps of dried fruit and bread that Candle had forced into his hands before he left.

The last time Liir had been so destitute in the Emerald City, he had gone to work in the Home Guard. Ready to improvise, he headed again to the main barracks campus near Munchkin Mousehole, in the lee of the low hill on which the Palace in its opulence squatted.

Boys, and a few girls, too, were running about the same sward on which he had once played gooseball with the bored soldiers. The grass was brown and flattened, weary of winter even before Lurlinemas Day, but the cries that rang out among the children seemed green enough to him. Unless he should run forward and capture the ball, and impress himself onto a team by dint of his swift responses, he would remain invisible to the children. Why not? He was a tallish, slightly ravaged young man, thinner, more ribby than the sleek soldiers who toyed with the kids.

He saw himself through their eyes: his cord-held hair, his green eyes, his new habit of ducking his head, scratching his elbows. A handsome enough beggar, maybe, but a beggar nonetheless, and too grown up to be thrown a bread roll for charity's sake. If the notion of charity still obtained here. He wasn't yet able to tell if it did.

Still, children at their games! It pleased him to watch. He remembered the children he had sung to, briefly, on the steps of a church when he first came to the Emerald City. He had smiled at them, had felt for them in a general sense, but he hadn't stood solid with them. Each time of life is such a prison, a portable prison. The children here on this fairway, the soldiers messing about with them, were no more like Liir than a Tiger was, or an elf or a—

"Cutting an old chum with impunity, and not blinking an eye. You've considerable nerve, you have."

Liir shook his head to register. A soldier at his left shoulder, breathing hard; he must have been among the fellows playing at gooseball, and come running up behind him. Hah. So much for the more sublime perception of the isolate.

"You don't remember my name any more than I yours." The fellow swept his damp blond hair off his sweaty brow. "What'd you do to deserve early retirement? *Our* tenures have been indefinitely extended with no right to petition otherwise."

Liir shook his head, wondering if he should play dumb, play it as a case of mistaken identity. Play wounded in battle? Play for time anyway. He hadn't worked out any particulars of strategy, just intentions.

"It's bon Cavalish, if you please. Trism, actually. You came into the service from this very field, and I was the one told you how."

Liir wrinkled a smile at him and shrugged. Work with what you have. *Trism*. Yes. A Minor Menacier . . . and in dragon husbandry, if he remembered correctly.

Coolly, Liir said, "That's a good eye you have for a distant acquaintance. I was standing there thinking how blind we all are to each other, and I didn't even recognize you."

"And I got you, but not your name."

"Ko, that's what I go by. Liir, commonly."

"Liir Ko. Right. You went off somewhere a few years back."

"I did indeed," said Liir, "but I don't want to talk about it, certainly not here."

"O ho," said Trism, and then, "O *ho*. A deserter? No."

"You'll get in trouble being seen with me."

"Trouble. That'd be fun." Trism looked this way and that. "Well, unless you're reenlisting voluntarily, you're making a big mistake showing yourself here. Or do you *want* to be caught? Are you spying for one of our enemies?"

"I don't even know who our enemies are," said Liir. "I never have."

"Well, if you've really gone and scampered, you count as one of them, so you better make yourself scarce. However, don't drift too far. The service is a bit more lenient in some matters than it used to be. They had to relax a few rules if they were going to keep us enlisted forever. We get a little city freedom, if you know what I mean. I'm sprung tonight till midnight. Hang about somewhere and we'll have a drink. Don't forget. Don't forget me." He gripped Liir's collar suddenly. "I haven't forgotten you."

✦ 3 ✦

TRISM WAS AS GOOD AS HIS WORD and was waiting at a sidewalk place in Burntpork, the low-rent district. "Welcome to the Cherry and Cucumber," he said, handing up a full pint of lager before Liir'd had a chance to take a stool. "They keep their license to serve real beer because they sponsor the annual Holy Action Day festivities."

"The what?"

"You're *way* out of touch. We can change that. Cheers."

The place was too empty at this hour for Liir to bring up the matter most pressing to him. Voices would carry. Scrawled in chalk on a slate above the bartender's station, though, was a message announcing: "Tonight, Fourth Comeback Tour, Sillipede Herself. 9:30. No tomatoes." The notice didn't actually promise a crowd, but Liir could hope. Or they could wander elsewhere.

Liir wasn't inclined to talk about himself much, and found that easy enough to manage. Trism didn't ask. He relaxed almost at once, and chattered at length about the military as if he and Liir had been best of friends back then. This one, that one, regulations by the book, funny pranks on supercilious superiors. "And what's become of Commander Cherrystone?" asked Liir as lightly as he could. He didn't want to be recognized as a deserter by someone with the power to slap him in chains for it.

"Dunno." Trism turned to survey the room, which, as hoped, was filling up with a noisier clientele, some of whom had been drinking before they arrived.

"We're not likely to meet a commanding officer here," said Liir, "I suppose."

"Anything's possible. Tastes vary. Doubt it, though."

On their third round, Liir began. "You were special forces, weren't you? Back then?"

"To the Unnamed God, we're all special," said Trism. Liir was unsure if he heard sarcasm in the rejoinder. "Minor Menacier back then."

"Husbandry, wasn't it?"

"Oh, the lad's sharper than he looks. Yeah, husbandry, for a time."

"Not now?"

"I don't like to talk about my work when I'm out larking."

"But I'm curious. Sounded very important. We dug the foundations for that new building—the stables."

"Basilica."

"That's right. I remember now. No stables below?"

"Look, it's Sillipede. The very one. A living legend. She must be ninety." An extremely odd, angular creature was being hoisted onto a small stage. Behind her, whisking spittle from the mouthpiece of her willow flute, stood a young woman dressed in little more than golden epaulets slapped strategically about her body. A couple of Bears opened their music cases and began to turn pegs to tune up: an Ugabumish guitar, a violinsolo. "So few Animals with real jobs, but if you drummed Animals entirely out of the music business, nobody'd hear a note."

Sillipede began to warble. She was so old that it was impossible to tell if she was a man or a woman, nor if she was trying to make an attempt to imitate either her own or the opposite gender. In the cracked and breathy voice, though, the singer still had considerable power, and the room quietened down somewhat. Liir had to wait for the first number to end before continuing his remarks.

"I mean, specifically, dragons," he said through the applause.

"Hush, you're not being polite," said Trism. "Isn't she something?"

"Something or something else or something else again. Maybe not to my taste. Do we have to stay?"

"And give up our good seats? Have one more beer and let's see the first set through, anyway."

Sillipede bumbled her way through some difficult patches, talking more than she sang. She lit a cigarette halfway through one number and burnt her fingers, and told her backup to can it. "I'm hardly myself tonight," she told the crowd, "what with this dreadful heathen holiday approaching. *Lurlinemas.* Can you believe the Emperor in his goodness allows any reminder of those archaic superstitions? Can you believe that he in his goodness? Can you believe his goodness? I mean, can you? I'm asking you a question here."

The room was silent. Was she spinning out a comic story or was she losing her marbles? She took a drag on her smoke.

"Don't get me wrong," she said. "I can see on the faces of those of you who still *have* faces that you're afraid you've wandered into a conventicle of traitors instead of a comeback concert. Please. Relax. If we get raided and we all end up in Southstairs, I'll lead singalongs on the weekends. I will. That's a promise."

The flautist relieved an itch beneath one of the epaulets.

"I'm not proselytizing. Neither *for* the Unnamed God nor *against* its holy un-name. That would be plain old sedition, and frankly at my age, I'm just not up to it." She made a face. "Sedition is unthinkable. Although to say something is 'unthinkable' is, of course, to have been able to think of it. And I'm at the age where I'm losing language faster than I'm gaining it. I don't know what sedition means anymore. I never said it. I never never said the word *screwy*, did I? Did I say the word *complicity*?"

Someone in the back muttered something a little ugly. Sillipede said, "I can see you back there squirming. You and your sour puss. Don't get out much, do we? You remind me of someone. You remind me of someone that I would find really annoying. What're you getting so feisty about? I'm just taking a cigarette break. Shooting the breeze. If you think I'm being unscrupulous, give me a break: I'm too old to have scruples anymore. Where would I put them?"

"What is she on about?" muttered Liir.

"She's going to end up either in prison or the ward for the incurably old," said Trism. He was red in the face. "Maybe you're right; we better go."

But they couldn't get up while she was in her monologue: that would single them out for her catcalling, draw attention their way. She'd be all over them.

She wandered a bit in the crowd. Now she looked more like an old man in makeup, now like an old woman trying to look young. She looked more human than anything else, though that didn't necessarily mean handsome. Liir prayed she wouldn't come over and start talking to him. He had a strong feeling she would.

Under the table, Trism reached for his hand and squeezed it. He was more nervous than Liir. This place wasn't sanctioned by the Home Guard, Liir guessed, and Trism would be in serious jeopardy if things got any hotter. Liir detached his hand.

"I'm a ditsy old relic, don't mind me," said Sillipede. "You young things take everything so seriously. But you don't remember the bad old days of the Wizard. The drought. How we lived back then. How we laughed! Hah. A lark. And hardly anyone stood up to him. Only some fool witch from the hinterlands. And we all know what happens to witches."

Someone hissed.

"These days are so much better," the creature said. "Ask Sillipede. Sillipede knows. I'm old enough to remember when the Ozma Regent was still the crowned head of the nation, and baby Ozma a little bundle of coos and poos. I'm so old I was already retired when the Wizard arrived and set things to rights. Hard times then! Things are better now, ain't they? Well, depends on your outlook, I guess. If things ain't actually better, they sure are *gooder.*

"These times," she continued, "so righteous! Everyone so much more moral! Put some clothes on your nakedness, girl, or the vice squad'll be down our throats. Or down your throat, anyway, if you look at 'em like that."

The flutist looked as nonplussed as the audience.

"You got to hold on to your values, if you can still reach them," said the chanteuse. "Buy some values, rent 'em, steal 'em if you have to. Sell 'em for a profit when tastes change. Whatever works. Is this a crock, or what?"

She regained the small stage and put her hand to her eyes, shading the flare of the lights. "I can see you. I know you're there," she said. "I know you're in there somewhere. I can wait." She signaled the Bear on bass and said, "A torch song about lost hopes, Skoochums, how 'bout. For old time's sakes. In the key of E, Harrikin. No, not B. I said E—E for Elphaba. One. Two. Three. Whatever."

The Bear lazily thwacked out a bass run, and Sillipede drew a breath, but then spoke again, interrupting the intro. "And that other problem, all that graffiti! I saw it again on my way here, scrawled on some library wall. 'Elphaba lives!' What's that supposed to mean? I ask you. Isn't it just too much? Why don't they keep their sloppy old slogans to themselves? Elphaba lives! As if."

She flicked her cigarette butt into someone's lager. "Now I just feel all riled up and alive. This ain't happened since I left double digits. So I am going to sing a beautiful old hymn to prove it to you. Anyone who's with the Emperor can stand and sing it with me, to show we're not just scratching our balls here, are we, folks?"

The band patched together an intro and Sillipede sauntered into a familiar melody. The patrons of the place were irritated, a bit unnerved by the theatrics, and unsure who was being made fools of: the Emperor, the Unnamed God, Sillipede herself, or them—or anyone idiotic enough to take a position against the Palace. But the song was balm itself—devotional, a bit flowery, familiar. Complexities gave way to the simpler sentiments. People stood and sang in defiance of Sillipede's posturing. In the shadows and shuffling, Liir and Trism escaped. Trism grabbed Liir's hand as if he might try to duck away; Liir couldn't help squeezing back. He was wound up. *E for Elphaba.* It was as if, these years later, he'd finally attended her wake.

• 4 •

THEY WALKED ALONG a quay in the Lower Quarter. Elsewhere in Oz it was probably snowing, but with the warm smoke of ten thousand coal fires, Liir and Trism felt only a particulate moisture in the air, part rain, part mist. Flames burning in lampposts gave off a pulsing, melon-colored glow.

"Mustn't be late, I assume," said Liir.

"One can hear the bells of the basilica all over the City. These days of the New Piety, they ring on the half hour. We've some time yet."

"That place made you tense. Where're we going?"

"I've been there before, but not on Treason Night."

"You think that was treasonous?" Liir was aghast. "I thought it"—he governed his language—"only stupid."

"She'd do better to keep her opinions to herself. Or organize them first, anyway. I wasn't even sure what she was on about, but it takes something like whiskey courage to pretend that much skepticism about the Apostle Emperor. He's a good fellow. The people love him. I myself feel flattered to have met him personally."

"You have? Really? What's he like?"

Trism shot him a look. "Of course I have. I was with you the first time it happened. The night before you lot shipped out? Remember? He offered us his carriage. He was cynical and louche then, as I remember. A lost soul. His Awakening hadn't happened."

"The Emperor of Oz . . . no. Shell? Shell Go-to-hell Thropp?"

"The First Spear himself. Can you really not have known? Where *have* you been? The moon?"

The very paving stones on the quay seemed more slippery. "I don't get it. Everyone talks about the Emperor's . . . his virtue. Shell was the last person to have any virtue. He was a spy, wasn't he—didn't someone say? Anyway, he used extract of poppyflower to opiate the young women in Southstairs and fuck them silly. I know that for a fact."

"Well, who better to speak for the Unnamed God, then, than one who has sinned so egregiously? Talk about your recoveries . . . the Awakening happened, and he heard the voice of the Unnamed God, telling him to lead. You know his sisters were the two witches? Nessarose and Elphaba Thropp?"

Liir felt ill. "It's just too . . . uncanny. Too unlikely."

"Not as unlikely as all that. Who is exempt from the claw of salvation? The more sinful you are, the more likely salvation can take root. His father was a unionist minister, after all. A missionary, I think."

"He's a charlatan, Shell is."

"May have been once. Don't think so now. He believes he was Awakened in order to lead Oz through this desperate time."

"Are we so desperate that we need the likes of him—"

"Well, you tell me," said Trism. His voice had gone lower, intimate. He leaned in and almost put his chin on Liir's shoulder. "How desperate are any of us at any given moment? Hmmm? Are any of us so desperate that we might, say, attack an unarmed rural settlement at night and burn it into the river?"

Liir pivoted to glare at Trism, who reached out and pinned Liir's right arm behind his back, whispering, "You shitty little creep."

"Let me go. What is this? A one-person tribunal? A vendetta? Let me go. Where are we?" In the mist Liir had lost his bearings. "How do you know anything about me? And what's it to you? I was doing the Emperor's *work,* Trism. Your precious leader. His bidding. Let me go."

"I'm going to beat your head in and then shove your sorry carcass into the water." By now Trism had both of Liir's hands behind his back, and Trism was kicking at cobbles randomly, to find one that was loose and use it for braining.

Liir struggled. Trism, in military trim, was fitter and had had the advantage of surprise. To yell wouldn't help: a police force would side with Trism at once. "Look," Liir said, trying not to sound terrified. "I'm bone tired. What do you care about what happened south of Qhoyre? Aren't you a company man? Head office mastered that situation in a flash, I've heard."

"I heard what *you* did. How could I not? Soldiers gossip worse than housewives. Because of that attack, the Quadlings around Qhoyre struck out at Cherrystone's garrison. You lost some of your buddies, buddy. And then the Emperor called up his brand-new defensive system and deployed it against the natives."

Liir began to get it. "Oh ho. But that was your specialty. Those were your dragons."

"I was one of the team. Prime Menacier of the division. Right. And I'd been told the dragons were to be held in abeyance, paraded for show on Holy Action Day. The annual display of military might and moral purpose. Scare the rabble and comfort the nervous. Nothing like good defenses to allow citizens to sleep well at night."

"And you believed every word of what was told you, and never meant to hurt a fly. I know that story. Let me go, Trism. Come on. You're hurting me."

"I've only started to hurt you. Get used to it. Because of your fucking about, the dragons were called up from their catacombs. And you haven't seen merciless until you've seen those beasts at work."

Liir was near to spitting. "I have seen merciless, Trism. As it happens. I was attacked by your little trained pets."

It was Trism's turn to start, and with the advantage, Liir tried to pull away. He half managed, but they ended up in a tumble on the pavement, fighting. They rolled in puddles and a plod of horse dung, and Trism ended up on top, his knees on Liir's chest.

"I'm going to kill you. I saw you standing there on the playground, and I thought: there *is* an Unnamed God, and it has delivered you to me to kill. Your cruel actions have sentenced me to a life more wretched than anything you have known. Once the military strategists saw what the dragons could do, nothing for it but that they should be used again. Trained more precisely. My life is *chained* to the job of perfecting the killing capacity of those creatures." He was as close to wailing as yelling, and Liir saw now what he hadn't noticed so far: Trism bon Cavalish was a shattered person.

"Kill me then," Liir said. "It'll make you feel a whole lot better, I can just tell. And maybe me, too, the way things are going. But hear me out first. It was the Emperor's word that started this whole thing. He required Cherrystone to invent an incident. Maybe he wanted a reason to launch a dragony attack all along, I don't know. I was doing the bidding of my company commander."

"And that's all I'm doing, and between us there's hundreds and hundreds dead, and more hundreds living in terror, and even more hundreds ready to kill us back, if they could only find a way."

Liir let Trism sob. Well, he didn't have much choice. Trism's nose dripped on Liir's face, but Liir couldn't lift his arms to wipe it off. "We're more or less in the same boat, you know," Liir said in as even a voice as the sentiment allowed, when Trism had regained some composure. "We've both done some serious damage."

Trism took a huge breath, nodded, and then removed his knees from Liir's chest. Liir sat up and, as discreetly as he could, shook the snot off his forehead.

• 5 •

THEY WALKED ACROSS the Law Courts Bridge and disappeared into the alleys and courtyards of the Lower Quarter. The place teemed with charlatans, addicts, and runaways; it stunk of sizzling night sausage and sewage, and rang with the laughter of the mad. We belong nowhere else, thought Liir; better get accustomed to it.

They could talk, though, without fear of being overheard; and in not looking at each other they could say more.

Trism bon Cavalish was the chief dragon master. He wasn't governor of the dragon stables, but he trained the creatures with a sure hand and a regulating eye. He had the longest tenure on the staff. His work required him to follow the exploits of the dragons and fine-tune their training.

He knew that a pack of dragons from the west had returned with a broom and a cape, though he didn't know where this bounty had come from. Liir, of all places! Trism knew about the scrapings of the missionary maunts, among, it turned out, several dozen others.

"Scrapings," said Liir with a shudder. Candle had mentioned such a thing. "I hardly know what it means . . ."

The claws are sharp as razors, oppositional pinchers like a human thumb and forefinger, Trism explained. A human can build a miniature ship in an empty jeroboam, and a dragon can remove a face with as few as nine incisions.

Trism was curt. "Don't ask me for the rationale. I know one thing: the dragons only go after the young. They're trained that way." He squared his shoulders. "*I* trained them that way. The theory is that when the young are brought down in their prime, it is more—alarming— useful—than if some old codger or crone is bumped off."

• 253 •

Why hadn't the dragons scraped Liir's face? He was young enough. Maybe they thought the broom and cape were all the trove they needed. Or maybe they saw something in Liir that stopped them.

"But maunts!" Liir said. "Young women devoting their lives to the service of the Unnamed God? It doesn't figure."

Trism explained that the old maunteries, with their traditions of independence, didn't suit the leadership style of the Emperor. The Apostle of the Unnamed God—

"What's all this about the Apostle?"

"That's what the Emperor calls himself. The humblest of the humble has been exalted by the Unnamed God. So the Apostle feels obliged to exercise the authority granted him." It seemed that some of the maunteries about Oz were led by older women raised in an archaic scholastic tradition. Some superiors were becoming dangerously out of touch with the needs of the common folk, and fell to asking bothersome questions about the spiritual authority of the Emperor. Such foment could only erode the confidence of the nation.

"Is that it?" asked Liir. "Is this a moment of foment?"

"I'm not privy to the thinking. Information's meted out on a need-to-know basis. But I've heard the western tribes were close to uniting by treaty, to defend against City interests in their land. The dragon attacks could confound the tribes, cause them to mistrust one another, if they didn't know who was behind the attacks.

"The faces of those young missionaries you mention," Trism concluded, working to maintain his composure. "They've been cured and stored. They're going to be taken out at the next Holy Affairs Day and exhibited. A point is going to be made."

There was worse still. The dragons—there were several dozen of them—were fed on the corpses of freshly killed humans. That bloody diet helped stoke the dragons with the strength needed to fly the hundreds of miles to the west. The cadavers were imported directly from a killing chamber in Southstairs, where a fresh supply was always available, thanks to the culling campaigns of the Under-mayor.

"Chyde," intoned Liir. "The guy with the rings."

Trism was nonplussed. "Is Shell the spy, or is it you?"

"I get around. Find the company I deserve. Go on."

"Well, with all that folderoodle, human corpses freshly bled and rendered into cutlets, do you wonder I am a wreck? The dragons weren't my idea, but I was elevated to the position, and now they're under my supervision."

"Whose idea were they? Shell's not that clever."

Trism cast Liir a dark look. "Who can believe anyone anymore? But I met Shell again—as Emperor I mean, of course—a while ago. I had a private audience, not long after his Elevation to the Imperialcy."

Liir folded his arms and leaned against a parapet. They'd walked on, climbing out of the Lower Quarter as the streets climbed. The lights of the alleys of the Burntpork district burned below the escarpment. "Do tell."

"He was humility personified, Liir. Make that face if you like. You distrust everything. He's a little thicker about the waist, very quick of wit and . . . almost tender, I guess. His Awakening has given him a largesse and a zeal. He talked about it. Why shouldn't he lead? 'Choosing the lowliest among us,' he said, indicating himself. 'A fornicator and a sot.' He seemed pretty shocked. 'What am I but a shell—waiting to be filled with the spirit of the Unnamed God?' "

"What form did his Awakening take, I wonder? I thought people who heard voices were generally considered lunatics."

"Who knows. He grew up in the thick of it, though, didn't he? He'd had those two powerful sisters; next to them he must always have felt like shredded cabbage."

"Are we talking about the same Shell? Come on!"

"Come on yourself. Suppose everyone in your family was thought to be wicked. Even were called *Wicked,* almost as a title—"

But they were, thought Liir; it was my family, too, or as good as.

"—what would you have done in Shell's place—as . . . alleviation? Compensation? Damage control? Shoot, he may have believed the next flying house or flying bucket of water was meant for him. You'd sign on with a Higher Authority if you were he, wouldn't you?"

"Shell was about the last one I'd have fingered for a low self-image. Surprise, surprise. Now he works out his inferiority at the helm of the nation . . ."

"He sees it as destiny. He showed me a page torn out of a book of magic. The Scarecrow found it in the Wizardic apartments after the abdication. It was in an indecipherable script, but it had been laboriously translated. I suppose by the Wizard. 'On the Administration of Dragons' it said."

Liir felt creepy. He knew that the Wizard had wanted Elphaba's Grimmerie. She had sworn it would never happen. This sounded like a bit of it. How had it gotten here?

"He convinced me it was the right thing to do," continued Trism. "I believed him, mostly because he believes himself. He's not lying; he's not the sham that the Wizard was, or misguided like Glinda the Glamorous, establishing libraries wherever she planted her jeweled scepter. Neither was he the ineffectual front man of a cabal of bankers, like the Scarecrow. He's the genuine article."

"The genuine article of what?" It was Liir's turn to scorn. "He convinced you to take part in something so heinous?"

"He asked me. What could I say? It was like the Unnamed God came down—"

"Isn't the Unnamed God actually unnamed so that you can't confuse it with someone named Shell Thropp?"

"I'm just telling you, since you asked. We've all heard that the bankers in Shiz have been withdrawing investments from the Free State of Munchkinland. Lord Chuffrey was the chief architect of that strategy. Sanctions against the Munchkins. They're not small enough already, bring them to their little knees. The exercise of dragon power was billed as a necessary lead-up to an annexation of Restwater in western Munchkinland. Well, the Emerald City needs the water, you know."

"All that bores me. You still knew what you were training dragons to do."

"I did," said Trism. "The dragons were the Second Spear."

If the Seventh Spear could immolate Bengda, what might the Second Spear be capable of? And the Emperor, the First Spear? "Can't you ask for a reassignment?"

"Dragonmaster bon Cavalish? Reassigned? Don't be absurd. They couldn't replace me. I'm too valuable. My assistants are assigned to the stables on a quick rotation so they can't learn too much. There's no replacement trained to take my place. Not yet anyway, it's all too new. In the development and testing stages."

"You could just leave. Scamper, as you put it. The way I did."

"That would make me feel better for about an hour. It would do no good beyond that. The dragons would still be there. Someone else would figure out how to hum them through their assignments. I'm talented, but I'm not a freak; I'm not indispensable. Besides, I have a family. They'd be fatally mortified if I disappeared in disgrace—and singled out for reprisals, like as not."

"A family." Liir whispered the word as if it meant *gelignite*. He felt cold, as if he was offended that his potential murderer no longer thought him worth the effort to kill. Falling from a great height again, and no warning. A *family*.

"What's *that* look for? I mean parents. Citizens of some standing. From good lines. Also a lunk of an older brother, simple in the head. Not such a good iteration of the bloodlines."

And Liir didn't crash-land but was rescued by that answer.

They were walking, circling, in the mist. It was a clammy night to be out on the street, but neither of them wanted to stop in another establishment. The mist thickened to a fog, and bells rang out. Ten-thirty. Someone emptied a chamber pot out an upper window, and the soldiers ducked together into a doorway just in time to escape being wasted. It put Liir in mind of the time they met, huddled in an archway, sheltered from a hailstorm.

For the first time since Quadling Country, Liir felt the appetite for a perguenay cigarette.

They kept on. Dragons. Where had they come from, these creatures of myth and mystery? Had a cluster of eggs been uncovered in some landslide in the Scalps, or in a mud-pocket in the badlands of Quadling Country? Trism wasn't certain.

Liir didn't have to ask about the more basic *why*. Not if the Emperor's aim was to make rural people cower. If a dragon was really a flying lizard, the original lizard of Oz was the Time Dragon. The foundation myth of the nation. In a subterranean cavern, deeper even than Southstairs, sealed over by earthquakes and landslides, the Time Dragon slept. He was dreaming the history of the whole world, instant by instant.

Trism was thinking along the same road. "I can tell you the inspiration," he said, and—a little pompously—recited the words of the anonymous Oziad bard.

> *"Behold the floor of rhymeless rock, where time*
> *Lies sleeping in a cave, a seamless deep*
> *And dreamless sleep, unpatterned dark*
> *Within, without. Time is a reddened dragon.*
>
> > *The claws refuse to clench, though they are made,*
> > *Are always made in readiness to strike*
> > *The rock, and spark the flint. Then to ignite*
> > *The mouth of time that, burning hot*
>
> *And cold in turn, consumes our tattered days . . ."*

"You have it down cold."

"And it goes on

> > *". . . then the burst*
> > *Of whitened sulfur spark. The fuse is lit.*
> > *The dragon's furnace starts to roar and ride*
> > *And time, being dreamt within, begins outside."*

Liir was awed. "You've had some schooling before the service."

"We had to memorize great quaffs of *The Oziad* in primary lessons at St. Prowd's," said Trism. "I was a day student on a bursary. Got top honors though."

"Well, it's awfully, uh, grand," said Liir. "The Time Dragon dreams up when we're born, when we're to die, and whether for lunch we'll get the roast pfenix stuffed with creamed oysters at the head table at St. *Prowd's,* or the day-old ploughman's, the roadsweeper's budget lunch?"

"If the unlettered farmers of Munchkinland and the factory workers of Gillikin believe that their fate is being determined by how the Time Dragon dreams them up, they don't need to bother to take responsibility for their actions or for changing their class and station in life."

"You too," said Liir. "You were brought through primary school to the services, and the Time Dragon dreamed you there at the head of this horrible stable. But you don't know what he's going to dream you to do next. Maybe it's scamper and leave those dragons to their fate."

"I said already. The family."

They came to a newsstand shuttered up for the night. ELPHABA LIVES was scratched in char on the boards. The family! Hah. "They think they own her," Liir said, suddenly disgusted. "The Witch would be foaming at the mouth. She was a flaming recluse and a crank." Even the handwriting had an intimate, proprietary look to it somehow.

"What do you care?"

Liir changed the subject. "Maybe it's your job to kill the dragons. Maybe that's why you're there. Maybe that's why our paths crossed again today."

"Are you *insane*? I couldn't do that."

"You could kill me, or at least you told me that you would. And I'm the least little lick of flame in your past. If it wasn't Qhoyre, if that hadn't worked, your superiors would have set up some other straw threat. I was being used no less than you are now. But I left, Trism. I did. You could, too."

"I told you. The parents," he said. "I'm trapped."

"How would it work?" said Liir. "Quick and permanent? Burn the stables down? Slice their heads off?"

Eleven-thirty bell. Time to start back for the barracks.

"Poison?"

"Didn't you hear me?" said Trism. "They'll kill my next of kin."

"Not if you didn't do it," said Liir. "I'll do it. I'll leave a note saying

I did so, and that I kidnapped you as a hostage. You'll be exonerated. They can't kill my next of kin—I don't have any."

He didn't add: Anyway, by some rumors, Shell is my next of kin, our holy Emperor. Let them go after the First Spear, if they must.

✦ 6 ✦

"TELL ME," said Liir as they stood outside the sentry gate, screwing up their courage, "how do you mesmerize a dragon?"

"It's not mesmerism, quite. I focus and I—hum—"

Liir raised an eyebrow. "Sweet nothings?"

"Nothing sweet."

"Come on."

Trism balked, but Liir pushed. They were both avoiding the risky moment of trying to get into the base. "Oh, all right," snapped Trism. "Truth is, my family's not all that exalted, despite the fancy 'bon' in my surname. Gentlemen farmers in Gillikin a couple of generations ago, but the gentlemanly part couldn't be afforded during the drought, and they farmed to eat after a while. I won a few hog-calling contests, which brought more shame than glory to the family, and then I did some sheepdog trials, too. I guess I have a knack. Proved there was dirt under the fingernails; it made my folks crazy. They were trying to breed up.

"Goes something like this," he said. "But I'm not telling you the whole whack: I've picked up the benefits of need-to-know. So this is the general stuff. I get up close to a dragon, which is hard work by itself. They're skittish and inbred, given the stocks we have to work with. Takes time. You have to be totally still and selfless as possible, become like a rag doll in their pen, till they relax. When they do, their breathing changes; it slows. I come in close and mount them. No, you can't ride a dragon, I mean I just climb up the pinions of their wings and settle my chest on their long strong neck, and straddle them. I crook my knees around the forward phalange of their wing. I circle the neck with my arms, the way I'd choke a man if I had to, only gently of course. This makes their ears fill with blood and stand up. It's arousal, basically. They're suggestible but also hugely intelligent, and I hum into their ears. Usually the left one, don't know why; it tends to cock backward a little more, I think."

"It *is* sweet nothings!"

"Shut up. I hum, line by line, the shape of the task at hand. If I hum a dragon to sleep, he sleeps—and I could jump up and down on his sensitive wings without waking him. If I hum him to fly, to hide, to hunt, to act alone, to be a team, to unlatch his dangerous claws, to cut, to scrape, to preserve, to return . . ."

"But you didn't hum four dragons to bully a boy-broomist out of the air and confiscate his broom . . ."

"No. And that's the worrying thing. I didn't. How would I know he'd be there? How could I?"

"Well," said Liir, "we're not a moment too soon, are we. But listen: why don't you just hum the dragons into docility? Or make them fly themselves into dead and deadening Kellswater?" Burning letters of thatch drowning in Waterslip.

"I don't think I could. I've always guessed that dragons are, essentially, antagonists. They take to attack more easily than to, say, flying in military formation."

"You could try."

"Not now. Not tonight." Trism cast a sideways glance at Liir. "I wouldn't trust myself to be able to concentrate so intently. One lapse of focus and I'm the midnight snack."

"No, don't try tonight," agreed Liir hurriedly.

Trism threw his military cloak around Liir's shoulders to finish what camouflage they could manage. "On we go, then, and see what happens."

THE SENTRY WAS yawning and ready for his relief to arrive. He was nodding over a pamphlet that looked suspiciously like "The Pieties of the Apostle," the tract printed at Apple Press Farm. Anyway, its arguments must have proven leaden and soporific; he waved Liir and Trism through the guardhouse without a second glance.

At this hour, the yard was largely deserted. Without opposition Liir and Trism circled about to the basilica with the stables beneath.

Since the dragons needed to be stabled, and yet their claws kept honed for precise military use, the stalls wanted constant cleaning. Dragon fewmets tended to corrode dragon claws. But some months before, Trism explained, sloppy stablehands had left behind a bucket of cleansing solvent helpful in disinfecting the floors of their stone stalls. A dragon had lapped up a quart and died in its sleep an hour later.

Several kegs of the germicide, already tapped and ready for dispersal, stood in the cleaning shed. Trism had keys.

Liir didn't want to look at the dragons. The coma he'd been in had blunted the memory of their attack, and that was fine with him. Still, out of his peripheral vision he allowed himself to take in the golden blur, the furnace heat, the sharp ammonia pong of breath and semen-sweet skin, the sound of deep-throated dragon purring.

But the first dragon turned its nose up at the bucket of risk.

"Not thirsty?" whispered Liir, when hearing Trism's report.

"Dragons are smart," said Trism. "That's why they're so trainable. They learn fast and they remember. This dragon may have seen the other die, or smelled his death and associated it with the smell of the cleanser. Maybe if we disguise it somehow."

The first bell after midnight. They had to work fast in order to have time to get away.

"If they won't drink, maybe they'll eat," said Trism at last. "Come on, the provisions cellar is down this way."

Into a chilly storeroom they tumbled. Bricks of ice laid out on slate stones kept the meat cold. At least it was bundled in old newsfolds and tied with string, so they didn't have to look at it closely. The parcels were sloppy, more mounded than squared off, about the size of saddlebags.

"Stop, don't retch," said Trism roughly. "The dragons will smell your stink and be put off their supper. Don't think of this as human flesh. It's the delivery of a necessary medicine, that's all. And may the Unnamed God have mercy on these poor quartered souls, and on ours."

"And the dragons'," added Liir, but now he wanted to see them, wanted to remember that attack, their canny strength. He needed to block out the thought of what they were carrying, armload by armload, up the stairs, but when he could no longer do that—peppery tears an inch thick in his eyes, all of an instant—he steadied himself:

You poor corpse, you thought you had died in vain, selected for slaughter by Chyde. You didn't. You're bringing down the House of Shell. In the most ungodly way, you're doing good. Bless you.

They doused the parcels with the poisonous decoction. As if they were tossing lighted coals into pools of flammable fluid, Liir and Trism dashed up and down the central corridor of the dragon stables, and along the several transepts, and lobbed the midnight snacks over the stout stone-ribbed doors. Those dragons who dozed woke up and ripped the packets open with their teeth. They ate so vigorously that small glistening gobbets of flesh spun in the air.

Only when the last one was done did Liir allow himself to climb up on a bench and look down into a stall.

The dragon faintly gave off its own coppery light. It was working at its meal without hesitation, snuffling with greed. The forearms twisted with a terrifying capacity for grace. The claws retracted, clicked, leaned against one another in efficient opposition, and gleamed a horny blue-silver. Then the creature turned and looked at Liir. Slobber fell from the back of its jaw as it slowed its eating. The intelligent eye—he could only see one—was gold and black, and its iris, shaped more like a peapod than a marble, rotated from a horizontal to a vertical slit, and widened.

He'd been recognized. This was one of the very beasts that had attacked him.

The creature reared up and slapped its heavy wings forward so that its body arced backward, slamming against the rear wall of the chamber. The snout raised and the mouth opened, and bloody teeth moved into position, and a sound issued that was not a bellow nor a snort, but the beginning of a dragon trumpet volley.

"Shit, that's not good," said Trism, grabbing him by the shoulder. "Let's get out of here."

"They're raising an alarm," said Liir.

"They're dying, and they know it, and at least one of them knows why."

· 7 ·

TRISM AND LIIR STOPPED at the top of the landing. In one direction, the stairs continued farther up, to the vaulted basilica proper. The door to the outside, through which they'd come, stood ajar. There was no sound of anyone dashing about to see what, if anything, was wrong. Maybe dragons snorted and bellowed in their sleep all night long, and this was nothing new.

Liir waited. "What?" said Trism.

"I'm not leaving without the broom. I've promised myself that."

"No reason you shouldn't have it back. But we'll have to hurry." Trism fitted a key into the only other door opening off the landing.

"Wait here," he said. "Inside is the stuff of nightmares."

Liir followed him in regardless. In their treason the two men were bound together, at least for the night, and Liir didn't want to lose sight of his accomplice.

The sloped ceiling suggested the long narrow room was a shed appended to the basilica. Probably built low so as not to interfere with the colored windows giving into the sacred space above, Liir thought. Unheated at this hour, the room reeked with the juices of pickling agents and tanning acids.

Trism used a quickflint to light a portable oil lamp. "Keep your eyes down, if you're going to follow me in here," he muttered, shielding the light from the glass chimney with one hand. "The broom is in the far cupboard, and I'll have to fiddle with the lock." He hurried between tall slanted tables on which some sort of piecework was in progress.

"How much danger are we in?" asked Liir.

"You mean in the next five minutes, or for the rest of our short, sorry lives? The answer's the same: lots."

The small light went with Trism toward the cupboard. In the returning shadows, Liir moved nervously and disturbed a pile of wooden hoops about a foot across. They clattered to the floor. "Shhh, if you possibly can," called Trism in a hoarse whisper.

Picking up the materials, Liir listened to the sounds. The dragons below, snorting and nickering, and their wings like vast bellows pumping. The jangle of Trism's key ring, heavy old iron skeletons throttling against the glassy tinkle of smaller jewel case keys. The snap and thrust of a lock being pulled back, and then the rustle of dried sedge and straw. The broom. Elphie's broom. Again.

He had to see it, as Trism turned; he looked up in something like love. Trism had the Witch's cape looped ungainly over one arm, and the broom under his elbow, as he fiddled to close the closet again and lock its door. Then he turned, and held the light up so he could see his way back to Liir. He was smiling. So, too, in a sense, were the semblance of faces that sprung out of the shadows on the inside wall of the chamber. Ten or twelve or so, plates of face: creepy voodoo stuff, Liir thought at first. The scraped faces, repaired with catgut twine where needed, were strung with rawhide cord inside beech-wood hoops like the ones Liir had upset.

"Shhh, will you shush?" said Trism. "I told you not to look."

✦ 8 ✦

SOME MOMENTS LATER, when at Liir's insistence they had finished removing the dozen remnants of human countenance, and had stored them in two satchels, Trism said, "If you're really serious about leaving a note claiming responsibility, now's the time to do it. Can you manage ink and a pen?"

"I know how to write," said Liir. "I didn't go to St. Prowd's, but I *can* write."

"Shut up. I mean, are your muscles shaking too much to control the nib?"

He had to work at it. The third parchment was good enough to serve.

I abducted your craven dragonmaster and aborted his evil work. He will pay for his offenses against lonely travelers.

Signed, Liir son of Elphaba

"Son of Elphaba?" said Trism. "Not *the* Elphaba?" He looked at Liir with a new respect, or maybe it was outright disbelief. Or dawning horror?

"Probably not," said Liir, "but if no one can prove it so, it's equally hard to disprove, isn't it?"

Trism looked at the note again. "Is *craven* overdoing it a bit?"

"Let's go."

"I hope this is only rhetoric, that I'll pay for my offenses."

"You will pay, Trism. You will. We all do. You'll pay, but you won't pay me." He clutched the broom. "You've already paid me."

As they hurried away, the noise rose. The poisoned dragons were falling into fits, roaring, throwing themselves against the walls of their stables. The basilica above shook with it.

◆ **9** ◆

THEY DIDN'T DARE present themselves at an inn or a hotel at that hour of the night, and all of the gates of the City were closed. After skulking about in the fog, they eventually hopped a fence in one of the City's small private cemeteries, and found a lean-to used for wheelbarrows and digging supplies. The mist turned to a thunderous rain, sheeted with weird winter lightning. There, under the cape, they huddled for warmth, and shuddered. Just before they fell asleep, Liir murmured, "No humming, now."

They rose before dawn. Trism had enough coin in his pocket to buy them milky tea and a few cream biscuits from the first street vendor. They argued about the best way to leave the City without detection, but their bravery had subsided. They chose Shiz Gate because the welfare of the Emerald City and the northern province of Gillikin were the most tightly entwined, and the traffic there the heaviest.

Providence provides: that's why it's called providence. They shambled through Shiz Gate by helping an old merchant whose wagon had suffered a split wheel on the cobbles. The sentries at Shiz Gate paid them little mind, deep in gossip of their own about the attack on the basilica the night before. Word of it was abroad already.

Once through, they abandoned the hapless old man in his search for a wheelwright, and ambled north until they came to a high road looping back. Hatless, in civilian clothes, they meandered westward, the gleaming profile of the Emerald City always at their left shoulders. The sun rose, shone for a while, and then became cloaked in cloud. By nightfall they'd reached the outskirts of Westgate. Liir wanted to keep on toward the Shale Shallows, until he could recognize one of the tracks that led southeast through the oakhair forest, between the great lakes, and back toward Apple Press Farm.

But their limbs, by now, would go no farther, so they counted up their coin. As night fell, colder than the one before, they presented themselves at the door of a ramshackle tavern and inn on the main Kellswater Road. A sign reading WELCOME ARMS dangled on a broken hinge from the lamppost. The Gillikin River ran close by, gurglingly, and bare willows hung over it like ghostly harps.

"Oh, there's not much by way of rooms tonight, only two," said the matron, a tall spindly older woman whose unkempt grey hair spilled from her bonnet. "The locals shivareed a new married couple last night, don't you know, so the best room is a mess. I wouldn't put my own disgusting mother in there. They'll pay, that lot, but meanwhile I'm shy of chambers. I don't want to give you the big room, as I often have a party arriving from the City an hour after the close of gates, don't you know, and they pay government rates. Very nice little sinecure for a widow on her own. But up top a'that there's a space not much used. No fireplace, mind, but I'll gift you with extra blankets. You're young and hot and you won't notice."

She rustled them a supper, buckled mutton with a side of tadmuck, stringy and dried out but warm enough to satisfy. Perhaps a bit lonely, she poured them drinks of yellow wine, and kept them company through the first bottle and the second. But then there were horses in the yard, and she stirred herself to her feet, yawning. "It's the trade I was hoping for, so if it's all the same to you, gentlemen, I'll leave you to a good slumber if you please."

They found their way. The flight of steps led only to their chamber. The small room was an architectural afterthought, the result of a failed attempt at dignity, a mansarded cap on the larger guest dormitory below. Cold, indeed. More a storage space with a feather bed in it than a chamber for guests. A tall round-topped, gabled window was set in the middle of each slanting wall.

Liir sat down, weighted with fatigue and a little tipsy, on the edge of a trunk. The thing was felted with dust. They shouldn't have to pay a penny for this attic.

Trism left to wash in the sink on the landing. Liir stared at shadows, seeing nothing. The smell, the sight, the notion of killing dragons—and what would Elphaba have thought of that?

But he wasn't Elphaba; most days he was barely Liir.

He'd gone to get the broom, only, so he could fly for the Birds, ambassador for them. Then they would pay him by looking for Nor—or so they said. How could he identify her? He didn't even know what she looked like after all this time.

Then, he'd done more. He'd murdered the herd of dragons. The Birds would be able to fly free now. He wouldn't need to fly with them or for them: he'd removed the deterrence.

Trism came back. "Asleep sitting up?" Water slicked down the blond hairs on his thighs. He didn't smell sweet and soapy, just less sour. His green tunic, unbuttoned at the neck and released from the belted leggings, was long enough to preserve modesty and serve as a nightshirt. "I think our dame has got the custom she hoped for, by the sound of it. More bottles opening downstairs. Hope they don't keep us awake; they'll be sleeping right under us."

Ratty brocaded drapes, dating from no later than the days of the Ozma Regent, hung thickly on either side of the windows. Liir regarded the four separate glimpses of night: night north, south, east, and west.

"Come to bed," said Trism. "It's freezing."

Liir didn't answer.

"Come on. Why not?"

"The moonlight," he said at last. "It's so—seeing."

"Well, I'm not going to go to sleep until you lie down. Do you

think I'm going to turn my back so you can stick a knife in me? I remember that line: *he will pay for his offenses.*"

"That was theatrical." Liir shuddered. "It's the moon, I guess," he
said.

Trism got up and moved across the floor, huffing in irritation. "Paranoia. Very attractive. No one can see in windows this high, Liir. But we'll
block the moon for you, then." The sills of the windows were three feet
from the floor, and the columnar bulk of the heavy drapes rose six feet
higher than that. Trism said, "Move, you," and nudged Liir off the trunk,
which he dragged to the first window. From there Trism climbed to the
windowsill, his clean bare feet pawing in the grit and dust for purchase.

He reached up. The curtains hadn't been shifted in decades, and they
resisted. He grunted. The light of the moon fell on his ear tips, his lifting shoulders as his fingers just grazed the center of the curtain rod and
walked their way east and west toward the edges of the drapes.

"Oh, company," he said. "Those horses in the yard—five of them.
They've got the Emperor's caparisons. This is a soldiers' sleepery."

"Welcome Arms. I suppose it figures." Liir came up behind to look.
As Trism stretched, the shirttail lifted above his shapely rear. Liir reached
out and settled his hands there, to support Trism should he fall, for the
ledge was shallow and Trism's balance precarious. Trism made a sound
in his throat.

He managed to dislodge the first volute of brocade an inch or two,
and a colony of blue moths, the size of penny blossoms just going by, issued forth and settled upon them both. A thousand pinches without
fingers.

The brocade shifted some more. The drapes were cut from an old
tapestry design. Once pink and yellow and rose, it was now the color of
dirt and ash, but the ravaged faces of society charmers still peered out
through threaded expressions. Moths are the death of brocade potentates
and hostesses, pavilions and rose arbors and islands in some impossible
sea. Moths eat such faces alive. The faces of living humans they merely
explore, and the peninsulas of their forearms, and the promontories of
their breastbones, and the shallows of their tympanic chests, which when
heard close up thunder too loudly for moths to notice.

"Right," whispered Trism hoarsely.

"Come on," Liir answered. "We have to be quiet. Maybe these soldiers aren't looking for us. Maybe she's too drunk to remember we're here. There's no way out, anyway. Not till they're asleep, at least."

"We could jump out the window into the river."

"Too late for that; we've already jumped. Anyway, I'm going to jump you now. Come on, to bed. It's just the next part of history, right? If we're going to be found, we might as well be found out."

◆ 10 ◆

DESPITE THEIR EXHAUSTION, they hardly slept. They clung to each other, making the least possible noise, and when it got too much to bear they buried their faces in pillows. Spent, at least briefly, they dozed, and Liir's last thought was: sleeping with the talent. A dragon mesmerist, of all things—what magic a body is—all that you couldn't know about the world packed up tightly in the flesh lying on your breast.

All the things Ansonby and Burny had known about—not about girls, but about people—how they felt when they were closer than clothes could ever be. How secret, still: how still, and secret. But a connection nonetheless, dared and decided: a new way of knowing, new burning letters falling through the air—and the words that could be spelled weren't all disastrous.

At last, in the deadest part of the night, they crept back into their clothes and braved the staircase. From the larder they nicked a hock of ham, and from the pasture by the river's edge they nicked two horses. Trism's way with dragons, it seemed, had suggested to him a language for comforting horses, too.

They led the horses away by the river's edge, where the noise of the water would afford the best cover. A mile out, Trism showed Liir how to climb into the saddle. Liir had never ridden before. "I'm not sure tonight's the best night for this lesson," he said. "Ow."

"It's the next part of history. Now, where are we going?"

"Are we going together?"

"We seem to be. For now, anyway."

Liir shrugged. "We've got to cross the Gillikin River and keep Kells-water on our right. South through the oakhair forest." As far as Apple Press Farm, he thought, but he didn't want to say that yet.

"I don't know these parts, but if we're crossing the river, let's not wait for a bridge. We'll ford it here where we can, and confound the soldiers if they come looking for their rides."

The moon was nearly down, but there was enough light for the horses to pick their way safely across the water. They gained the far bank, which rose to a prominence. Looking back, the fellows could see the Welcome Arms they'd abandoned. From here, with its smaller second story, it looked like a lopsided old boot.

"The Boot of the Apostle," said Liir.

"The Apostle only wears sandals, to judge by the graphics advertising that exhibit. That Apostle Muscle exhibit."

They rode till dawn, though at a safely slow pace, keeping to well-worn tracks. Gradually the sky lightened, cheerless and without bold character, the look of molasses dissolving in milk. They hoped a wind would arise to shift the scratchy snow and cloak their tracks, but it didn't.

By the time they could see their own breath in the cold dawn, they had reached the edge of the Shale Shallows. They could begin to move faster. They were now apparent to each other again, though in the daylight it was harder to meet one another's eyes. They didn't talk much.

Siege

SISTER APOTHECAIRE WAS drying her hair with a towel when Sister Doctor rushed into the ablutory. "He's back," she said.

Sister Apothecaire did not need to ask who *he* was. "With the girl?"

"No. With a boy. Well, a young man, I mean."

"Do up my veil snap, will you, Sister? I'm *hurrying*."

Along the stairs, they met Sister Cook. "Famished the both, malnourished the one, perhaps, though I'm not a doctor, being only the cook," she reported. "They're both deeply into their third helping of sausage and beans. The Superior Maunt is waiting in her chamber."

Indeed she was. Her hands were composed upon her lap, and her eyes closed in prayer. "Forgive me, sisters," she said when they came forward. "Obligation before devotion, I know. Won't you sit down?"

"We hear that Liir is back," said Sister Doctor. "We should like the chance to see him."

"To inspect him. To meet with him."

The Superior Maunt raised her eyebrows. Sister Apothecaire blushed. "I merely meant that it would be useful in our professional practice to know what the cause of his peculiar ailments actually was.

Likewise we are quite in the dark as to the treatment Candle applied that helped him to recover so."

"Of course," said the Superior Maunt. "And I'm eager to know as well. But I have other responsibilities this morning. The unexpected arrivals are breaking their fast in the refectory, I believe, but I have made an appointment to counsel our other guest in the small chapel. I don't believe I should break my appointment with her. So you will conduct the interview jointly and report to me."

"Yes, Mother."

She dismissed them, but then called after, "Sisters."

They turned.

"In women of your age and station, it is unseemly to pelt so. The young men will not have left."

"Pardon us," said Sister Doctor. "But of course the last time we hoped to find him, he *had* left."

"He hasn't asked as much yet, but I believe he's requesting sanctuary," said the Superior Maunt. "I'm afraid he won't be leaving very soon. You have time. Practice continence in your expression of enthusiasm."

"Yes. Indeed. Quite."

"You may go."

They stood there. "Go!" repeated the Superior Maunt wearily.

She closed her eyes again, but this time not in prayer. The new winter was approaching. Another winter in the mauntery of Saint Glinda. Fires that would not warm her papery skin. Fruit that would grow mealy in the larder. Increased agitation among the maunts, for when there was less work in the gardens there was more gossip and bitchery in the sewing compound. There would be new leaks to repair, and ague would knock a few of the old ones into the grave. She wondered if it would be her turn.

She couldn't hope for this. She didn't hope for it. But the rewards of the winter season seemed richer in her childhood memories, back before she had these tiresome women to govern—the silly affectations of Lurlinemas, which even professed maunts in their strictness remembered with pleasure—the spectacle of sunlight staining birch shadows into the snow like laundry blueing—the way snow fell up as well as down, if the wind had its way—of course, the way birds returned, stitching the spring back into place by virtue of melody.

It was the gardens of her girlhood she remembered most, the earliest blossoms. Jonquils and fillarettes and snowdrops, perfect as the Dixxi House porcelain bibelots that had adorned her mother's dressing table. She had not seen a fillarette in years, except in her mind. How sweet it was to regard!

She prayed for strength to last the winter out. These days, though, she rarely got into the fourth line of a beloved old epiphody before her mind skipped back through some pasture or garden walk of her youth.

Attend, she barked at herself, and stood with difficulty. The cold was already at work in her joints. She creaked as she readied herself for the morning conversation. Noting the raggedness of the face flannel with which she wiped her brow, she hoped that the mauntery's guest might have come to propose a sizeable donation. Or even a little one. But this was beyond what the Superior Maunt thought it was proper to pray for, so she didn't spend her prayer in that direction.

Wisdom is not the understanding of mystery, she said to herself, not for the first time. Wisdom is accepting that mystery is beyond understanding. That's what *makes* it mystery.

THE FELLOWS WERE NEARLY KEELING OVER into their coffee cups. "You've had no sleep, you've been riding all night," said Sister Doctor, disapprovingly. "It's a dangerous track at best, and foolhardy to venture upon if you don't know your way. Have you come from the Emerald City?"

"We've been round and about," said Liir.

Sister Doctor explained that she and Sister Apothecaire had briefly tended to Liir when he'd been brought in by Oatsie Manglehand, the captain of the Grasstrail Train. "Have you any recollection of that?" she pressed.

"I know very little about anything," he said. "I'm useless, pretty much."

"Any more cheese, d'you think?" asked Trism, draining his noggin of ale.

"You were here for weeks, I'm afraid," Sister Doctor remarked to Liir. "Without the ministrations of our community you should certainly have died."

"Perish the thought. I'm alive, for what it's worth."

"What Sister Doctor is trying to ascertain, in her skittery way, is how Candle did it," interrupted Sister Apothecaire. "She was mute as a lilac, and seemed not overly canny. Yet she managed a miracle with you."

"Professional curiosity requires us to ask how," inserted Sister Doctor.

"Professional jealousy requires it, too," admitted Sister Apothecaire.

"I don't know." The boy had a private look. "In any event, I wasn't consulted."

"Oh, she leached him, she took a lancet and bled him, she sucked his poison out, and a good thing, too," said a biddy on a bench nearby. They hadn't noticed her there.

"Why, Mother Yackle!" bellowed Sister Doctor in a matronizing manner. "Aren't you the chatty one today!" She shared a wrinkled expression with Sister Apothecaire. The dotty old thing. Ought to be in the solarium with the other silly dears.

"She's got a good instinct, that Candle," said Yackle. "The oafs are pleasant enough to bed, in their way, but it takes a daughter of Lurlina to draw out the milk only boys can make . . ."

"Shame and scandal on the house," said Sister Apothecaire. "Gentle-boys, forgive her. You know, their minds wander at that age, and the sense of propriety wobbles ferociously."

Liir turned to look at the woman. Her veil was pulled forward, but the splayed nostrils of her long rude nose showed. "Are you the one who directed us to the farm in the overgrown orchard?" he said.

"She never!" said Sister Apothecaire. "Liir, she's yesterday's potatoes, and mashed at that. Don't pay her any mind."

In a low voice, almost masculine in gruffness, Mother Yackle replied slowly, "I mind *my own business.*"

"Of course you do," said Sister Doctor.

"But if I were you, I'd send those soldiers' horses packing," continued Mother Yackle. "You don't want them found on the premises, I'd warrant."

Liir shrugged, then nodded.

"Look," said Sister Doctor, "this isn't the place to talk. Finish up, lads; we need to have a heart-to-heart."

But Trism had fallen asleep against the back of his chair, and Liir's eyelids were lowering as they watched. There was nothing for the maunts to do but show them to the cots in the guest quarters, and find blankets, and retreat.

• 2 •

LIIR, NEARLY ASLEEP, tossed his body back and forth on the lumpy straw of the bedding. It was as if he had been here before.

Well, he had, but in a feeble enough way. In childhood he'd been more aware of the hems of Elphaba's skirts, of the food in the wooden bowls. An awful lot of oatmeal mush. And more recently, he'd been broken and mindless, wandering his past in a feverish state. Even the night he and Candle had left the mauntery, and she had helped him move, as good as carried him on her back down the stairs, nearly, the halls had been dark. He'd collapsed into the donkey cart and slipped almost immediately into a real sleep, a sleep of fatigue and not one of voyage.

That was his first apprehension of Candle, he remembered. A slip of a thing with the strength and willpower of a pack horse. She'd been mostly naked, and Mother Yackle had thrown a cloak over her shoulders. Here in the mauntery again, Liir tried to lean into that recent memory, the way he had learned to steep himself in other memories. Maybe there was something yet to be understood about whether he'd actually slept with her, impregnated her . . . even more, whether and in what ways he might love her.

Now—a thousand difficult lonely miles away from Trism, who snored a yard to the east—Liir turned over, facing the wall. Candle was a cipher to him, sweet and elusive, and the memory was frail. There was nothing more he could unpack from it, nothing useful. To distract himself, in his heart and memory he walked about and examined the hull of the mauntery, doing a kind of spectral surveillance.

The place betrayed its origins as a gardkeep. It was a fortified house, here on a slight wooded rise, an oasis of trees in the Shale Shallows. The ground floor had no windows, and the front door was reinforced with iron bracing. Behind, the kitchen looked out on a greasy moat crossed by a simple drawbridge. The vegetable plots and cow barn were beyond.

The mauntery would afford little protection in a siege. The place was tall and, at this stage in its history, unsecurable for very long. In any effort to gain unlawful access, a modern police force might be slowed, but it wouldn't be stayed.

Still, at least a few cows could be swept into the parlor, and hay stacked up under the stairs. The fruits of the harvest crowded the shelves and larders, and the garde-manger was bulbous with blood sausage, dried muttock, and nine varieties of salami, to say nothing of cheeses. There was a mushroom cellar and a bin of desiccated fish fragments. And plenty of wine, and that wonderful rarity in a rural establishment, an indoor well.

In his dreams he checked the cupboards for rifles, he blew through each room to look for wardrobes that could be pushed against windows. He did not see the Superior Maunt asking questions of her esteemed guest about the payout schedule of a proposed beneficial annuity. He didn't see Mother Yackle nodding in her own morning nap in the sunlight. He didn't see nor overhear Sister Doctor and Sister Apothecaire squabbling gently in their shared cubicle about how they ought to proceed. The rooms were empty of novices, maunts, guests, spiders, mice, bedbugs, and any presence of the Unnamed God that he could determine.

What he saw, in the topmost room where he had lain, was a figure on a rush-bottomed chair, sitting away from the light, twisting her hands. Her dark hair was looped up on her head with no regard for neatness or propriety, just to get it out of the way. Her eyes were closed, but he didn't think she could be praying. He didn't know what she was doing. At her feet was a largish basket woven of twigs. He didn't look into it; he couldn't. Every now and then her shoeless foot would nip out from beneath the dark hem of her skirt and give the basket a little push, and because of its rounded bottom, the basket rocked for a time. Then the green foot would appear again, and start the rocking over.

HE WOKE WITH A START. It was sharp noon, and the house smelled of warm leek-and-cabbage eggery for lunch. Trism was still asleep, his hair rucked back against the pillow. The sound of cantering horse hoofs grew louder. Liir wanted to kiss Trism awake, but had the notion that the time for that was already over.

He did it anyway. Trism groaned, and made room, and after a while said, "We don't do this sort of thing in our circle."

Did he mean his class at St. Prowd's? His family? The Home Guard? Didn't matter. Liir replied, "Well, your circle seems to have widened, hasn't it."

"Or shrunk," said Trism, reaching for his boots.

◆ 3 ◆

"THEY'RE LOOKING FOR TWO men," said Sister Doctor.

"Indeed," said the Superior Maunt.

"One is said to have kidnapped the other."

"Our guests appear to be on a more familiar footing than hostage and abductor, don't you think?"

"Well—yes."

"So tell the soldiers we haven't seen the men they're seeking, and bid them good day."

"The thing is," said Sister Doctor, "they're said to be quite dangerous, these fellows. In an act of desecration, they imploded the Emerald City basilica of the Emperor by causing combustible dragons to—combust."

"How dreadful. I don't think our two look very dangerous, though.

Underfed, if you ask me, and perhaps undecided in their emotions, but not dangerous."

Sister Doctor came back. "I've been told that one of the two they're seeking is named Liir."

"I see. Well, tell them he's not here."

"Mother Maunt. I question your—propriety. Is that not a lie?"

"Well, if one of the two that they seek is named Liir, one is *not* named Liir. So answer in reference to that one, and say he's not here."

"That is devious, Mother Maunt."

"I'm old and muddled. Put it down to that, if you must comfort yourself," she replied sharply. "But I'm still in charge, Sister, so do as I say."

Sister Doctor came back a third time. "They are more explicit. The Commander says that they are seeking Liir Thropp, the son of the Wicked Witch of the West."

"As I live and breathe, Sister Doctor! You extend more respect for my authority than is useful. Need I come up with every rejoinder? Are you never to think for yourself? To the best of my knowledge it hasn't been conclusively determined that Liir is the son of the witch. So, again, since we cannot answer for certain that the person they seek is here, they must conduct their searches elsewhere. Give them my blessing and tell them to hurry, or do I have to come and do it myself?"

Sister Doctor yelled the message out the windows of the scriptorium. The Commander called back, "If you're not harboring felons, why are your doors blocked?"

"Spring cleaning."

"It's early winter, Sister Thudhead."

"We're behind schedule. We've been dreadfully busy."

"Busy harboring criminals?"

"I hate to be rude, but I've work to do. Good-bye."

By late afternoon the thud of stones against the door had become intolerable, and the Superior Maunt herself came to the window. The armed contingent had to interrupt the attack in order to hear her quavery voice.

"It's an inconvenient time to come calling," she said. "For one thing, ladies in community tending to have their menses together, you find an entire household of terribly cross and uncompromising people. We're not up to housing a garrison of soldiers, however rudely they pound on our doors. Please go away at once."

"Mother Maunt," said the Commander. "This household received its original charter from the Palace, and it is with the authority of the Palace that I come and demand access. Your studied resistance proves you are harboring criminals. We know they stayed at an inn last night, and they cannot have come much farther than here today."

"Matters of authority are perplexing, I agree," replied the old woman, "and I would love to stand here in the icy wind and discuss them fully, but my ancient lungs won't stand it. Our original charter, by way of our motherchapel in the Emerald City, does comes from the Palace, I'll concede. But I'll remind you that the Palace in question was the Palace of the crown of Ozma, many generations back, and in any instance we have earned the right to self-governance."

"The Palace of Ozma is long over, and it's the Palace of the Emperor that comes calling now. He is favored by unionist acclaim, and by dint of his apostleship you are under his bidding."

"He is a parvenu Emperor, and he does not speak for the Unnamed God to me," she cried. "And unless he asked for it, no more would I speak of the Unnamed God to him. I reject his expedient and proprietary faith. We stand here on our own chilblained feet, without apology and without genuflection."

"Is this an indication that the Mauntery of Saint Glinda has endorsed and even overseen the publication of recent treasonous broadsheets attacking the spiritual legitimacy of the Emperor?"

The Superior Maunt made a most uncharacteristic gesture.

"That's hardly an answer the courts would recognize. Good Mother Maunt," came the reply, "let us not distract ourselves with the luxury of theology—"

"For me it is no luxury, believe me—"

"I know the boy you are harboring. I met him when he was only a boy, at the castle of Kiamo Ko in the Kells. When fate brought him in my path again, not once but twice, I suspected he had the makings of a firebrand in him. I made it my business to convince him of the rightness of the Emerald City cause. He might have knowledge of Elphaba, or of her missing Grimmerie. I named him my secretary in Qhoyre. I promoted him. I fathered him as best I could. Now listen: he was not Elphaba's match. He could not be her son—too docile and biddable. But he should give himself up regardless. He has kidnapped a soldier of the Emperor and destroyed the basilica of the army."

"Commander," replied the Superior Maunt, "you can save your breath. And you can put down those archaic crossbows or whatever you're readying. We've got company that it would be unseemly for you to disturb."

She turned and beckoned. A figure appeared at the window and lowered a shawl off her forehead. The glitter in the eyebrows stood out in the falling light. Commander Cherrystone made a gesture and the men dropped their weapons as the Superior Maunt intoned, "The widow of Lord Chuffrey, Oz's former throne minister, making a religious retreat to the mauntery that bears the same name that she does. Lady Glinda."

◆ **4** ◆

A NOVICE OPENED THE DOOR for Liir and pointed him into the simple paneled parlor, and closed the door behind him without a sound.

"I was told you were in the country," said Liir.

"But I was," answered Glinda. "I am. I had intended to travel from Mockbeggar Hall, our—well, my—country house to come make a bequest to this mauntery. Lord Chuffrey has left me quite wealthy, you know, and I thought it time to help the women in their good works.

"But when my under-butler arrived last night on horseback with news of the attack on the basilica, I decided to change my schedule and come here straightaway. I have a commitment to this house, and I wanted my new bequest registered before there was any move toward disestablishment."

Her glamour was all the more ridiculous and appealing in this setting. "It's good to see a familiar face," said Liir.

"I suppose I shouldn't be surprised to find *you* here. After all, Elphaba was here for a while, you know. It's one of the reasons I like to support it."

"I know she was."

"She tended the dying."

"And the living," he said, remembering his dream of the basket. "I'm sorry about your husband."

"Oh, well." She waved her hand dismissively but then dabbed at her nostril with a scrap of lacy roundel. "We largely went our own ways; it was that kind of a marriage. Now he's gone his own way for good. I miss him more than I would ever have let on while he was alive. I suppose I'll get over it."

She cheered up almost instantly. "Now tell me about you. Last I remember, you were marching off to Southstairs to find some little friend or other. I lost track of what happened. Well, there was the court to manage, and various putsches to suppress." She regarded him. "No, I suppose it was ruthless of me to forget about you as soon as you left. I've never been good at keeping up with people. I'm sorry."

Liir remembered that he had momentarily hoped for Glinda as a mother. He pushed the thought aside. "You know the Emperor," he said. "None other than Shell. Elphaba's younger brother."

"Wouldn't she be surprised to know her brother had succeeded the Wizard!" She looked rueful.

"Surprised," said Liir. "That's one way to put it."

"Well, yes. She'd be outraged. Piety as the new political aphrodisiac. I suppose that's what you mean."

He shrugged. "What someone would feel after she's dead—that notion means little to me. She doesn't feel. All that's left of her—shades and echoes, and fading by the hour."

Glinda closed her breviary with a little slap. She hadn't been attending closely to her devotions anyway. "That pesky slogan you see scrawled everywhere is right. She does live, you know. She does."

Liir snapped at her. "I have no truck with that kind of sentiment. All butchers and simpletons 'live' in that sense."

Glinda raised her chin. "No, Liir. She lives. People sing of her. You wouldn't guess it, being you—but they do. There's a musical noise around her name; there are things people remember, and pass on."

"People can pass on lies and hopes as well as shards of memory."

"You refuse to be consoled, don't you? Well, that's as much proof as *I* could ever need that you're kin to her. She was the same way. The very same way."

• 5 •

THE SITUATION, the Superior Maunt concluded that evening, was de-cidedly unsettled. Scouting from the highest windows in all directions, the novices reported that several dozen armed horsemen showed signs of making camp in the Shale Shallows. They'd broken into the kitchen gar-dens and rooted about in the shed for squashes and such. "It seems un-feeling not to provide them with a meal," said the Superior Maunt, "but I suppose that might give the wrong impression."

Liir and Trism asked for an audience, and she sat with them on a bench at the base of a flight of steps. "We can't have the house put in danger on our behalf," said Liir. "Between Trism and me, while working in the Home Guard, we've been responsible for enough loss of life. We didn't know the dragons would explode. We didn't intend to bring down the basilica. We don't know if there was human death in that ca-tastrophe. We want to do no further damage, if we can help it. We shall give ourselves up to them."

"Since it may ease your minds on that score, I will tell you that I heard of no loss of human life in the collapse of the basilica," said the Superior Maunt. "It was midnight, after all. The place was deserted, even the side sheds and storerooms that escaped being crushed by falling de-bris. I suspect, however, your foes imagine the basilica was your real target, and the death of the dragons—how do they term it these days?—collateral damage. As to your suggestion that you should turn yourselves in, let me take it up in council before you make your decisions."

"What is council?" asked Trism.

"I don't know. I'm going to find out," she replied.

THEY GATHERED IN THE CHAPEL, the only room in the mauntery large enough to hold all inhabitants and guests. Evening devotions usually occurred on a basis of rotations, some maunts handling kitchen washup or geriatric babysitting while the rest sank into quiet prayer or early nap. Tonight the Superior Maunt requested the attendance of all, even those retired maunts like Mother Yackle who were on the edge of gaga.

Lady Glinda, though a benefactress, refused a seat on the dais up front, and she had removed her trademark diamond strutted collar for a quieter linen ruff. Liir and Trism, unfamiliar with these traditions, stayed standing. The older maunts were escorted in, in wheeled chairs when necessary; the novices took their places on their knees until the Superior Maunt indicated they should sit. "This is not prayer," she said. "Something like it, but not prayer, precisely."

She sat herself down, with difficulty. After a short silence, Sister Hymnody offered a provocatory in plaintone, though her sweet bell-like voice quavered. They were all on edge.

"Sisters, mothers, friends, and family. I shall be brief. Our tradition of charity, reinforced by our vows, brings us this evening into a conflict none of us has anticipated or experienced before. However generous the tithe of Lady Glinda, I doubt it will rebuild this house should the army of the Emperor sack it.

"We are a small house, a mission post on the road halfway between our motherchapel in the Emerald City and the rest of the world. Our isolation has been the cause of loneliness, at times, but also promoted peace and protection. Perhaps even provocation—but I pass over that. Tonight we are neither isolated nor peaceful. It is a truth we must accept.

"I am an old woman. I was raised as a novice in the venerable practice of obedience. Under the rubric of our order I followed instruction, including the one that required me, years ago, to take charge of this mauntery and govern it until death.

"I still believe in obedience. Even while soldiers camp outside our walls, and quite likely call for reinforcements, I must be obedient to the wishes of the powers that placed me here.

"As I speak these words, my dear friends, I hear in them an echo of the Emperor's remarks. He professes subservience to the highest aims and intentions of the Unnamed God. God is the mouthpiece and the Emperor is his striking arm. The First Spear.

"I have not met the Emperor, and I will not. I should decline an invitation were one offered. The Emperor has hijacked the great force of faith and diverted it to further the prosperity and dominance of the City. Who can argue with a man who has the voice of the Unnamed God speaking exclusively in his ear? Not I. I have never heard such a voice. I have only heard the echo that still reverberates, once the Unnamed God stopped speaking and the world took up with itself.

"In our house, we profess to believe that the Unnamed God has made us in its likeness and its image, and this should have enlarged us to be like the Unnamed God. I fear in the Emerald City, they have remade the Unnamed God in their image, and that has belittled and betrayed the deity. Can the Unnamed God be belittled, you ask. No, of course not. But the deity can go unrecognized, and return to mystery."

The sisters shifted. Many of the novices were ignorant of the Emperor's apostasy, and the shoals of theocracy were beyond their ability to navigate. The Superior Maunt noticed.

She stood. "Bring me two other chairs, one at my right and one at my left," she said. This was done.

"The Unnamed God retreats into mystery, and is not especially localized in my heart, my dears. Nor in the Emperor's. The mystery is as equally in your heart as in mine, and in . . . the spirit of the trees and the . . . the music of water. That sort of thing. In the memory of our elders. In the hope for the newborn.

"I break with the tradition of our house tonight, as the decisions now to be made involve your lives as well as mine. I am old; happily I would go to my sweet reward this evening were it provided me by a literal spear of the Emperor. I cannot ask the same of you. Therefore it is my wish that henceforth the mauntery—even if our residency here lasts only till dawn—shall be governed not by a single voice, but by a troika of voices. Were the disagreeables not outside our walls, I should invite your opinions and call for a ballot. Time prevents me from allowing that. In extremis, our family of maunts shall accept the leadership of three. Sister Doctor, will you rise to the chair?"

Sister Doctor gaped. She grasped Sister Apothecaire's hand briefly, and moved forward. Sister Apothecaire trembled and moved to the edge of her seat, perching for approach.

"I shall take the second seat," said the Superior Maunt. "I may be old, but I'm not dead."

The room was so still that the sounds of horses whinnying and stamping outside carried through the cold.

"The third chair I am reserving for the novice known as Candle," declared the Superior Maunt. "I have a notion we shall see her again. For how long, I don't know. But we need the wisdom of age, the strength of the fit, and the initiative of the young. From this moment forward, my absolute command over this establishment is dissolved. I shall enter it so in the Log of the House before I retire. Now, let us see how we get on."

Sister Apothecaire bit her lip and tried to feel more humble than humiliated.

Skirts rustled as the women shifted. Faint whispering, unprecedented in the chapel, sounded, like faraway wind. The Superior Maunt dropped her forehead into her fingers and breathed deeply, feeling that the world had changed utterly, and wondering how quickly she would regret this action.

In the stillness, Lady Glinda stood. Reticence not being her usual thing, she'd had about enough: and anyway, hadn't the Superior Maunt called for a collaborative spirit? "If I may speak," she began, in a tone that implied she knew she could not be denied, "even if the army breaks through the defenses of this mauntery, they cannot do you good women much harm. There will be no bloodshed or rape here. Not while I am in house. Make of it what you will, even though I am retired from what passed for public service, I am still seen as a friend of the government. I have the ear of every society power monger in the country. The army knows well enough they cannot abuse you while I am a witness—and they will not touch me. They daren't."

She added, "I am Lady Glinda," in case some of the younger novices hadn't cottoned on yet.

"It isn't the girls that are wanted," said Sister Doctor. "It is the boys."

"Don't underestimate what people in the throes of passion may do," said the Superior Maunt. "Our rectitude means little to the world beyond our walls, and the commitment of our lives is as cheap as throwaway grain on unuseful margins of field. Still, Sister Doctor, you are right. The army seeks two young men, but they do not know for sure that they are here."

Liir said, "I do not think the broom would carry two, but Trism could climb to the ramparts late at night, and fly to safety. That would leave only me, and whatever fate I have earned, I should face it by myself."

The room grew decidedly chilly. "So the rumors of the broom are true?" said Sister Doctor. The Superior Maunt took in some breath wetly at the corners of her mouth.

Liir shrugged but couldn't deny it. From the side, mad Mother Yackle called, "Of course the rumors are true. The broom came from this very house. I myself gave it to Sister Saint Aelphaba years ago. Am I the only one concentrating enough to know this?"

She might, an hour earlier, have been hushed, and the Superior Maunt began to speak. But Sister Doctor raised her hand and stayed the Mother Maunt's comment, and remarked, "You've been quiet for a decade, Mother Yackle, but of late you've come back to yourself somewhat. Have you anything to add we should know?"

"I don't talk when there's nothing to say," said Mother Yackle. "All I have to add is this: Elphaba should be here to see this hour."

"You have an uncommon association with—the Witch of the West."

"Yes, I do," said Mother Yackle. "I seem to have been placed on the sidelines of her life, as you might say, as a witness. I'm mad as a bedbug, so no one needs to attend, but I've taken some measure of her power. Oh!—but she *should* be here to see this hour."

"Mother Yackle? A guardian angel?" called Sister Apothecaire.

"Well—a guardian twitch, anyway," replied the old woman.

Liir trembled and thought of his lack of power, once again, and of his revery within these walls. Now he remembered what he hadn't seen before: that in the corner of the room where the green-skinned novice had sat rocking the cradle, a broom leaned against a chest of drawers.

"Are there other remarks?" asked Sister Doctor.

Shocked somewhat by the developments, the maunts muttered quietly, but no one else spoke until Sister Apothecaire stood and said, "Mother Maunt, I would like to applaud you for your courage and your wisdom."

Tears ran suddenly from the old maunt's eyes as her house, to a person, stood and paid their respects. Outside, the horses shied and the men started at the sudden rain of noise from the chapel windows.

THE BROOM, THOUGH, wouldn't carry Trism. In his hands it was no more than a broom. "I lack the proper spunk, it seems," he said.

"Maybe it has lost its power," said Liir, but in his own hand the thing leaped to life again, bucking like a colt.

"We might be able to manage a sleight of hand with only one man to hide," said Lady Glinda. "After all, as you pointed out, they are looking for a pair of you. Perhaps Trism could be passed off as my bodyguard. It was unlike me to have ventured here without a bodyguard, after all, though I did. Sometimes I like to confound even myself," she explained. "It isn't difficult."

"If the men who hold us under siege recognize Trism from the barracks at the Emerald City, he will be put under arrest," said Sister Doctor.

"Well, I used to be good at makeovers," said Glinda. "And I could do magic with a blush brush. He's got big shoulders for a maunt, but he's pretty enough, and a little peroxide on the facial hair, which is so conveniently blond—" She tossed her own curls. "Well, I never travel without it."

"I think not," said Trism in a steely voice.

"Then we'll have to take the chance we can pass you off as my servant," said Lady Glinda. "Liir will leave tonight, on the broom, and tomorrow morning I shall ride out with Trism at my side, and make no explanation. If you choose then to open your doors to the soldiers, they will find nothing untoward here. I shall wait outside your gate as an obvious witness until their search is completed. If they are that hungry for blood, they will not dally here but rush on elsewhere."

"But where will you go?" the Superior Maunt asked Trism. By now they had retired to her office, and she was sagging against the worn leather of her chair.

Liir looked at Trism. As much as could pass between them in a look, without words, passed: and another moment of possibility crashed and burned.

"If Trism can get through, he should try to find Apple Press Farm," said Liir. "He might smuggle Candle to safety elsewhere. The Emperor's soldiers are headed vaguely in that direction, and the site has been discovered and ripped up by thugs and vandals at least once already. It seems to have been used as a clandestine press for the printing of antigovernment propaganda."

"Yes," said the Superior Maunt modestly, "so I've been told."

"For you, I would try to find that farm," said Trism. "And I will take the scraped faces, that they not be found here when the army does its ransack."

"As for me," continued Liir, "I've learned something from you." He looked at the Superior Maunt, who was tending to nod. "I promised to try to complete an exercise, and I did this much: I helped rid the skies of the dragons that were attacking travelers and causing fear and suspicion among the outlying tribes. I will finish my work before anything else happens. I should let the Conference of the Birds know that, for now, they are free to gather, to fly, to conduct their lives without that undue threat. With the help of the Witch's broom, and unimpeded by dragon-fings, I can manage that shortly.

"Beyond that," he said, "I have other scores to settle. I set out years ago to find Nor, a girl with whom I spent some childhood years."

"But, Liir," said Sister Doctor, "the Princess Nastoya is expecting your return."

Liir started. "I had assumed she'd have died long ago."

"She's been trying to die, and trying not to die, a complicated set of intentions," said Sister Doctor. "She mentioned you, Liir."

"I don't know what I can do for her. I do not have Elphaba's skills, neither by inheritance nor by training."

They sat silently as he worried it out. "In the choice of what to do next, I'm troubled. On the one hand, you say the Princess Nastoya is old and suffering and wants to die."

"Yes," said the Superior Maunt wearily. "I know the feeling."

"On the other hand, Nor is young and has a life ahead of her, and perhaps it is a greater good to help her first, if I can."

They waited; the wind soughed a little in the chimney.

"I will return to Princess Nastoya," he told them. "I know I won't be able to help her to sever her human disguise from her Elephant nature. I'm not a person of talents. But if I can give her the loyalty of friendship, I'll do that."

"You would help an ancient crone over a disappeared girl?" said Sister Doctor. Her sense of medical ethics flared.

"Young Nor found her own way out of Southstairs," said Liir. "Whatever else has been done to her body or her mind, she clearly has spirit and cunning. I shall have to trust that her youth will continue to protect her. And maybe she doesn't need my help now—though I won't rest until I know it for sure. Meanwhile, Sister Doctor, you say that the Princess Nastoya has asked for me. Ten years ago I made a promise to try to help; I owe her my apologies if nothing else. And if I can report conclusively to the Scrow that it was not the Yunamata who were scraping the faces of solitary travelers, I may be able to help effect a treaty of faith between the two peoples."

"Is it hubris to aim for such a large reward?" asked Sister Doctor.

"No," said the Superior Maunt, her eyes now closed.

"No," said Liir. "The Superior Maunt has shown me that tonight. If we share what we know, we may have a fighting chance. This house, as a sanctuary, may survive. The country, and its peoples, may survive."

"The country," said the Superior Maunt. Her mind was sliding sleepward. "Oh, indeed yes, the country of the Unnamed God . . ."

"The country of Oz, be what it may," said Liir.

In a semblance of a toast to hope, they raised imaginary glasses of champagne, as the Superior Maunt began to snore.

SOMETIME LATER THAN MIDNIGHT, Sister Apothecaire showed Liir and Trism to an attic. A window gave out conveniently to a place where two matching peaks of roof on either side sloped together to form a valley between them. Corbelling protected this section of roof from the view of people on the ground.

Sister Apothecaire said, "Sister Doctor mentioned your intentions to me, Liir. I'm glad to have the chance to add what Sister Doctor forgot about. The Princess gave us a message to give you—but of course you had disappeared by the time we got back. She said something about Nor and the word on the street about her. I don't recall precisely, but she has something to say to you."

Liir reached inside the Witch's cape. In the interior pocket, he felt for the folded-up drawing of Nor by her father. He winced at the memory of the childish writing—the chunky downstrokes, the blocky uncials. *Nor by Fiyero.*

Sister Apothecaire wrapped Liir's cape the more tightly around his chest to make sure it wouldn't flap and draw undue attention as he tried to make his escape. She tucked extra loaves of bread and a parcel of nuts into his lapels, and bade him Ozspeed. Then she retreated to give them privacy for their good-byes.

"Neither of us may make it, you know," said Trism. "Before noon tomorrow we may both be dead."

"It's been good to be alive, then," said Liir. "I mean, after a fashion."

"I'm afraid I got you into this," said Trism. "I saw you on the ball pitch and thought I would take my revenge on you. I didn't mean this much revenge—either that you should die, or that we should part like this."

"I was looking for you, too, sort of—you just saw me first," Liir answered. "It might have been the other way round. Anyway, what does it matter? Here we are. Together a moment longer, anyway."

After a while, Trism managed to say, "Are you sure you can fly in this condition?"

"What condition is that? I've been in this condition my whole life," Liir answered. "It's the only condition I know. Bitter love, loneliness, contempt for corruption, blind hope. It's where I live. A permanent state of bereavement. This is nothing new."

They kissed each other a final time, and Liir mounted the broom of the Wicked Witch of the West, and felt it rise beneath him. He did not look back at where Trism stood. He had few talents, did Liir, and while flying a broom was one of them, he wasn't practiced enough to risk breaking his neck.

His other talent, though, was a distillation of memory into something rich and urgent. He guessed, in the hours or years remaining to him, he would remember the effect of Trism clearly, without corruption, as a secret pulse held in a pocket somewhere behind the heart.

The exact look of Trism, though, the scent and heft of him, the feel of him, would probably decay into imprecision, a shadowy form, unseen but imagined. Hardly distinguishable from an extra chimney in a valley formed by pantiled roofs of a mauntery.

The Eye of the Witch

FLYING AT NIGHT.

He kept low at first, scarcely twice the height of the highest trees. The winds tunneling beneath the cloud cover were ill-tempered, as if out to tumble him. Below, the oakhair forest twitched in the winter gale, looking like the pelt of a great beast lumbering along for midnight rendezvous with sex or supper.

Then the clouds thinned, and the air grew colder still. He remembered more of the attack by dragons than he wanted to—it kicked up a sick feeling. He couldn't manage much more height than he'd achieved so far. Still, with a quick flip of his head left, right, he could make out the southernmost cove of Kellswater and the bay where the Vinkus River debouched into Restwater. From this vantage both lakes looked hard and dead as slate.

He crossed the dark line drawn by the Vinkus River. Now he was halfway to Kumbricia's Pass, which meant that Apple Press Farm was somewhere below. How was Candle faring? He thought of pulling down and seeing.

You could, he said to himself. Now you needn't worry about scaring her, for if you show up in the middle of the night, she'll be ready: she'll have divined the present and sensed your approach, and prepared the tea for your arrival. And the blankets, and the fire, and the bed, though you're not ready yet to go to her bed again, even chastely.

But no, no, he continued—no. What if she was with someone else? Or what if she'd left? Or what if Commander Cherrystone recognized Trism and arrested him, and tortured him into revealing Liir's hiding place—and thence discovered Candle? And kidnapped *her*—as he had done Nor all those years ago!—as a kind of reprisal against the slaughter of the dragon contingent, the ruin of the basilica?

Liir was learning to think in terms of consequence. He gave due credit to the strategies and devices of the Emperor. In any case, though, concern for Candle would distract Liir from completing his mission, as he had promised her to do. Let Trism get there safely and see to her needs, if he could, if he would. Time enough for me to show my sorry face and find out what's going to happen next.

For now, he would finish what he'd started: at least this much.

He might have caught sight of the farmhouse roof winking, or he might be miles and miles off. He didn't know, and it didn't matter. He kept his eyes trained on the foothills of the Great Kells, which from this height were already beginning to swell, less an actual shape than a shift in the grade of shadow.

The wind strengthened as it rushed down the eastern slopes of Oz's mountainy spine. He lost speed, and it took more effort to keep the broom on course. Like riding a horse in a raging river, he imagined, now that he had some experience of horseback riding under his belt, as it were. Finally he had to come down to earth entirely, from exhaustion. He found a shepherd's summer lean-to, abandoned for the season, and stretched out underneath the cape and fell promptly asleep, the broom between his arms and along his chin like the boniest of lovers.

+ 2 +

AT DAWN, THE WINDS RELENTED, and the mountains burned in pinkish light. He finished the small meal provided by Sister Apothecaire and
pressed on.

Kumbricia's Pass was defined by a color of evergreen specific to the
suspended gorge that widened apronlike as it dropped toward the Vinkus
River plain. How foreboding the uprights of the cliffs on either side—
how much more fortress the landscape provided than Liir had been
aware. No wonder the Yunamata, the Scrow, and the Arjiki had never
knuckled under to the industrial strength of Gillikin or the military
might of the Emerald City. And no wonder the dragons had been an important development—they would have had to work to flap their way
along this wind-chased passage, but they would have managed. If the
dragon population had expanded, and a whole fleet of them had become
available for maneuvers, they could have rained destruction even upon
the distant populations of the widespread Vinkus.

And might yet, Liir knew. The strategic knowledge that had devel-
oped those dragons into weapons wouldn't have been lost because Trism
defected or the basilica collapsed. If nothing else happened, it was only a
matter of time before another Trism came along to do the bidding of his
superiors and raise up perhaps an even mightier army.

Yet today had dawned, and tomorrow could not be foreseen. No
magician in the world had yet mastered the art of prophecy, so far as Liir
knew. Not a single venerable bishop with his channels to the divine, nor
any tiktok mechanism of subtle apprehension, nor even the best-taught
sorcerer with the keenest of inner eyes, had ever accurately foretold so
much as whether the rain would hold off for the picnic. It was Time Yet
to Come that possessed the strongest force of all, a magic mightier than
the Kells themselves, a magic greener than all of green Oz. Inscrutable,
terrifying, and exhilarating at once.

+ + +

HE FOUND HE COULD NOT FLY above Kumbricia's Pass. His broom bucked to one side or another, as he'd heard a horse instructed to cross a risky bridge might do. He didn't know whether this was mere exhaustion, a flagging of his will, or some sort of wizardic or magnetic obstruction he didn't understand. He allowed himself to drop, by a series of long, scalloped declines, till at last he found landfall in a clearing, and continued his voyage by foot.

It took time to locate the spot where he had been interviewed by General Kynot, the crusty old Cliff Eagle—the island in the hanging tarn. The place seemed deserted. He could see nothing but random feathers and the inevitable mess of droppings. Maybe they'd moved on to a cleaner lobby somewhere.

On foot he continued west, losing track of time. One of the drawbacks of flying on the broom was that his nose became frozen, and the air at a certain height, while clean of grit, was also curiously scentless. Kumbricia's Pass, by contrast, was a festival of odors.

In the nest of the cape, he settled for an afternoon nap and didn't wake up until dawn . . . and he wasn't even sure it was dawn of the next day, or some day further on.

Nonetheless, he was rested at last, rested in a deep way, and better able to spy winter berries in the thickets, and chichonga pods, and the occasional scatter of walnuts on the ground. Dozens of streams leapt from either side of the great gorge and crisscrossed, occasionally islanding the floor of the pass into hillocks. He didn't go thirsty. He felt that the longer he pressed on, the stronger he became.

At last Kumbricia's Pass made its final abrupt turn before opening out above the beautiful bleak expanse, as far as the eye could see, of the rolling prairie known as the Thousand Year Grasslands. In the shallow caves and along the ledges of the westward face of the Kells, nearly deafened by the constant wind, Liir met up with what remained of the Conference of the Birds.

Their numbers had dwindled in the short time since Liir had left Kumbricia's Pass. When General Kynot spied Liir standing there—so much for the vigilance of their sentries!—he lop-winged over and indicated, with a strict jerk of his head, that they should retreat into the gorge for a bit of a chin-wag.

A few Birds saw the General's intentions, and braved the buffeting winds to join the colloquy. Several dozen gathered, including the Wren named Dosey, who cued in the blind, hobbledy Heron.

"We see you've reclaimed your broom," began the General without formality. "I'm to understand it is not functioning as a vehicle for flight anymore, or you wouldn't have come on foot. And you would have come sooner."

"I came as quickly as I could," said Liir. "What's happened?"

"We've lost half our number," said the General, "or near to it. The Yunamata rushed us, and since we were scared to take high wing, we were caught in a series of nets and traps they'd erected across a narrow part of the Pass. Scarcely a one of us hasn't lost companion or kin."

"That's not like them," said Liir. "Or not like their reputation. They're a peaceable people."

The General glared at Liir. "We've had to leave the Pass, lest it happen again. We're cornered against the sky up here, on display to preying dragons, and without adequate supply of grubs and worms."

Liir said, "I'm sorry about the Yunamata attack. That's the Emperor's strategy—to keep his foes busy nipping at one another. That has to stop. There's no way to survive without our making peace among ourselves."

"Begging your pardon, sir," shrilled the Wren to Liir, and the General was too dispirited to bother correcting her terminology. "One population can't make peace with another by force."

"There are possibilities," said Liir. "The time of the dragons is done, at least for now. You can fly again. *We* can fly again. And before the next threat might come, we have to maneuver ourselves into . . . a coalition. No, not that: a nation."

"Which nation is that?" snapped the General.

"Witch nation!" tittered a Dodo. "I likes that, I do."

"You called a Conference about the raiding skirmishes of dragons," Liir reminded them. "The dragon fleet has been destroyed. But those dragons were a tribe, too: ill-used, malevolent, raised up to strike out, imprisoned by their training. It gave me no joy to poison a dragon, even one that has attacked and killed your kind and mine. Yet the moment is here to fly again. Not just home, not just yet: but fly into the storm. The Emperor has already sent out a guard to hunt me down, and he and his ilk will hardknuckle anyone who gets in his way. No one in the Emerald City can stand up to him, for he claims the divine right of the elect—not elected by people, but by the Unnamed God. Who can dispute that? We are all elect, for here we are, and we must fly for our lives. We must show ourselves to be a company. He sent dragons to scare the skies: we will fly ourselves as a flag right back at him."

General Kynot pretended to peck at his chest for vermin. When he raised his head, his eyes were dry again. "It is not easy to trust the wisdom of a human person," he admitted. "Like so many humans, you could be lying. Leading us into a trap. Promising us freedom, and tricking us into an ambush of yet more dragons. Yet we have so few choices but to trust. After all, you are the son of the Witch."

"Don't base your decision on a false premise," said Liir. "I will never know for sure who my parents were. And even if I did, the son of a witch can be as wrong as anyone else. Let us fly because you are persuaded we should, not because I say so."

"I vote yes," said Dosey.

"So do I," said the Heron, "though I can't fly anymore, of course."

"I didn't *call* for a vote," said Kynot.

"That's why I voted," Dosey replied.

"Witch nation! Witch nation!" said the Dodo.

THEY LAUNCHED AT NOON, maybe ninety Birds, swooping westward into the buffeting winds that ran the span of the prairie to build up enough strength to crash against the Kells.

The venture almost scattered them at once. The Wrens tumbled like husks of dried pinlobble; the Ducks shat themselves silly; the Night Rocs couldn't see in the widest daylight Oz had to offer, and nearly brained themselves by wheeling backward into the peaks.

Liir was giddy and vertiginous. The broom shot out over a rocky sward, so low that he could make out the surprised expressions of wild highland goats. Another instant and he was fifteen times higher than the highest tower of Kiamo Ko, and a silver river winked in the sunlight below him, narrow as a bootlace.

Just fighting to stay together took the better part of an afternoon. When they finally reached air space beyond the forested foothills, above the nearest start of the endless grassland, where the power of the wind diminished, they settled to rest and feed and count their number. Four of their ninety had been lost in the first descent out of Kumbricia's Pass.

But there were grassland grubs and beetles, and the backwash of mountain rills to splash in, so they made their first encampment.

IT TOOK A FEW DAYS of rehearsal for the Night Rocs to learn how to maneuver by daylight, but the Grasslands were forgiving. After hours of uninhibited flight, with no dragons approaching, the Birds grew braver and flew in a looser formation.

For the time being they avoided other populations, though far below them they delighted in the spectacle of wild tsebra wheeling and cantering in their winter migration toward the south, a flurry of black and white markings against the brown ground, an alphabet in the act of writing the story of tsebra migration. Or notes, singing a mythic history.

Draffes, their long tawny necks swaying, saluted them in their high-pitched voices. Liir couldn't hear them, but Kynot said that evening that sentient Draffes were living among draffes, in apparent harmony.

A small band of Vleckmarshes flew up to greet the flying Conference (Kynot would not allow the Birds to call themselves Witch Nation, despite the Dodo's pleading). At the sight of Liir on the broomstick, the Vleckmarshes made common cause with the travelers, and flew alongside.

Then a bounty of Angel Swans, who usually kept to themselves out of pride for the whiteness of their mien, gave wing. So too a noisy clot of Grey Geese, who were wintering together on the banks of a nameless broad winter lake that appeared and disappeared in different places every year, they said.

The Conference flew in waves, the bigger birds working harder, providing a breakfront against the wind, the smaller birds in the slipstream, and lower, in case of attack by air. It was Dosey who spotted the tents of the Scrow, arrayed in the usual geometric precision against the trackless blanket of earth.

Liir did not want to approach the camp, not yet. But General Kynot, agreeing to serve as an emissary, dove out of formation and whipped around the camp until he could decide which tent belonged to the Princess Nastoya.

That night, the Conference having settled under a shelter of windthorn hedge, Kynot reported to Liir.

"I found one who could speak to me, an old scholar named Shem Ottokos," said the General. "I told him you were abroad, but he said he didn't need me to tell him that. He had been able to make you out with his naked eye, because the cape unfurls so blackly against the scrim of the evening. He had the tent lifted for his queen to see, and though she is mostly blind now, she said she could make you out against the sky. He thinks it was the clot of the Conference she was seeing, its whole mass. She wants to see you, said Ottokos. She has something to tell you. Whether you can help her or not."

"If she agreed to meet me later, she can tell me then," said Liir. "Did she?"

"The Scrow rarely travel during this time of year, and they haven't settled any peace with the Yunamata. Ottokos does not know if he can convince the tribal elders to pull up camp and brave Kumbricia's Pass. He doesn't know how to talk to his people about this. But I explained about the extermination of the dragons. Perhaps Ottokos will be persuasive."

"If Princess Nastoya still has time, we have time," said Liir. "It is her time that we need to read, not ours."

NORTHWARD, BEATING AGAINST THE ICY WINTER gusts known in some circles as the Farts of Kumbricia; northward and northward, and the Thousand Year Grasslands went white under drifts of frost. The snow was lipped and patterned by the wind into shapes like the imbricated scales on a fish. Now out of sight of the Kells, now back; now joined by a throng of Snow Geese, five hundred strong, now by a mystic Pale Crane, her partner, and her senile though quite energetic mother.

At last, because the smaller Birds feared freezing to death, and the food stock grew scarce, the Conference wheeled eastward. Kynot had a notion that they could most safely cross the Kells again at the point where the Arjikis had built their mountain villages. If nothing else, there would be the chance of a barn in which to roost, or a bonfire around which to warm themselves. It was rough work, though. Once more suffering the churning of wind against the hard breast of the Kells, the Conference sought a lower altitude, which took more time but afforded quicker shelter should a storm come up.

The weather was with them, at least. Day after day the sky was peerless blue, if pinion-quaking cold. Under snow squalls or rain clouds the Conference would have fumbled. But they always had the chance to move on: this kept the smaller birds brave.

They came at last to the highland valleys and white wastes of the Arjiki stronghold of Kiamo Ko. Liir did not care to alight there, but the nights were drawing in earlier and earlier, and he had no choice but to see it as a blessing.

His rump sore, and almost unable to uncurl his spine from the arched position in which he flew, he landed on the cobbles of the courtyard with 220 of the smaller Birds, while the larger ones waited formally outside for an invitation. The monkeys shrieked, though whether it was out of terror or welcome, Liir couldn't tell. Chistery met him at the top of the steps to the main hall.

"I suppose you've asked me, for old time's sake, to join you," he said. "I'd come if I could. But I don't think my wings are up to it."

"You can't have had news of our intentions," said Liir.

"You're a message, that's all," said Chistery. "No one can watch you raveling and unraveling up the columns of mountain air without knowing you intend to be seen. I'll tell you, my heart was in my throat though, as you came nearer. I thought to myself, It's Elphaba herself."

"No, it's only me," said Liir. "How's Nanny?"

"Past her prime. For the fourth decade in a row, I'd say. She's having a sandwich of egg and dried garmot. Do you want to go up?"

"I suppose I'd better. May we stay here?"

"You needn't ask," said Chistery, slightly hurt. "Until someone else comes to claim it, the house is yours."

Nanny sat up in bed, looking gently at her bread crusts. When she saw Liir, she smiled and patted the bedclothes. "Don't worry, I won't wet," she said. "I've already gone."

"Do you know who I am?" asked Liir.

"Ought I?" She didn't sound worried about it. "Is it Shell?"

"Decidedly not."

"Good. I didn't like Shell very much." She held out the pieces of bread. "I saw the Birds coming, and I saved them something from my lunch."

"That's nice of you."

"Actually, the bread was a bit stale. But maybe they won't notice. It's nice to see you again, whoever you are. Just like old times." She patted his hand. "I never could tell what was going on then, either, but now I don't mind so much."

"Nanny?"

"Hmmmm?" She was beginning to drift off to sleep.

"Did you ever hear of someone named Yackle?"

One eyelid of Nanny's cocked open. "Might have done," she said warily. "Who wants to know?"

"Only me."

"Days a lifetime ago are clearer to me than today. I don't even know what sex I am anymore, and I can remember what I got in my Lurline-mas basket when I was ten. A tin cannikin full of colored beads—"

"Nanny. Yackle."

"I met someone named Yackle once," said Nanny. "I always remembered it because her name reminded me of jackal. Like the jackal moon, you know."

"Where?"

"She had a little commercial enterprise, if you call it that, in the Emerald City. The Lower Quarter, downslope of Southstairs, if you know where that is."

"I do."

"I went in to have my tea leaves read and to ask a question about Melena. Your grandmother."

Liir didn't bother to correct her.

"Yackle was an old crone without much time left, I'd guess. But she still had talent. She gave me a few words of advice, read me the riot act about my petty filching, and told me Elphaba would have a history. Can you believe it!"

"How did she know about Elphaba?"

"Silly. I told her, of course. I told her Melena had given birth to a green daughter. I bought whatever Yackle could provide as a corrective agent to ensure the second child didn't come out green. And she didn't, did Nessarose. Neither did Shell. Only our Elphie. A history! Can you believe that?"

"Must be a common name."

"Yackle, you mean? Don't know about that. Never heard it again. Why do you ask?"

"Do you think Elphaba will have a history?"

"She does already, ninnykins! I just saw her flying up the valley as large as a cloud. Her cape went out behind her, a thousand bits in flight. Nearly touched the peaks to the left and the right. If that's not a history, what is?"

CHISTERY SAW HIM OUT. "You're welcome here anytime," he said. "This is your house."

"She always loved you best, you know," said Liir, grinning as he laced the braces at the clasp of the Witch's cape.

"Considering what she was like, is that a compliment or an insult?" replied the Snow Monkey. "Fly well."

BY THE TIME THEY NEARED the Emerald City, half a month later, the Conference of the Birds was six thousand strong. They'd had to slow down as they grew larger, for fear of midair accidents, but east of the Kells the winds were less harsh. As the Conference crossed the Gillikin River, coming into sight of the smart little villages and spruce knolls and brick factories and millhouses of the rolling Gillikin tableland, its shadow grew more definite by the day.

Liir had no intention of attacking the Emerald City. The Birds were not warriors, and the Conference, or Witch Nation, wasn't military in makeup. Liir didn't want to see Shell, nor the Lady Glinda, assuming she had returned to take up residence in her Mennipin Square town house for the winter season.

He only wanted that they should be seen.

It was nearing evening when they approached the walls of the City from the north. The sun was sagging against a few distant scraggly clouds, heading pinkly for its rest, and then it disappeared behind the horizon. The western sky would remain glassy bright for a half hour yet.

As workers clocked off at the Palace, as the boulevards were thronged with people heading for supper, and as the indigent went to their own work of begging for coin against starvation, the Conference wheeled into place. Anyone looking north at the display of Birds, from the inn called Welcome Arms on the banks of the Gillikin, say, would read only cloud: an invasion, a plague, a disaster. The same impression struck those looking, from the northwest of the city, at the Birds swimming like an ocean away from them.

From the Emerald City, though, from every west-facing window of the Palace, the intention was unmistakable. The Conference of Birds had rehearsed to perfection. They flew in formation for viewing from the east. They were the Witch, hat and cape, skirt and broom, shadowy face tucked down against the wind, but beady-eyed bright. Liir, on his broom, followed General Kynot, whose superior navigational system gave him his location. Liir on his broom played the keen black eye of the Witch.

Was Shell there, wondered Liir, knuckles on some marble windowsill, Lord High Apostle Muscle himself, Shell Go-to-hell Thropp, First Spear, Emperor of Oz, Personal Shell of the Unnamed God? Did he lean forward and squint at the holy ghost of his remonstrating sister, and rub his eyes?

Six thousand strong, they cried in unison, hoping that the echo of their message would be heard in the darkest, most cloistered cell in Southstairs as well as the highest office in the Palace of the Emperor. "Elphaba lives! Elphaba lives! Elphaba lives!"

Raising Voices

♦ I ♦

THE CONFERENCE HAD GROWN too large for a single speaker to address it. On the morning it disbanded, therefore, two delegates from each species met with General Kynot and his loose affiliation of ministers, which included the Wren, the Dodo, and the most aggrandizing of the Grey Geese, a gander who had appointed himself.

Liir was invited, too. He asked the birds to keep an eye out for Nor. "You go everywhere, you see everything," he said.

"We stay clear of humans when we can," replied the Grey Goose, "present company accepted. Pro tem."

"It's probably futile," Liir agreed. "Still." He walked about with the drawing of *Nor by Fiyero*. "She used to look like this. She's older by now, of course."

"All people look alike to me," murmured a Vleckmarsh.

"She's simply beautiful," said the blind Heron.

"Well, thanks just the same," said Liir, tucking the paper away.

The General gave a rambling address that confused everyone, including himself. "To conclude," he conceded, "we go on to new work. The Birds run a risk of reverting to behaviors less than helpful. Now, I don't mean to besmirch the fine Ostriches from the Sour Sands, who because they don't fly were not part of our Conference. But we all know what Ostriches are rumored to do when faced with a crisis. We must not retreat into our claques and clans. Wary of human settlements—yes, who wouldn't be? Let's not be stupid about humans. But wary of one another? A little less so, if we can manage."

"And a little more chatter amongst us," added Dosey the Wren. "In ways we are only beginning to understand, we are the eyes of Oz."

"When can Witch Nation have a reunion?" asked the Dodo. "This was fun."

"The boy-broomist must go and make his own nest. And I?—off and away to my family," said the General. "The wife, you know, and there was a new clutch of eggs last spring. But there are the families of those Birds who were heinously trapped and slain by the Yunamata. Those families should be contacted, if we can figure out how."

"I'll take care of that, sir," said Dosey.

"You take care of yourself, missie."

"Should this be an annual event?" asked the Dodo. "Ought I be taking notes? I mean mental notes, at least?" But the General had lifted himself onto the hump of a sudden, warmer breeze, and whatever he answered over his shoulder could not be heard in the cheer that went up to bid him good-bye.

✦ 2 ✦

LIIR DIDN'T ASK THE GREY GOOSE for company, but the Goose followed along behind. It was a problem. The Goose was too regal to be servile, and too beautiful; he made Liir feel like a chimney sweep who hadn't seen a bath in a month. The Goose called himself Iskinaary.

They flew from the southern edge of the Emerald City and headed straight out across Restwater, keeping east of the isthmus between the lakes. If the mauntery of Saint Glinda had been torched, Liir didn't want to know about it yet.

Where the Vinkus River seeped along flat-bouldered steps into

Restwater, they stopped to get their breath, and they surprised a fox out of a clump of wrestlebush. The fox dove at Iskinaary and wrenched his wing, but Liir clobbered the fox with the broom, and the fox let go. His wing drenched in blood, Iskinaary shed unashamed tears at his disfigurement. Closer examination proved that the damage was, indeed, slight. Nonetheless, if they were to proceed together, they'd need to go on foot.

"I don't mind a chance to give my legs some exercise," said Liir.

"That's the most disingenuous thing I've ever heard," said Iskinaary. "And it's not as if you have particularly handsome legs."

"They walk faster than yours do, I've noticed."

"If you want to walk faster, you'll have to carry me."

Iskinaary was heavy to carry, and for all his beauty he still smelled very much like a Goose. Still, Liir didn't mind that the trip would take a little longer. So much had happened. A chance for reflection was welcome.

He was returning now, having accomplished something at last—a set of dragon murders, regrettable, but there you go. He was eager to know how his accomplishment would fit in the house. What he and Candle would be like together now. He had no experience of a happy return, ever. He would hardly know what to say, where to smile. He hoped that not knowing might seem wonderful.

He knew more about human warmth, too, from Trism. How that knowledge would translate in the presence of Candle was a puzzle to anticipate with excitement.

When they reached the Disappointments south of the Vinkus River, it was sunset, and the cold dusk made them shiver. But there was evidence of the tiny flower known as Shatter Ice—four little bluets in a nest of the tiniest emerald leaves—which meant the hump of the winter had been passed, and spring, however long it took to arrive, had started on its way.

ISKINAARY'S WING HAD MENDED a bit—not much—by the time they approached the series of wooded knolls in which Apple Press Farm was hidden.

"You're not planning on staying and becoming domesticated, I assume," said Liir. "I mean, it'd be fine to see you, umm, swanning about our meadows, but I can't expect that would give you anything approaching professional satisfaction."

"I have my own ambitions," said Iskinaary. "I'm intelligent as well as gorgeous, you know. Leave it to me."

"To be more specific," said Liir gingerly, "I'm not necessarily inviting you to take up residence with us permanently. No hard feelings."

Iskinaary shrugged, as much as a Grey Goose could shrug. "Makes no difference to me what you say," he replied. "I wasn't waiting for an engraved invitation. I'll follow my own instincts. We Animals still *have* instincts, you know."

"Touché. And your instinct is?"

"To keep my own counsel."

They entered the woods, slopping through mushy hillocks of drifted snow. "And, being instinct rich, Iskinaary, have you any opinion what *my* instincts are?"

"You're not untalented," said Iskinaary, overlooking the slight sarcasm in Liir's tone. "You're even rather smart. For a human. You keep excellent company."

"Yourself."

"Exactly. Furthermore, from what I've observed, you have a talent for reading the past."

"What does that mean?"

Iskinaary honked. "What it sounds. There are very few who can read the future. And you've mentioned this Candle of yours can read the present. But reading the past is a skill in and of itself. It's not just knowing the past. It's feeling it. It's deriving new strength and knowledge from it—learning from it all the time. It's my own guess that this was intended to be the great strength of human beings, when the Unnamed God came up with the notion of you. Sadly, like so many good ideas, it hasn't quite worked out in practice."

"Thank you very much."

"No insult intended."

"I didn't know you believed in the Unnamed God."

"I was speaking metaphorically. I assumed you'd get that. Is this the place you're looking for?"

It was. The low roofs of the dependences, and the main structure of the house itself, and the big barn room in which the broken press presumably still stood. Perhaps it could be made to work again.

They came the long way around, to approach from the open meadow by the front door. There they found that Liir's invitation had been accepted. Nine tents were erected in the meadow, as perfectly aligned as the casual ramble of the fences would allow. Eight subordinate tents made a square, and the Princess Nastoya's tent stood centrally.

With her canny ways, and for all the advance warning of this contingent of Scrow, Candle ought to have known he was coming. Nonetheless, she seemed surprised. Surprised, and flustered, large and slow, even redder of face than her natural coloring suggested was possible. Perhaps blood pressure problems? Or had she been experimenting with native rouges?

He approached her cautiously—as if she were a young novice, not a farm bride. He took her hands and held them, and found out that even now he didn't know how he felt. "I've flown the world," he said.

"Welcome home from the world." Her face was tucked down, as if she were shy. A new shyness.

"Candle," he said, "has the fellow called Trism come here?"

She looked up at him from under a wrinkled brow. "He said you'd ask for him. I couldn't be sure of him; he seemed a soldier of some sort. Well, now you've asked, and right off. Though I'd have thought you'd enquire if I was all right first! All these guests, and me in this state!"

"Of course—of course. But I can see you're all right. And I don't know if Trism survived."

"Well, he did," she said, summarily. "Oh, Liir," she continued, her voice now sounding as if he'd only been gone an hour, and she'd missed him for sixty full minutes, "look what's happened, and I wanted to greet you on our own." She spread her hands at the meadow.

"I know," he said. "I invited them."

"I'm glad you finally arrived to greet them, then. They've been here a week, and my careful larder is just about bare. The one older fellow speaks a rude sort of Qua'ati, but I can't make out a thing from the others."

The Scrow were trying to brew a kind of tea out of the bark of apple trees and such sap as was running in the maples. They wrinkled their noses at it and hardly seemed to notice Liir's arrival.

"In the family way, I note," said Iskinaary pointedly, slipping into Qua'ati effortlessly, "or are you just big-boned, my dear?"

Indicating the Goose, Liir said to Candle, "This is my . . ." He paused; the word *friend* seemed inappropriate.

"Familiar," supplied the Goose.

"Oh, please!" said Liir. "Is *that* what you're on about?"

"Don't mind me, I'll just settle here with the stupid hens," snapped Iskinaary.

"I'm not a witch, nothing near!" said Liir. "You're going on the grossest sort of hearsay."

"Get on with your task, and I'll be the judge," said the Goose. He shifted about three inches to one side and turned elegantly still, which gave him the effect of being statuesque while allowing him to eavesdrop with impunity.

Liir picked up Candle's hands again. He wanted more from her, he willed it so. She let him thumb her palms for a moment, then she pulled her own hands away.

"So Trism got here unharmed?" he said.

"The dragon master? He did," she said, her face turned away again.

"Where is he?"

"He couldn't stay."

Cautious. Gentle step, here. "Why not? Candle?"

She began to lift a huge urn of water from the table in the yard; he took it from her.

"Candle. What happened? Was he all right?" Suddenly Liir had no trust: not in his own apprehensions of Trism, nor of Trism . . . nor even of Candle. Trism, after all, had once wanted to kill him. "Did he treat you poorly?"

"This water needs taking out to the Princess," she answered. "She's being laved round the clock. I've been preparing it with essence of vine-gar, as that priestly prince instructed me to do."

"What happened? What passed between you and Trism? Candle!"

"Liir. What could pass between us? He didn't speak Qua'ati. And I could understand what he chose to tell me, but not answer him—I don't speak that bossy a tongue. I have a small voice, a half-voice. As you know."

In succession, Liir thought a half dozen crises. She knows I loved him. That I love him. That he loves me? That he loves her?

That she loves him?

What was this verb *love* anyway, that could work in any direction?

Did he hurt her?

"Candle. I beg of you."

"Don't beg," intoned Iskinaary, standing on one foot. "Remember General Kynot. Don't beg. Never beg."

"We'll talk later," she said. "Now, if you'd take that water to your guest? And then you'd better do what you came here to do."

"I came here to be here! With you."

"And this band of ragamuffins who preceded you? They are, what? The relatives?"

Tears pricked his eyes. "Don't be preposterous, and don't be mean! I've been away, Candle. Doing what you asked. Getting something done. Anything. Learning where I wanted to be."

"I have my bad moments," she admitted, wiping her own face. "It hasn't been easy. Let's not talk. Go straight to work, and help that old sow if you can."

"She's an Elephant."

"Whatever the beast she is."

"Candle!"

"I didn't mean it like that. Liir, you startled me. Carrying this child is hard work. I haven't been myself."

He could see that.

"Did Trism leave parcels for me?"

"Two packets in the press, hanging on strings from the ceiling, to keep the mice from them. The mice are very interested. Are you going to haul this water to the invalid, or shall I? I have other work to do now. Washing. The old woman runs through a dozen towels a day."

She picked up a basket of wet laundry and wobbled outside to an old apple tree, where she began to sling the clothes on drooping branches to dry. She's hurting, he thought: even I, dull as I am, can see that. But from what? My long absence? My affection for Trism? Or is the child inside her making her sick, draining her blood, eating her liver from within, kicking her pelvis sore with its ready heels?

• 3 •

He wasn't up to dealing with Princess Nastoya yet, and the Scrow seemed to have settled in nicely. Hell, she'd been dying for a decade, she could die some more for another ten minutes before he finally had his reunion with her.

Stung by Candle's reticence, he wandered into the barn to retrieve the parcels. If Trism had gotten them here safely, then he must have managed to elude Commander Cherrystone. Glinda's glamour had worked once again, and riding at her side as her factotum, Trism had played the shadowy manservant, a known quantity. He'd been smuggled out of the mauntery safely.

But what had happened here? Had he followed Liir's directions and found Candle in residence, beautiful and reticent and large with child? Had Trism resented the notion of a Candle? Had he been stung by the fact that Liir had never mentioned her pregnancy? Had he assumed Liir was the father?

Had Trism been cruel to her?

Liir took down the parcels, struck by the thought that the workings of the human heart could be as various and imperturbable as the workings of human communities. He didn't know enough of love in all its forms to compare, to choose, to sacrifice, to regret. Held in Trism's soldier arms, he'd been strengthened; held in Candle's loving regard, he'd been strengthened, too. Now the only thing holding him was Elphaba's cape. Was her mantle of penitential solitude to be his, too?

He wiped his eyes and opened the parcels. In the slanting light through the barn door, he wheeled out the hoops of face. Now that he knew what they were, they seemed less grotesque—no less terrible than a drawing or a dream of someone. A flat disc not unlike a mirror. They'd had lives, these people, as puzzling as his. No one would ever know what those lives were like, though.

"Well," said Iskinaary, who'd followed him in, "as I live and breathe. Is this what they mean by a human shield?"

"They're the faces of the dead."

"You're in here studying them, when you have a dying woman out there in a tent, waiting for your attention?" Iskinaary was incensed.

Liir looked at them, shaking his head. From the distance he heard the first few notes of a melody. Candle had taken down the domingon again. Whom was she calling with it? The baby within her? Come out, come out? Or Liir himself, stuck in his indecision, his confusion?

"I'm quite an expert at music, as I have perfect pitch. Unusual in a Goose," said Iskinaary. "She's got a way with that instrument. She could play the eggs right out of a mama Goose."

"I heard her encourage the yard animals to sing," said Liir. "I mean really sing, not just bray and cackle."

"Singing lightens the load," said Iskinaary, who looked about ready to deliver an aria himself. He cleared his throat. But Liir suddenly snatched up the hoops from the ground and turned on his heel.

"If she can be persuaded," he said, "maybe she can help the load lighten. She's so weighed down herself—but she's a kind person. What a good idea!"

"Thank you," said Iskinaary, his feathers ruffled. Denied an audience, he hummed to himself in a desultory fashion, but shortly thereafter he followed Liir to find out what his good idea had been.

LIIR INTRODUCED HIMSELF to the man called Lord Ottokos.

"We've met before," said Shem Ottokos, "though since then, you've grown up and I've grown old."

Liir explained what he hoped Candle might do. If she would.

Shem Ottokos seemed to find nothing peculiar in the proposal. "Your wife is very kind, even in her heavy condition, and your husband seemed equally kind."

"She is not my wife, and I have no husband," said Liir. "Indeed, I have no talent except the idea for this. And I do not know if it will work."

"I will tell the Princess Nastoya that you have arrived," said Ottokos. "She is in grave distress, and it is hard for her to talk anymore. But I believe she is still able to hear and understand. I must believe this: it is my job."

Liir took the scraped and treated faces of the dragons' victims into the orchard, faintly budding already, though the ground was still wet with old snow. He hooked the thirteen hoops upon notches of apple tree branch, as near to body height as he could guess each one had required when attached to a living body. The damp sheets and toweling fluttered like liquidy limbs beneath.

+ **4** +

SHE PUT ASIDE her domingon when he approached and asked her for her help. "Don't do it for me," said Liir. "Do it for her."

"I'm already doing laundry for her," said Candle. "I have no more strength."

"You know people and you know kindness. Your music sang me back to life. You have that skill. It's called knowing the present. You could make the barnyard sing. I only ask that you know the present of Princess Nastoya, and play her constituent parts to their own places."

"You think like a witch. I am not a witch, Liir."

"I am not a witch and I am not thinking like one. I am trying to learn from history. I am trying to figure out what happened in the past, and work to use that knowledge again. You played in my past, and brought me my life. Perhaps you can play her death to her."

"I don't feel well." She rubbed her eyes with her forefingers. "Frankly, I haven't been sleeping. I don't know that this pregnancy is going as it should, but there's no one to ask."

"You don't feel as badly as Princess Nastoya does."

"Liir!"

He caught her at the elbow. "Tell me what happened!" he said roughly. "Tell me what happened with Trism!"

"Leave me be, Liir," she said, crying, but when he gripped her arm harder, she said, "He told me to come away with him. He said whoever had followed the two of you so far would not give up that easily. He said the mauntery would be burned, and its members tortured until they disclosed the whereabouts of this satellite operation. Oh, don't look at me like that. Of course the maunts know about this place! Why else would Mother Yackle have sent us here? Or the donkey know the way? Think, Liir!"

"He told you to leave with him?"

"He said I should go with him, for protection: that it is what you would want me to do."

Liir was stunned. "Why didn't you do it, then?"

"I trusted you," she said, a little abrasively, "how do I know whether to trust another soldier? He could have been abducting me to kill me and my child. He could have been lying. He could have been doing it to hurt you. Though now I see he meant more to you than I reckoned."

What he heard mostly was her possessive pronoun: *my child*. Not *ours*.

"And he didn't stay," said Liir, in a voice nearly as small as hers.

"No, he didn't," she answered. "Generally, people don't. They come, they go. He left. The Scrow came. For all I know your Commander Cherrystone will be here in time for tea, and Mother Yackle for the washing up."

♦ 5 ♦

THE SCROW RETINUE carried the Princess into the orchard and set her down on a blanket. She was grey; her legs had swollen like bolsters, her scalp was nearly bald. She'd lost her eyebrows and her eyelashes, which gave her sightless eyes a horrible eggy look. Her chin bristled with enough hair to wipe farm boots clean.

Liir could hardly put this collaboration of bones and muscles and foul odors together with his childhood memories of meeting Nastoya the day or two after Elphaba had died. He didn't try. The Princess was beyond language, groaning and leaning into a screw of physical pain that seemed to implicate the entire orchard. He could never apologize for having abandoned his promise to her for so long. Neither could she speak whatever message she'd had for him. It was too late now.

Lord Ottokos retained his composure. He spoke to her about every shift of limb and placement of pillow. Unsuccessfully he tried to dribble some water into her mouth, but even at this late moment he was afraid he might drown her before she could be divided from her disguise. She would have to go to her death, if this worked, thirsty.

She was prostrate on the ground, her head rolled back, giving her chin some prominence for perhaps the first time in a decade.

"We're ready," said Ottokos. He stood with a gnarled old staff, a bit of sourwood into which iron thorns had been pounded. It looked like a mace of some sort, a scepter, and Lord Ottokos was ready to assume the leadership of the tribe.

Liir nodded at Candle, who had come equipped with an old milking stool. She sat down clumsily. Her legs went wide, but there wasn't enough lap on which to hold her instrument. She had to balance it on an overturned washtub. Still, she looked at Princess Nastoya with a complicated expression, and presently she began to play.

The others in the company had not been invited, but they lined the edge of the orchard, knuckles locked, a Scrow position of reverence. The Goose stood near Liir, a foot or two back, both deferential and significant. It wasn't clear if he was Liir's familiar, or if Liir was his interpreter.

♦ 317 ♦

Candle began by dissecting chords and distending them into arpeggios. She chose the lighter modalities at first, but quickly shifted into more subtle variations. The Princess was uncomfortable on the ground, and her blankets were already getting soaked in the snow.

"To grow a death," murmured Liir, holding Candle's shoulders, "you must plant a life."

She shook him off. He began to walk the perimeter of the orchard, trying to see from different angles. Was there something more he could do? He should be doing? Candle was hard at work, and no doubt Princess Nastoya was doing her own, but was more help needed, in this mission of nothing but mercy?

One stretch of the orchard. Another.

"Liir," whispered Candle as he neared her. "I am very uncomfortable here. It is not like six months ago. I can't keep this up for long."

She rotated the instrument a quarter turn and splayed her fingers, cocking them laterally, and she flat-struck the alto quarter, trying a sprigged quadrille, a dance of spring.

The third side of the orchard. Iskinaary wandered over as if at an evening reception honoring the recent work of a well-regarded painter. "You might try concentrating on the past," he said.

"I don't know her past," said Liir. "I don't know a thing about it, except that she knew Elphaba."

"I don't mean her past," said Iskinaary. "She knows her own past well enough, somewhere in there. I mean the others. Even in death, we are a society, after all."

Liir turned and looked at the Scrow, standing a distance away, but then he saw what Iskinaary meant. It wasn't anything the living could do—it was the human dead who were best equipped to call the human disguise off Nastoya. They could beckon it forward, if Candle could play the scraped faces to sing.

But the playing was her talent, and the singing was theirs—it was his job to listen. To witness their histories, and cherish them in memory, his only talent. He had looked into the Witch's crystal ball, after all, and had seen her past, even if it had nothing to do with him. He had stumbled upon his own reveries without benefit of any gazing globe. Maybe his only job was to listen. That much he could do.

◆ 6 ◆

I WAS THE FOURTH OF FIVE CHILDREN, and I loved the way sun warmed stone. Just before lunch, on the flagstones of the terrace, I used to dance barefoot with my mother for she loved it too.

I was happy enough in my marriage, and happier still when I was widowed, though happiness seems incidental to a good life.

I never wanted to take the cane my father gave me, and I picked it up and broke his nose with it, and he laughed so hard he fell into the well.

I made things with colored threads, little birds and such.

I always wanted to go to university at Shiz, as some of my friends would do, but boys like me weren't allowed.

I believed in the Unnamed God and accepted the mission set me because God would take care of everything: the Emperor said so.

I once took off all my clothes and rolled in a field of ferns, and had an experience I never told anyone about.

I was at the ceremony in Center Munch when the cyclone dropped the house on Nessarose, and I saw it with my own eyes, but I lost my ribbon on the way home.

I loved how milk tastes, and the way hills go blue with cloud markings, and my baby sister, her hair black as a beetle brush.

I loved it when I was alive.

I loved it when I was alive, too.

Forget us, forget us all, it makes no difference now, but don't forget that we loved it when we were alive.

LIIR HEARD SOMETHING from each hoop. Every face sang as Candle provided accompaniment. The bud-notched trees shook with the force of their voices, though there were no tongues, and little enough left of lips, and no wind to pass through the aperture and turn their mouths into flutes.

Reminded of human life, the corporeal part of Princess Nastoya melted into the snow. All that was left of her human disguise shook off—a spin of charcoal smoke, smudged in the air like incense. It stood, finding its feet, before it dispersed, and the voices fell silent.

There was nothing left on the blanket but a massive She-Elephant. The Scrow all closed their eyes and began to weep. Her eyes opened and her head rolled back. Her eyes met Liir's for an instant. Her neck snapped.

No Place Like It

FTER AN HOUR, Lord Ot-
tokos indicated that a surgeon should come forward with a saw. The
small bowl-stomached woman went to work at the Elephant's right tusk
and removed it in just a few minutes. Then she sawed an inch of disc off
the wider end. The tusk being hollow at the wide end, the disc formed a
ring with an aperture several fingers wide. The surgeon fitted this on the
point of the other end of the tusk, and handed the relic to Ottokos.

He bowed and accepted it. In turn he fastened it to the staff he had
prepared. When finished, the staff was a six-foot stake crowned by an
arched prong of Elephant tusk, an ivory smile without a face around it.

"I will lead under the influence of Nastoya," he said in a quiet voice,
and this calmed the Scrow from their weeping.

What influence is that, thought Liir; a shard of bone, a makeshift
totem?

That, and memory. Maybe all the influence needed.

THE SCROW HAD lived so long under the leadership of Princess Nastoya
that they hardly knew what to do when she was gone. With effort,
everyone tugging at once, they managed to get her body onto the cart

that had brought Candle and Liir to Apple Press Farm. Then they began the long trudge back to their tribal homeland. They would burn her on a pyre when they arrived, and the scraped faces besides, and not a moment too soon. Nastoya had never smelled very fine while alive, and now she was a health hazard as well.

Lord Ottokos insisted Liir should accompany them through Kumbricia's Pass in case the Scrow delegation met up with the Yunamata, and trouble flared. "It's the last thing you can do for Princess Nastoya, finishing the task she asked of you back when the Witch first died," he said. "See her bones to safety, anyway."

Liir decided to leave the broom and the cape behind. He wouldn't fly while in the company of the Scrow, and after departing from them, he mightn't be able to fly back, anyway. Kumbricia's Pass had been resistant to his flying above it.

After packing the hooped faces alongside Nastoya's carcass, Liir bade Candle and Iskinaary a quick good-bye. "Mind each other," he said. "Iskinaary, keep watch."

"I can watch over myself," said Candle. "You forget I can read the present."

"Can you read what is in my heart?" he asked. If so, tell me what it is, he continued to himself. Tell me, so I can tell you back.

Candle held his hands but wouldn't meet his eyes. Perhaps, the nearer the baby was to birth, the more she despaired of ever having said it was his. Would he ever be able to map any part of her mystery?

He set out once more, with a sense that his life would be rich in setting outs, and perhaps poorer in homecomings.

THERE PROVED LITTLE DRAMA on the high ground. One evening the Yunamata materialized out of nothing, naked as Birds, painted in tribal markings. They approached the corpse of Princess Nastoya, carrying the lighted roots of hagtooth bush that they used in their own funeral rites. They sang, and melted away again in rather unseemly haste.

At the final gorge, where the Conference of the Birds had departed for its circuit around western Oz, Liir said a quick and perfunctory good-bye to Lord Shem, Prince Ottokos, and turned home with a heavy heart.

The accomplishments of the last six months had been irrelevant, he decided, for all but Nastoya. Was that the only accomplishment that mattered?—that somehow you not bungle your own death? Everything else that had happened in his short adult life had been frothy and mean-ingless, ultimately. Passionate, yes—yes, that, indeed. Passionately felt, but without shapeliness or worthy outcome.

The dragons were dead: some people were still walking about, igno-rant of how their tired lives might otherwise have ended up with a scraping. That much was good. Stack that up against the cursed lives of those Quadlings who daily had to remember their own dead, lost at the burning of the bridge at Bengda. The bit of thatch falling, a letter in the air, flaming and drowning.

And doubtless there were still disconsolate prisoners in Southstairs, and misguided soldiers in barracks, and those abject poor who had sur-vived the cleaning out of Dirt Boulevard. And that kid named Tip, whose granny had probably sold him already for a better brand of cow, a broom, a new pot for the hearth.

To be sure, the airborne Conference of the Birds—a great show, if nothing else. But what did it mean? Where did it get anyone? For all Liir knew, that juvenile spectacle would give the Emperor better leverage to draft additional soldiers, to tax for newer weapons, to dictate for more control over the crown city of Oz. A flying witch made out of birds! In another generation that would have been called pleasure faithism: as if spectacle itself could convince one of anything.

Yet the world was a spectacle, its own old argument for itself. End-lessly expounded with every new articulation of leaf and limb, laugh and lamb, loaf and loam. Surely there was *something* in the world lovely enough to counter the dread of being alone, a solitary figure untroubled by ambition, unfettered by talent, uncertain of a damn thing?

The great force of evil? Shell, Emperor Quake-in-your-Boots, nam-ing himself the Spear of the Unnamed God? Or the next despot, or the one after that?

The colossal might of wickedness, he thought: how we love to locate it massively elsewhere. But so much of it comes down to what each one of us does between breakfast and bedtime.

Remembering Princess Nastoya, he thought: *Sever us from our disguises.* Then he flinched, almost in disgust: was that a prayer?

How he wished the Elephant Princess had been able to deliver whatever message that Sister Apothecaire had advertised she had for him. Another slim hope dashed, so many slim hopes waiting to rise in its wake.

A message about Nor, and the word on the street. Could Princess Nastoya, with her massive ears, actually have learned Nor's whereabouts? Surely she'd have found a way to tell him?

Nor, lovely Nor, wherever she was. He didn't know where, he might never know, except she was in his memory—like everyone else. There, and drawn on the piece of paper secreted into the inner pocket of the Witch's cape. He saw it in his mind's eye, clear as day, the drawing, the coffee-colored wash suggesting the gleaming highlights of preadolescent, perfect skin, the letters written in Nor's peculiar, crabbed printing.

It was as if the burning letter had spelled something, suddenly, just before it was quenched in black water. The thought came like a spasm, and he harvested it before it disappeared. He unpacked the Princess Nastoya's promised gift.

The word on the street. *Elphaba Lives!*

Nor's handwriting.

WHEN HE GOT BACK to the farm a little after dusk, perhaps a week later, he knew at once that it was deserted. One knows those things about an old farmstead. Iskinaary was gone, and the donkey, and the hens had scattered. For a minute he wondered if Trism had come back for Candle, and now—angry at Liir for his quizzical ways, or herself taken with handsome Trism—she'd changed her mind, and cast her lot with him.

Or perhaps Trism's warning had been accurate, and Commander Cherrystone and his band had found Apple Press Farm at last. Found a way to avenge the slaughter of the dragons.

It mattered, and would matter more tomorrow. For now, he was alone, as before. As usual. It was a condition he'd need to get used to, or to tolerate never getting used to—not exactly the same thing, more's the pity.

He walked through the house. Her domingon was gone, which suggested deliberation, but the dishes were unwiped, still crusty with porridge, which suggested haste. Had she taken the broom? No, there it was, put up on the mantelpiece out of harm's way.

He built up a small fire in the kitchen to take the edge off the chill. There was precious little with which to make a meal. As he stood trying to think, though, he heard a barracking in the boggy land some way south of the farm. Thrashing through underbrush, he found the goat hidden in thickets, tied to a tree, sorely in need of milking, and cross as blazes.

He led it back to the barn, and milked it in the shadows of the broken press, glad he had learned one skill at least.

Then, in the dark corner of the stair hall where they left the trash for tipping into the dump beyond the orchard, he nearly tripped over the Witch's cape. He picked it up to shake it out and hang it on a hook, and the lump of dead matter rolled off the hem into the corner.

Oh, oh oh oh. So this was it. The baby had come, come early, he guessed; he didn't know all that much about the calendar as it pertained to babies. It must have come too soon, and it had been dead on arrival, or it had died at once. And Candle had been alone, poor thing—alone but for that vainglorious Goose. How misguided that Liir should have felt the need to honor the corpse of Nastoya and leave Candle to face a possible childbirth or a stillbirth alone, with only a silly Goose to hiss for help.

He had hauled the dead carcass of an Elephant across the mountains on a cart; he had tried to hear the testimonies of people who had had their faces scraped. He had murdered dragons and people. He could bear to touch the small corpse of a human child.

So he picked it up. He held it at a distance. Tears started, though why? He hadn't believed this was his child, and there was no new reason to believe it now. It was just another child, just another inevitable fatality, the next crude accident of the world, and not the last.

He maneuvered its cold form closer. Cold, though not icy; this death had to have just happened. Had the scraped faces sung the fetus to a death, as they'd sung Princess Nastoya?

Maybe the child had been born dead this very morning, as he was making his approach. And a rosy morning it had been, the sun strengthening, and the inane involuntary return of a green blush to the skin of the world. He had even sung a bit of his own. Not his usual way!—he'd yodeled some nonsense syllables, thinking: Maybe it will be all right. Maybe Candle. Maybe Trism. Maybe something will work.

The form was cold. Was it a normal infant size, or smaller? He didn't know human infants. He nestled it against his neck, and thought he felt its mouth move.

Gingerly he stepped from the stair hall into the kitchen. Was it warming up? Or was it just his own heat he felt, reflecting back at him?

In the feeble light of the new fire, he moved it again, shifted it to rest along his forearm. It was a pretty corpse, and now he could see it had been a girl. Its umbilical cord was an unholy mess. Maybe Iskinaary had helped to sever it. It didn't bear thinking about.

The corpse twitched and cried, and stretched a little. He wrapped it from stem to stern, forehead to toes, making sure its dab of a nose had access to air. Then he carried it closer to the fire, in case corpses liked to be a little warm before they were fed milk.

Elphaba had kept a basket rocking at her feet, once: a basket was just the thing. Was there an old onion basket somewhere in the keeping-room belowstairs? He'd find a basket.

He found a basket.

He fed her by dripping goat's milk through a cheesecloth into her pursing mouth. She took the false sucket well enough. She had Candle's Quadling face, already: those beautiful rhomboids that made such splendid cheekbones.

Of course Candle would flee, if she'd given birth to a child and thought it had died. Imagine the panic. Of course she would. Maybe she'd go back to the mauntery, as the Superior Maunt had suspected she would. At least for a time: to recover herself. What an ordeal she'd had. The lonely pregnancy, the lonely delivery, and then—whatever it was that had happened with Trism. And all of Liir's absences. Of course she would flee.

She might come back. She might.

He sat with the infant most of the night. For a while he spread out the cape and even managed to sleep a little—he kept her in the basket, though, so he wouldn't roll over onto her by accident and crush her.

In the first black wash of dawn, he woke up comforted with a different thought. Candle could see the present. Perhaps she'd known he was almost home. What if she had fled—what if a guard of Commander Cherrystone's battalion had indeed found the farm, and she'd led them away, diverted their attention? Drawn them off scent? The mother bird pretends to have a broken wing, to lead predators away from her nestlings in the grass. Candle had as much instinct as a mother bird.

So she knew that Liir would be back in time to rescue the girl, give it a burial if needed, feed it if not. She'd hid the goat for him to find.

She wasn't leading danger away from him, but from the baby. She could take care of herself; they didn't want her, after all. But she was relying on Liir to save her baby, whether he believed it was his or not.

Imagining that, anyway, helped him open his eyes.

There was heavy rain in the morning. The light was greyish and mossy with the low clouds. He had to concede that the baby wasn't a corpse, really. She was alive. Maybe she'd been born stone cold. But she was alive now.

Still smeared with her birth blood, and the watery beginning of her little feces. He took her to the doorway and held her up in the warm rain. She cleaned up green.

A LITTLE PATIENCE, and we shall see the reign of witches pass over, their spells dissolve, and the people, recovering their true spirit, restore their government to its true principles.

—Thomas Jefferson, 1798

From *Wicked*

THEY CONDUCTED THEIR LOVE AFFAIR in the room above the abandoned corn exchange as the autumn weather came lop-leggedly in from the east: now a warm day, now a sunny one, now four days of cold winds and thin rain.

✦   ✦   ✦

ONE EVENING THROUGH THE SKYLIGHT the full moon fell heavily on Elphaba sleeping. Fiyero had awakened and gone to take a leak into the chamber pot. Malky was stalking mice on the stairs. Coming back, Fiyero looked at the form of his lover, more pearly than green tonight. He had brought her a traditional Vinkus fringed silk scarf—roses on a black background—and he had tied it around her waist, and from then on it was a costume for lovemaking. Tonight in sleeping she had nudged it up, and he admired the curve of her flank, the tender fragility of her knee, the bony ankle. There was a smell of perfume still in the air, and the resiny, animal smell, and the smell of the mystical sea, and the sweet cloaking smell of hair all riled up by sex. He sat by the side of the bed and looked at her. Her pubic hair grew, almost more purple than black, in small spangled curls, a different pattern than Sarima's. There was an odd shadow near the groin—for a sleepy moment he wondered if some of his blue diamonds had, in the heat of sex, been steamed onto her own skin—or was it a scar?

But she woke up just then, and in the moonlight covered herself with a blanket. She smiled at him drowsily and called him "Yero, my hero," and that melted his heart.

My MOTHER was a westerne woman
And learned in gramarye

–K. Estmere, 1470,
collected in *Reliques of Ancient English Poetry*, 1765

✦ ACKNOWLEDGMENTS ✦

THANKS ARE DUE to the team at ReganBooks, starting with Judith Regan and including Cassie Jones, Paul Olsewski, and Jennifer Suitor.

Thank you to David Groff, Betty Levin, Andy Newman, and William Reiss for commenting on early drafts of *Son of a Witch*.

Thank you to Haven Kimmel and to Eve Ensler, for encouraging words sent at precisely the right moment.

Thank you to Harriet Barlow, Ben Strader, and the company of Blue Mountain Center, New York.

Thank you, again, to Andy Newman, for defending the ramparts as usual, and to Lori Shelly, for able assistance at every wicked little thing.

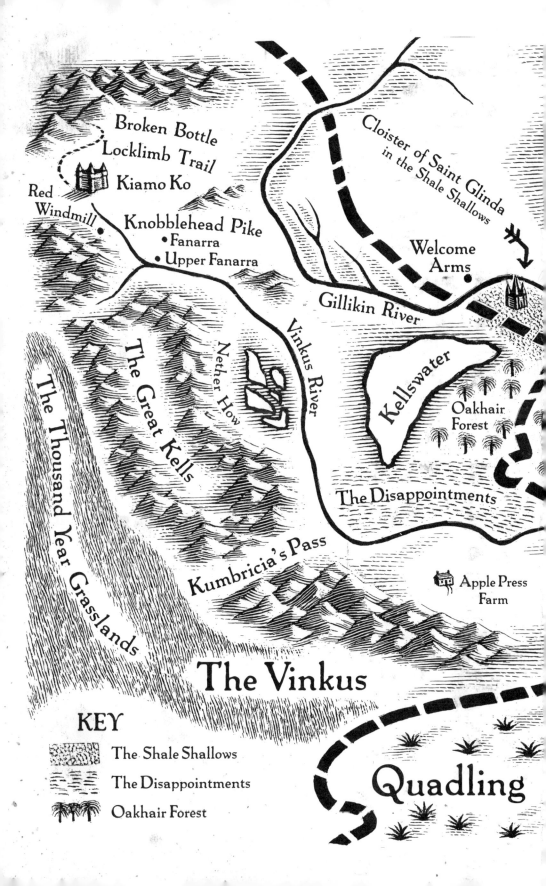